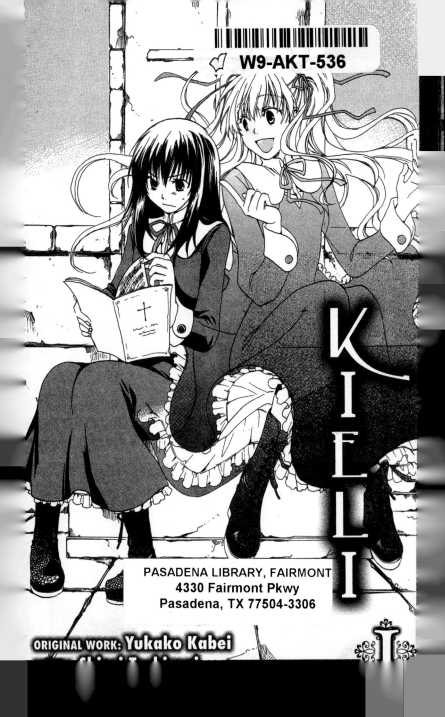

KIELI

ORIGINAL WORK: **Yukako Kabei**

CONTENTS

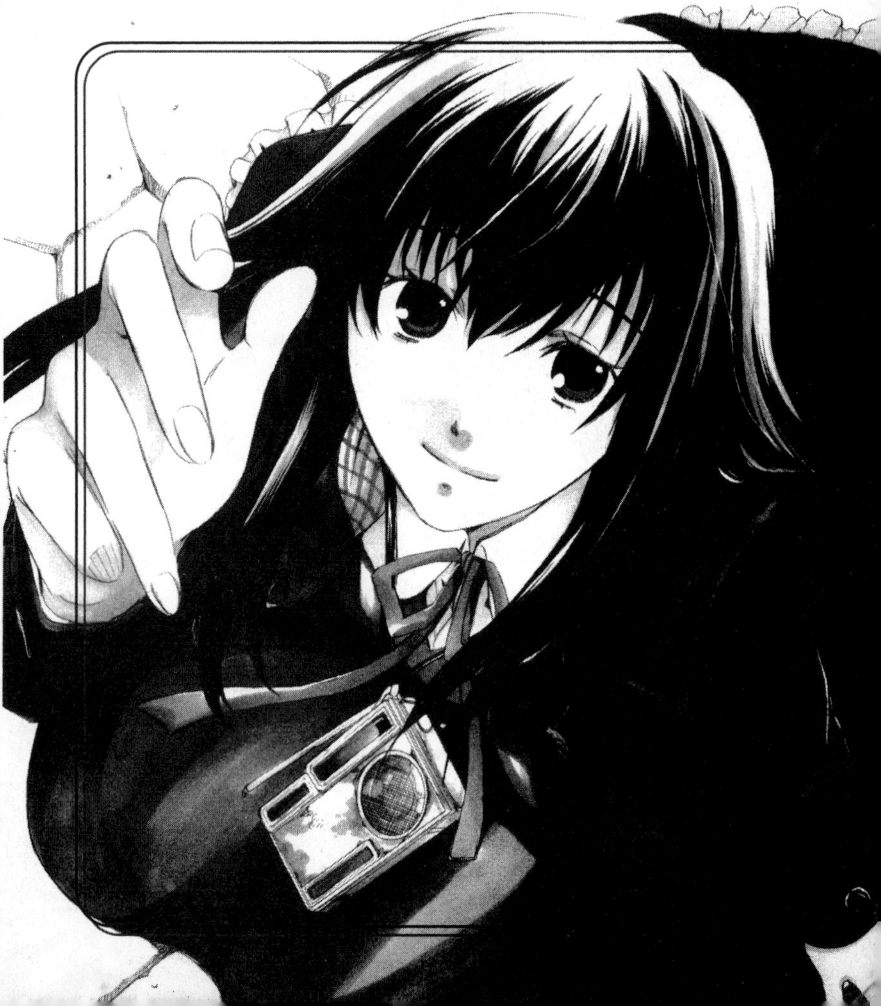

CHAPTER 1

ROOMMATE

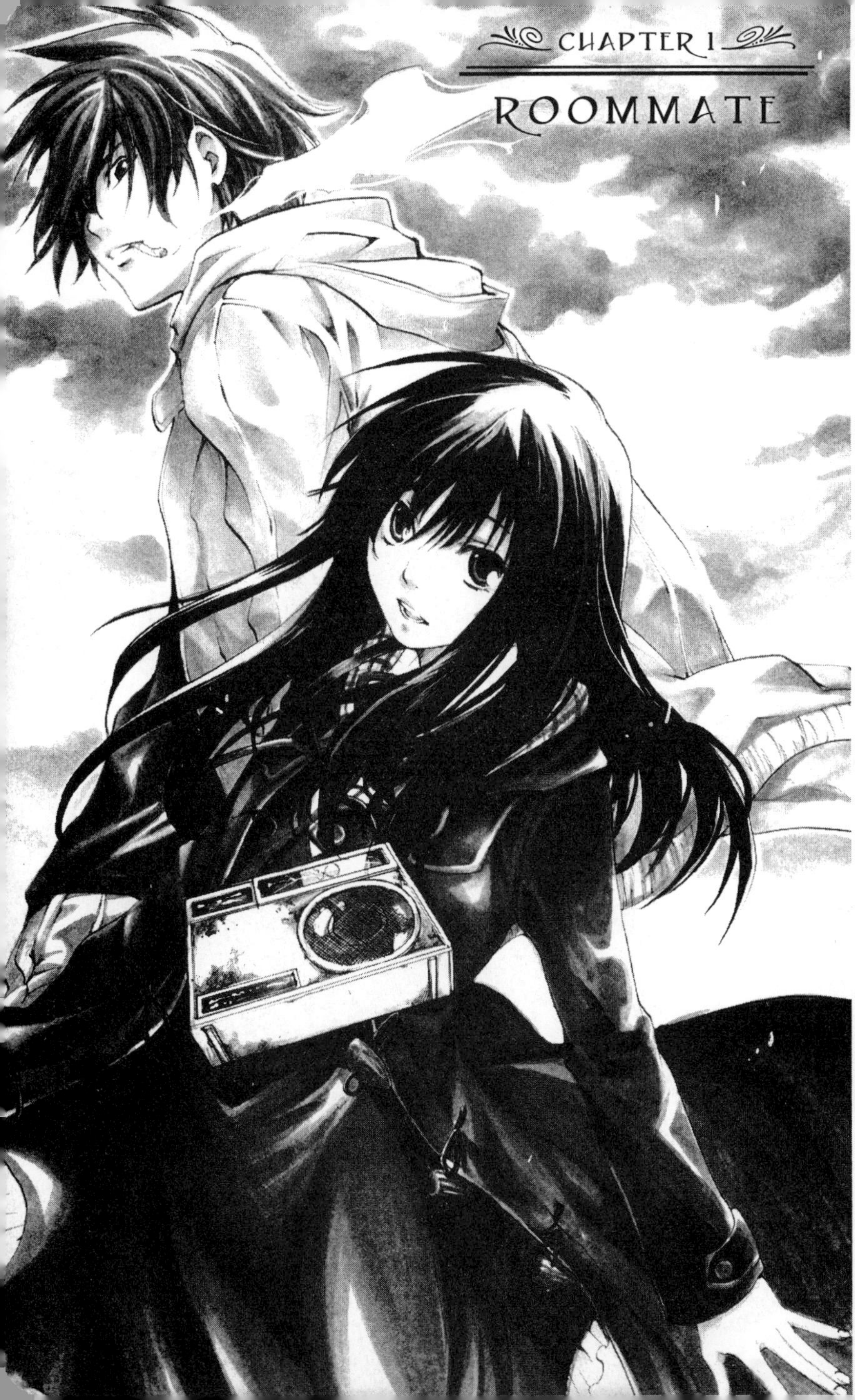

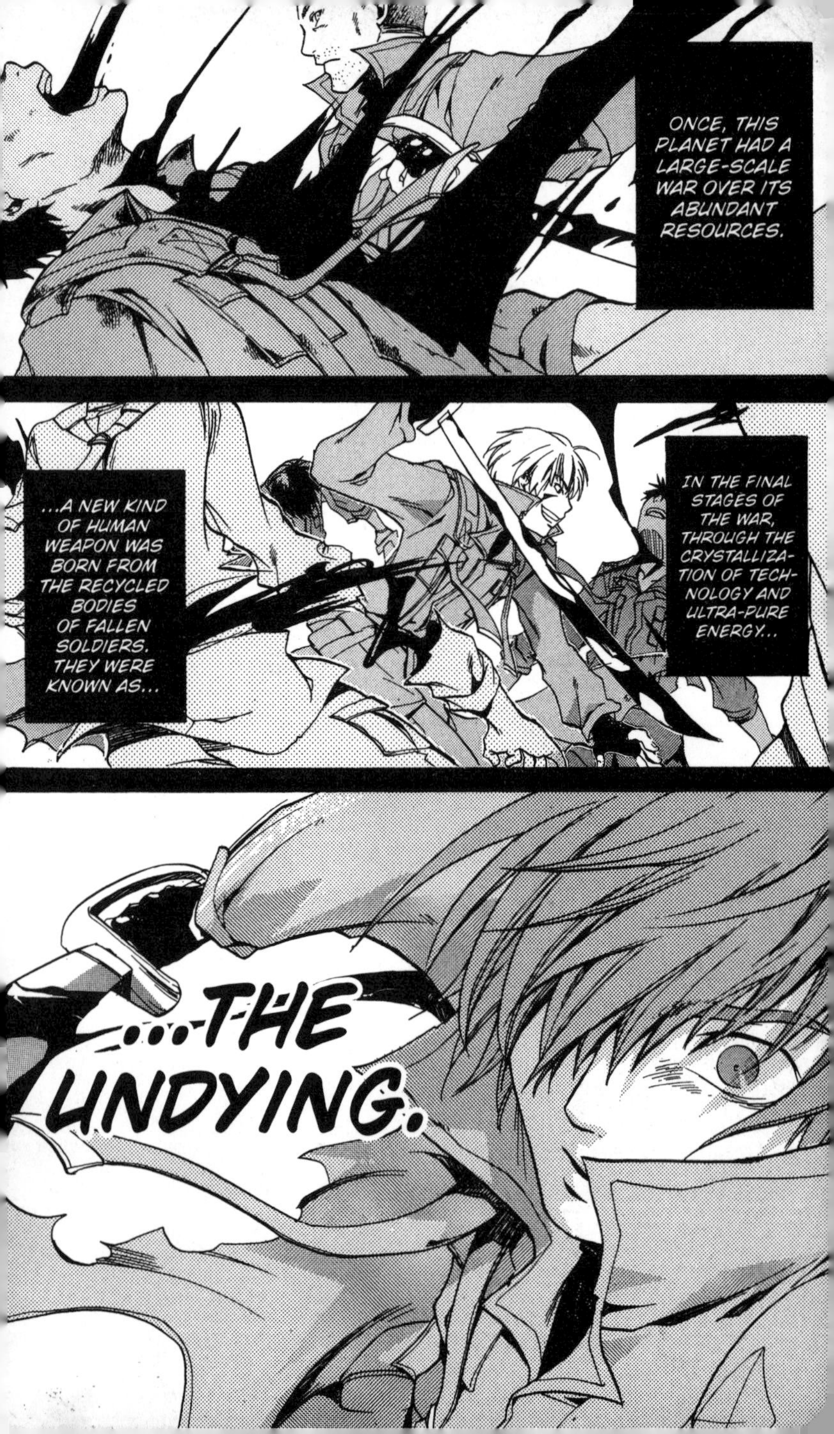
ONCE, THIS PLANET HAD A LARGE-SCALE WAR OVER ITS ABUNDANT RESOURCES.
IN THE FINAL STAGES OF THE WAR, THROUGH THE CRYSTALLIZATION OF TECHNOLOGY AND ULTRA-PURE ENERGY...
...A NEW KIND OF HUMAN WEAPON WAS BORN FROM THE RECYCLED BODIES OF FALLEN SOLDIERS. THEY WERE KNOWN AS...
...THE UNDYING.

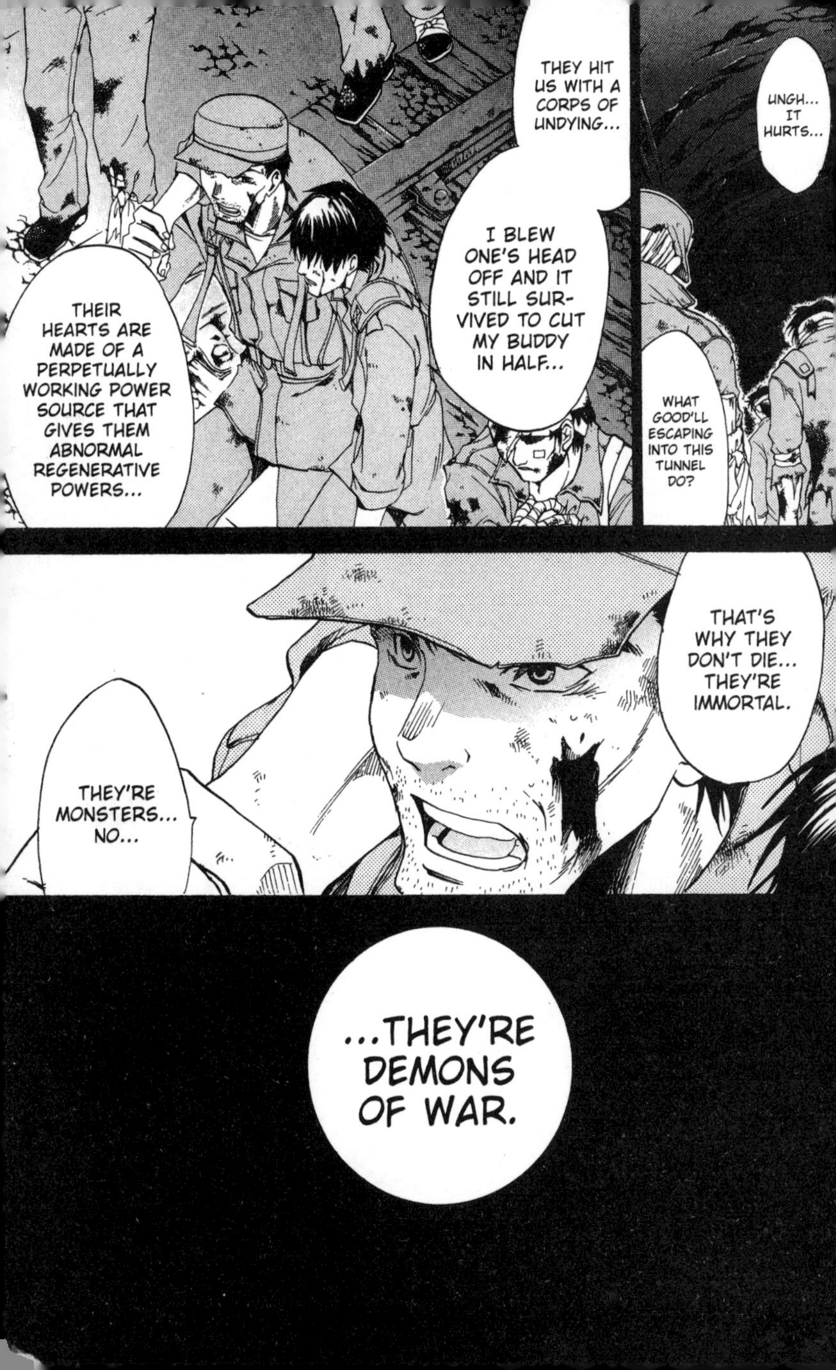
UNGH... IT HURTS...
WHAT GOOD'LL ESCAPING INTO THIS TUNNEL DO?
THEY HIT US WITH A CORPS OF UNDYING...
I BLEW ONE'S HEAD OFF AND IT STILL SUR-VIVED TO CUT MY BUDDY IN HALF...
THEIR HEARTS ARE MADE OF A PERPETUALLY WORKING POWER SOURCE THAT GIVES THEM ABNORMAL REGENERATIVE POWERS...
THAT'S WHY THEY DON'T DIE... THEY'RE IMMORTAL.
THEY'RE MONSTERS... NO...
...THEY'RE DEMONS OF WAR.

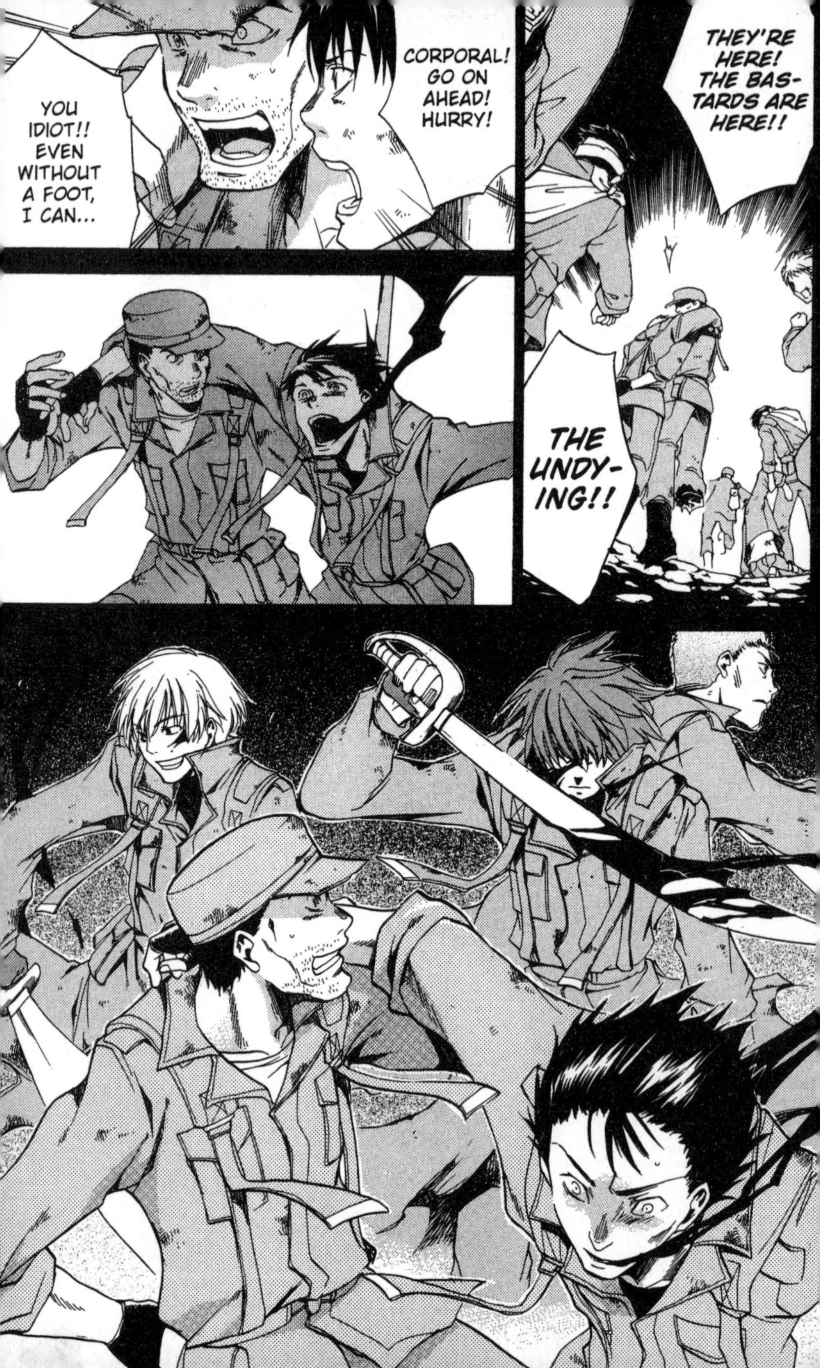
THEY'RE HERE! THE BASTARDS ARE HERE!!
THE UNDYING!!
CORPORAL! GO ON AHEAD! HURRY!
YOU IDIOT!! EVEN WITHOUT A FOOT, I CAN...

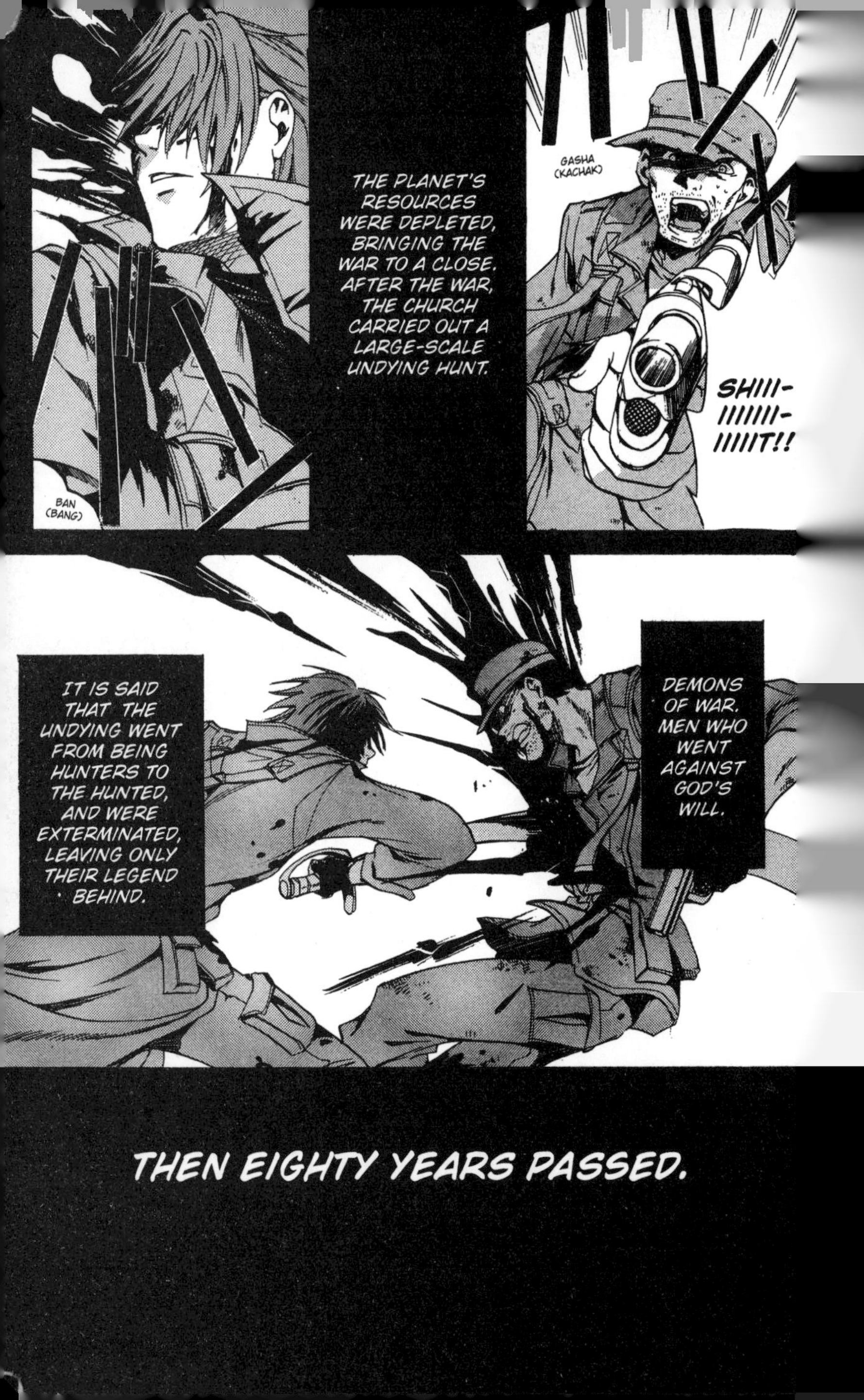
GASHA (KACHAK)
SHIII-IIIIIII-IIIIIT!!
THE PLANET'S RESOURCES WERE DEPLETED, BRINGING THE WAR TO A CLOSE. AFTER THE WAR, THE CHURCH CARRIED OUT A LARGE-SCALE UNDYING HUNT.
BAN (BANG)
DEMONS OF WAR. MEN WHO WENT AGAINST GOD'S WILL.
IT IS SAID THAT THE UNDYING WENT FROM BEING HUNTERS TO THE HUNTED, AND WERE EXTERMINATED, LEAVING ONLY THEIR LEGEND BEHIND.
THEN EIGHTY YEARS PASSED.

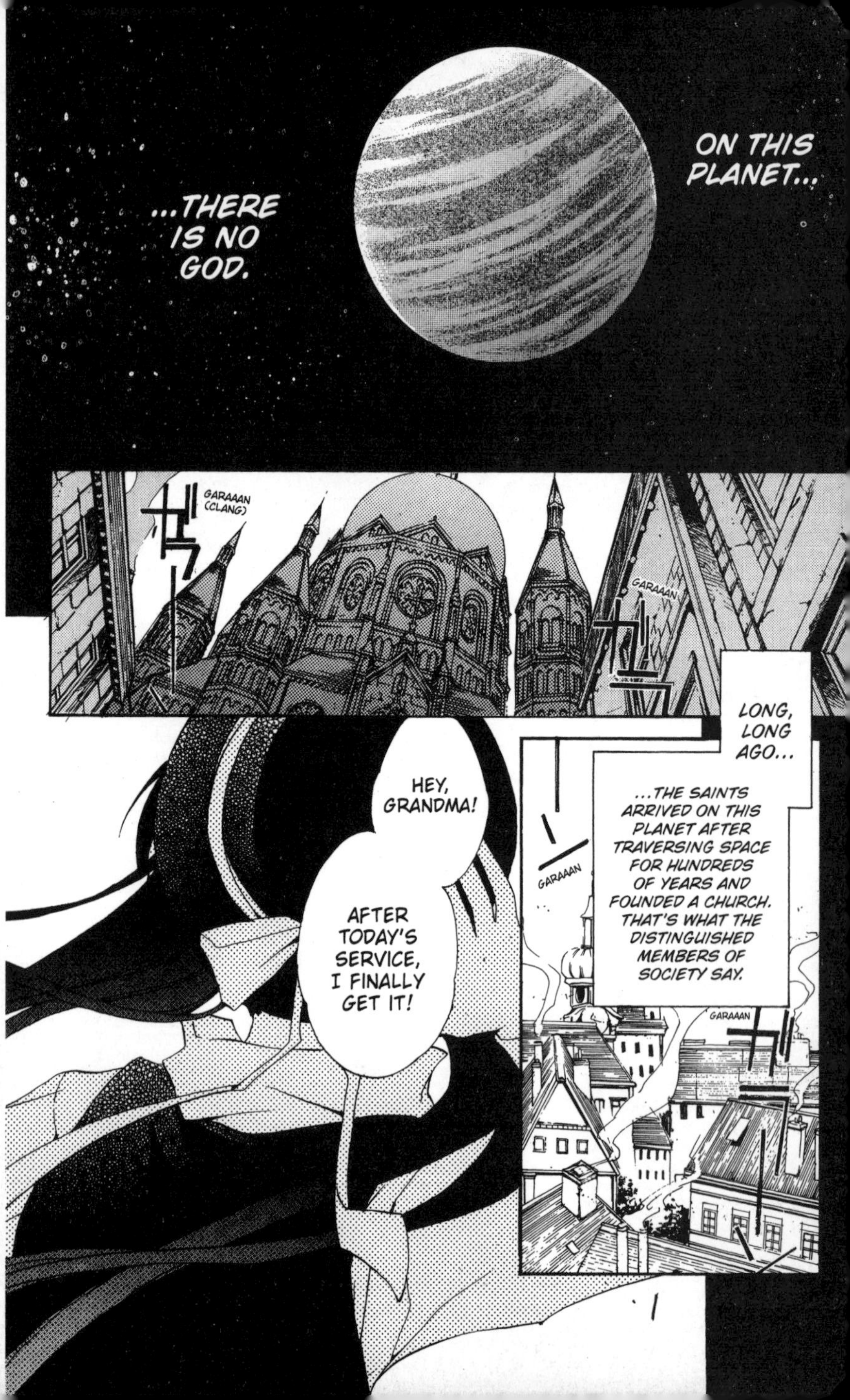
ON THIS PLANET...
...THERE IS NO GOD.
GARAAAN
GARAAAN (CLANG)
LONG, LONG AGO...
...THE SAINTS ARRIVED ON THIS PLANET AFTER TRAVERSING SPACE FOR HUNDREDS OF YEARS AND FOUNDED A CHURCH. THAT'S WHAT THE DISTINGUISHED MEMBERS OF SOCIETY SAY.
GARAAAN
GARAAAN
HEY, GRANDMA!
AFTER TODAY'S SERVICE, I FINALLY GET IT!

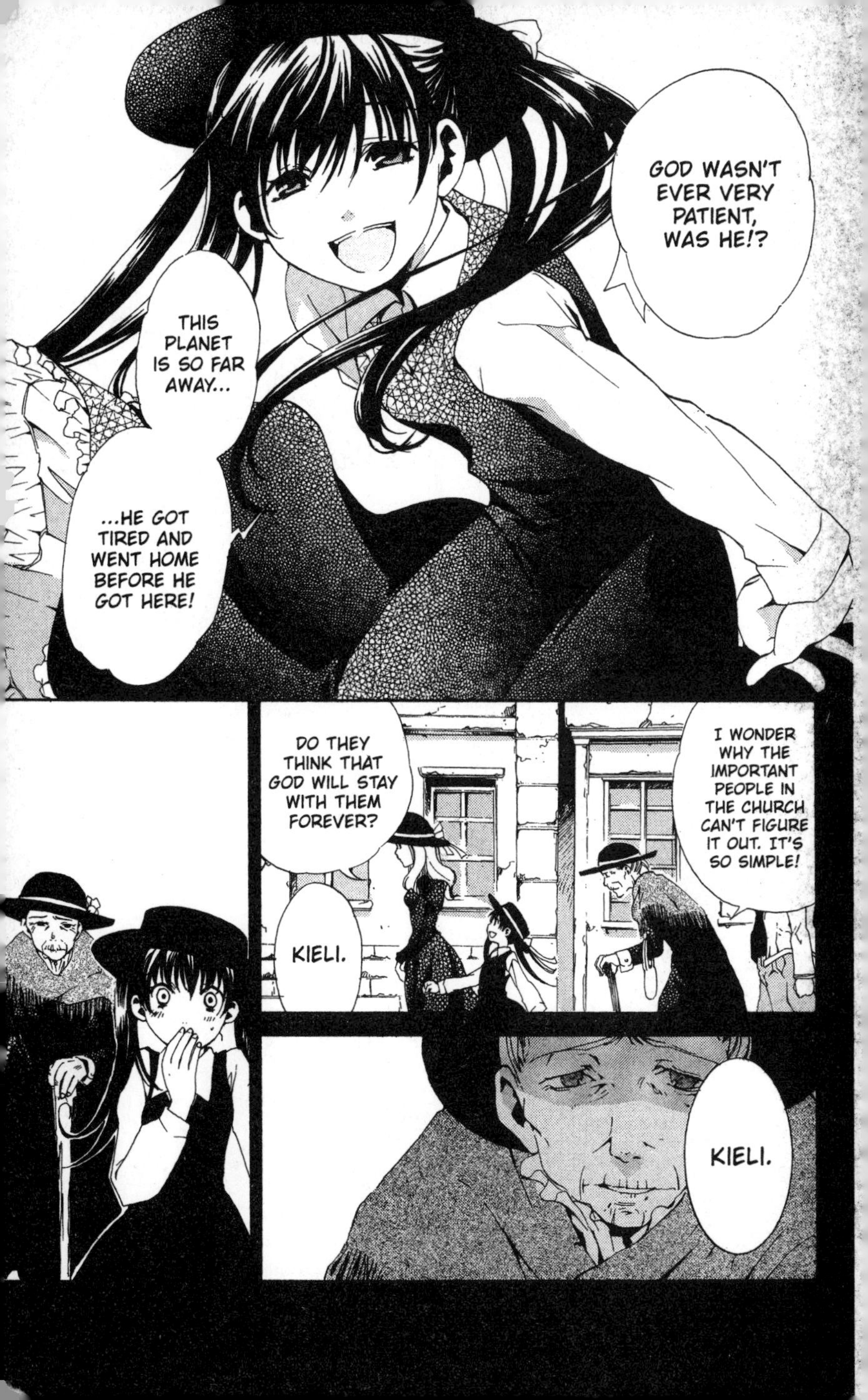
GOD WASN'T EVER VERY PATIENT, WAS HE!?
THIS PLANET IS SO FAR AWAY...
...HE GOT TIRED AND WENT HOME BEFORE HE GOT HERE!
I WONDER WHY THE IMPORTANT PEOPLE IN THE CHURCH CAN'T FIGURE IT OUT. IT'S SO SIMPLE!
DO THEY THINK THAT GOD WILL STAY WITH THEM FOREVER?
KIELI.
KIELI.

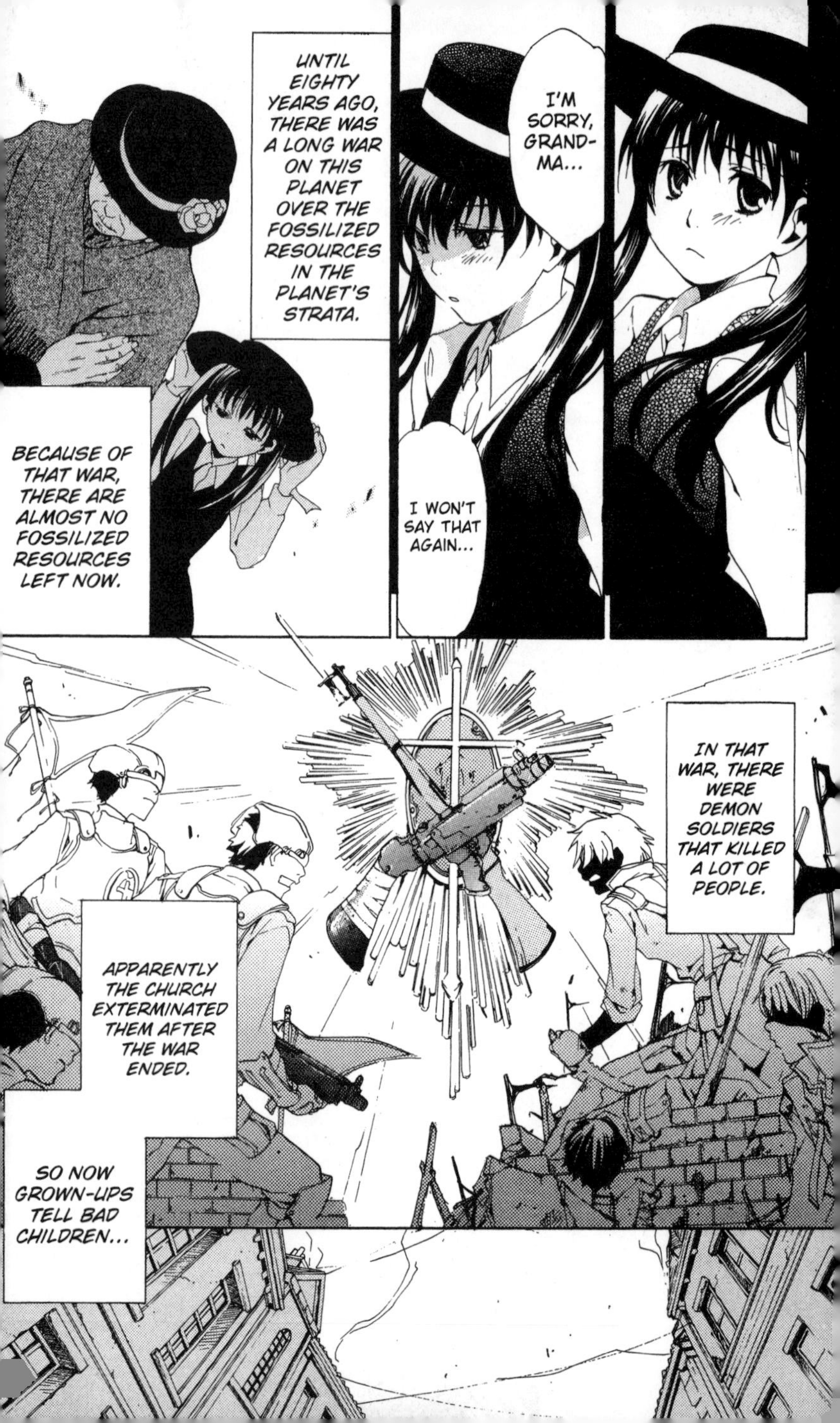
I'M SORRY, GRAND-MA...
I WON'T SAY THAT AGAIN...
UNTIL EIGHTY YEARS AGO, THERE WAS A LONG WAR ON THIS PLANET OVER THE FOSSILIZED RESOURCES IN THE PLANET'S STRATA.
BECAUSE OF THAT WAR, THERE ARE ALMOST NO FOSSILIZED RESOURCES LEFT NOW.
IN THAT WAR, THERE WERE DEMON SOLDIERS THAT KILLED A LOT OF PEOPLE.
APPARENTLY THE CHURCH EXTERMINATED THEM AFTER THE WAR ENDED.
SO NOW GROWN-UPS TELL BAD CHILDREN...

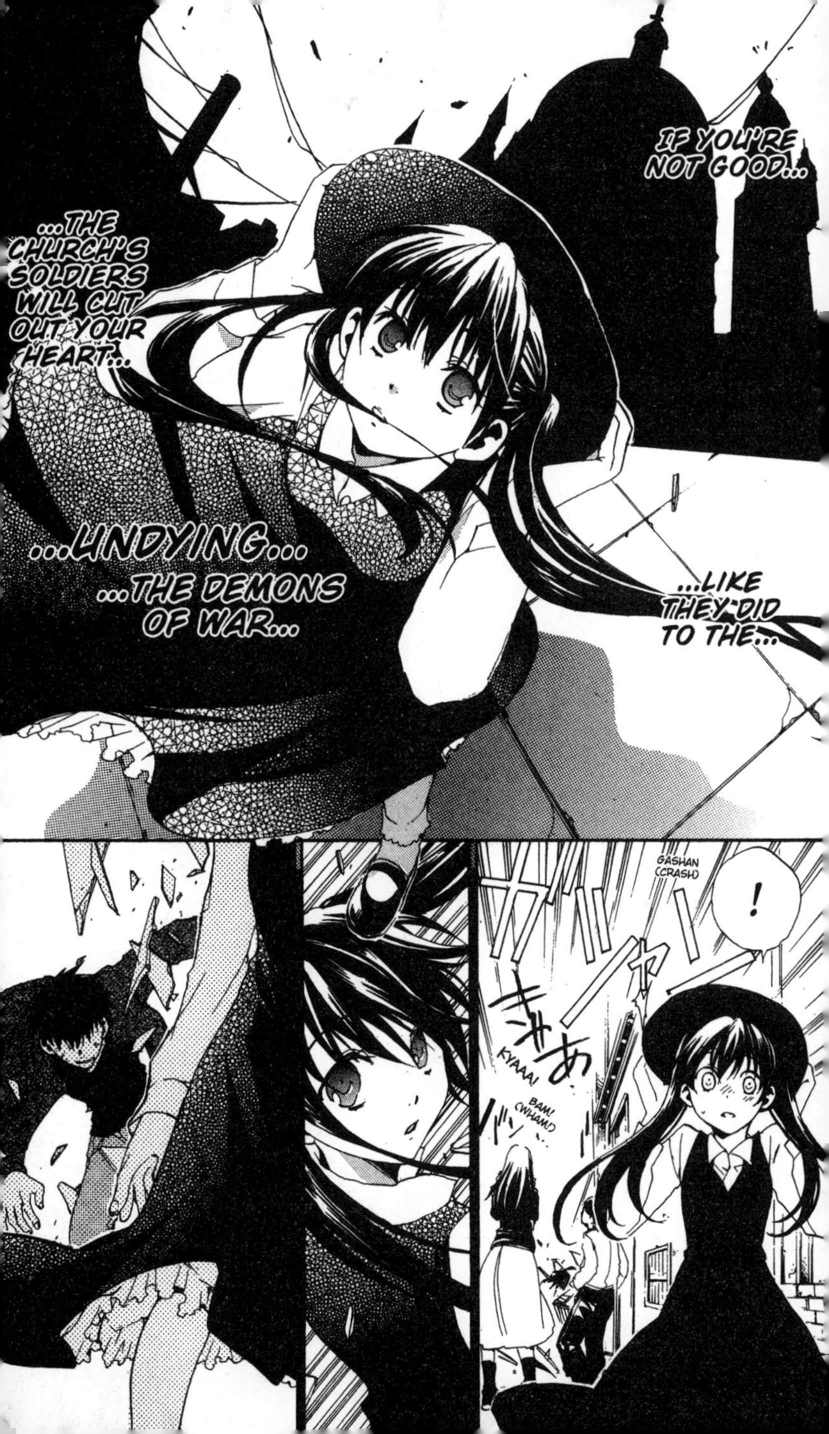
IF YOU'RE NOT GOOD...
...THE CHURCH'S SOLDIERS WILL CUT OUT YOUR HEART...
...LIKE THEY DID TO THE...
...UNDYING...
...THE DEMONS OF WAR...
GASHAN (CRASH)
!
KYAAA!
BAM! (WHAM!)

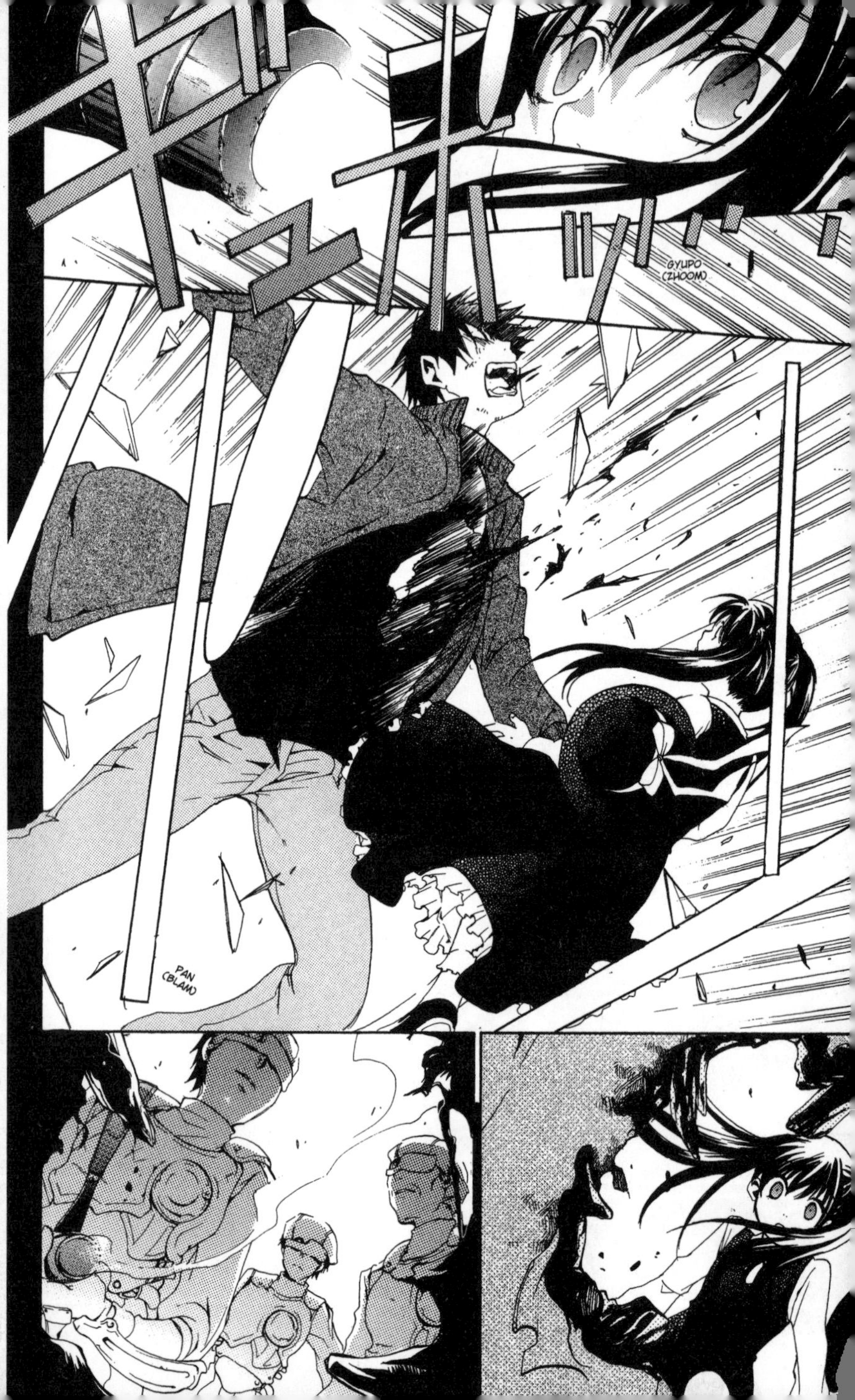
GYUPO
(ZHOOM)
PAN
(BLAM)

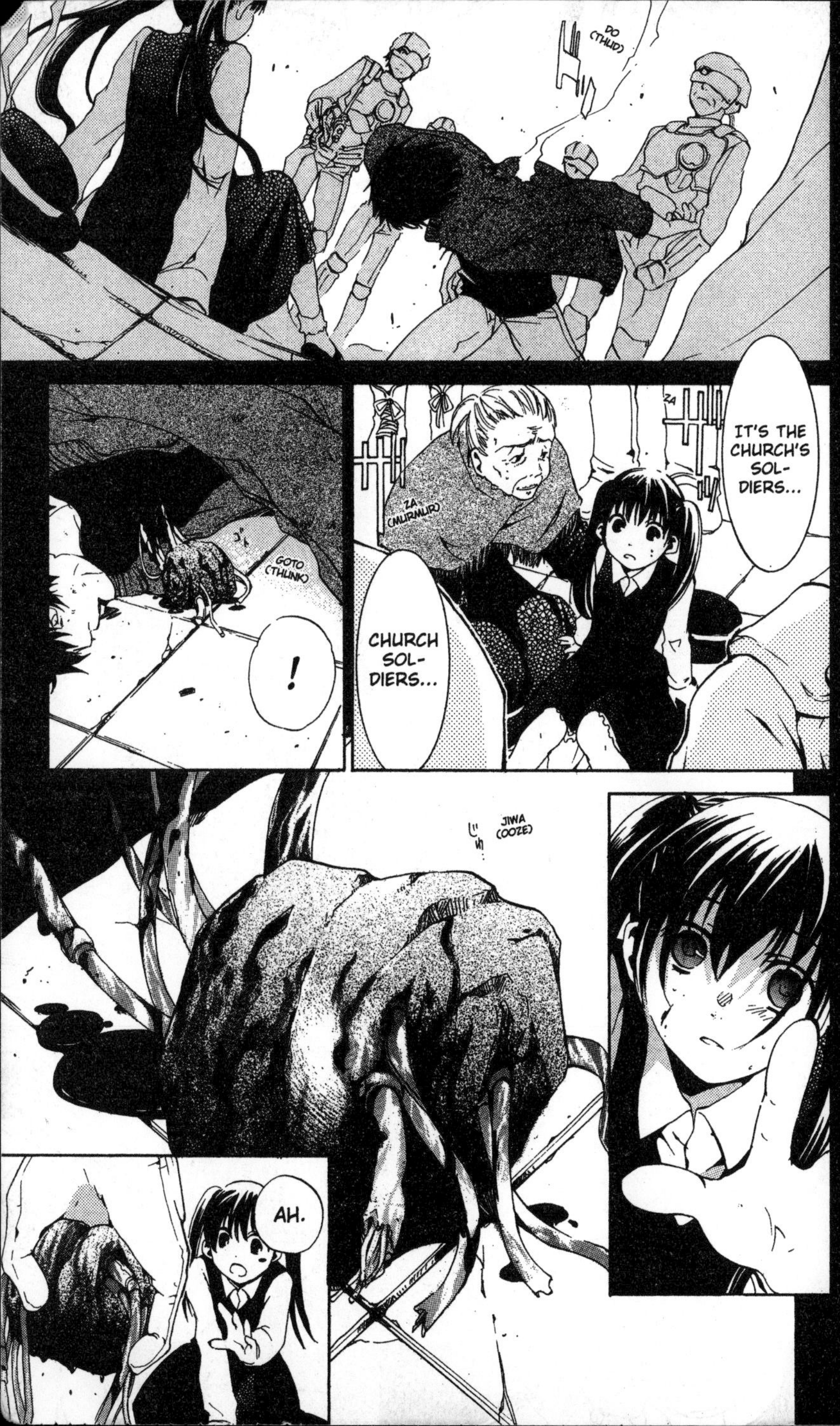
DO (THUD)
ZA
IT'S THE CHURCH'S SOL-DIERS...
ZA (MURMUR)
CHURCH SOL-DIERS...
GOTO (THUNK)
!
JIWA (OOZE)
AH.

WE'VE JUST EXECUTED A WICKED MAN. THERE'S NOTHING TO WORRY ABOUT.

YOU DIDN'T SEE ANYTHING.

A HEART MADE OF BLACK STONE...

...CHURCH SOLDIERS AND CARBONIZATION GUNS...

...WAS THAT...

...WAS THAT A DEMON OF WAR FROM THE STORIES...

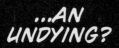

...AN UNDYING?

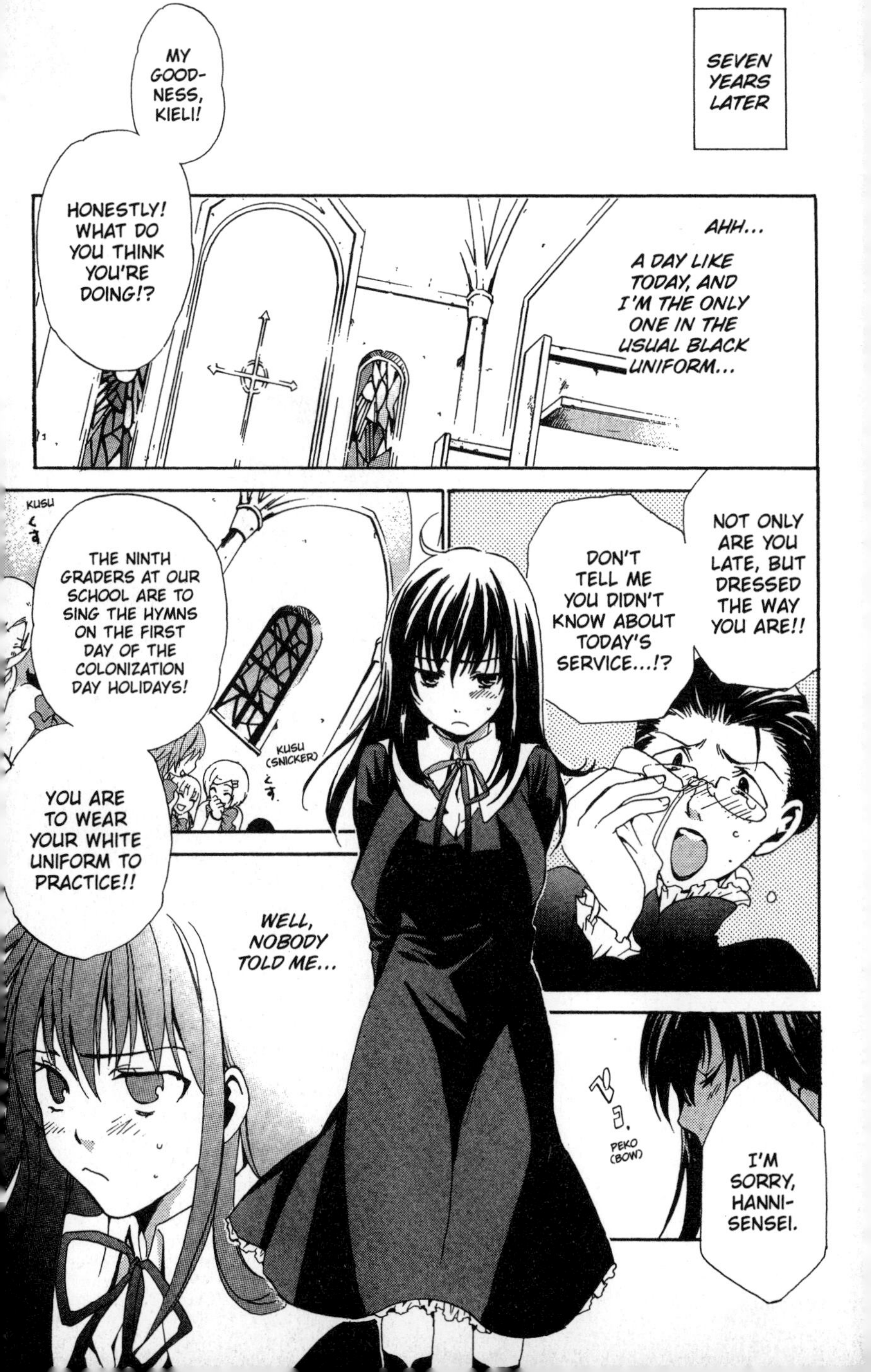
SEVEN YEARS LATER
MY GOODNESS, KIELI!
HONESTLY! WHAT DO YOU THINK YOU'RE DOING!?
AHH...
A DAY LIKE TODAY, AND I'M THE ONLY ONE IN THE USUAL BLACK UNIFORM...
NOT ONLY ARE YOU LATE, BUT DRESSED THE WAY YOU ARE!!
DON'T TELL ME YOU DIDN'T KNOW ABOUT TODAY'S SERVICE...!?
KUSU
THE NINTH GRADERS AT OUR SCHOOL ARE TO SING THE HYMNS ON THE FIRST DAY OF THE COLONIZATION DAY HOLIDAYS!
KUSU (SNICKER)
YOU ARE TO WEAR YOUR WHITE UNIFORM TO PRACTICE!!
WELL, NOBODY TOLD ME...
PEKO (BOW)
I'M SORRY, HANNI-SENSEI.

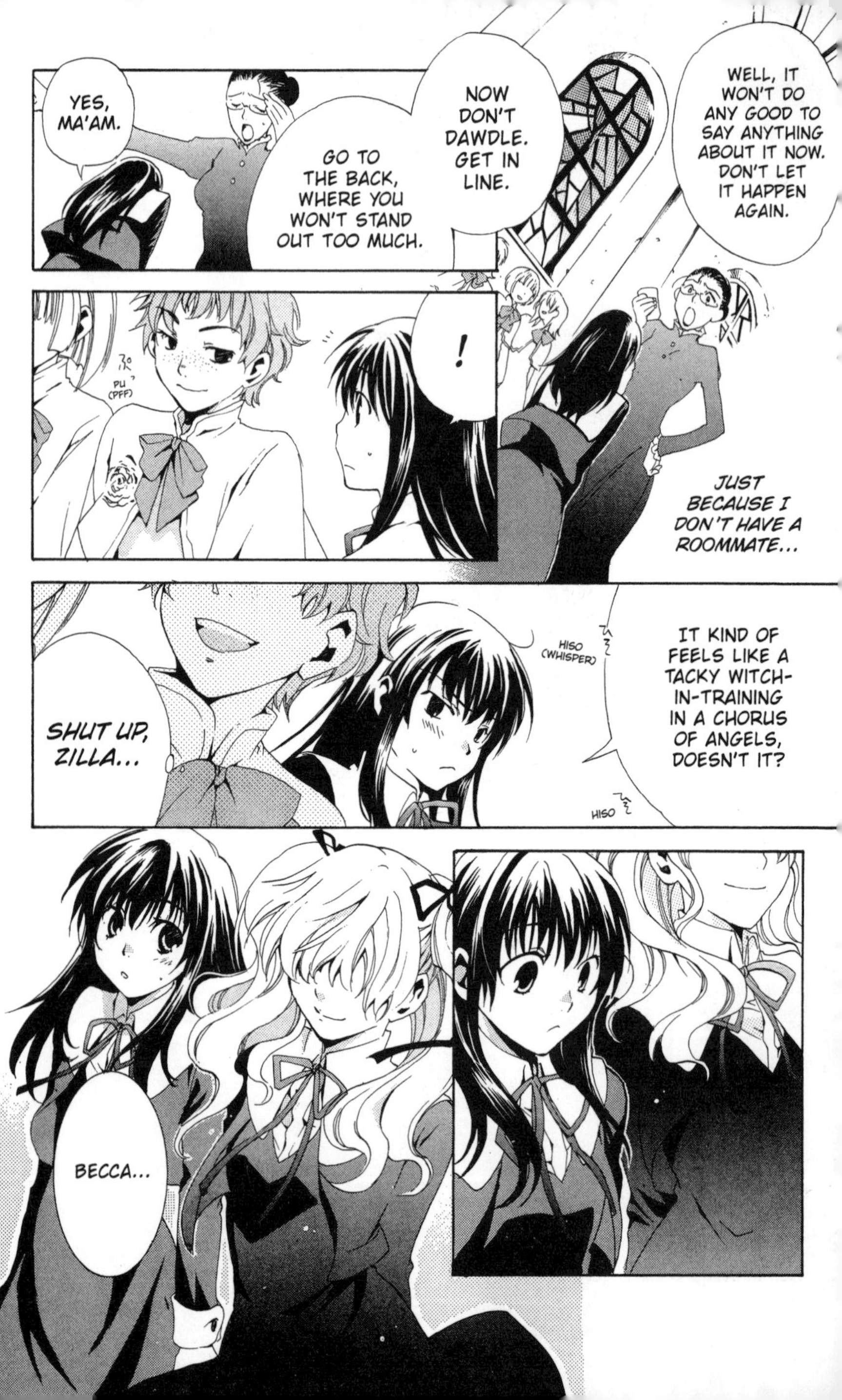
WELL, IT WON'T DO ANY GOOD TO SAY ANYTHING ABOUT IT NOW. DON'T LET IT HAPPEN AGAIN.
NOW DON'T DAWDLE. GET IN LINE.
GO TO THE BACK, WHERE YOU WON'T STAND OUT TOO MUCH.
YES, MA'AM.
JUST BECAUSE I DON'T HAVE A ROOMMATE...
!
PU (PFF)
HISO (WHISPER)
IT KIND OF FEELS LIKE A TACKY WITCH-IN-TRAINING IN A CHORUS OF ANGELS, DOESN'T IT?
HISO
SHUT UP, ZILLA...
BECCA...

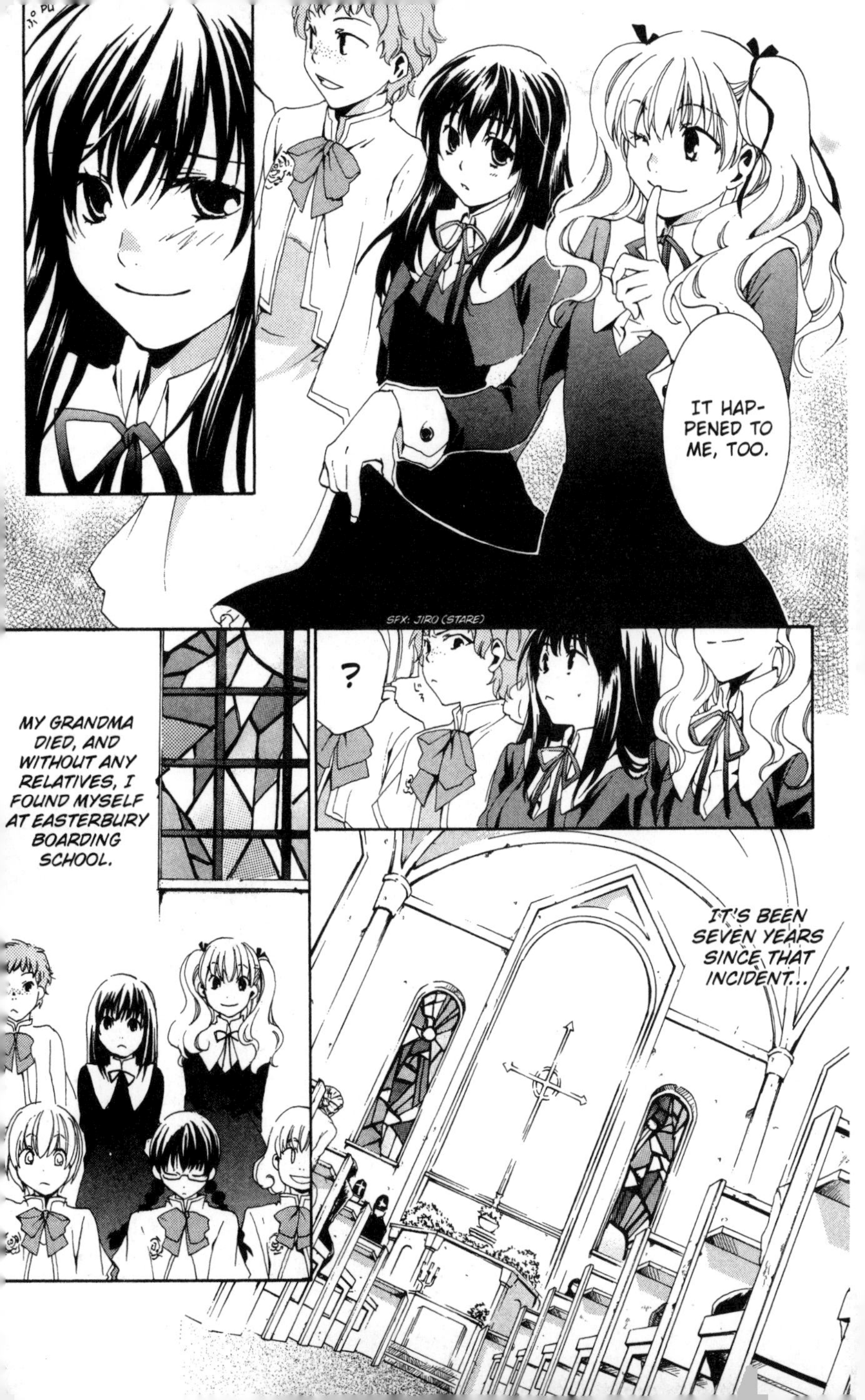
IT HAP-PENED TO ME, TOO.
ぷ PU
SFX: JIRO (STARE)
?
MY GRANDMA DIED, AND WITHOUT ANY RELATIVES, I FOUND MYSELF AT EASTERBURY BOARDING SCHOOL.
IT'S BEEN SEVEN YEARS SINCE THAT INCIDENT...

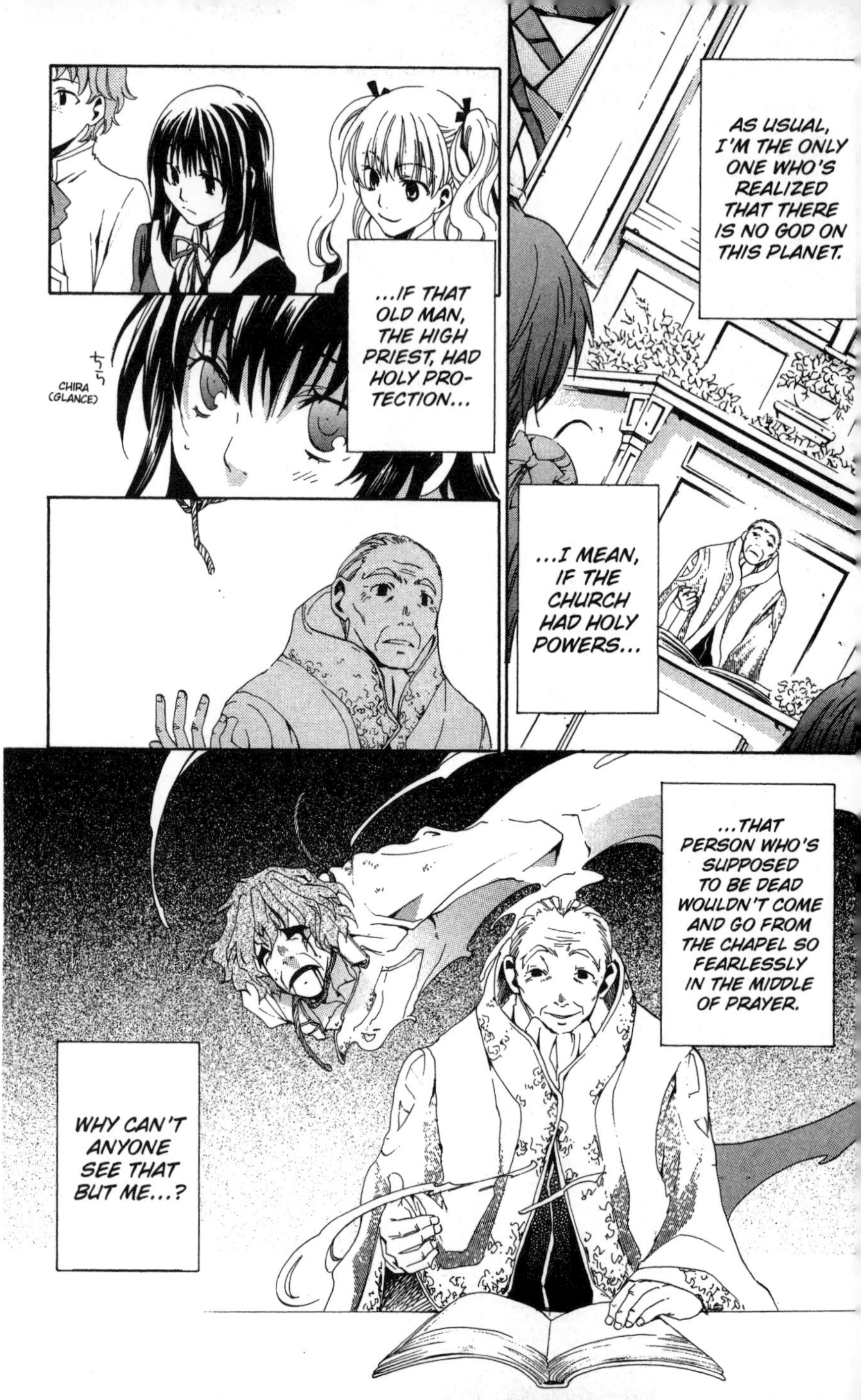
AS USUAL, I'M THE ONLY ONE WHO'S REALIZED THAT THERE IS NO GOD ON THIS PLANET.
...I MEAN, IF THE CHURCH HAD HOLY POWERS...
...IF THAT OLD MAN, THE HIGH PRIEST, HAD HOLY PROTECTION...
ちら
CHIRA (GLANCE)
...THAT PERSON WHO'S SUPPOSED TO BE DEAD WOULDN'T COME AND GO FROM THE CHAPEL SO FEARLESSLY IN THE MIDDLE OF PRAYER.
WHY CAN'T ANYONE SEE THAT BUT ME...?

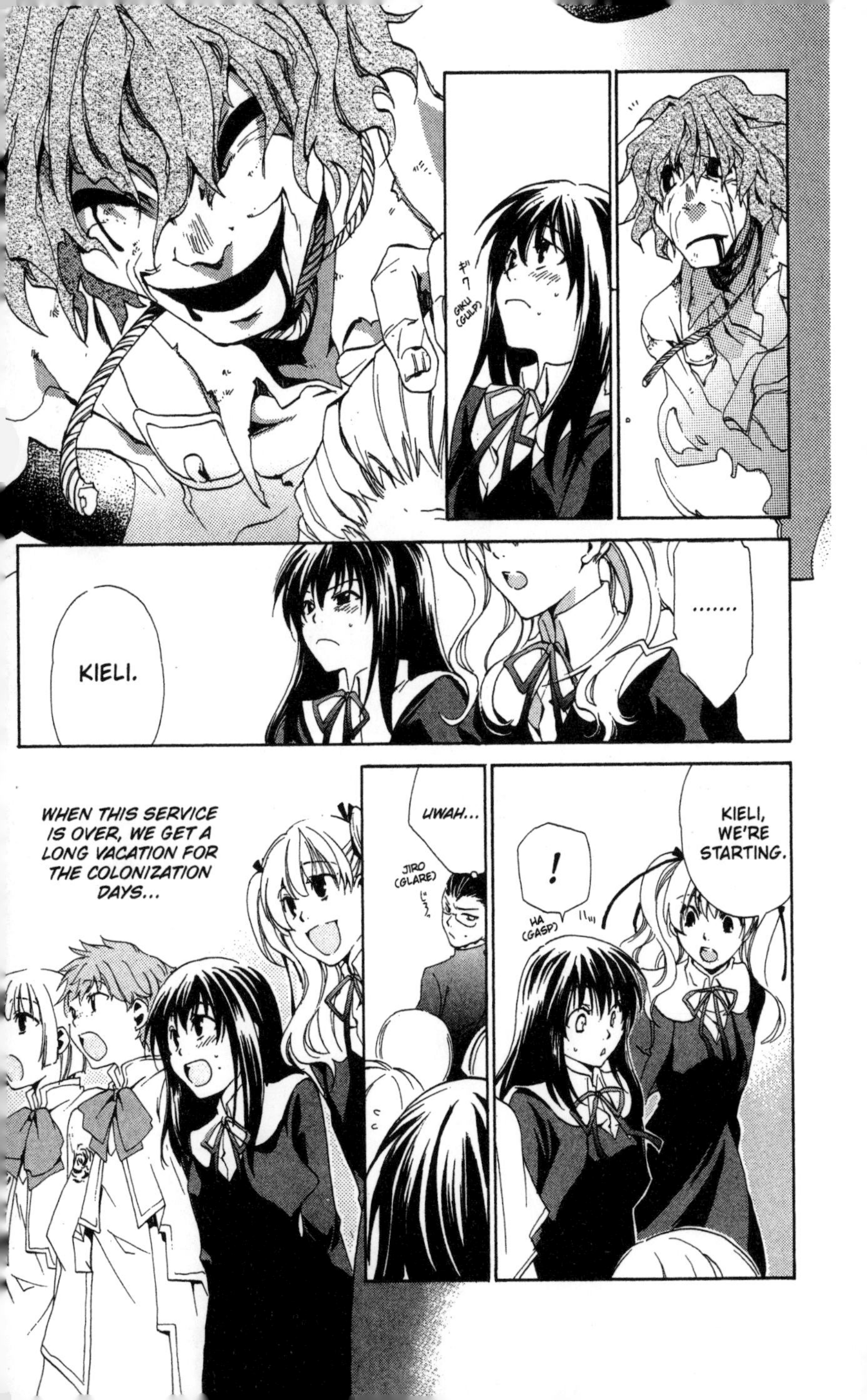
GIKU (GULP)
....
KIELI.
KIELI, WE'RE STARTING.
!
HA (GASP)
UWAH...
JIRO (GLARE)
WHEN THIS SERVICE IS OVER, WE GET A LONG VACATION FOR THE COLONIZATION DAYS...

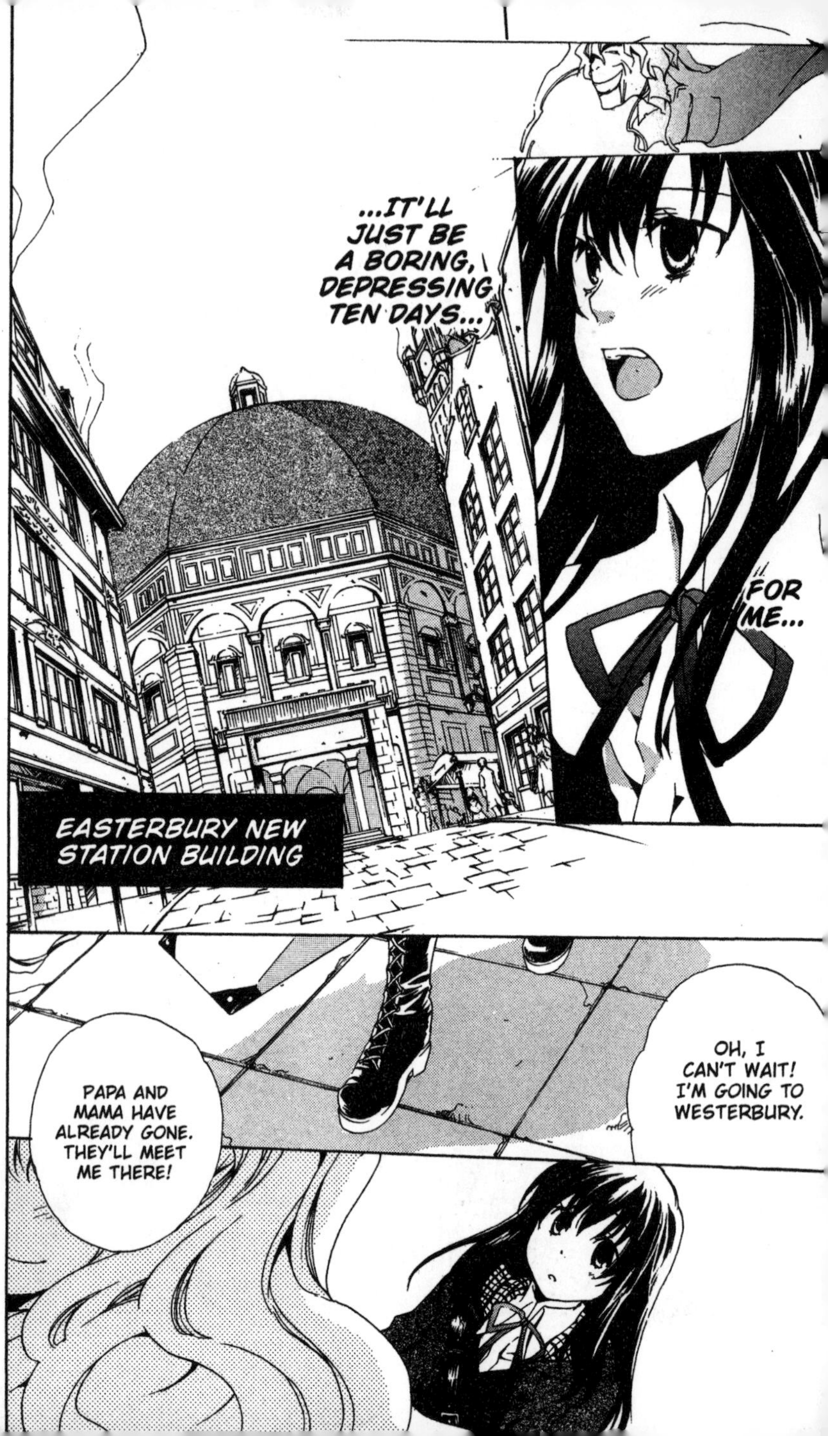
...IT'LL JUST BE A BORING, DEPRESSING TEN DAYS...
FOR ME...
EASTERBURY NEW STATION BUILDING
OH, I CAN'T WAIT! I'M GOING TO WESTERBURY.
PAPA AND MAMA HAVE ALREADY GONE. THEY'LL MEET ME THERE!

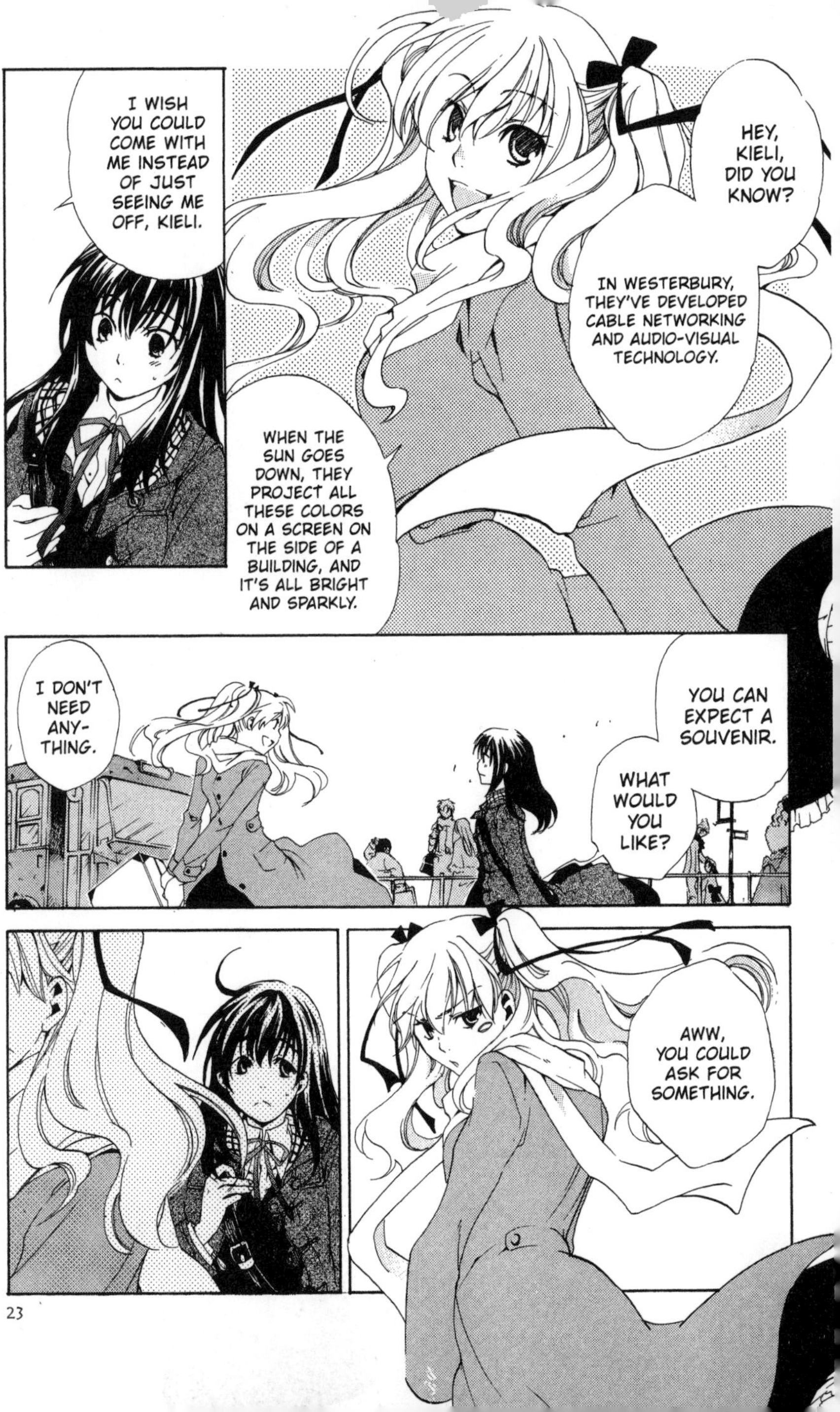
HEY, KIELI, DID YOU KNOW?
IN WESTERBURY, THEY'VE DEVELOPED CABLE NETWORKING AND AUDIO-VISUAL TECHNOLOGY.
WHEN THE SUN GOES DOWN, THEY PROJECT ALL THESE COLORS ON A SCREEN ON THE SIDE OF A BUILDING, AND IT'S ALL BRIGHT AND SPARKLY.
I WISH YOU COULD COME WITH ME INSTEAD OF JUST SEEING ME OFF, KIELI.
YOU CAN EXPECT A SOUVENIR.
WHAT WOULD YOU LIKE?
I DON'T NEED ANYTHING.
AWW, YOU COULD ASK FOR SOMETHING.

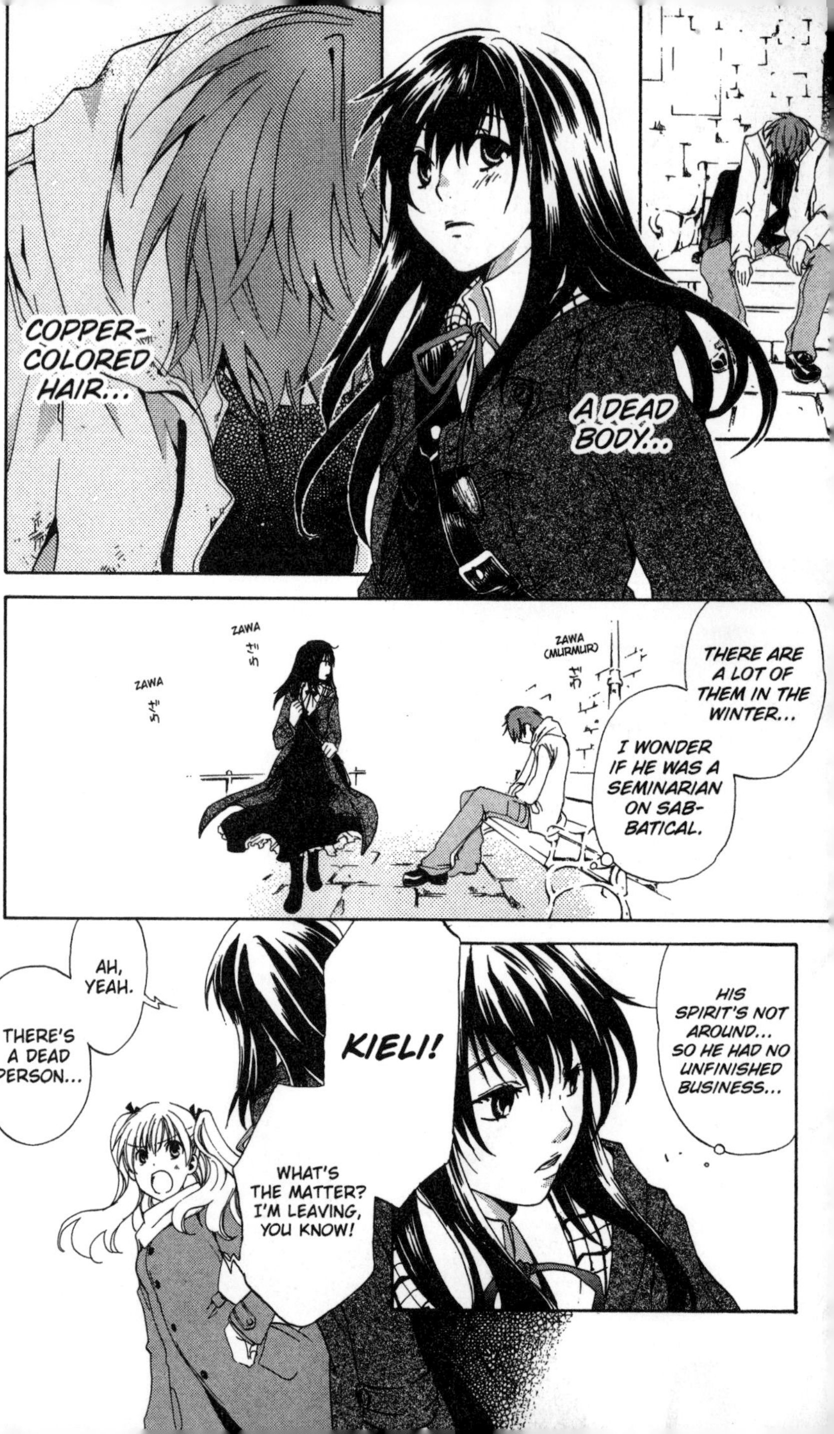
A DEAD BODY...
COPPER-COLORED HAIR...
ZAWA (MURMUR)
THERE ARE A LOT OF THEM IN THE WINTER...
I WONDER IF HE WAS A SEMINARIAN ON SAB-BATICAL.
ZAWA
ZAWA
HIS SPIRIT'S NOT AROUND... SO HE HAD NO UNFINISHED BUSINESS...
KIELI!
AH, YEAH.
THERE'S A DEAD PERSON...
WHAT'S THE MATTER? I'M LEAVING, YOU KNOW!

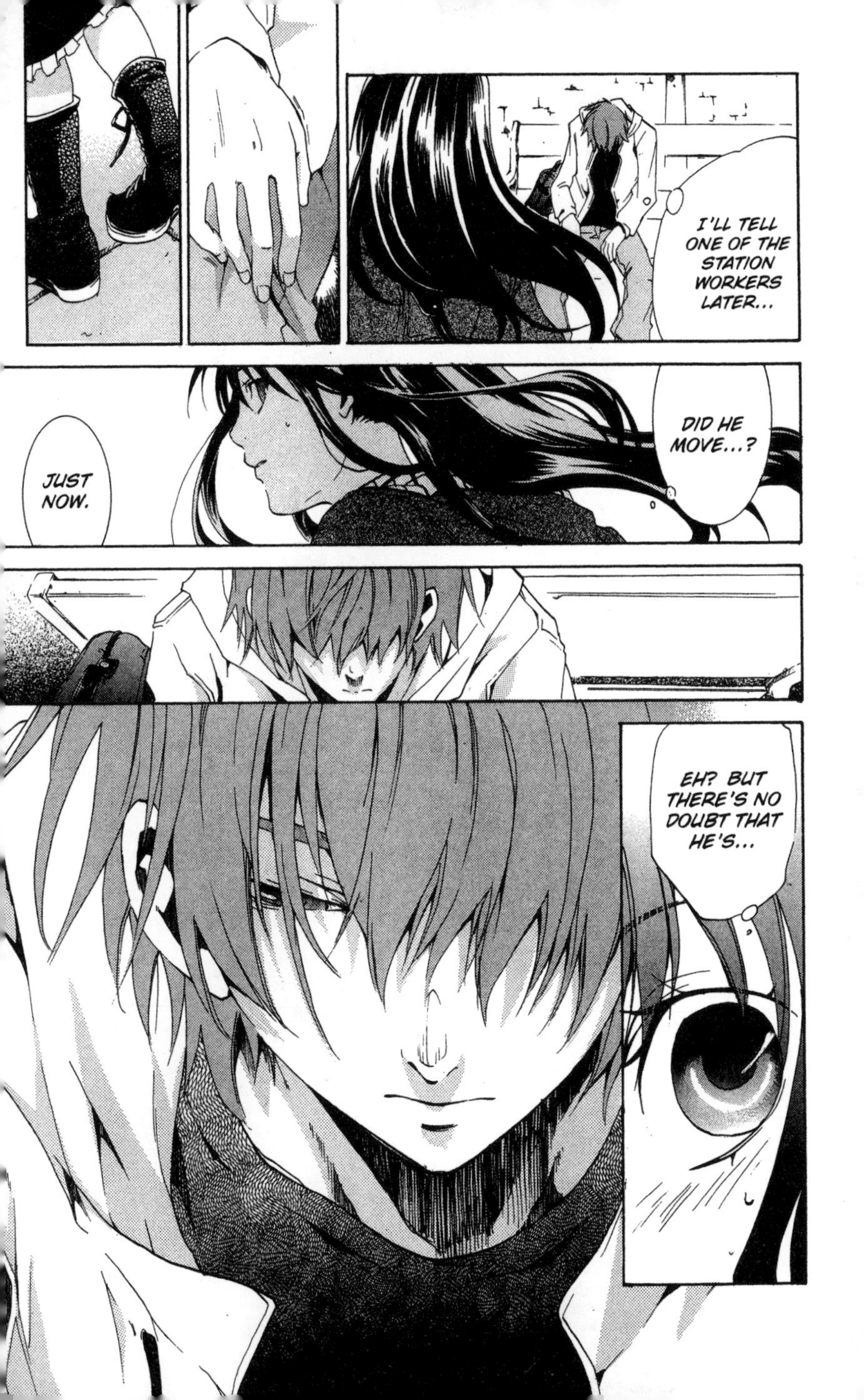
I'LL TELL ONE OF THE STATION WORKERS LATER...
DID HE MOVE...?
JUST NOW.
EH? BUT THERE'S NO DOUBT THAT HE'S...

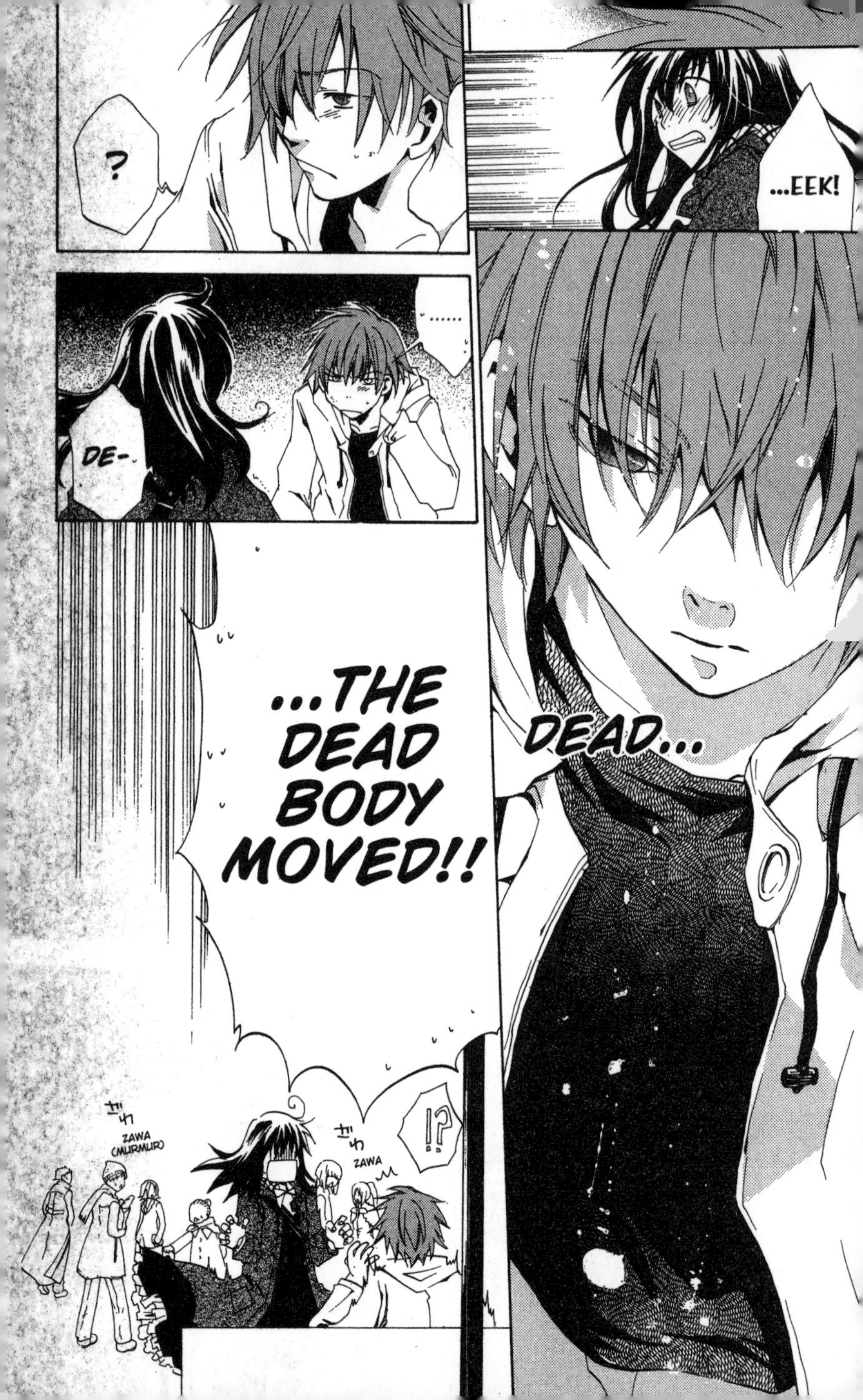
...EEK!
?
DEAD...
......
DE-
...THE DEAD BODY MOVED!!
!?
ざわ
ZAWA (MURMUR)
ざわ
ZAWA

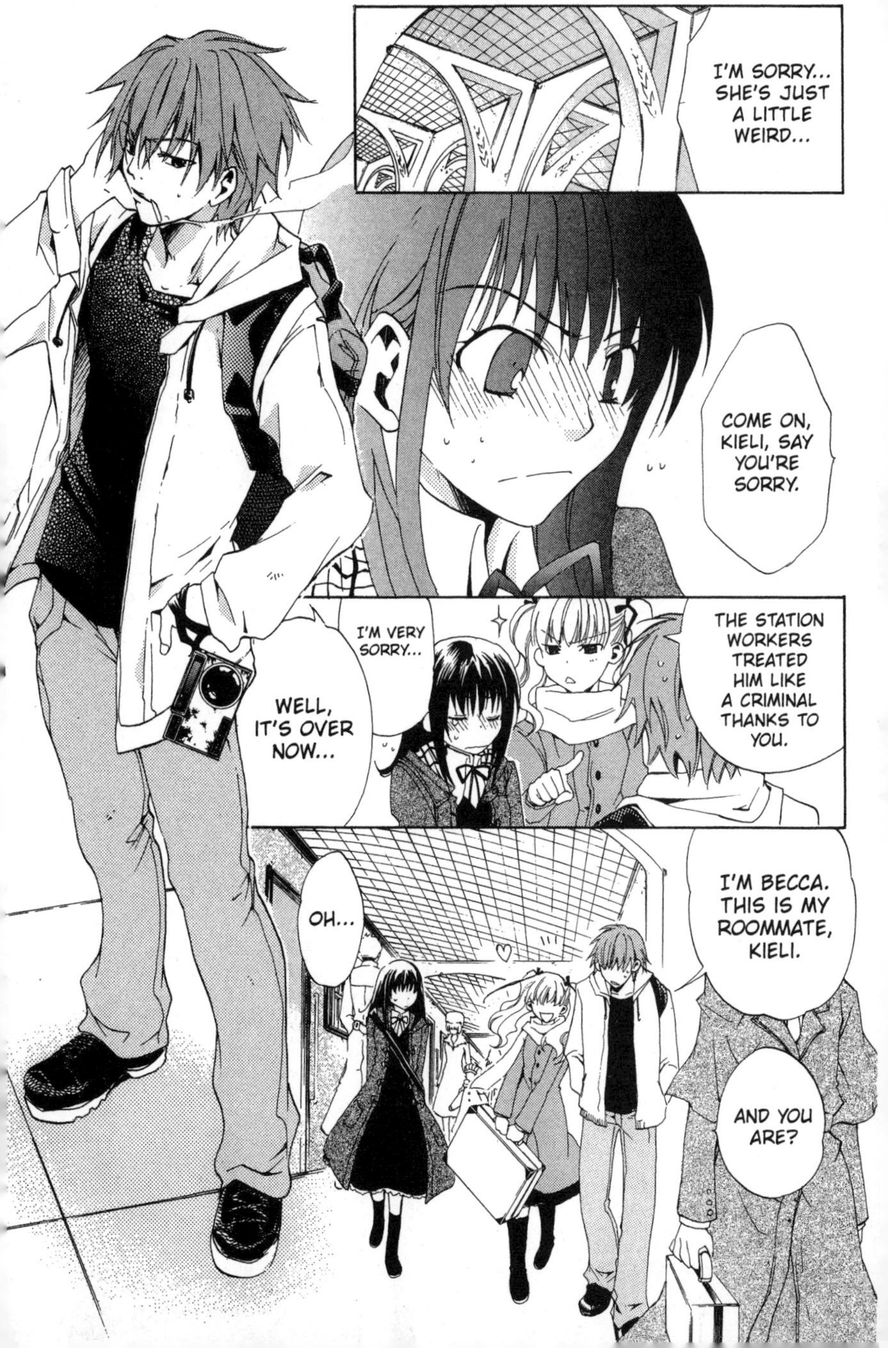

I'M SORRY... SHE'S JUST A LITTLE WEIRD...
COME ON, KIELI, SAY YOU'RE SORRY.
THE STATION WORKERS TREATED HIM LIKE A CRIMINAL THANKS TO YOU.
I'M VERY SORRY...
WELL, IT'S OVER NOW...
I'M BECCA. THIS IS MY ROOMMATE, KIELI.
OH...
AND YOU ARE?

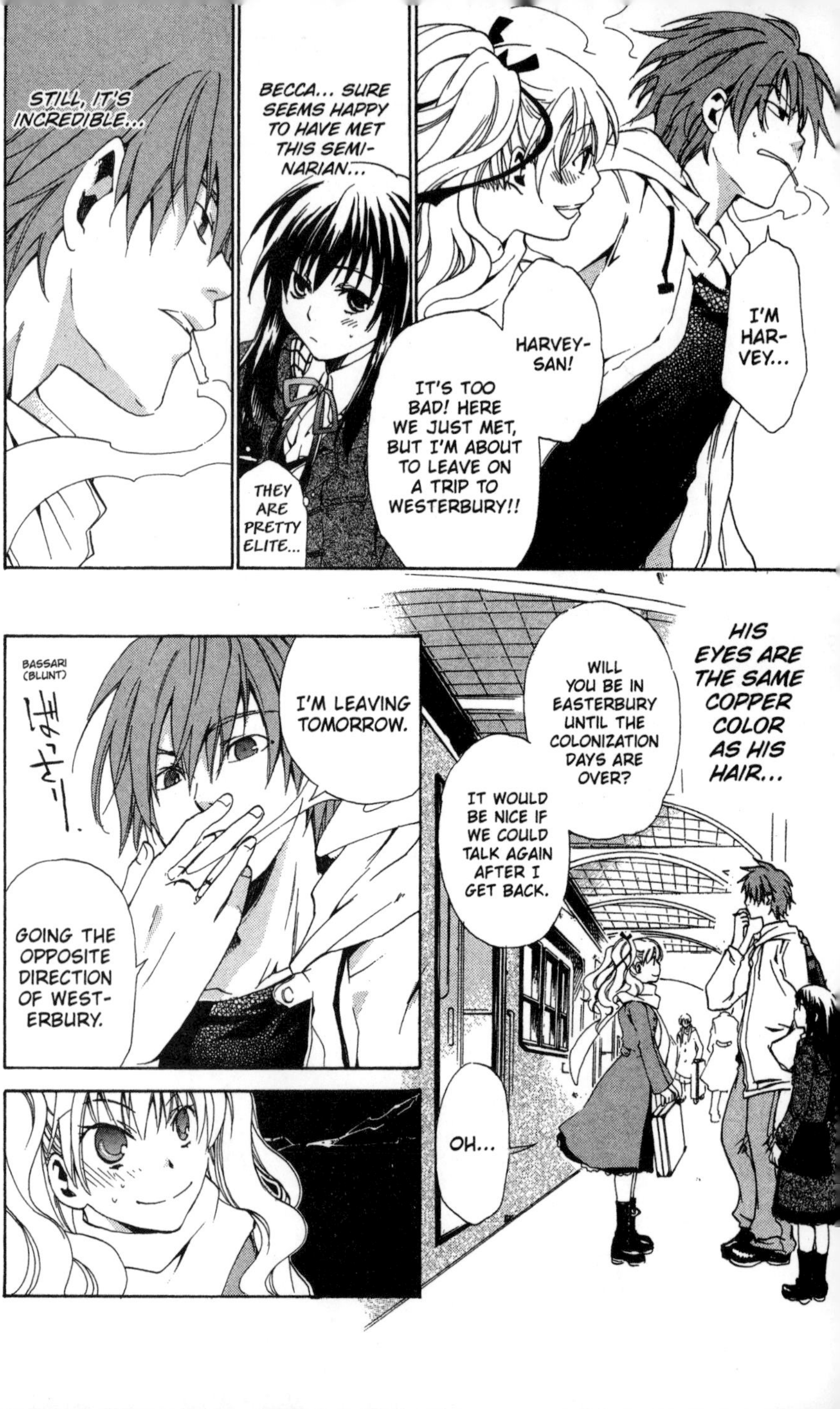
I'M HARVEY...
HARVEY-SAN!
IT'S TOO BAD! HERE WE JUST MET, BUT I'M ABOUT TO LEAVE ON A TRIP TO WESTERBURY!!
BECCA... SURE SEEMS HAPPY TO HAVE MET THIS SEMINARIAN...
THEY ARE PRETTY ELITE...
STILL, IT'S INCREDIBLE...
HIS EYES ARE THE SAME COPPER COLOR AS HIS HAIR...
WILL YOU BE IN EASTERBURY UNTIL THE COLONIZATION DAYS ARE OVER?
IT WOULD BE NICE IF WE COULD TALK AGAIN AFTER I GET BACK.
OH...
I'M LEAVING TOMORROW.
BASSARI (BLUNT)
GOING THE OPPOSITE DIRECTION OF WESTERBURY.

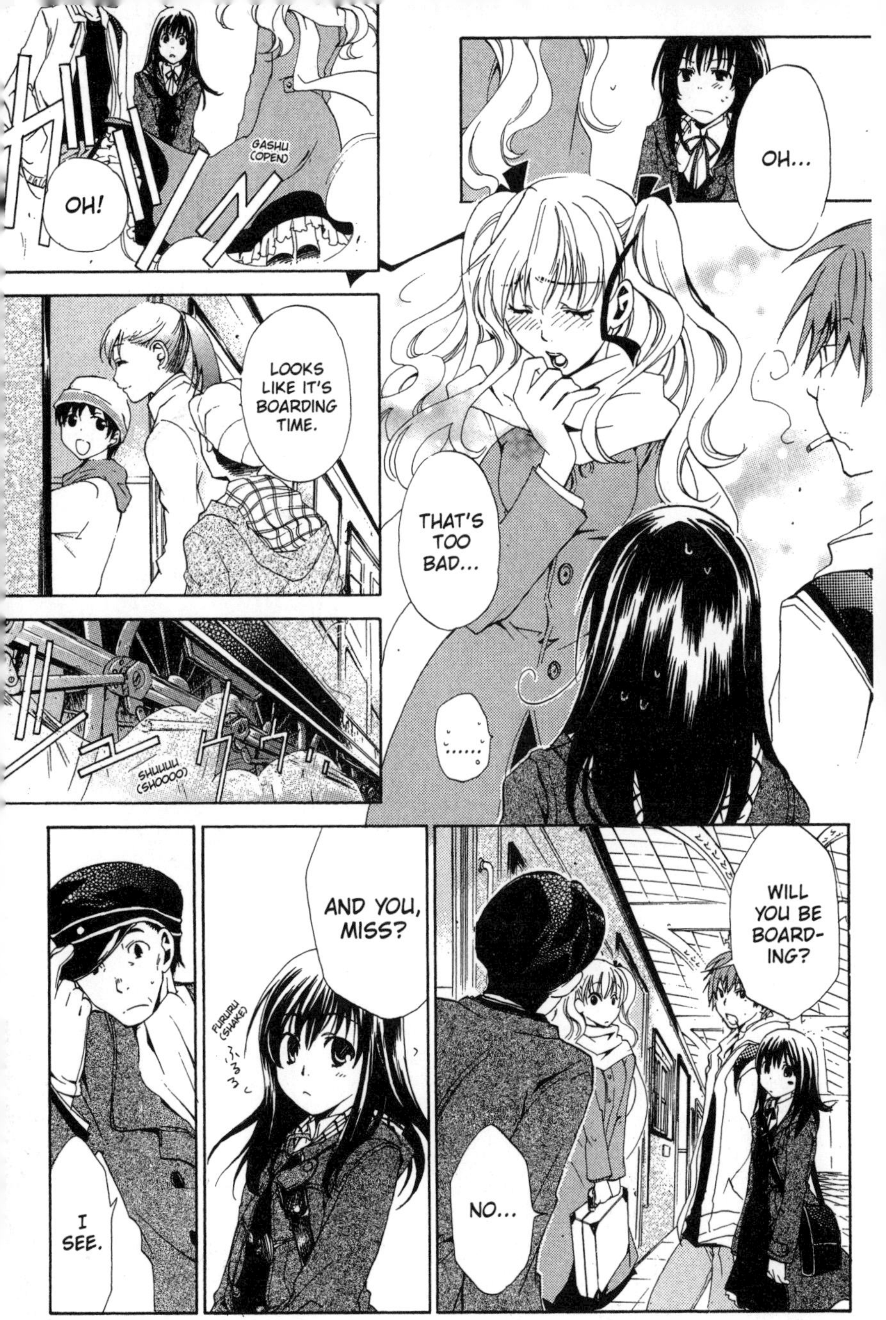
OH...
THAT'S TOO BAD...
......
OH!
GASHU COPEND
LOOKS LIKE IT'S BOARDING TIME.
SHUUUU (SHOOOO)
WILL YOU BE BOARD-ING?
NO...
AND YOU, MISS?
FURURU (SHAKE)
I SEE.

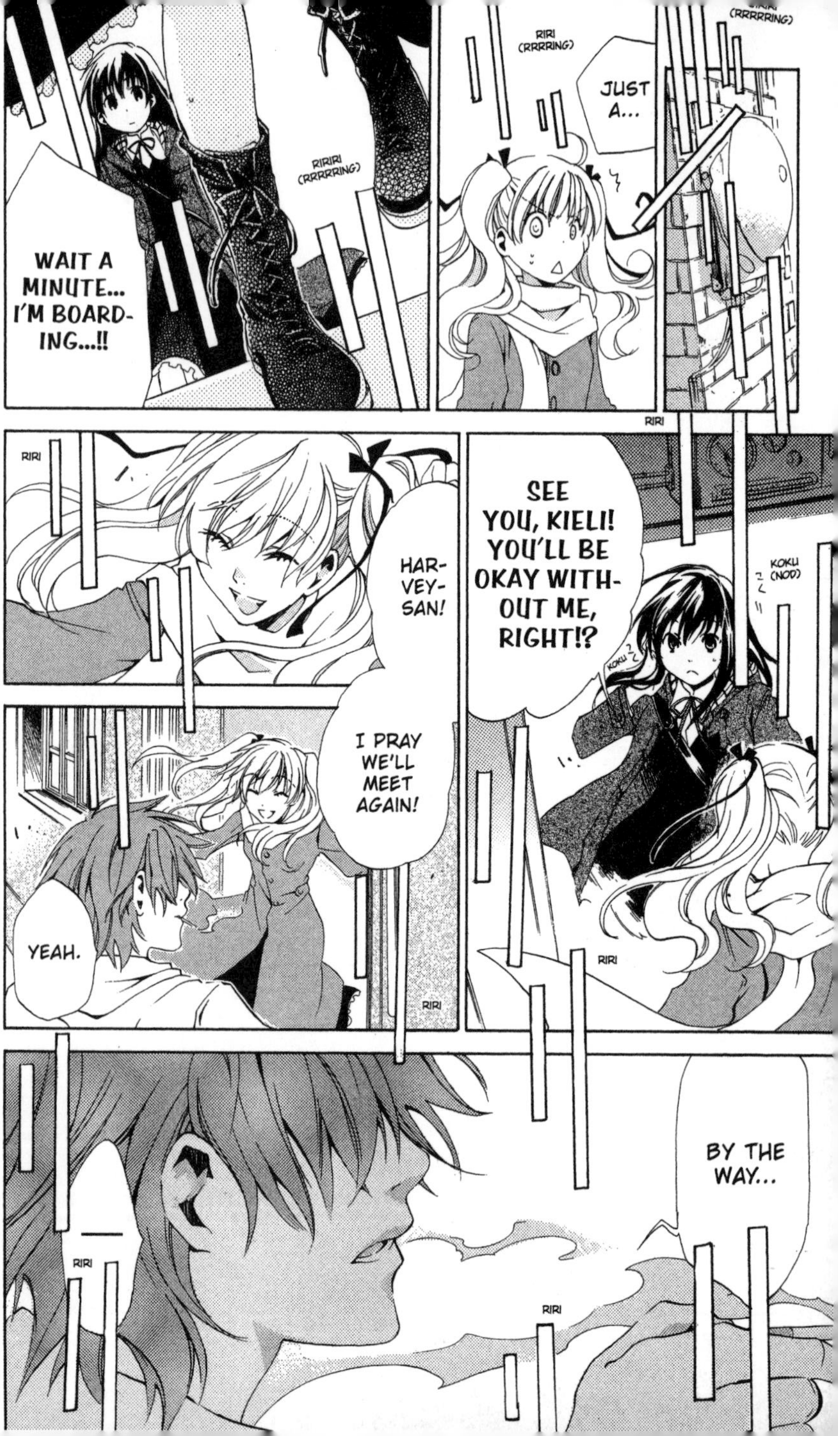
(RRRRRING)
RIRI (RRRRING)
JUST A...
RIRIRI (RRRRRING)
WAIT A MINUTE... I'M BOARD-ING...!!
RIRI
SEE YOU, KIELI! YOU'LL BE OKAY WITH-OUT ME, RIGHT!?
KOKU (NOD)
KOKU
RIRI
RIRI
HAR-VEY-SAN!
I PRAY WE'LL MEET AGAIN!
YEAH.
RIRI
BY THE WAY...
RIRI
—
RIRI

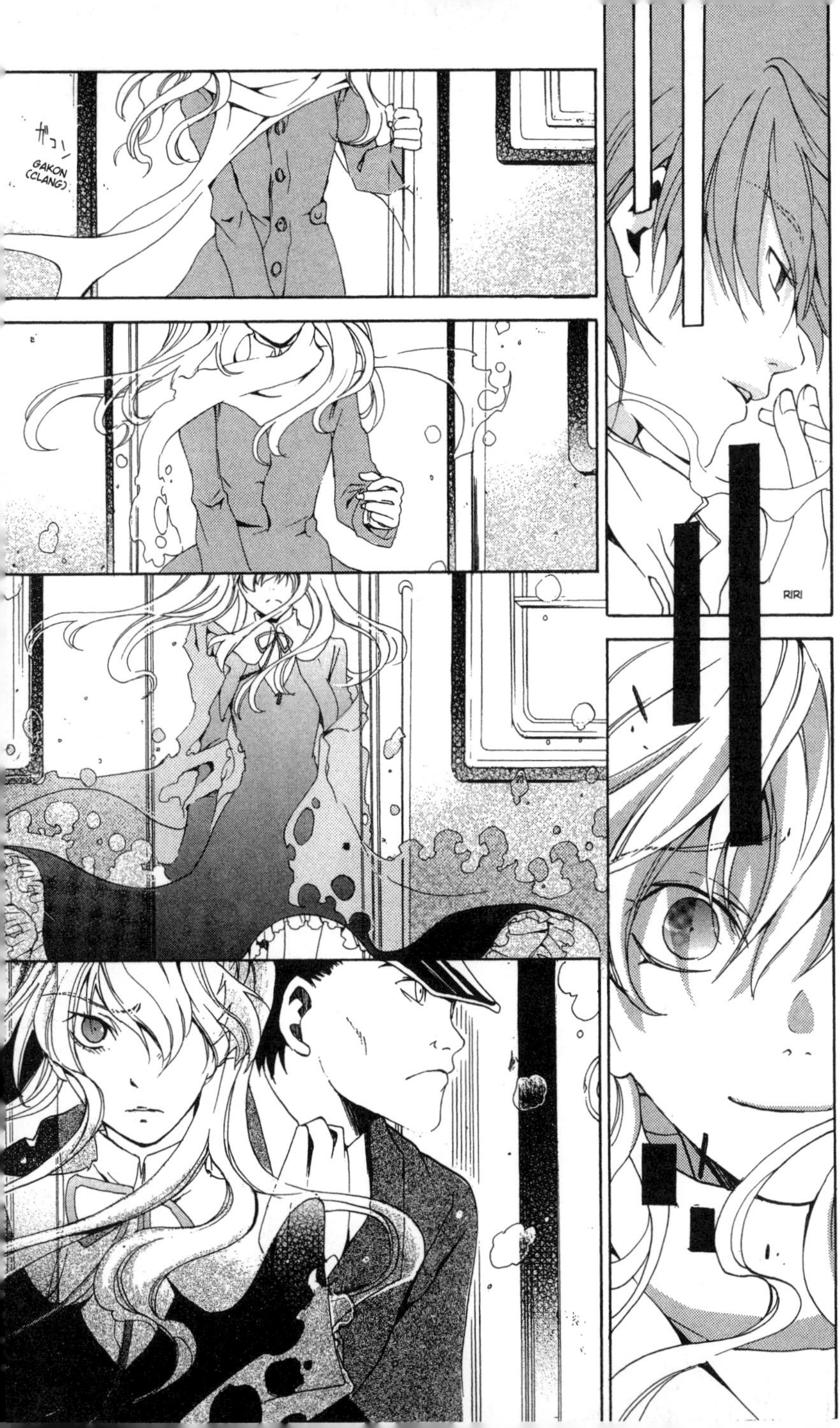
RIRI
ガコン
GAKON (CLANG)

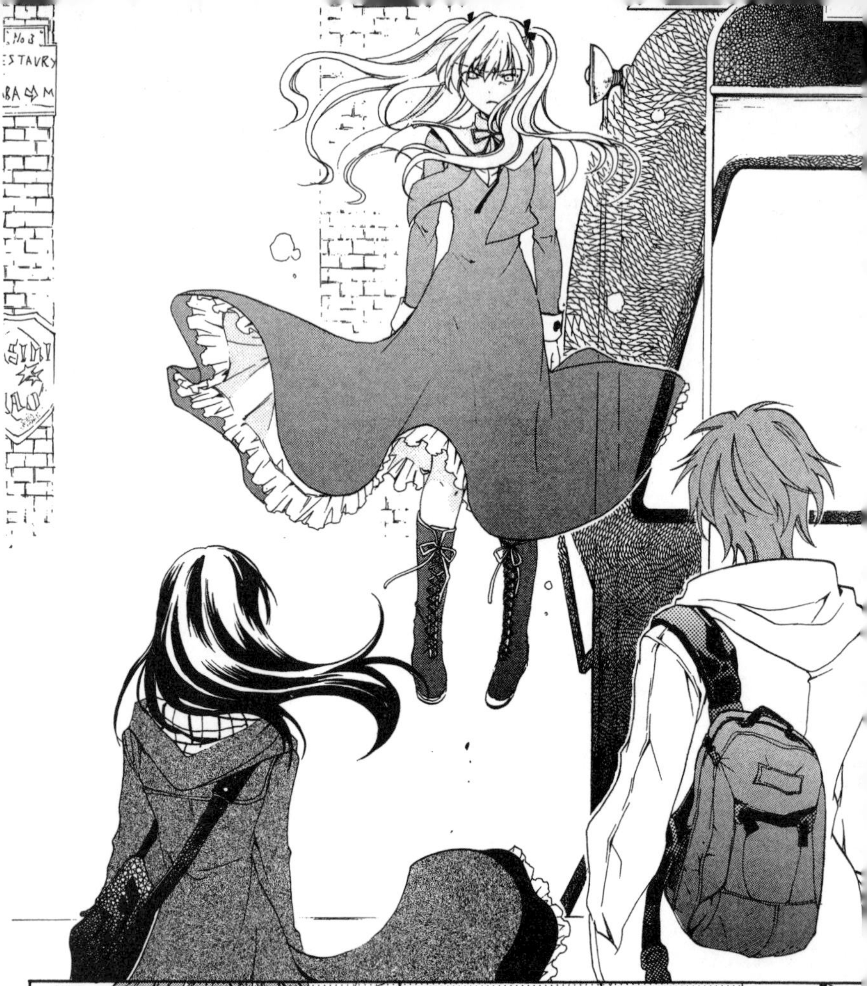

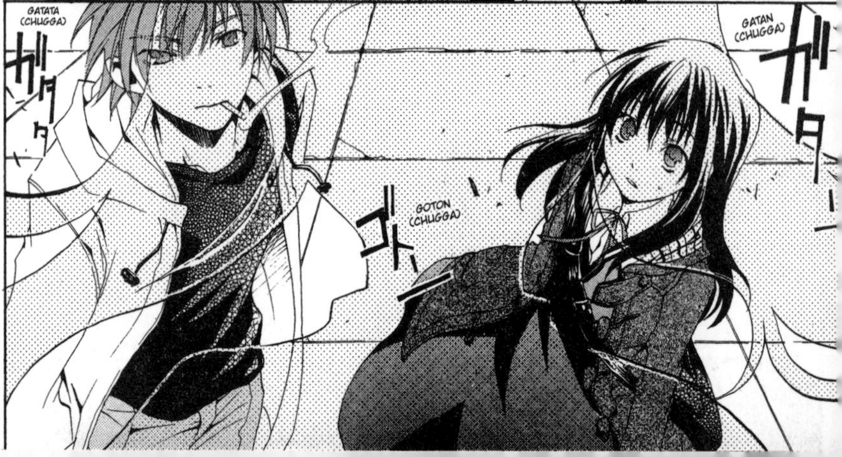
ガタン
GATAN (CHUGGA)
ゴトン
GOTON (CHUGGA)
ガタタ
GATATA (CHUGGA)

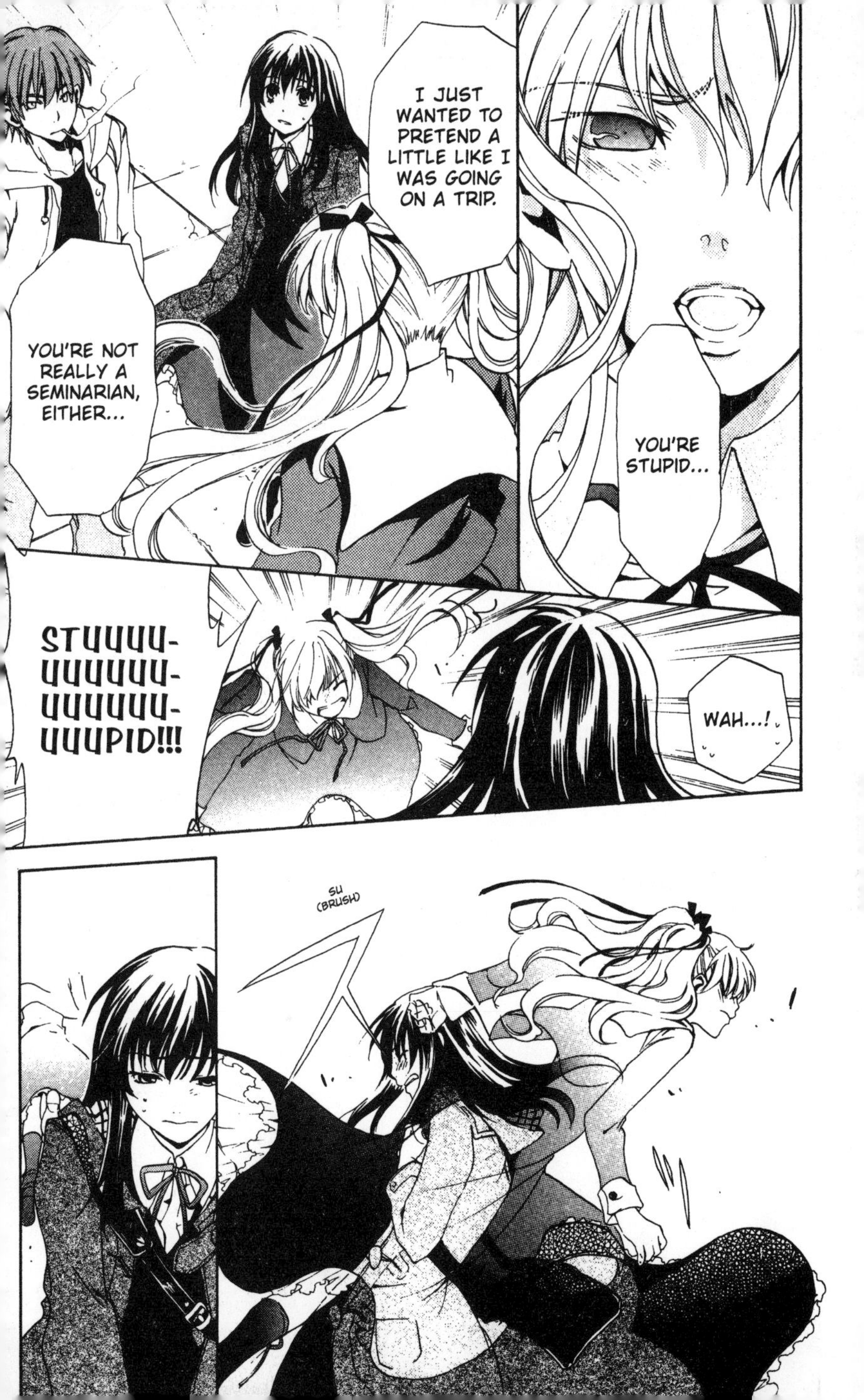
YOU'RE STUPID...
I JUST WANTED TO PRETEND A LITTLE LIKE I WAS GOING ON A TRIP.
YOU'RE NOT REALLY A SEMINARIAN, EITHER...
WAH...!
STUUUU-UUUUUU-UUUUUU-UUUPID!!!
SU (BRUSH)

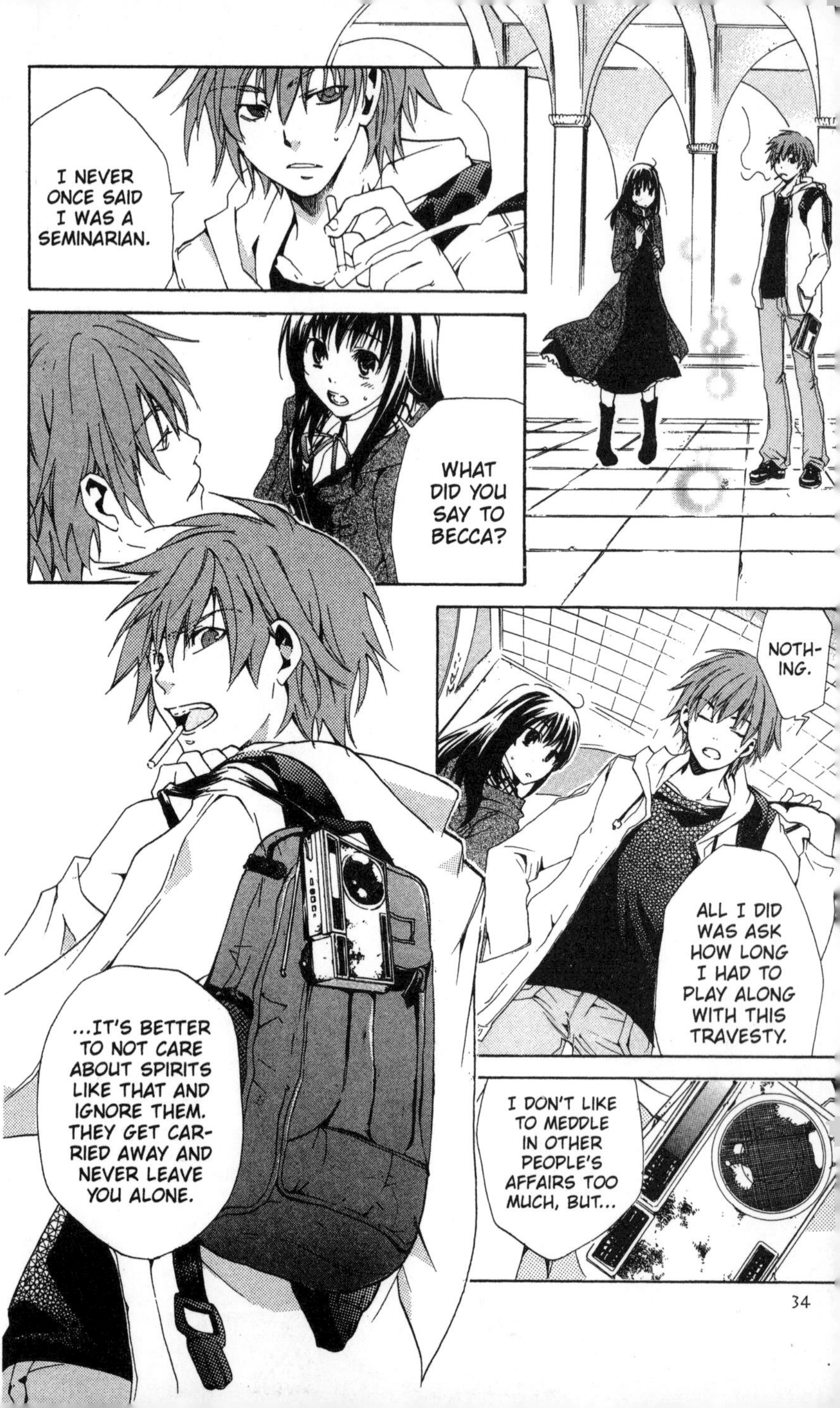
I NEVER ONCE SAID I WAS A SEMINARIAN.
WHAT DID YOU SAY TO BECCA?
NOTH-ING.
ALL I DID WAS ASK HOW LONG I HAD TO PLAY ALONG WITH THIS TRAVESTY.
I DON'T LIKE TO MEDDLE IN OTHER PEOPLE'S AFFAIRS TOO MUCH, BUT...
...IT'S BETTER TO NOT CARE ABOUT SPIRITS LIKE THAT AND IGNORE THEM. THEY GET CAR-RIED AWAY AND NEVER LEAVE YOU ALONE.

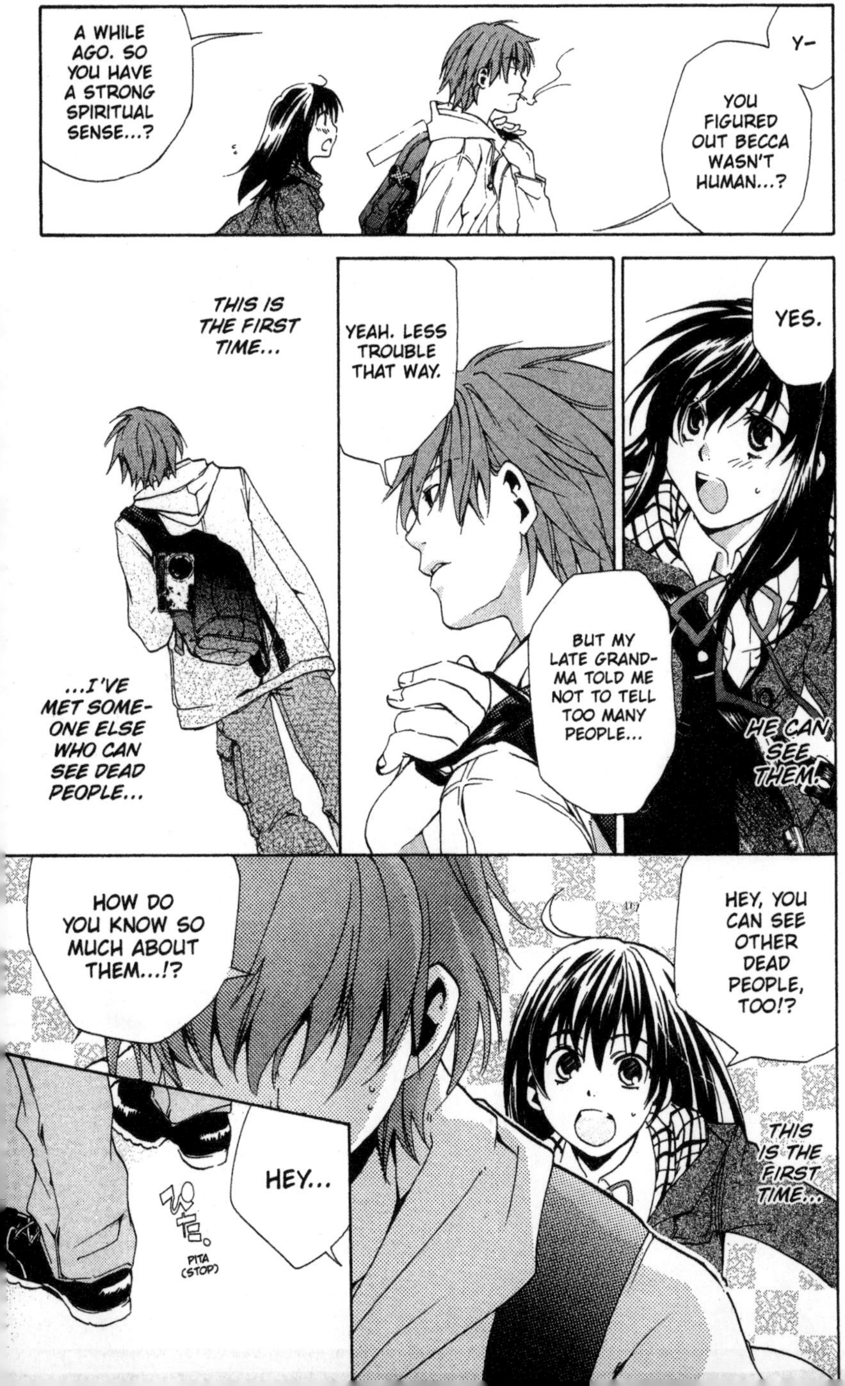
Y-
YOU FIGURED OUT BECCA WASN'T HUMAN...?
A WHILE AGO. SO YOU HAVE A STRONG SPIRITUAL SENSE...?
YES.
BUT MY LATE GRAND-MA TOLD ME NOT TO TELL TOO MANY PEOPLE...
HE CAN SEE THEM.
YEAH. LESS TROUBLE THAT WAY.
THIS IS THE FIRST TIME...
...I'VE MET SOME-ONE ELSE WHO CAN SEE DEAD PEOPLE...
HEY, YOU CAN SEE OTHER DEAD PEOPLE, TOO!?
THIS IS THE FIRST TIME...
HOW DO YOU KNOW SO MUCH ABOUT THEM...!?
HEY...
ぴた。
PITA (STOP)

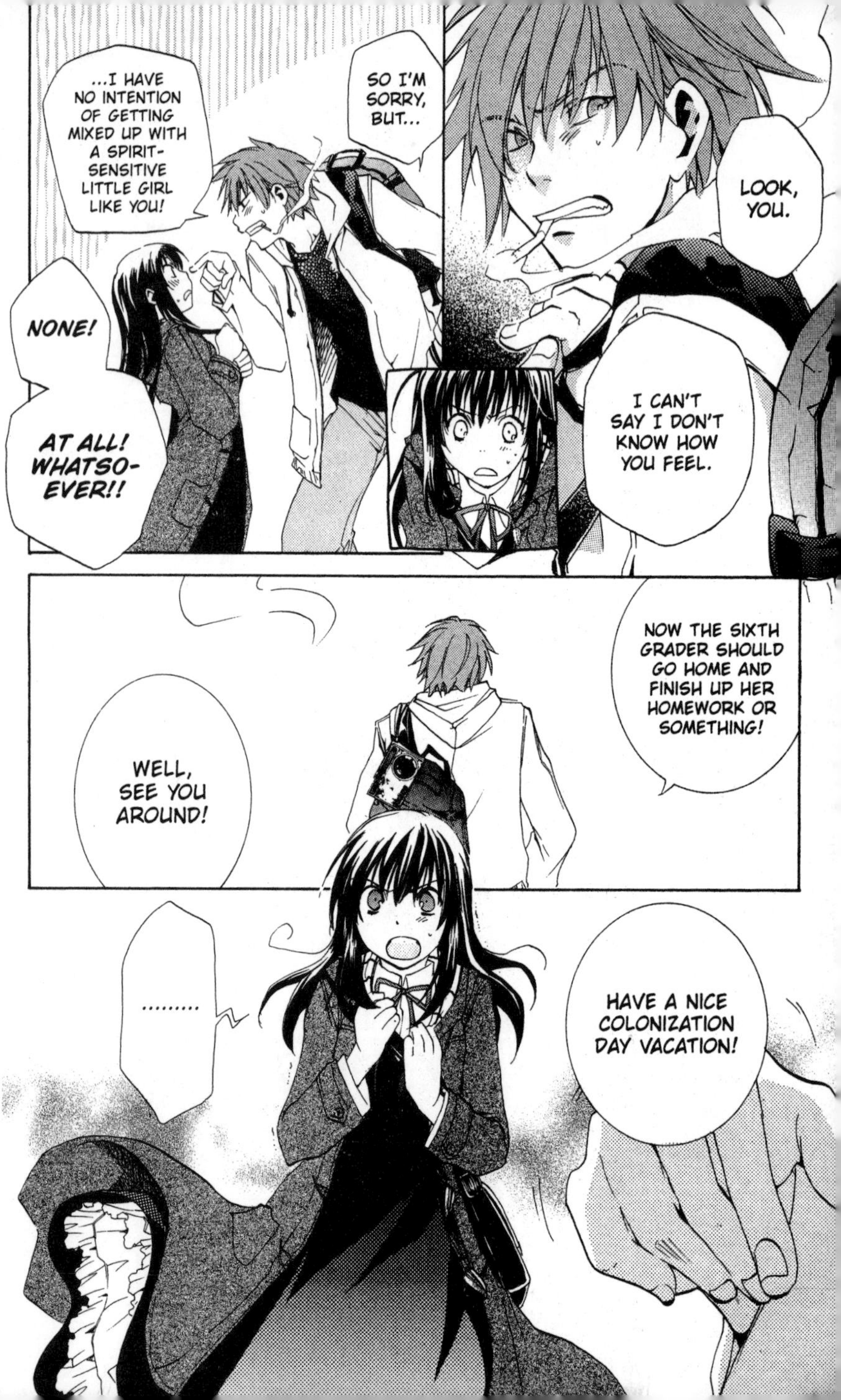
LOOK, YOU.
I CAN'T SAY I DON'T KNOW HOW YOU FEEL.
SO I'M SORRY, BUT...
...I HAVE NO INTENTION OF GETTING MIXED UP WITH A SPIRIT-SENSITIVE LITTLE GIRL LIKE YOU!
NONE!
AT ALL! WHATSO-EVER!!
NOW THE SIXTH GRADER SHOULD GO HOME AND FINISH UP HER HOMEWORK OR SOMETHING!
WELL, SEE YOU AROUND!
HAVE A NICE COLONIZATION DAY VACATION!
....

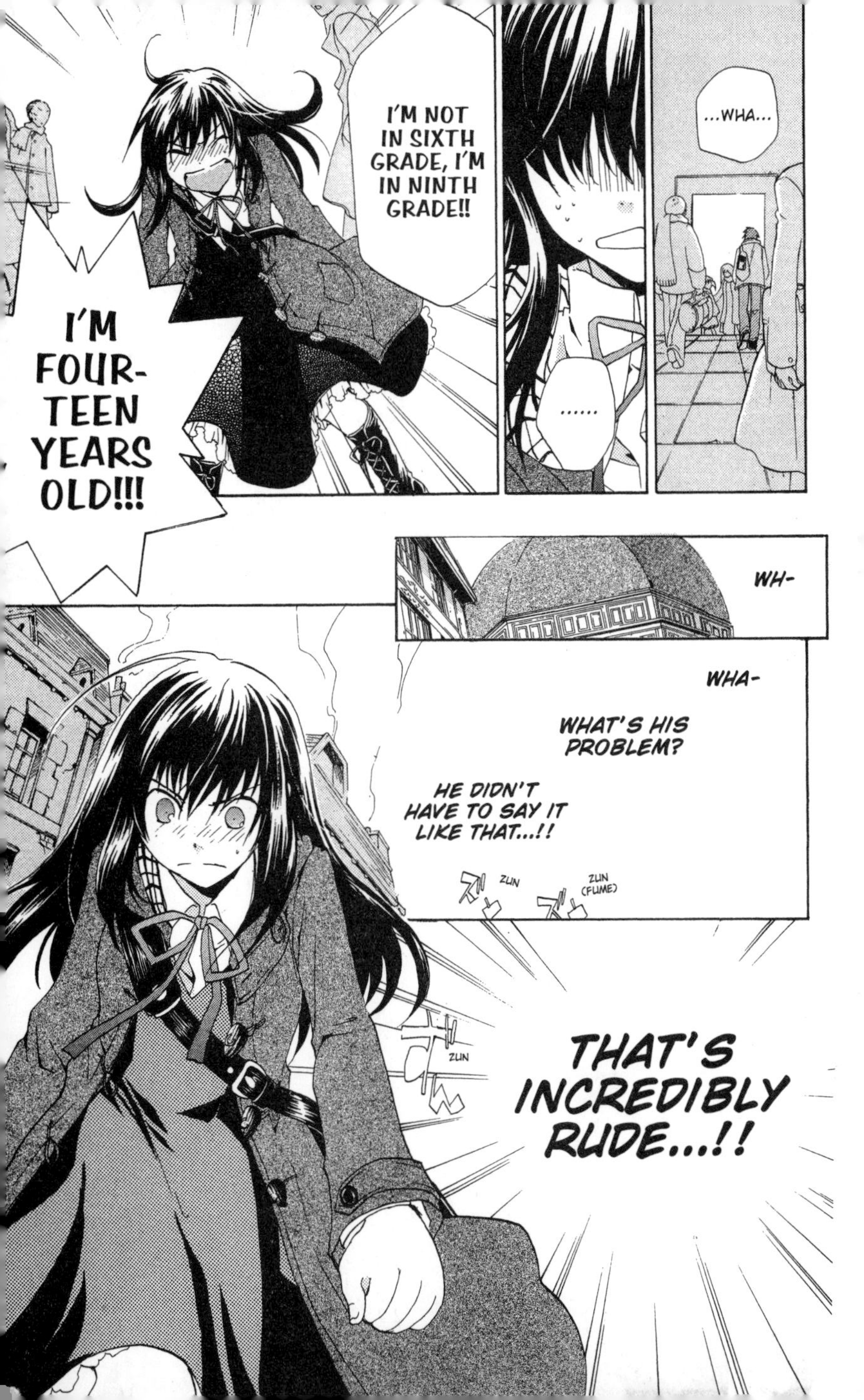
...WHA...
......
I'M NOT IN SIXTH GRADE, I'M IN NINTH GRADE!!
I'M FOUR-TEEN YEARS OLD!!!
WH-
WHA-
WHAT'S HIS PROBLEM?
HE DIDN'T HAVE TO SAY IT LIKE THAT...!!
ZUN (FUME)
ZUN
ZUN
THAT'S INCREDIBLY RUDE...!!

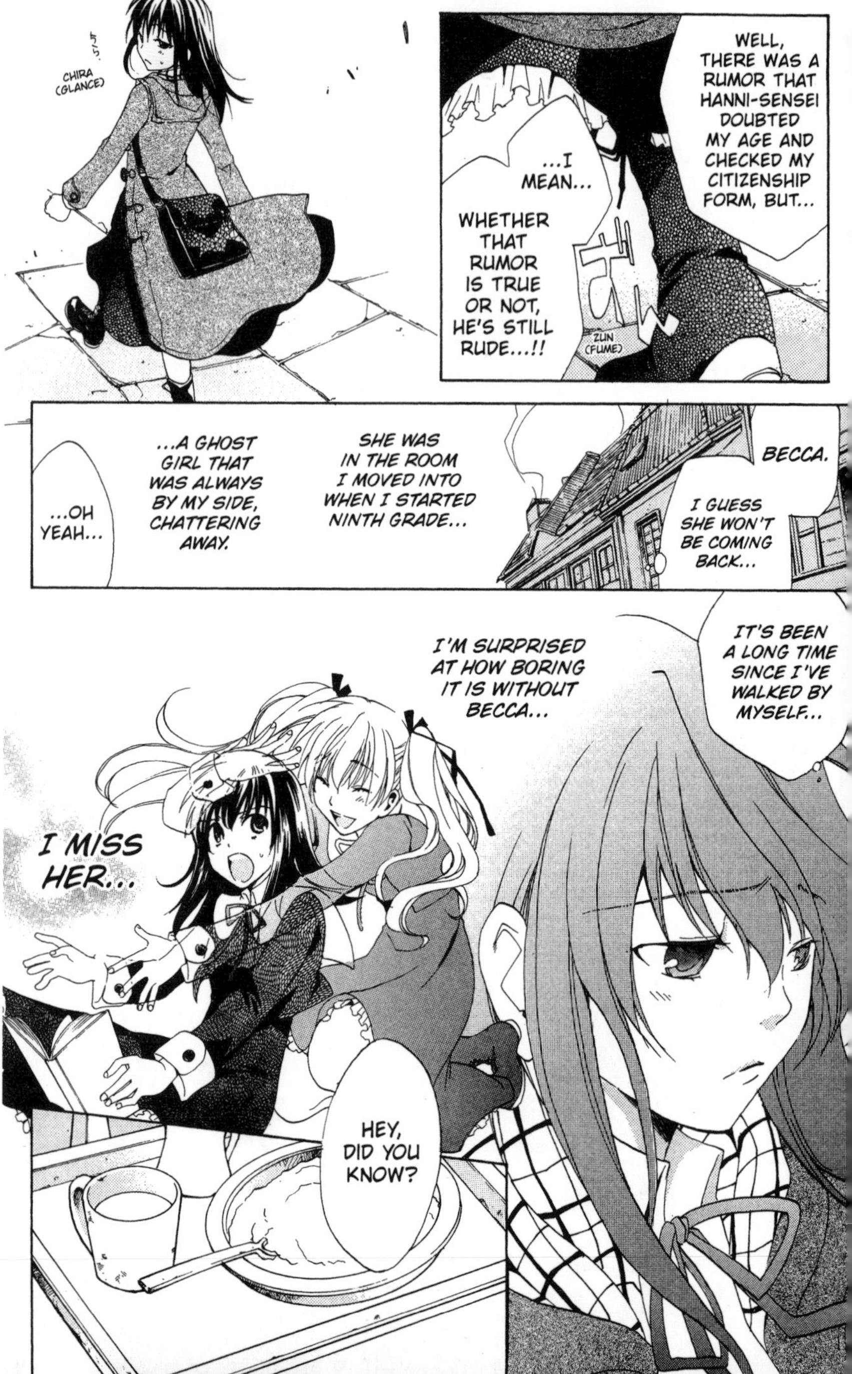
WELL, THERE WAS A RUMOR THAT HANNI-SENSEI DOUBTED MY AGE AND CHECKED MY CITIZENSHIP FORM, BUT...
...I MEAN...
WHETHER THAT RUMOR IS TRUE OR NOT, HE'S STILL RUDE...!!
ZUN (FUME)
ちら
CHIRA (GLANCE)
BECCA.
I GUESS SHE WON'T BE COMING BACK...
SHE WAS IN THE ROOM I MOVED INTO WHEN I STARTED NINTH GRADE...
...A GHOST GIRL THAT WAS ALWAYS BY MY SIDE, CHATTERING AWAY.
...OH YEAH...
IT'S BEEN A LONG TIME SINCE I'VE WALKED BY MYSELF...
I'M SURPRISED AT HOW BORING IT IS WITHOUT BECCA...
I MISS HER...
HEY, DID YOU KNOW?

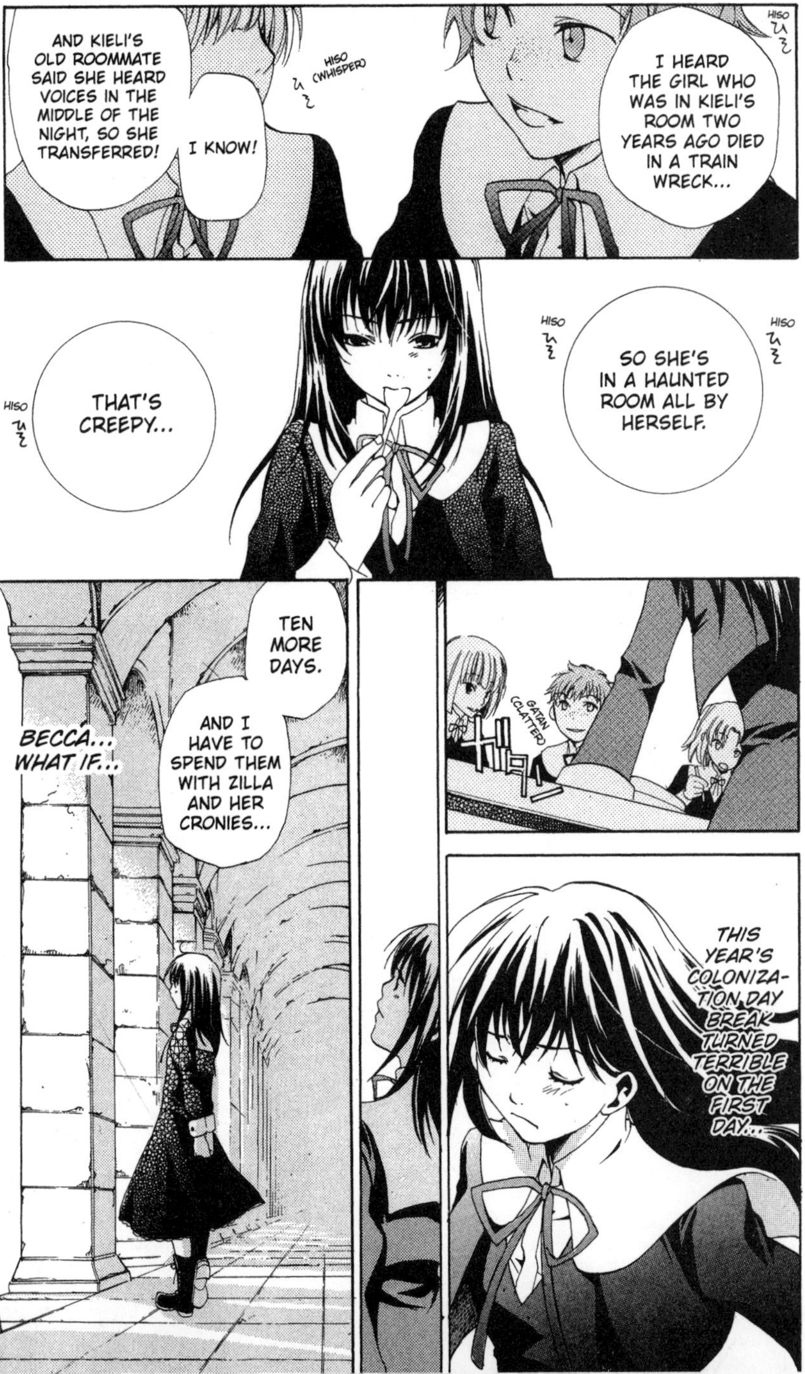
HISO
I HEARD THE GIRL WHO WAS IN KIELI'S ROOM TWO YEARS AGO DIED IN A TRAIN WRECK...
HISO (WHISPER)
I KNOW!
AND KIELI'S OLD ROOMMATE SAID SHE HEARD VOICES IN THE MIDDLE OF THE NIGHT, SO SHE TRANSFERRED!
HISO
SO SHE'S IN A HAUNTED ROOM ALL BY HERSELF.
HISO
THAT'S CREEPY...
HISO
GATAN (CLATTER)
THIS YEAR'S COLONIZATION DAY BREAK TURNED TERRIBLE ON THE FIRST DAY...
TEN MORE DAYS.
AND I HAVE TO SPEND THEM WITH ZILLA AND HER CRONIES...
BECCA... WHAT IF...

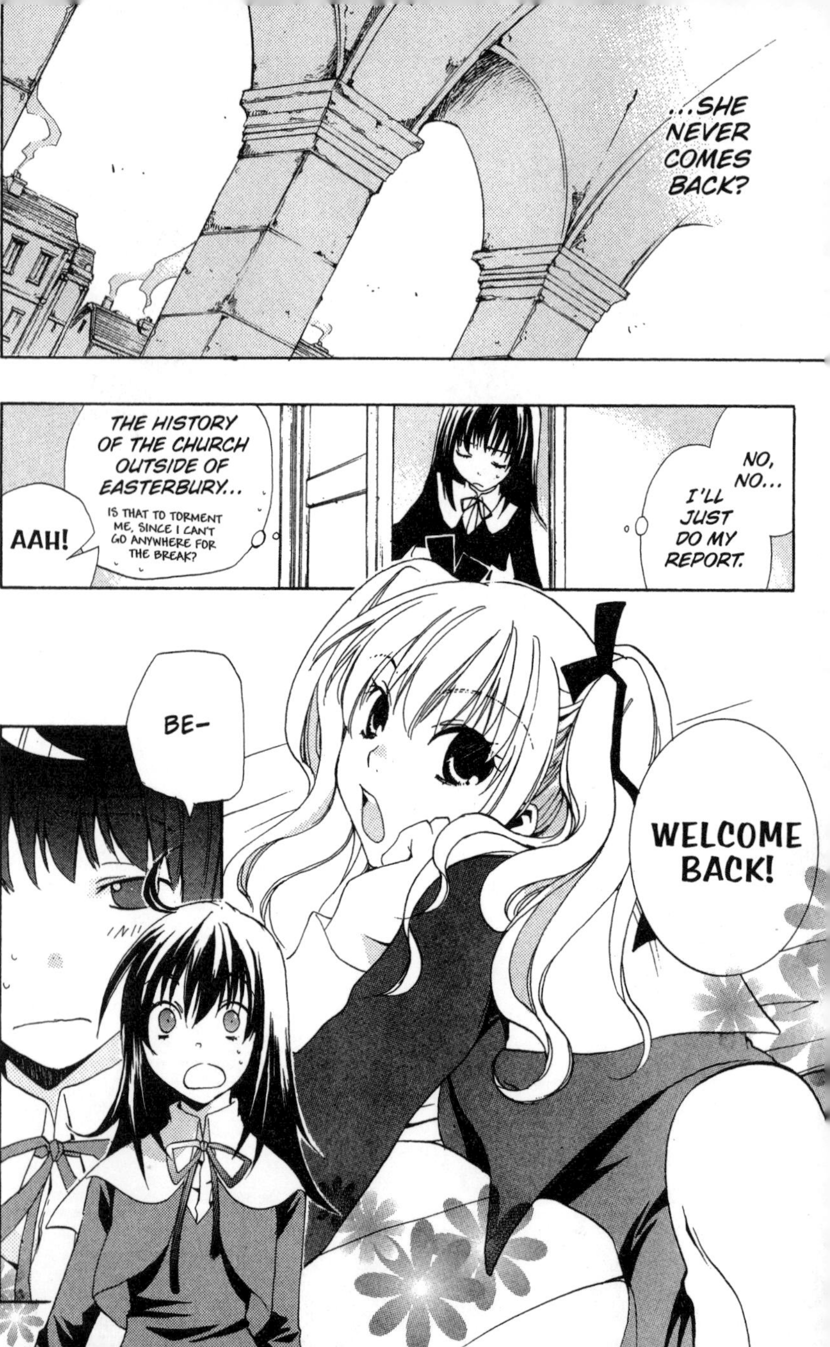
...SHE NEVER COMES BACK?
NO, NO... I'LL JUST DO MY REPORT.
THE HISTORY OF THE CHURCH OUTSIDE OF EASTERBURY...
IS THAT TO TORMENT ME, SINCE I CAN'T GO ANYWHERE FOR THE BREAK?
AAH!
WELCOME BACK!
BE-

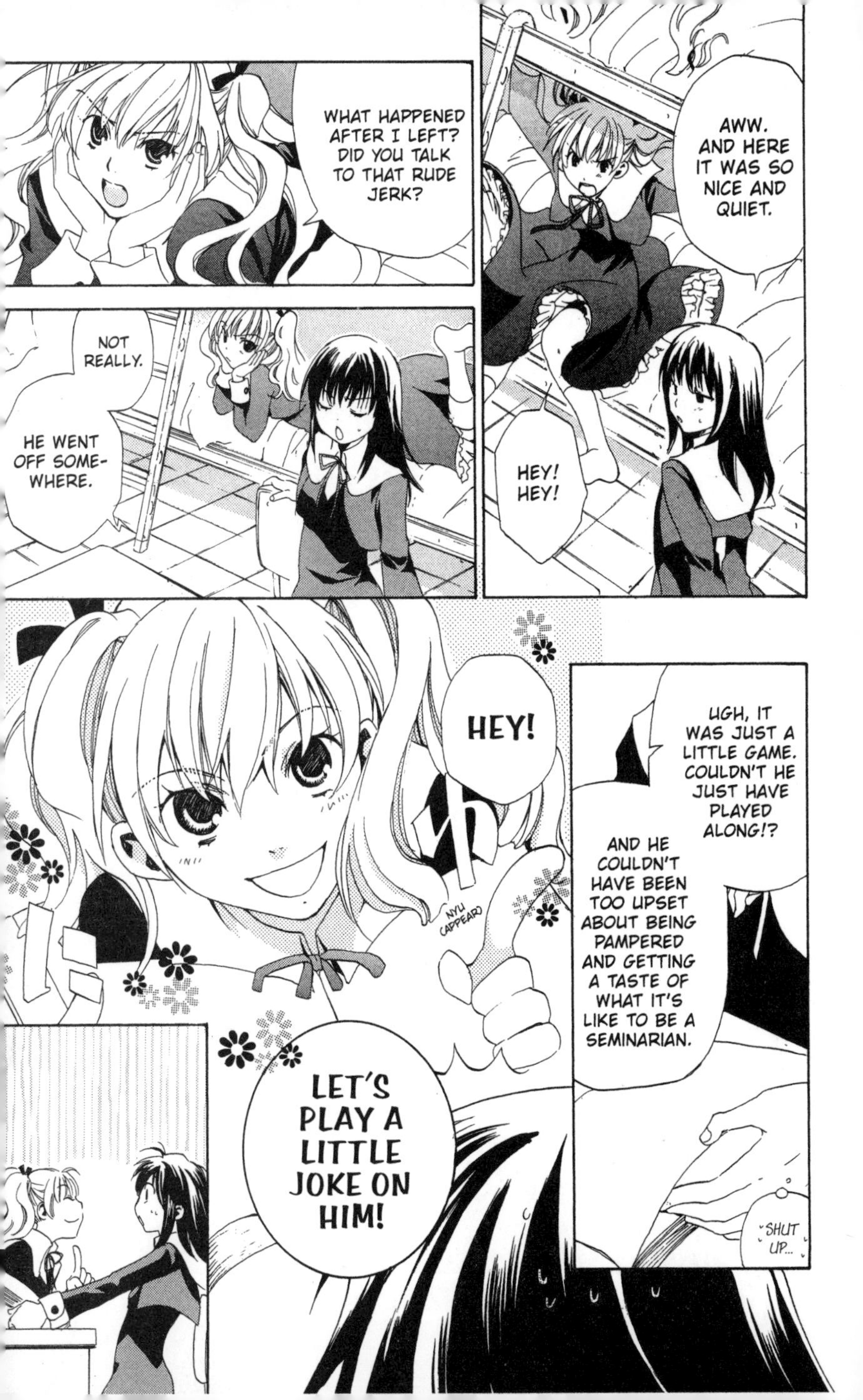
AWW. AND HERE IT WAS SO NICE AND QUIET.
HEY! HEY!
WHAT HAPPENED AFTER I LEFT? DID YOU TALK TO THAT RUDE JERK?
NOT REALLY.
HE WENT OFF SOME-WHERE.
UGH, IT WAS JUST A LITTLE GAME. COULDN'T HE JUST HAVE PLAYED ALONG!?
AND HE COULDN'T HAVE BEEN TOO UPSET ABOUT BEING PAMPERED AND GETTING A TASTE OF WHAT IT'S LIKE TO BE A SEMINARIAN.
SHUT UP...
HEY!
NYU (APPEAR)
LET'S PLAY A LITTLE JOKE ON HIM!

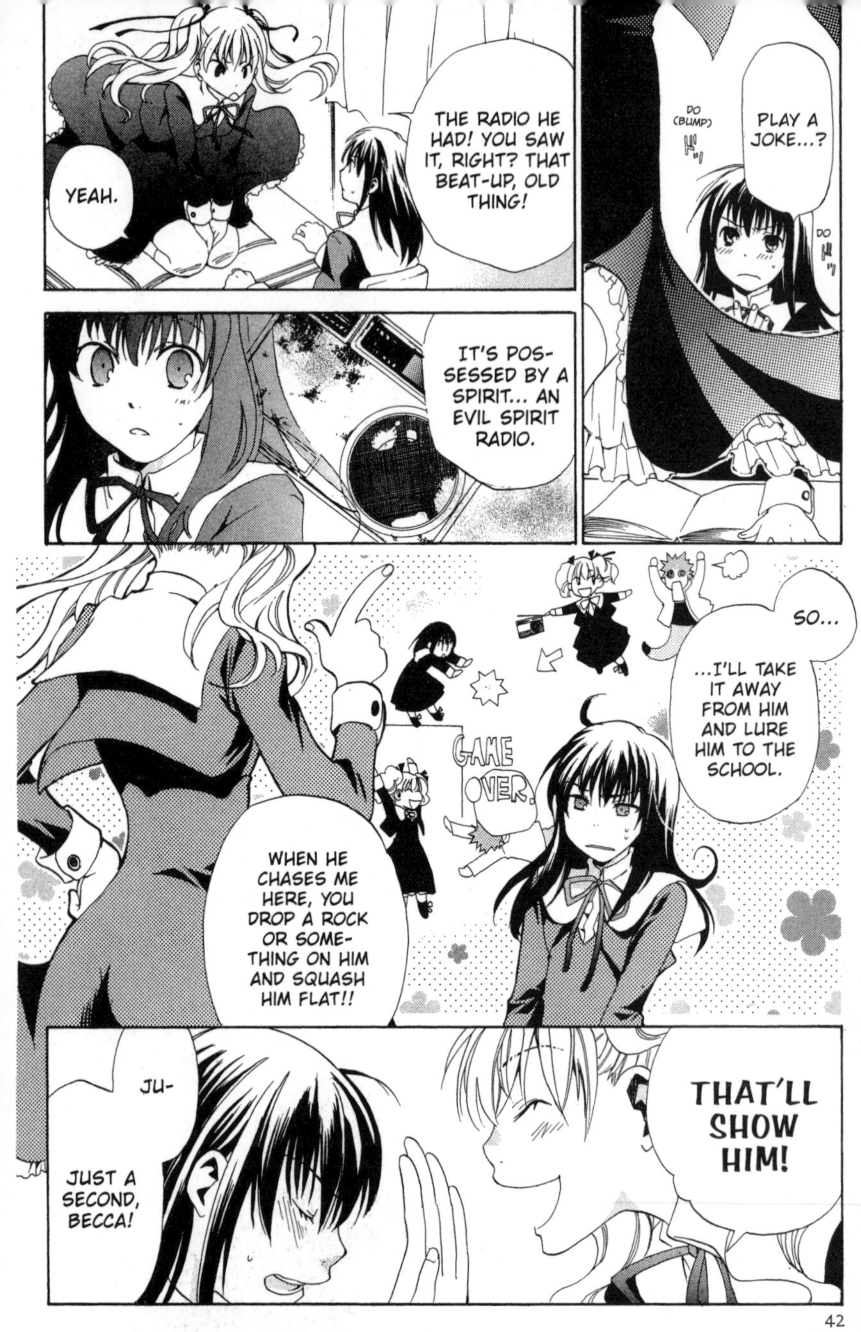
DO (BUMP)
PLAY A JOKE...?
DO
THE RADIO HE HAD! YOU SAW IT, RIGHT? THAT BEAT-UP, OLD THING!
YEAH.
IT'S POSSESSED BY A SPIRIT... AN EVIL SPIRIT RADIO.
SO...
...I'LL TAKE IT AWAY FROM HIM AND LURE HIM TO THE SCHOOL.
GAME OVER
WHEN HE CHASES ME HERE, YOU DROP A ROCK OR SOMETHING ON HIM AND SQUASH HIM FLAT!!
THAT'LL SHOW HIM!
JU-
JUST A SECOND, BECCA!

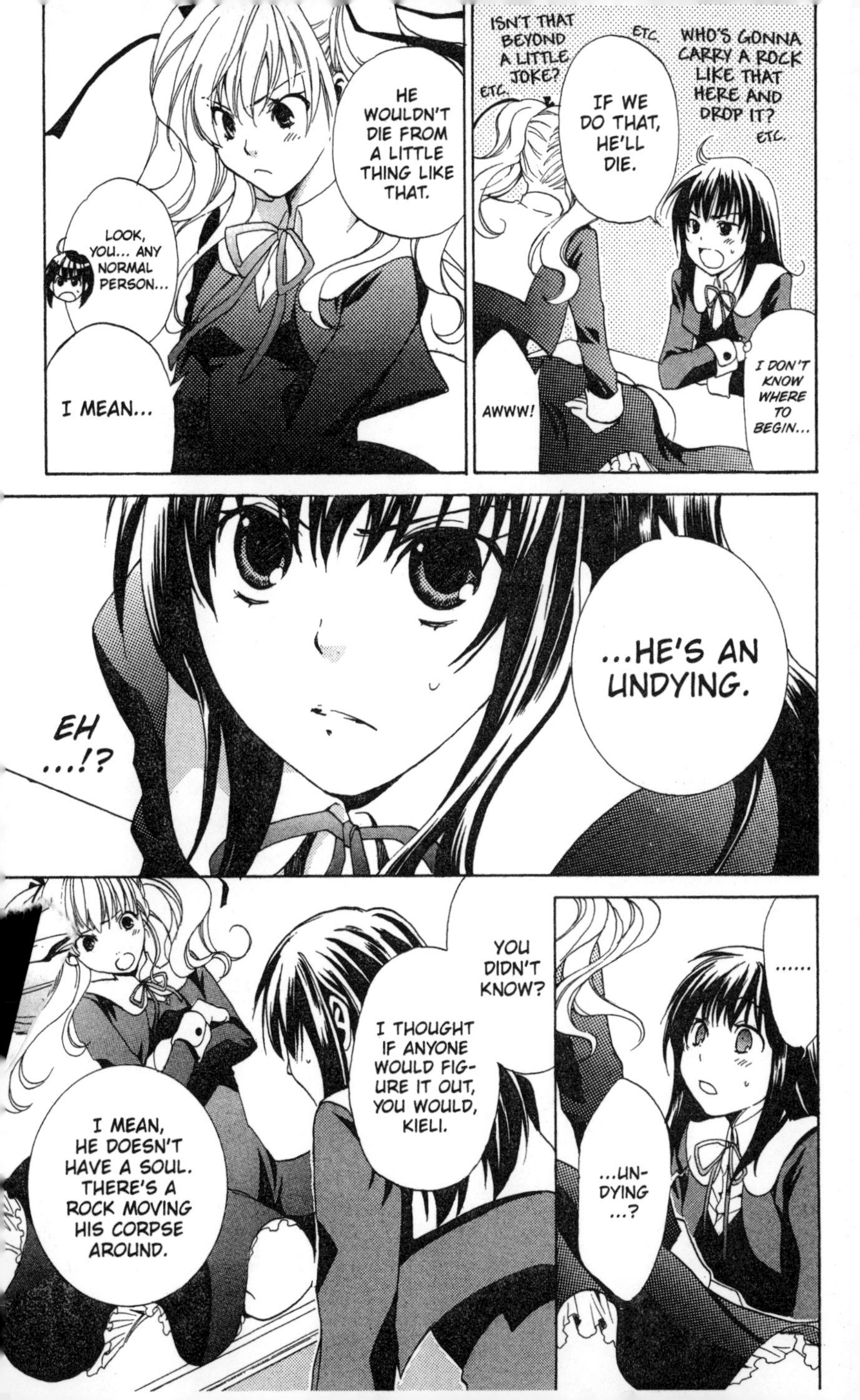
WHO'S GONNA CARRY A ROCK LIKE THAT HERE AND DROP IT?
ETC.
ETC.
ISN'T THAT BEYOND A LITTLE JOKE?
ETC.
IF WE DO THAT, HE'LL DIE.
I DON'T KNOW WHERE TO BEGIN...
AWWW!
HE WOULDN'T DIE FROM A LITTLE THING LIKE THAT.
LOOK, YOU... ANY NORMAL PERSON...
I MEAN...
...HE'S AN UNDYING.
EH ...!?
......
...UN-DYING ...?
YOU DIDN'T KNOW?
I THOUGHT IF ANYONE WOULD FIG-URE IT OUT, YOU WOULD, KIELI.
I MEAN, HE DOESN'T HAVE A SOUL. THERE'S A ROCK MOVING HIS CORPSE AROUND.

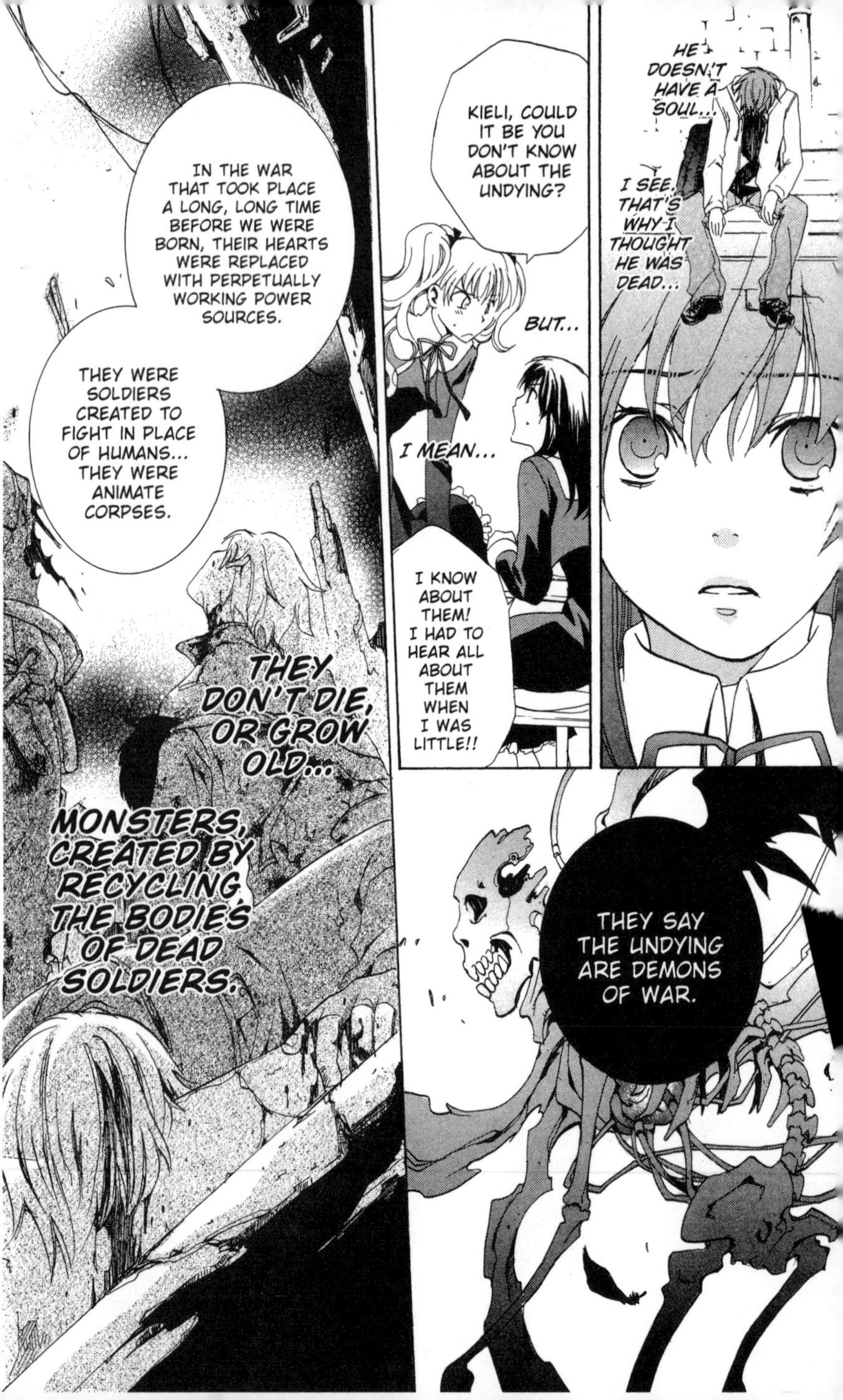
HE DOESN'T HAVE A SOUL...
I SEE. THAT'S WHY I THOUGHT HE WAS DEAD...
KIELI, COULD IT BE YOU DON'T KNOW ABOUT THE UNDYING?
BUT...
I MEAN...
I KNOW ABOUT THEM! I HAD TO HEAR ALL ABOUT THEM WHEN I WAS LITTLE!!
THEY SAY THE UNDYING ARE DEMONS OF WAR.
IN THE WAR THAT TOOK PLACE A LONG, LONG TIME BEFORE WE WERE BORN, THEIR HEARTS WERE REPLACED WITH PERPETUALLY WORKING POWER SOURCES.
THEY WERE SOLDIERS CREATED TO FIGHT IN PLACE OF HUMANS... THEY WERE ANIMATE CORPSES.
THEY DON'T DIE, OR GROW OLD...
MONSTERS, CREATED BY RECYCLING THE BODIES OF DEAD SOLDIERS.

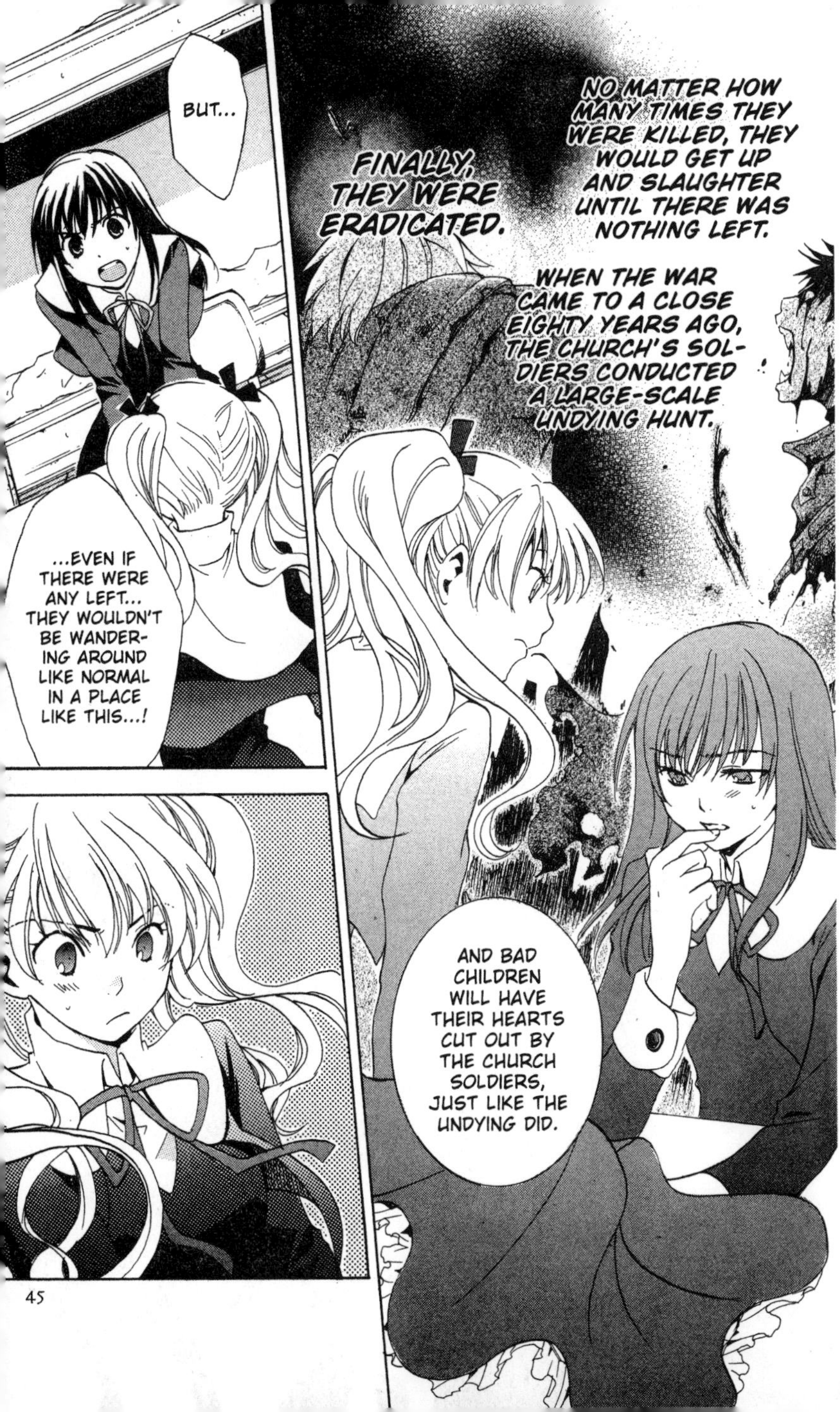
NO MATTER HOW MANY TIMES THEY WERE KILLED, THEY WOULD GET UP AND SLAUGHTER UNTIL THERE WAS NOTHING LEFT.
WHEN THE WAR CAME TO A CLOSE EIGHTY YEARS AGO, THE CHURCH'S SOL-DIERS CONDUCTED A LARGE-SCALE UNDYING HUNT.
FINALLY, THEY WERE ERADICATED.
AND BAD CHILDREN WILL HAVE THEIR HEARTS CUT OUT BY THE CHURCH SOLDIERS, JUST LIKE THE UNDYING DID.
BUT...
...EVEN IF THERE WERE ANY LEFT... THEY WOULDN'T BE WANDER-ING AROUND LIKE NORMAL IN A PLACE LIKE THIS...!

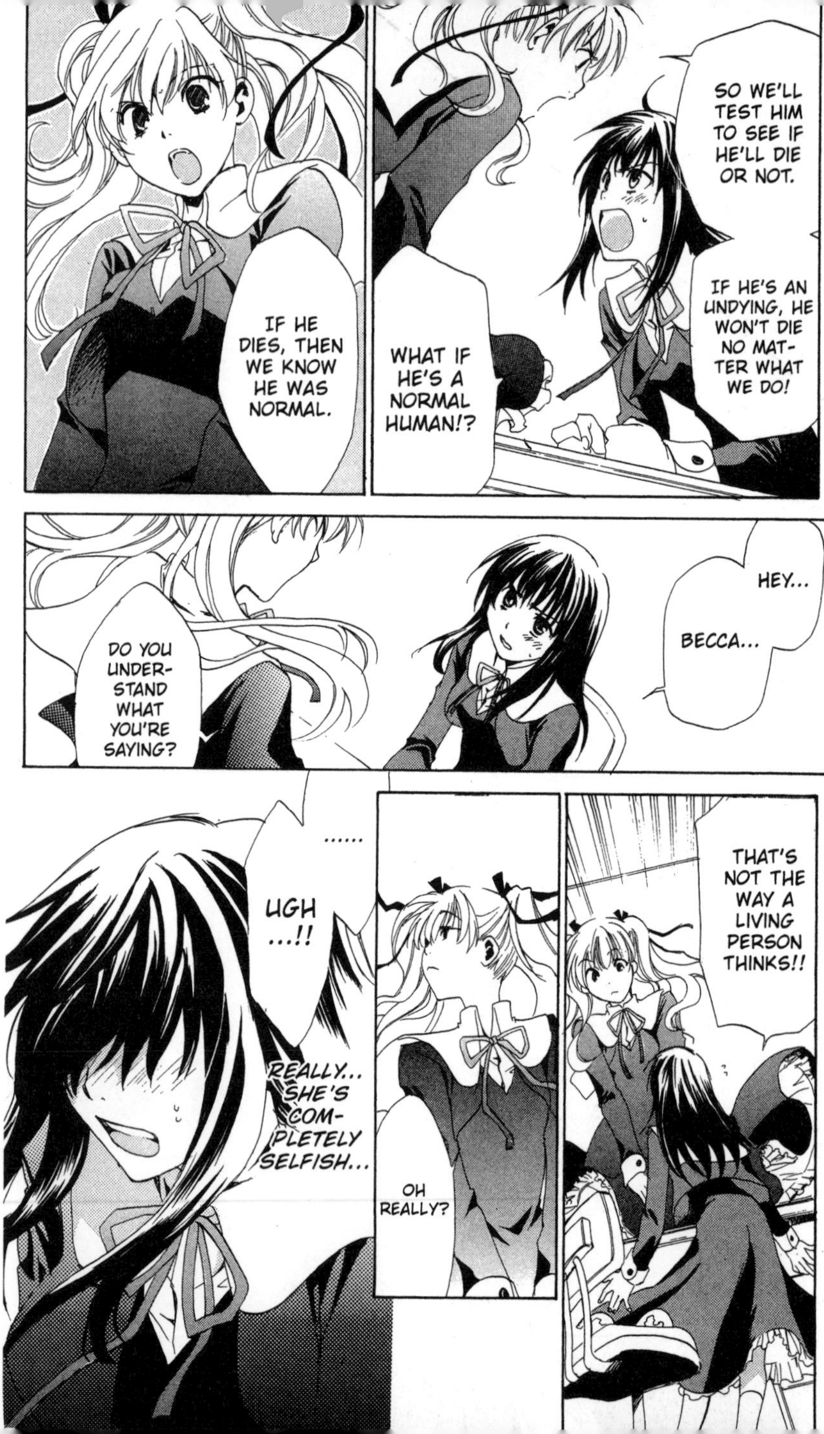
SO WE'LL TEST HIM TO SEE IF HE'LL DIE OR NOT.
IF HE'S AN UNDYING, HE WON'T DIE NO MAT-TER WHAT WE DO!
WHAT IF HE'S A NORMAL HUMAN!?
IF HE DIES, THEN WE KNOW HE WAS NORMAL.
HEY... BECCA...
DO YOU UNDER-STAND WHAT YOU'RE SAYING?
THAT'S NOT THE WAY A LIVING PERSON THINKS!!
OH REALLY?
......
UGH ...!!
REALLY... SHE'S COM-PLETELY SELFISH...

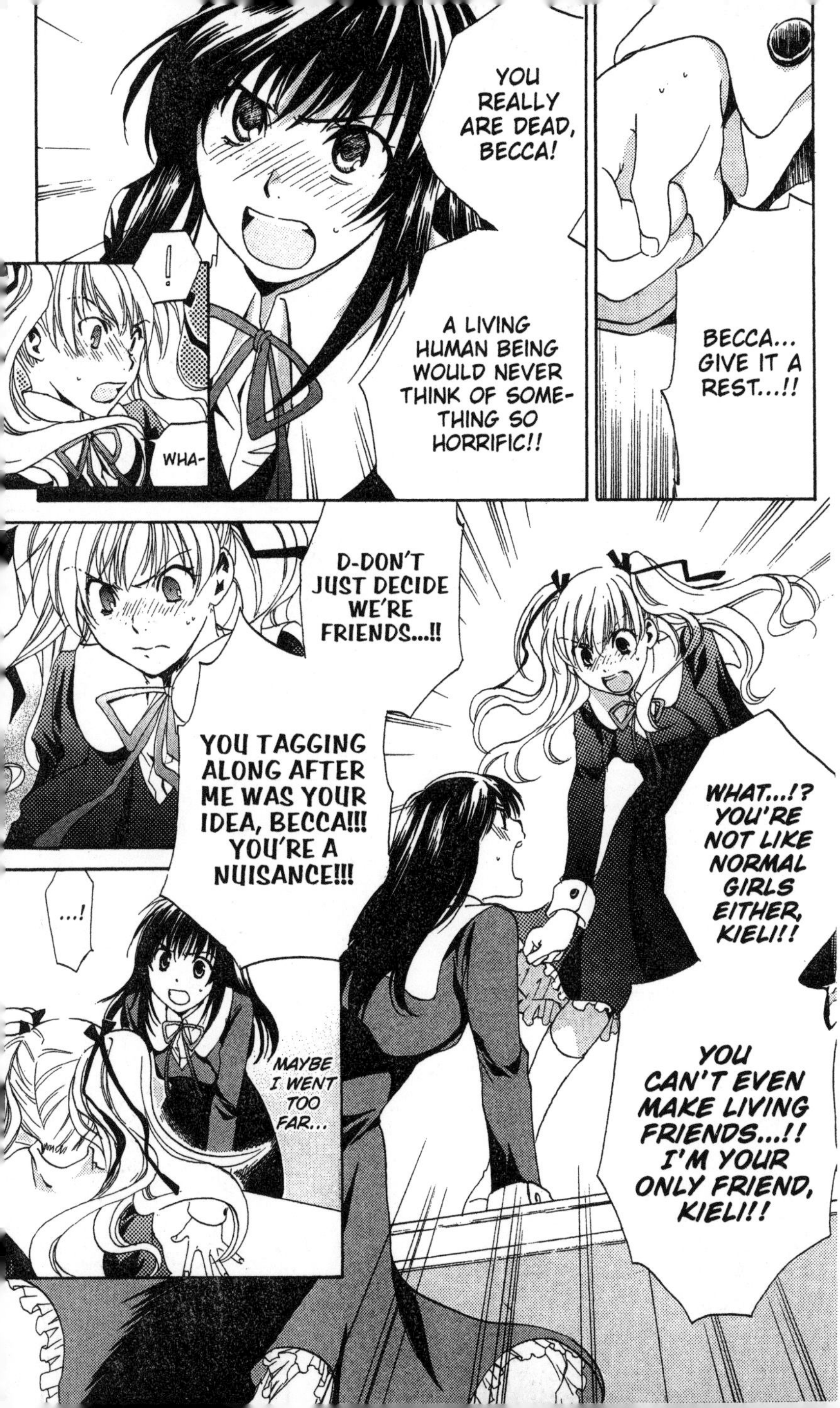
BECCA... GIVE IT A REST...!!
YOU REALLY ARE DEAD, BECCA!
A LIVING HUMAN BEING WOULD NEVER THINK OF SOME-THING SO HORRIFIC!!
!
WHA-
WHAT...!? YOU'RE NOT LIKE NORMAL GIRLS EITHER, KIELI!!
YOU CAN'T EVEN MAKE LIVING FRIENDS...!! I'M YOUR ONLY FRIEND, KIELI!!
D-DON'T JUST DECIDE WE'RE FRIENDS...!!
YOU TAGGING ALONG AFTER ME WAS YOUR IDEA, BECCA!!! YOU'RE A NUISANCE!!!
...!
MAYBE I WENT TOO FAR...

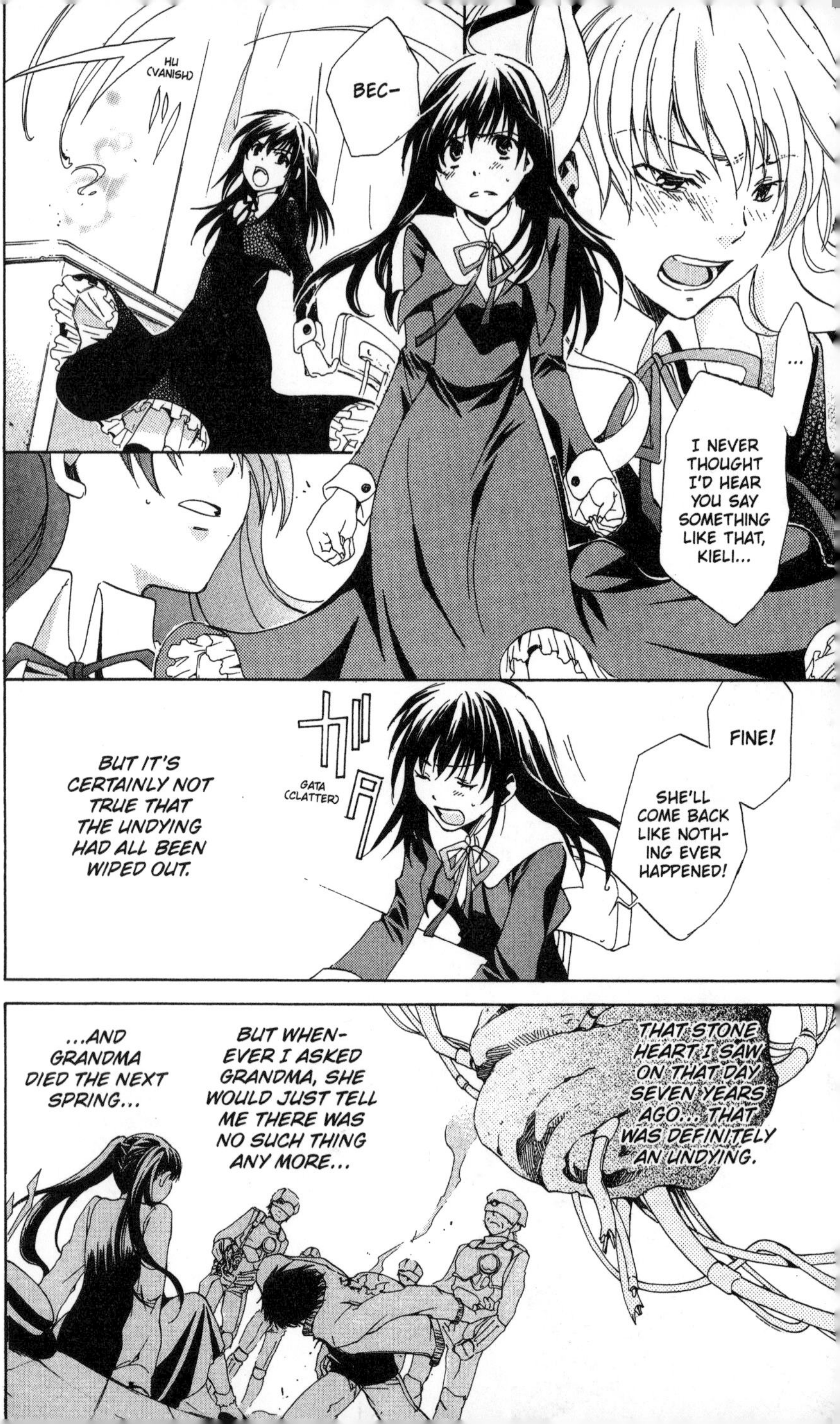
...
I NEVER THOUGHT I'D HEAR YOU SAY SOMETHING LIKE THAT, KIELI...
BEC-
HU (VANISH)
FINE!
SHE'LL COME BACK LIKE NOTHING EVER HAPPENED!
GATA (CLATTER)
BUT IT'S CERTAINLY NOT TRUE THAT THE UNDYING HAD ALL BEEN WIPED OUT.
THAT STONE HEART I SAW ON THAT DAY SEVEN YEARS AGO... THAT WAS DEFINITELY AN UNDYING.
BUT WHENEVER I ASKED GRANDMA, SHE WOULD JUST TELL ME THERE WAS NO SUCH THING ANY MORE...
...AND GRANDMA DIED THE NEXT SPRING...

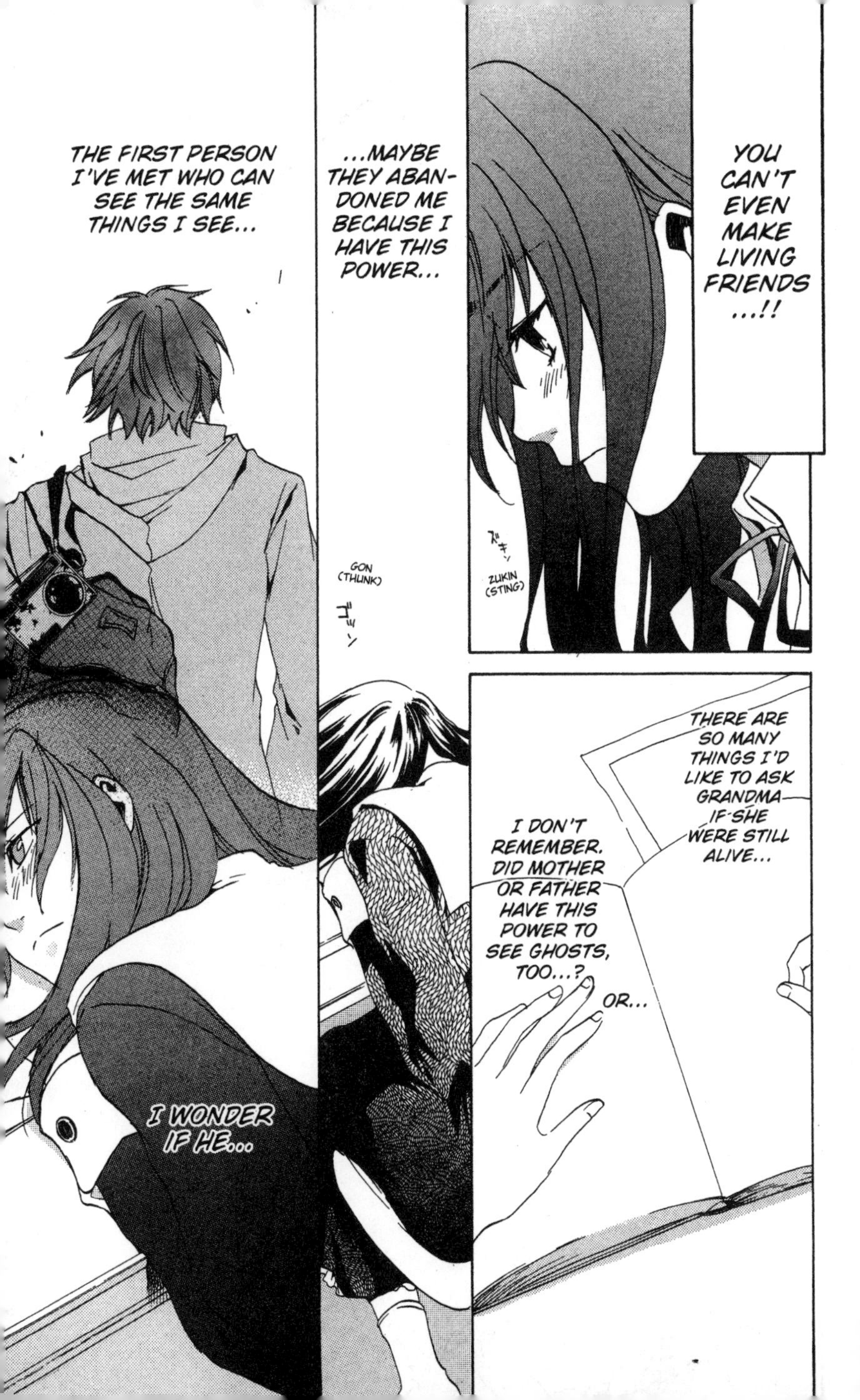
YOU CAN'T EVEN MAKE LIVING FRIENDS ...!!
ZUKIN (STING)
THERE ARE SO MANY THINGS I'D LIKE TO ASK GRANDMA IF SHE WERE STILL ALIVE...
I DON'T REMEMBER. DID MOTHER OR FATHER HAVE THIS POWER TO SEE GHOSTS, TOO...?
OR...
...MAYBE THEY ABANDONED ME BECAUSE I HAVE THIS POWER...
GON (THUNK)
THE FIRST PERSON I'VE MET WHO CAN SEE THE SAME THINGS I SEE...
I WONDER IF HE...

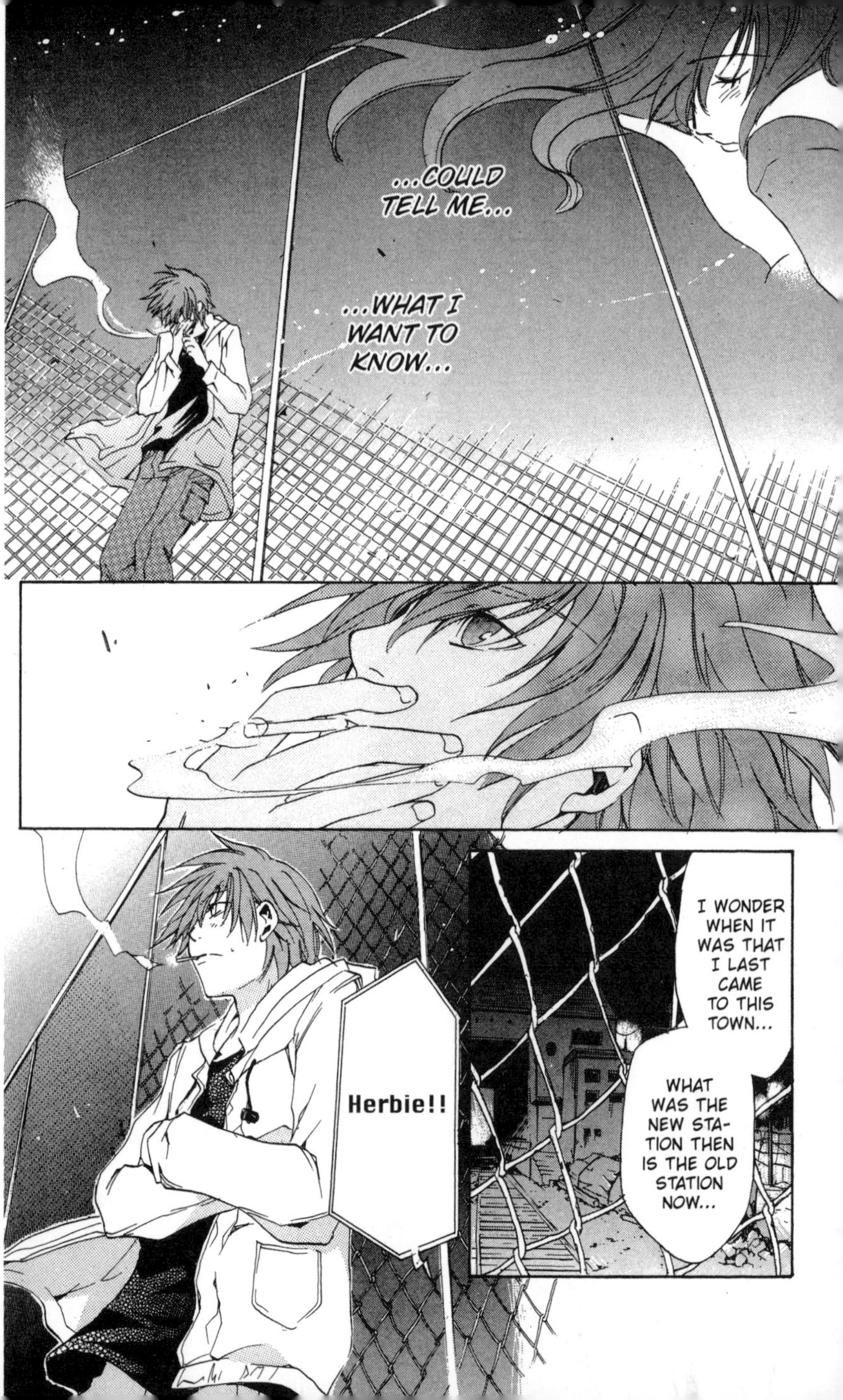
...COULD TELL ME...
...WHAT I WANT TO KNOW...
I WONDER WHEN IT WAS THAT I LAST CAME TO THIS TOWN...
WHAT WAS THE NEW STATION THEN IS THE OLD STATION NOW...
Herbie!!

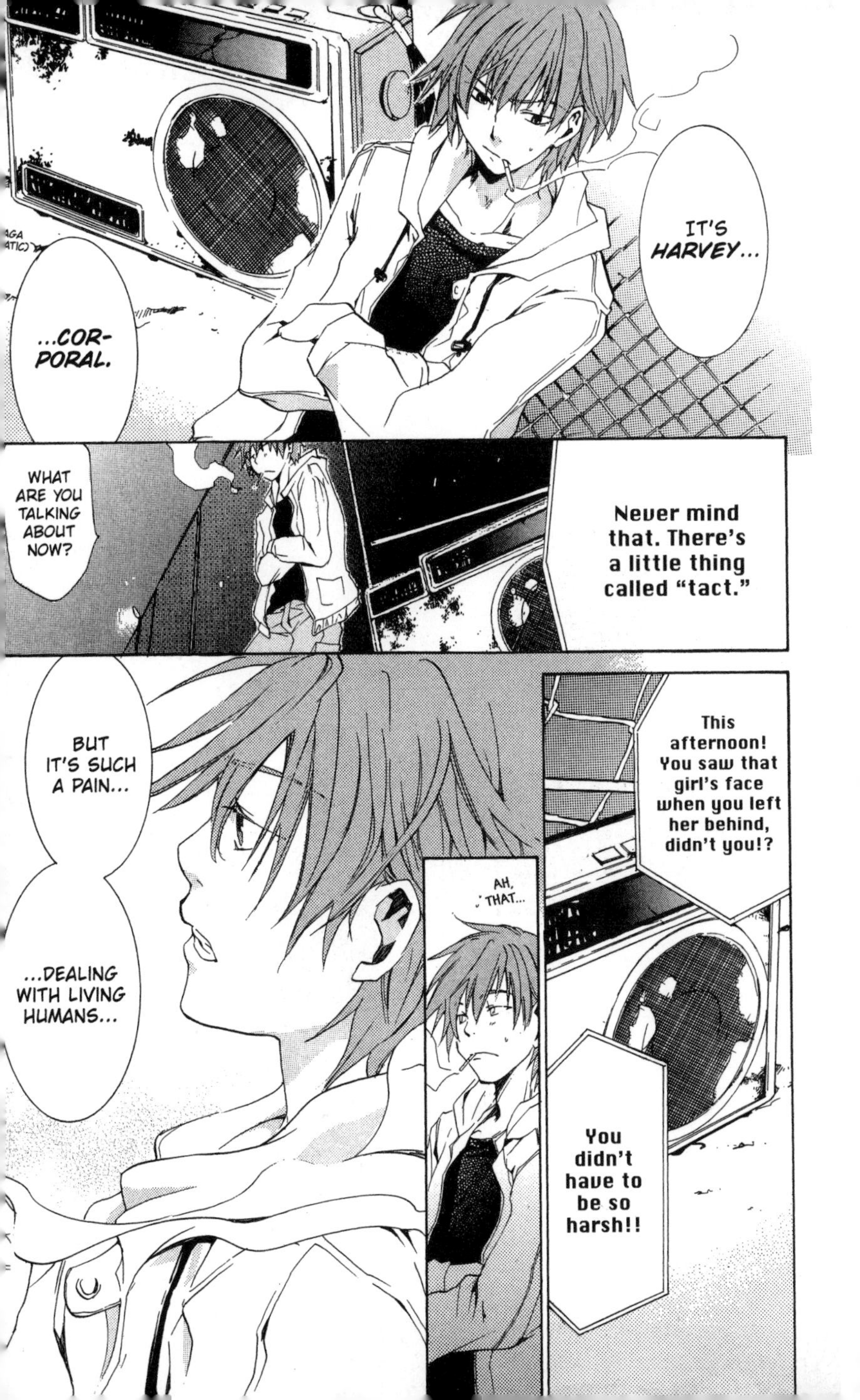
IT'S HARVEY...
...CORPORAL.
Never mind that. There's a little thing called "tact."
WHAT ARE YOU TALKING ABOUT NOW?
This afternoon! You saw that girl's face when you left her behind, didn't you!?
AH, THAT...
You didn't have to be so harsh!!
BUT IT'S SUCH A PAIN...
...DEALING WITH LIVING HUMANS...

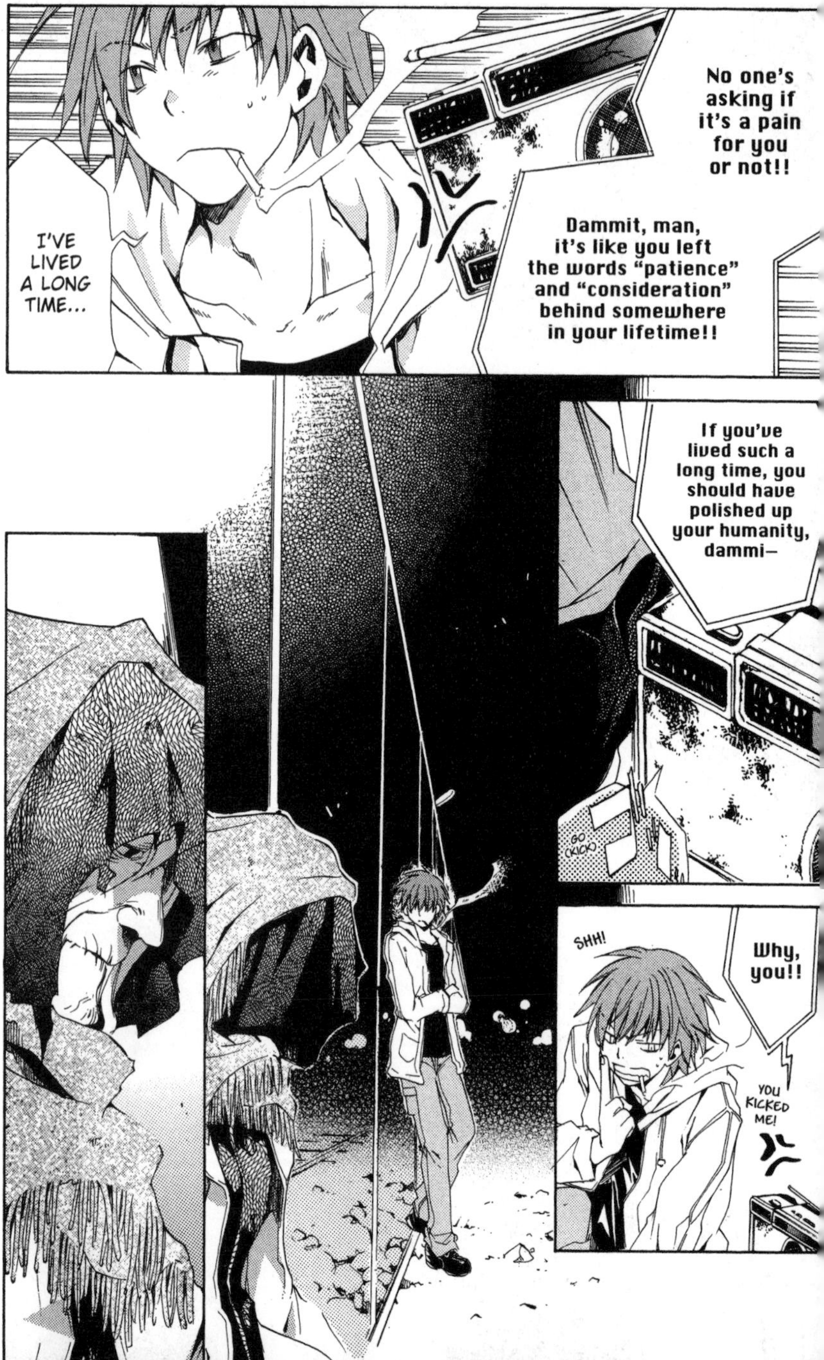
No one's asking if it's a pain for you or not!!
Dammit, man, it's like you left the words "patience" and "consideration" behind somewhere in your lifetime!!
I'VE LIVED A LONG TIME...
If you've lived such a long time, you should have polished up your humanity, dammi–
GO (KICK)
Why, you!!
SHH!
YOU KICKED ME!

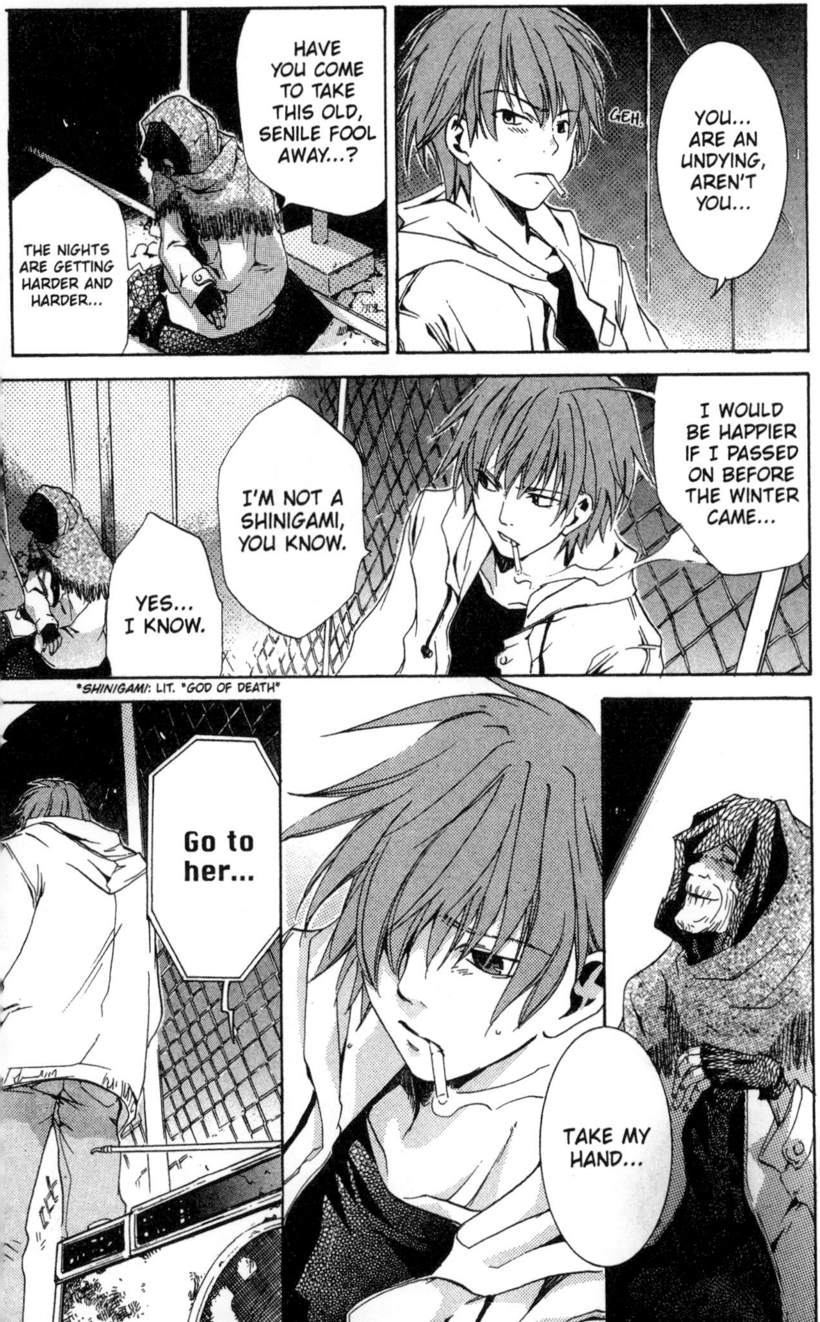
GEH.
YOU... ARE AN UNDYING, AREN'T YOU...
HAVE YOU COME TO TAKE THIS OLD, SENILE FOOL AWAY...?
THE NIGHTS ARE GETTING HARDER AND HARDER...
I WOULD BE HAPPIER IF I PASSED ON BEFORE THE WINTER CAME...
I'M NOT A SHINIGAMI, YOU KNOW.
YES... I KNOW.
TAKE MY HAND...
Go to her...
*SHINIGAMI: LIT. "GOD OF DEATH"

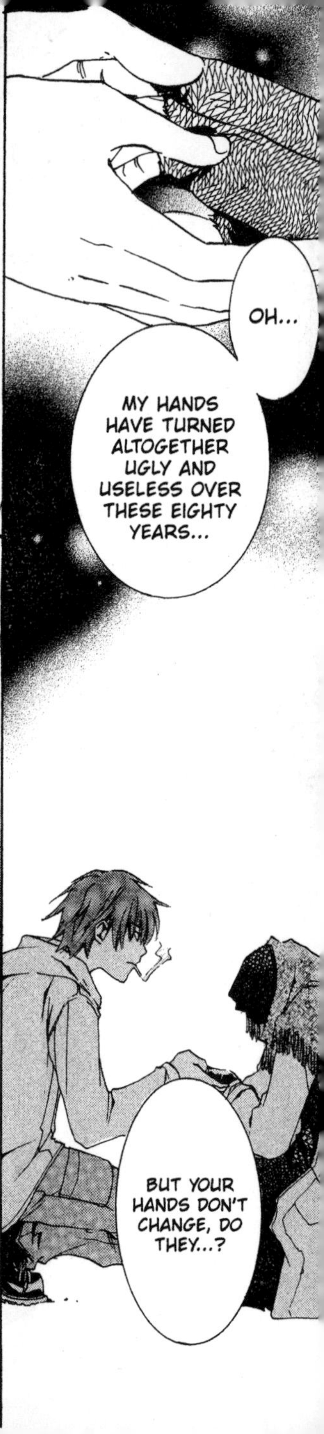
OH...
MY HANDS HAVE TURNED ALTOGETHER UGLY AND USELESS OVER THESE EIGHTY YEARS...
BUT YOUR HANDS DON'T CHANGE, DO THEY...?

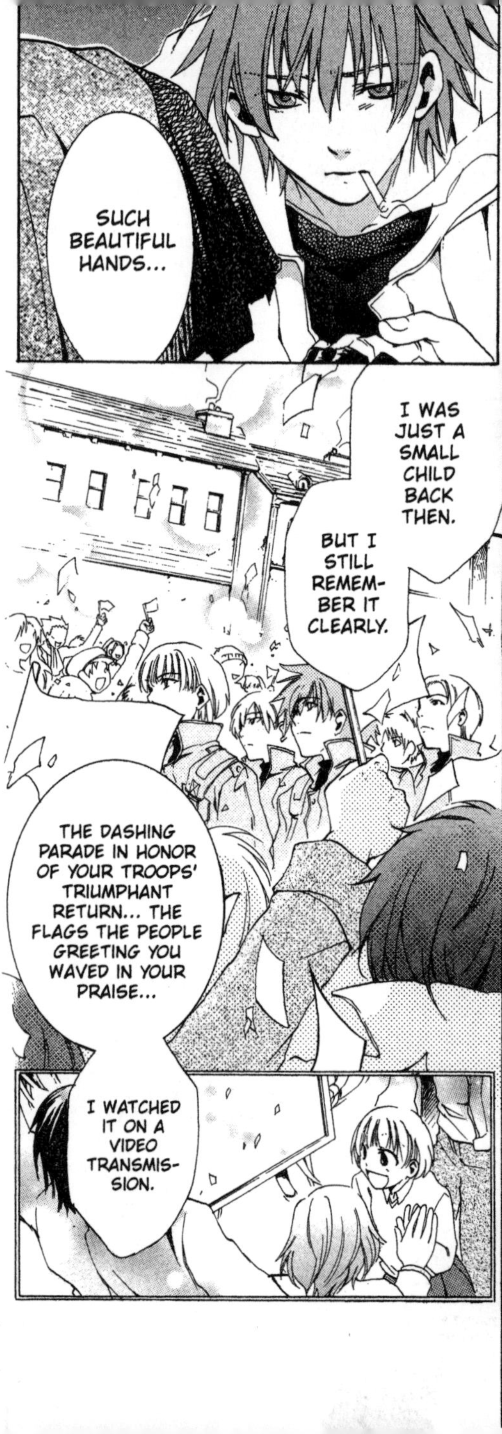
SUCH BEAUTIFUL HANDS...
I WAS JUST A SMALL CHILD BACK THEN.
BUT I STILL REMEMBER IT CLEARLY.
THE DASHING PARADE IN HONOR OF YOUR TROOPS' TRIUMPHANT RETURN... THE FLAGS THE PEOPLE GREETING YOU WAVED IN YOUR PRAISE...
I WATCHED IT ON A VIDEO TRANSMISSION.

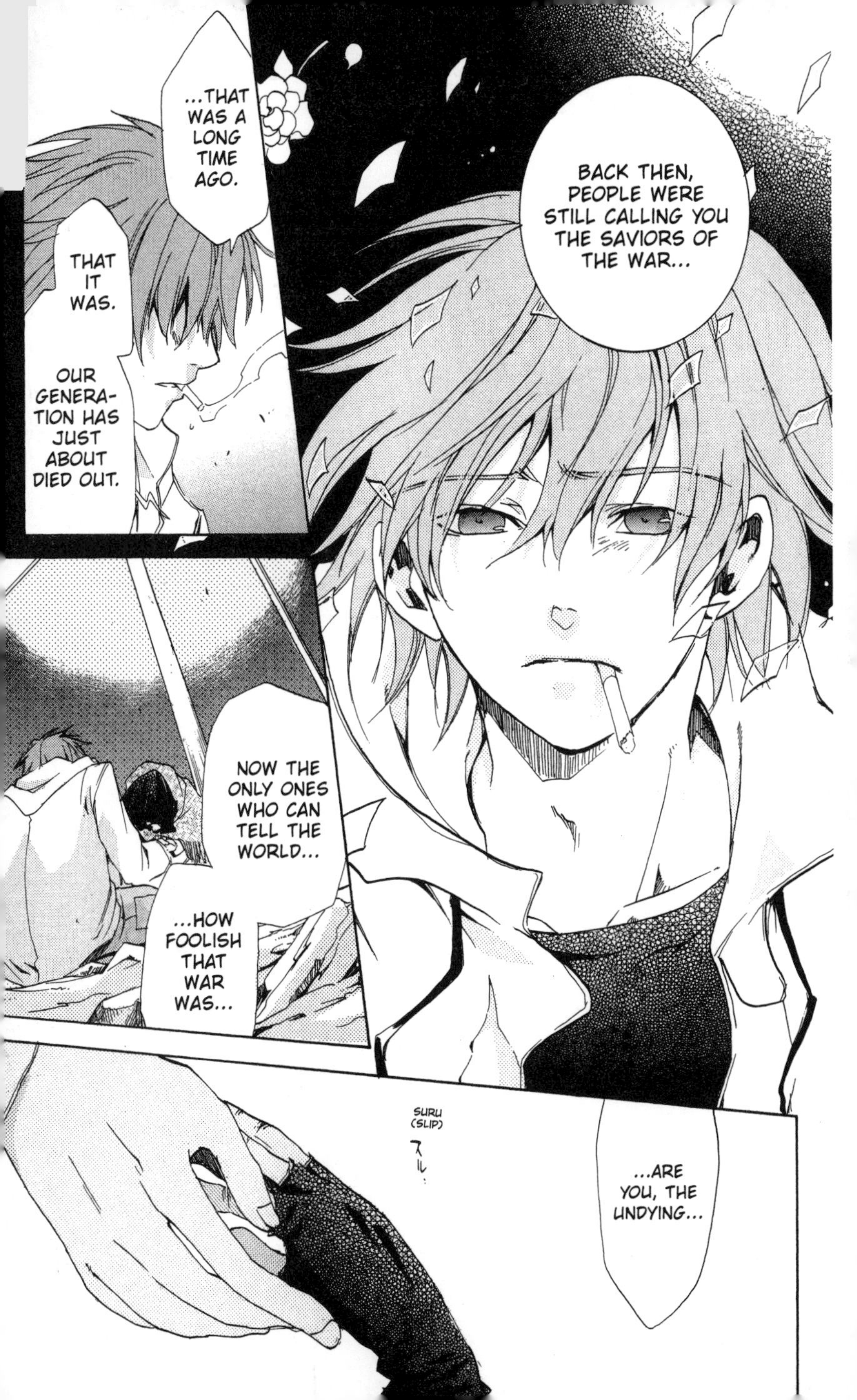
BACK THEN, PEOPLE WERE STILL CALLING YOU THE SAVIORS OF THE WAR...
...THAT WAS A LONG TIME AGO.
THAT IT WAS.
OUR GENERATION HAS JUST ABOUT DIED OUT.
NOW THE ONLY ONES WHO CAN TELL THE WORLD...
...HOW FOOLISH THAT WAR WAS...
...ARE YOU, THE UNDYING...
スル
SURU (SLIP)

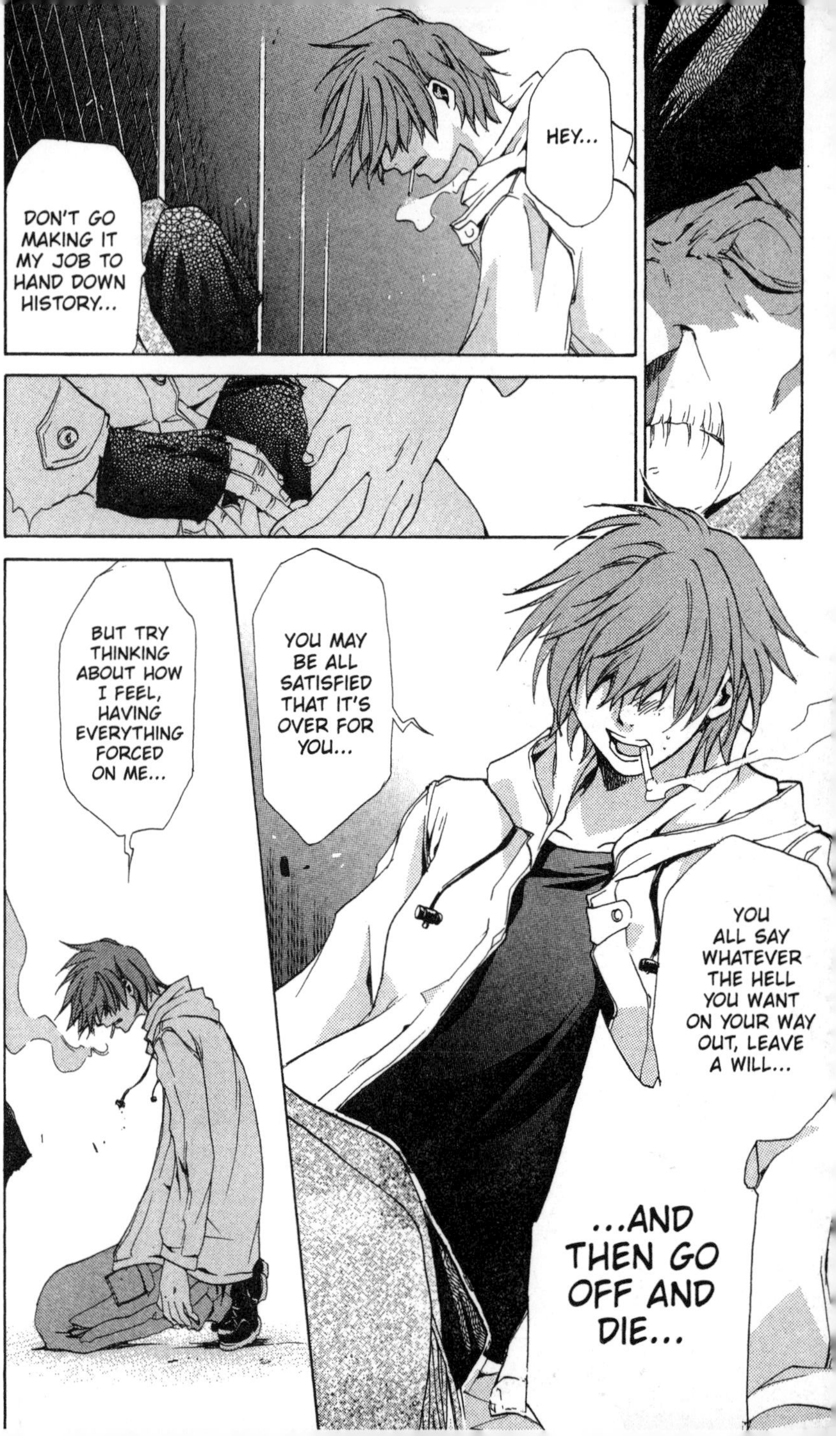
HEY...
DON'T GO MAKING IT MY JOB TO HAND DOWN HISTORY...
YOU MAY BE ALL SATISFIED THAT IT'S OVER FOR YOU...
BUT TRY THINKING ABOUT HOW I FEEL, HAVING EVERYTHING FORCED ON ME...
YOU ALL SAY WHATEVER THE HELL YOU WANT ON YOUR WAY OUT, LEAVE A WILL...
...AND THEN GO OFF AND DIE...

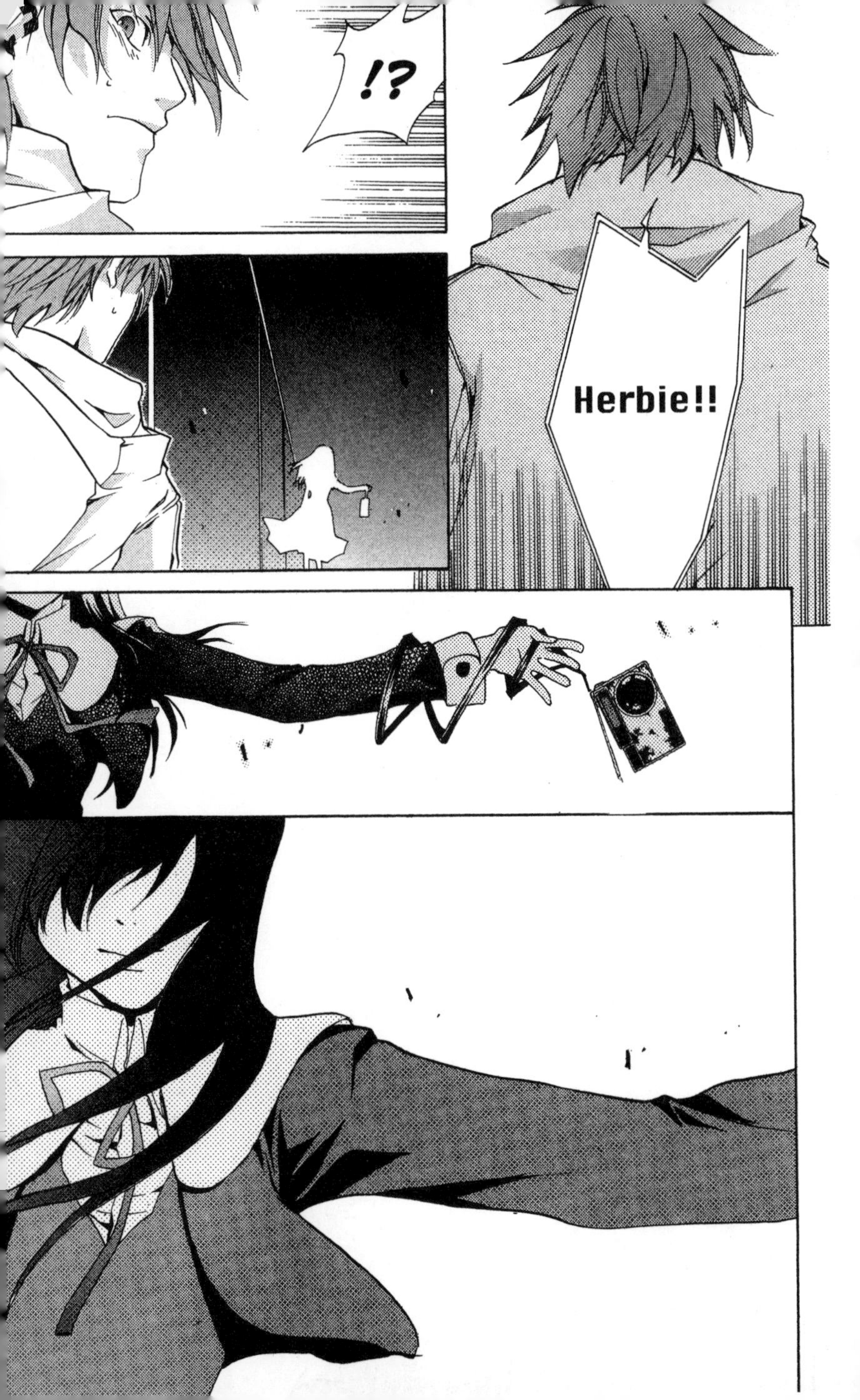
Herbie!!
!?

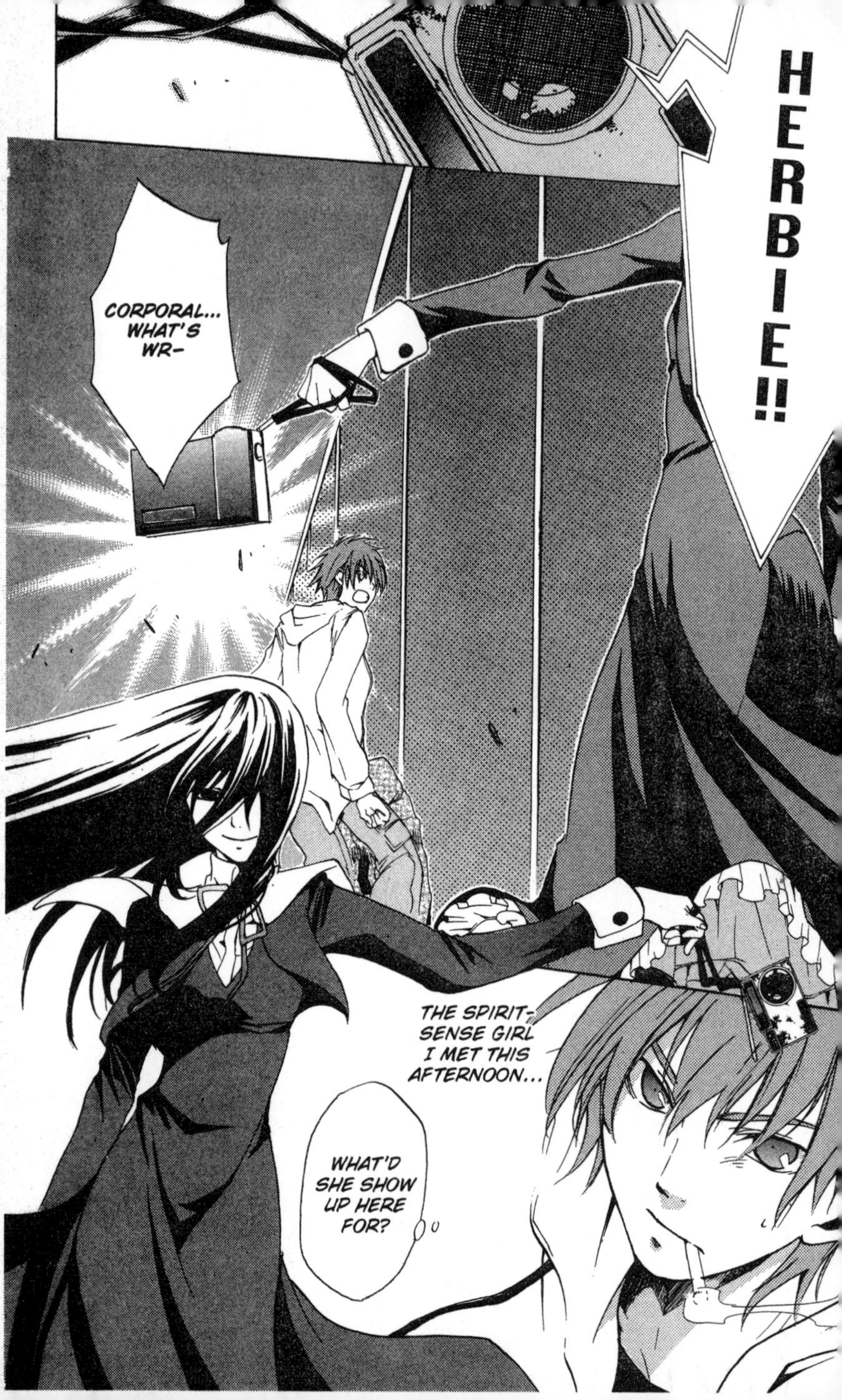
HERBIE!!
CORPORAL... WHAT'S WR-
THE SPIRIT-SENSE GIRL I MET THIS AFTERNOON...
WHAT'D SHE SHOW UP HERE FOR?

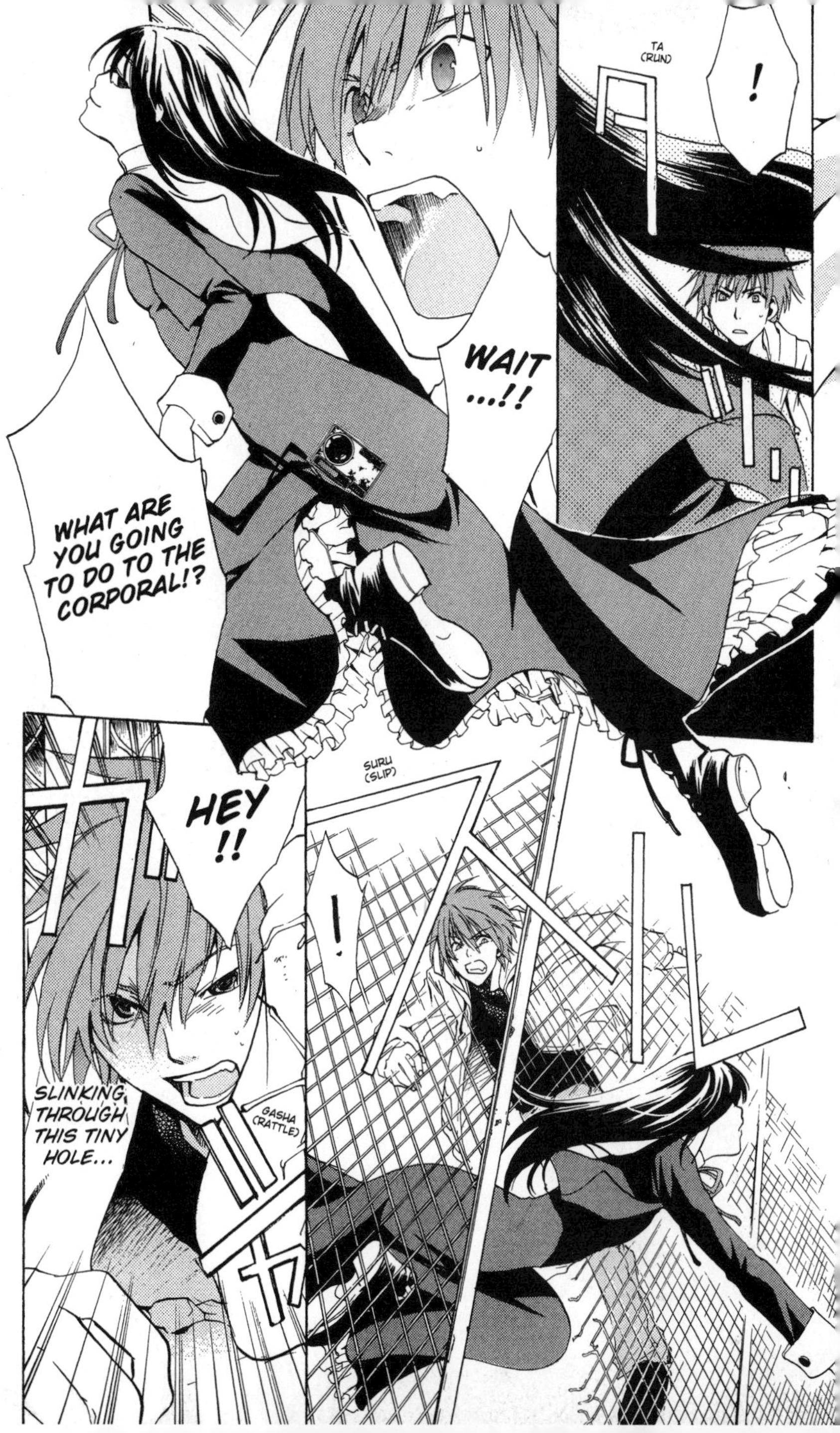
TA (RUN)
!
WAIT ...!!
WHAT ARE YOU GOING TO DO TO THE CORPORAL!?
SURU (SLIP)
!
HEY !!
GASHA (RATTLE)
SLINKING THROUGH THIS TINY HOLE...

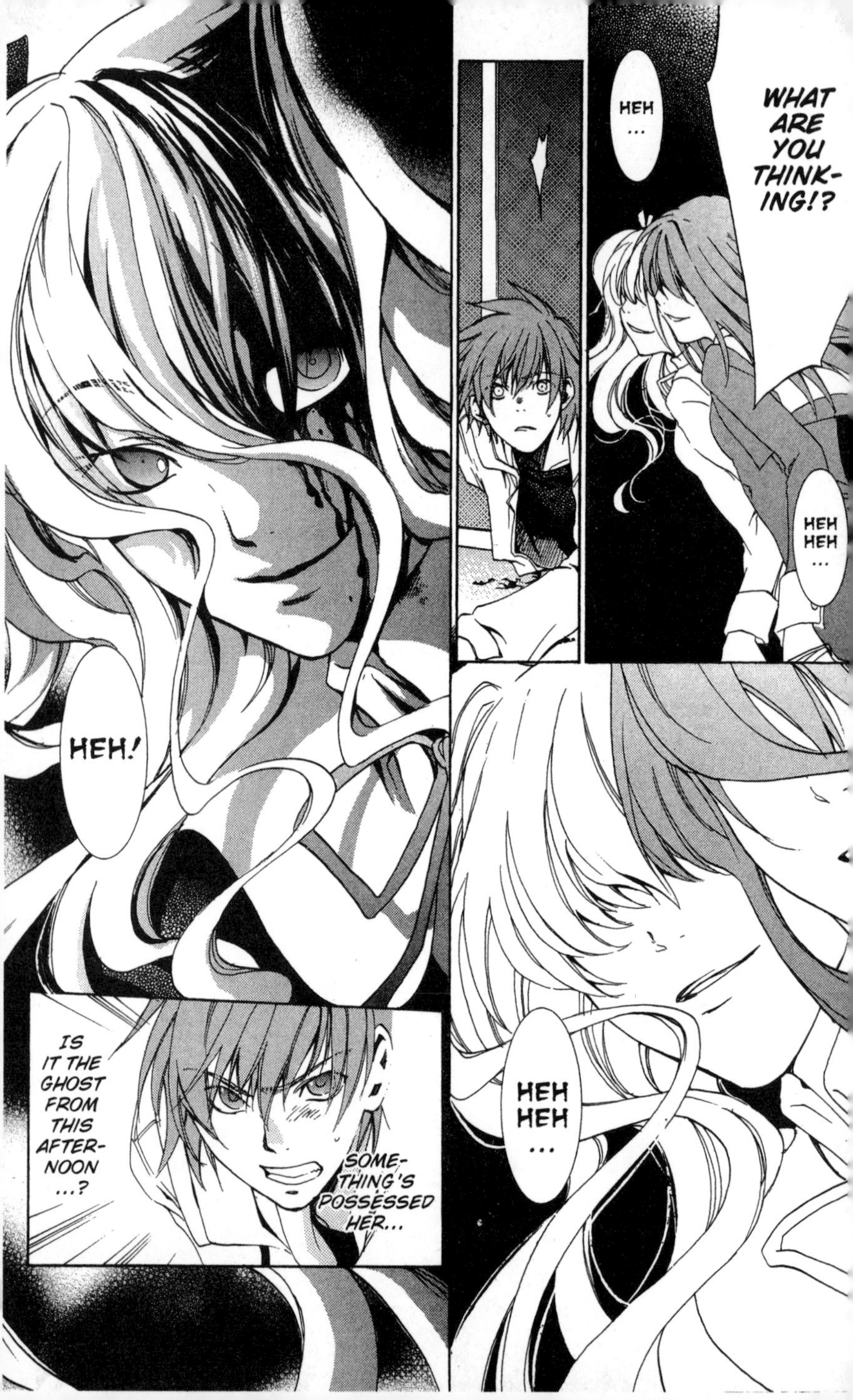
WHAT ARE YOU THINKING!?
HEH HEH ...
HEH ...
HEH HEH ...
HEH!
SOMETHING'S POSSESSED HER...
IS IT THE GHOST FROM THIS AFTERNOON ...?

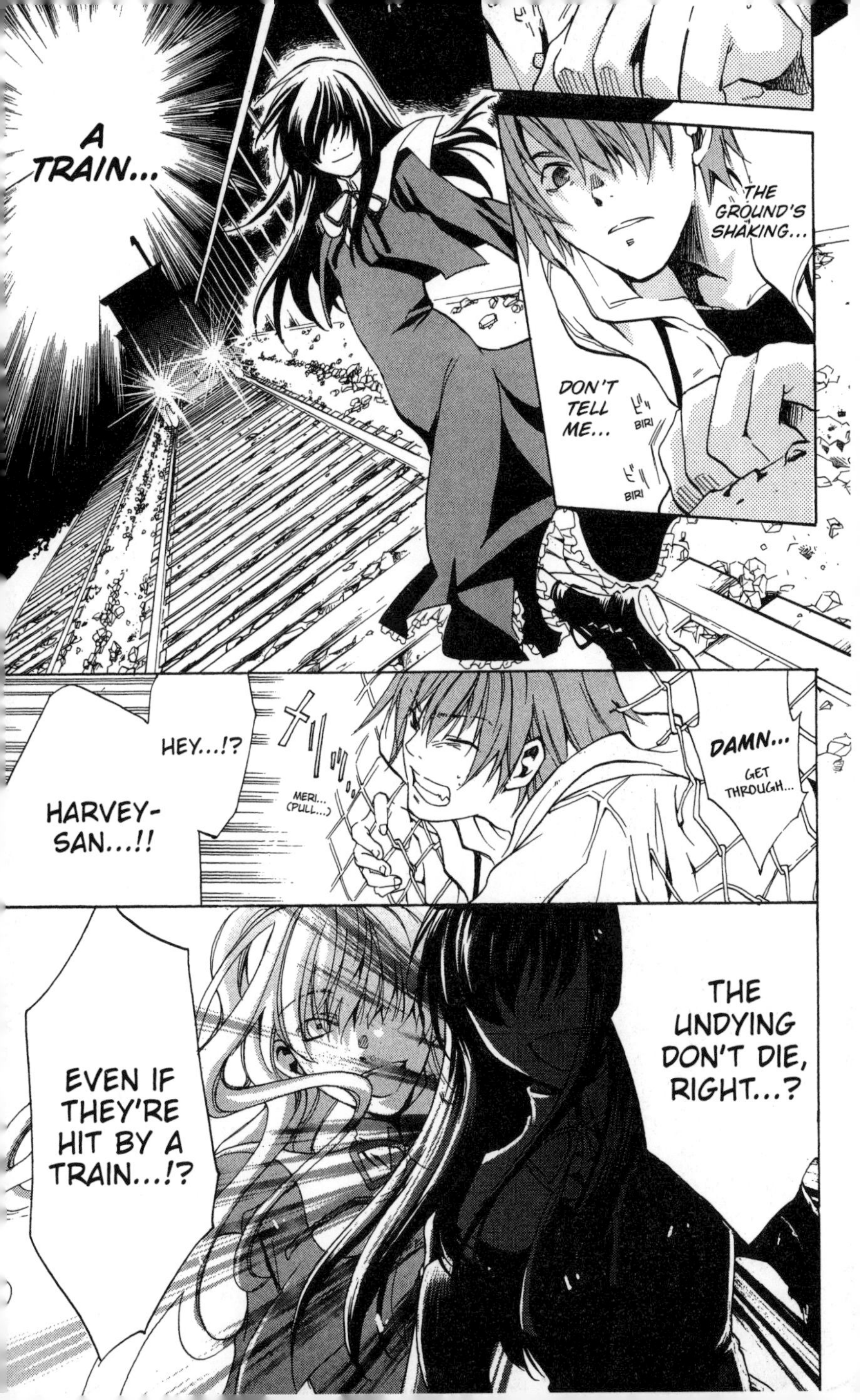
THE GROUND'S SHAKING...
DON'T TELL ME...
BIRI
BIRI
A TRAIN...
DAMN...
GET THROUGH...
MERI... (PULL...)
HEY...!?
HARVEY-SAN...!!
THE UNDYING DON'T DIE, RIGHT...?
EVEN IF THEY'RE HIT BY A TRAIN...!?

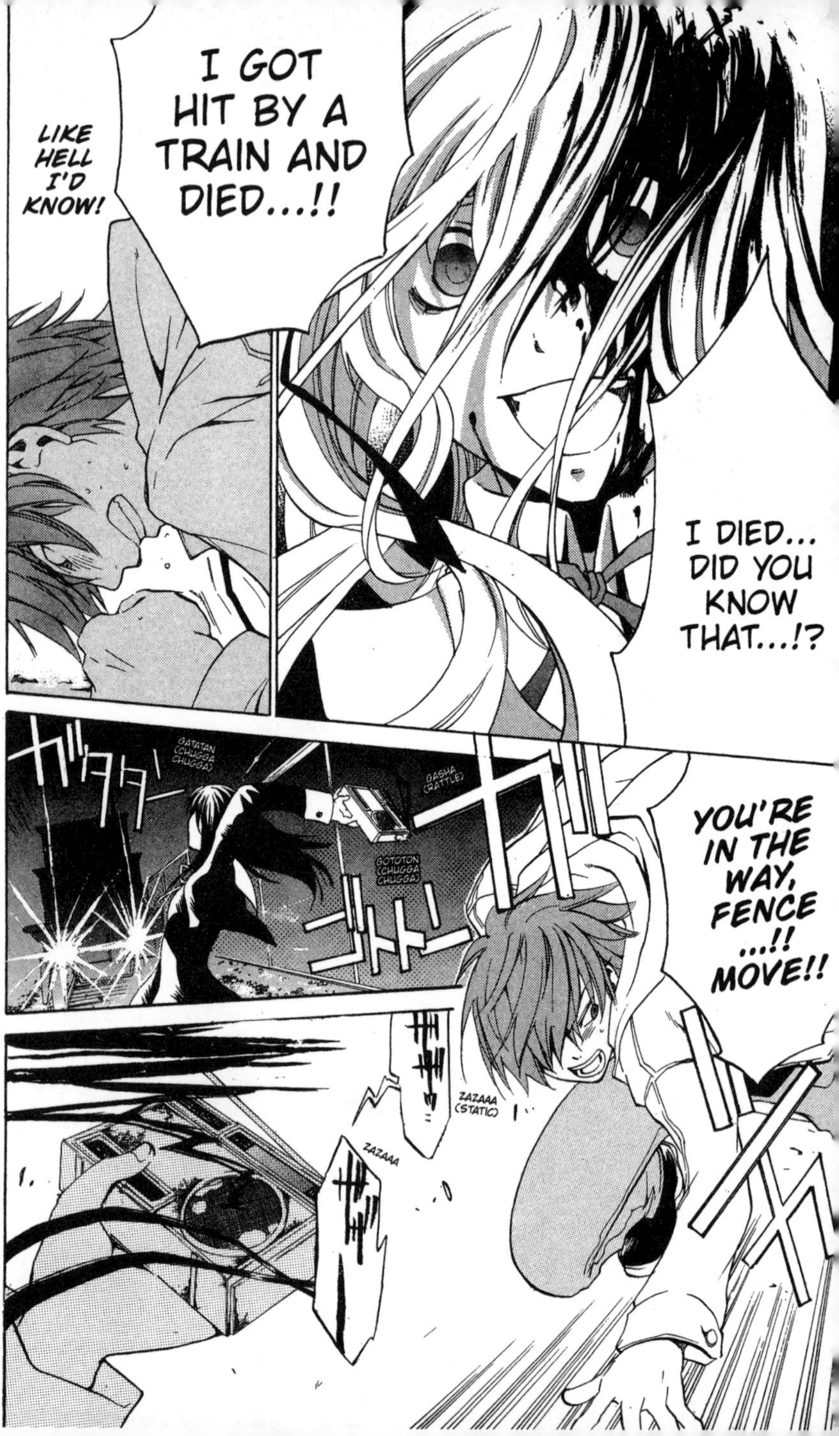
I DIED... DID YOU KNOW THAT...!?
LIKE HELL I'D KNOW!
I GOT HIT BY A TRAIN AND DIED...!!
YOU'RE IN THE WAY, FENCE ...!! MOVE!!
GASHA (RATTLE)
GATATAN (CHUGGA CHUGGA)
GOTOTON (CHUGGA CHUGGA)
ZAZAAA (STATIC)
ZAZAAA

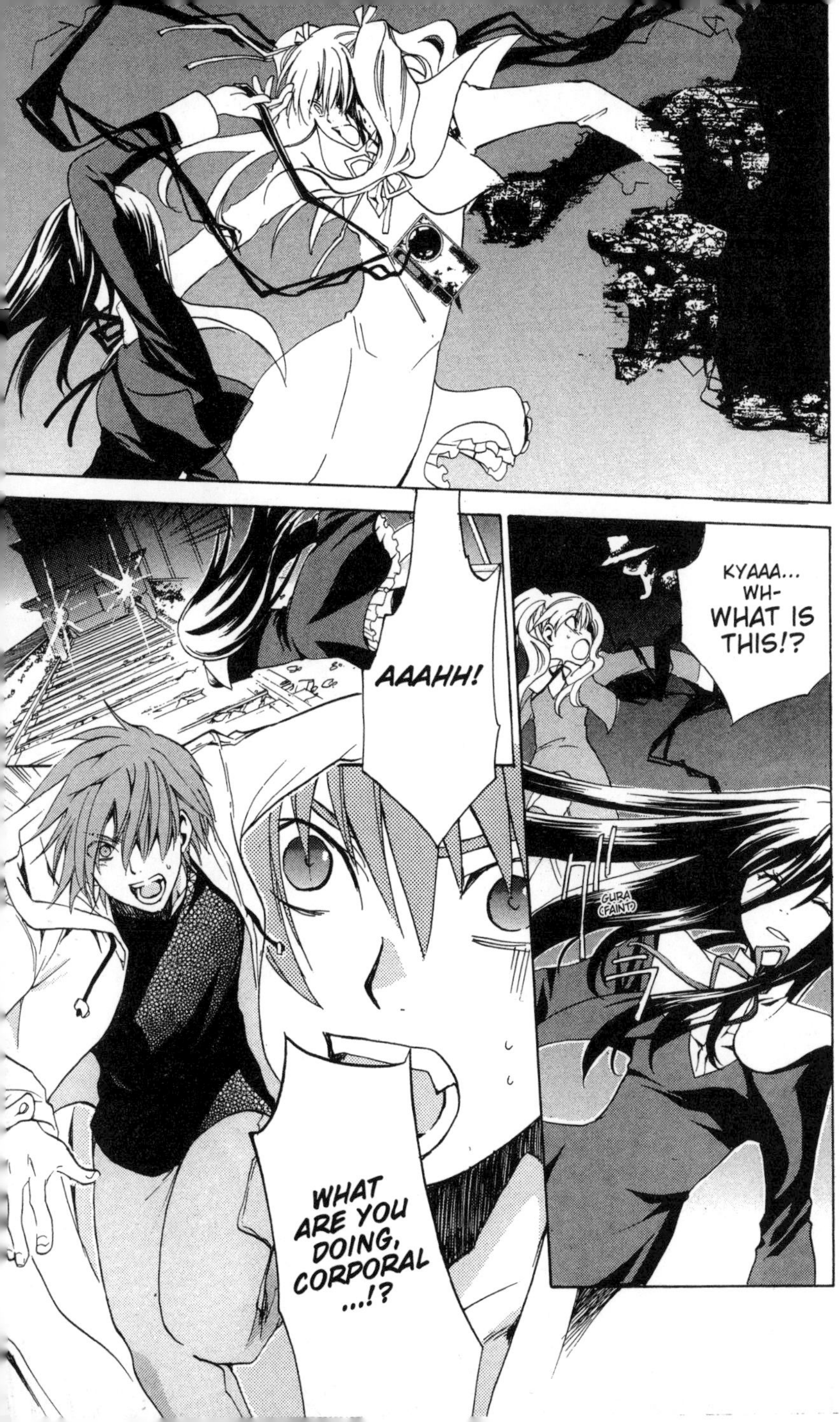
KYAAA... WH- WHAT IS THIS!?
GURA (FAINT)
AAAHH!
WHAT ARE YOU DOING, CORPORAL ...!?

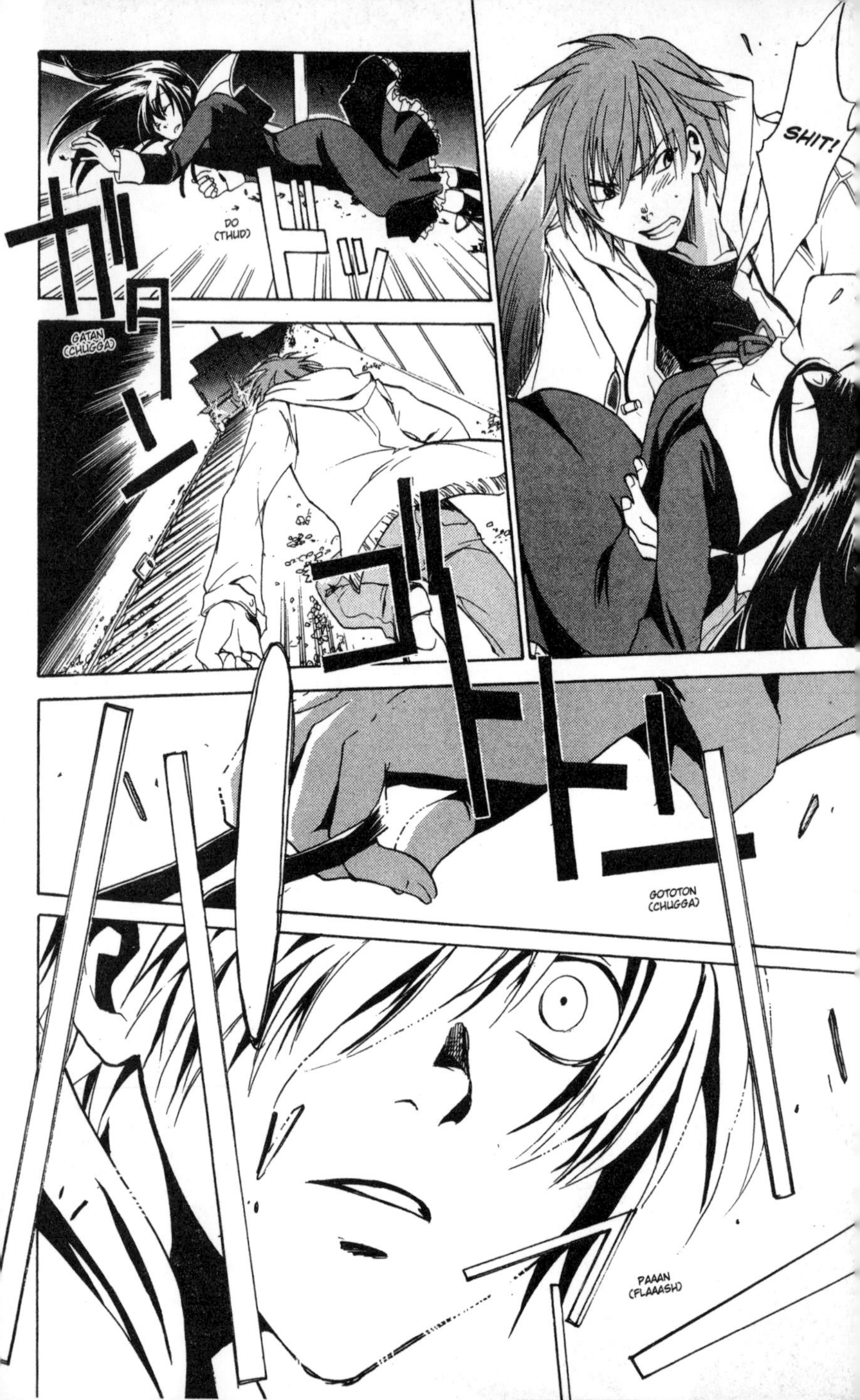
SHIT!
DO (THUD)
GATAN (CHUGGA)
GOTOTON (CHUGGA)
PAAAN (FLAAASH)

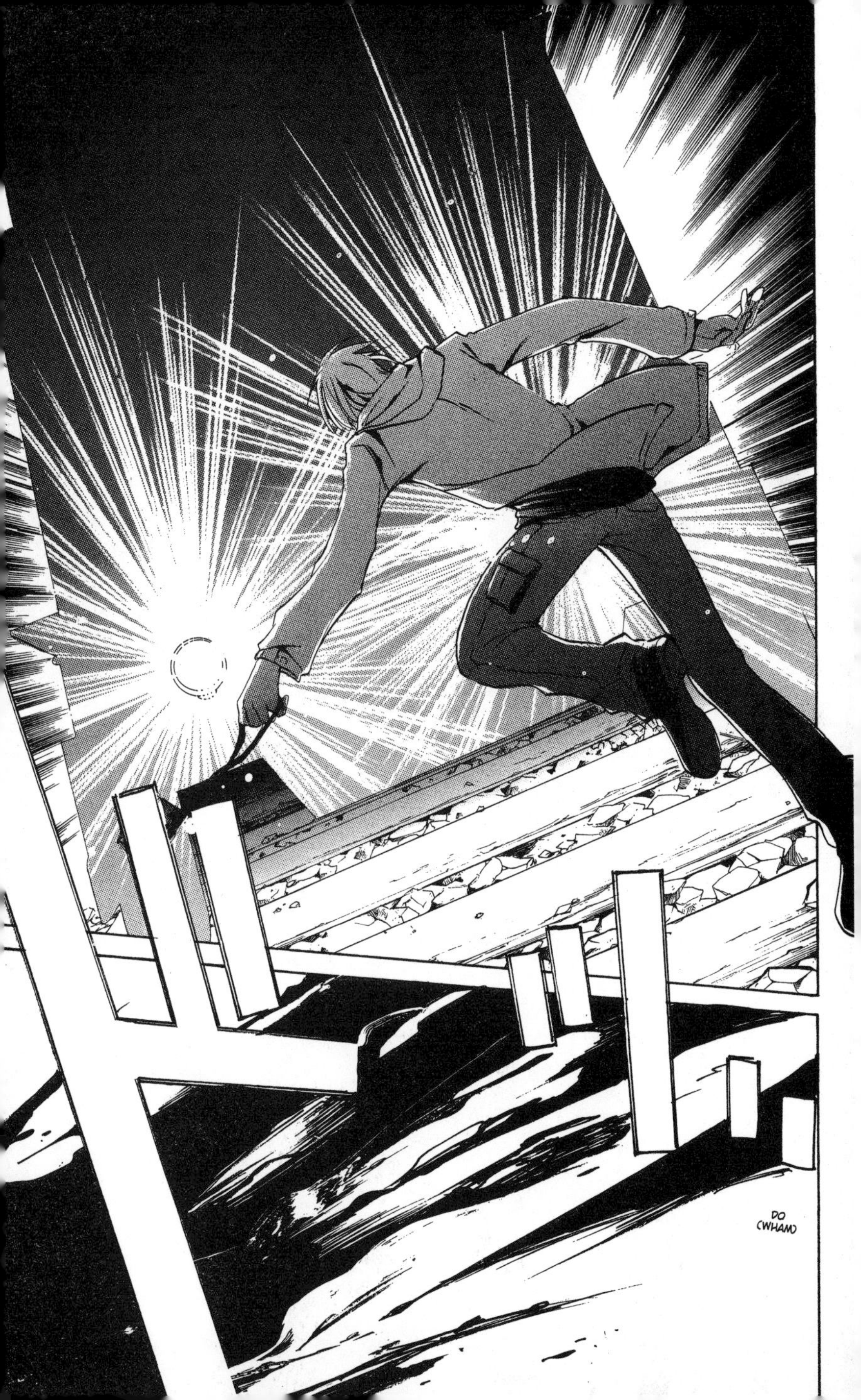
DO
(WHAM)

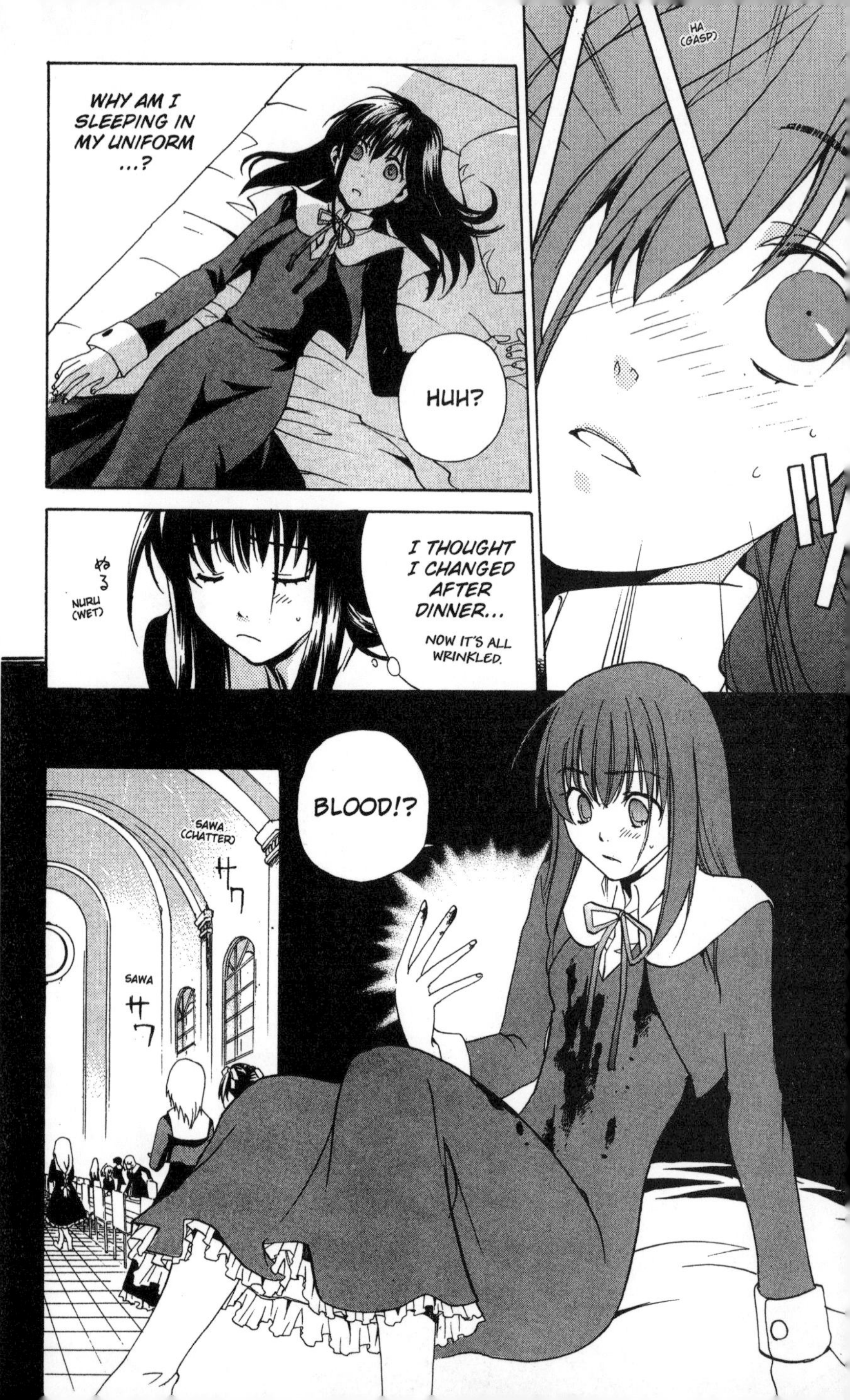

HA (GASP)
HUH?
WHY AM I SLEEPING IN MY UNIFORM ...?
I THOUGHT I CHANGED AFTER DINNER...
NOW IT'S ALL WRINKLED.
ぬる
NURU (WET)
BLOOD!?
サワ
SAWA (CHATTER)
サワ
SAWA

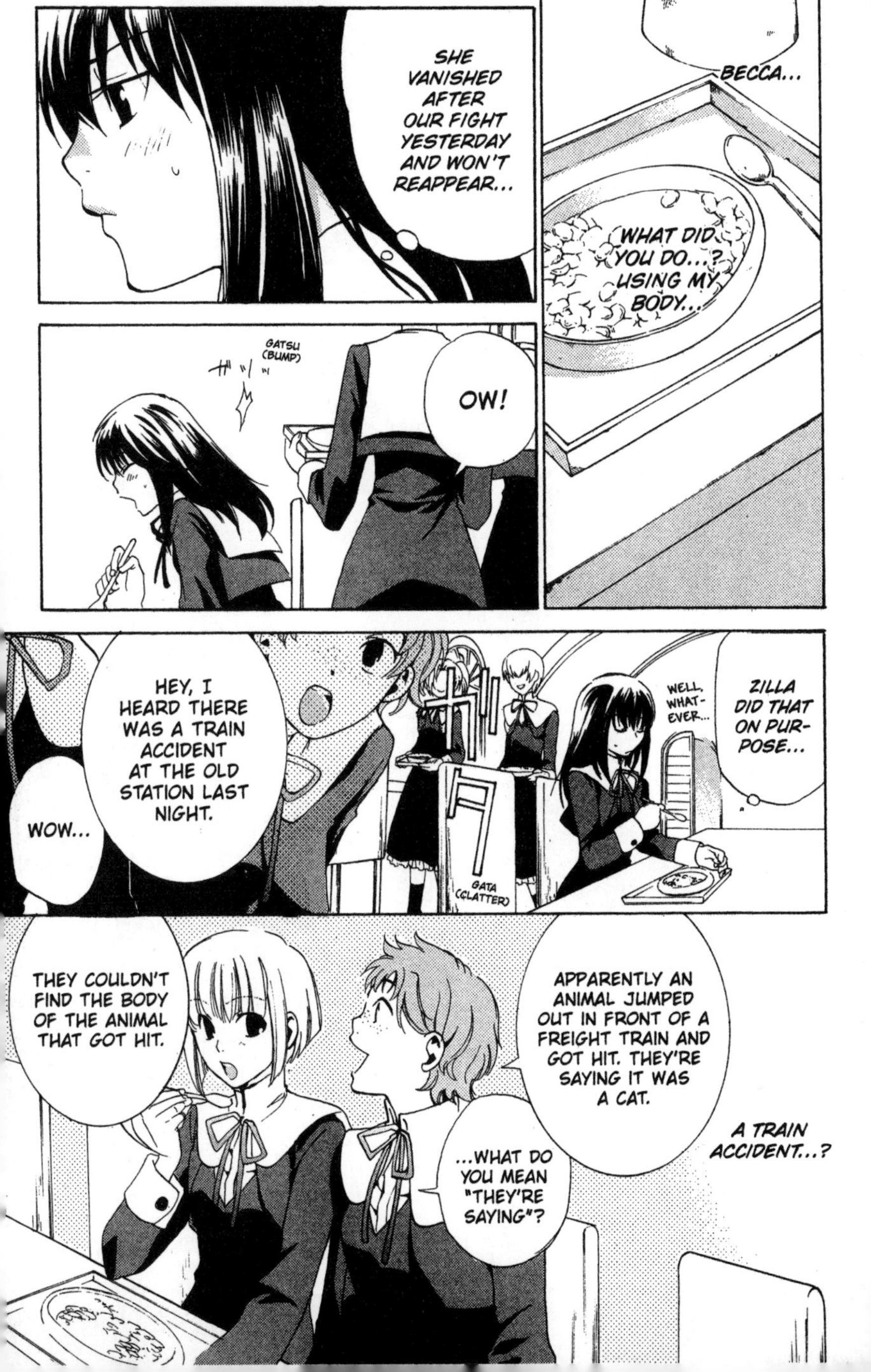
BECCA...
WHAT DID YOU DO...? USING MY BODY...
SHE VANISHED AFTER OUR FIGHT YESTERDAY AND WON'T REAPPEAR...
OW!
GATSU (BUMP)
ZILLA DID THAT ON PURPOSE...
WELL, WHATEVER...
GATA (CLATTER)
HEY, I HEARD THERE WAS A TRAIN ACCIDENT AT THE OLD STATION LAST NIGHT.
WOW...
A TRAIN ACCIDENT...?
APPARENTLY AN ANIMAL JUMPED OUT IN FRONT OF A FREIGHT TRAIN AND GOT HIT. THEY'RE SAYING IT WAS A CAT.
...WHAT DO YOU MEAN "THEY'RE SAYING"?
THEY COULDN'T FIND THE BODY OF THE ANIMAL THAT GOT HIT.

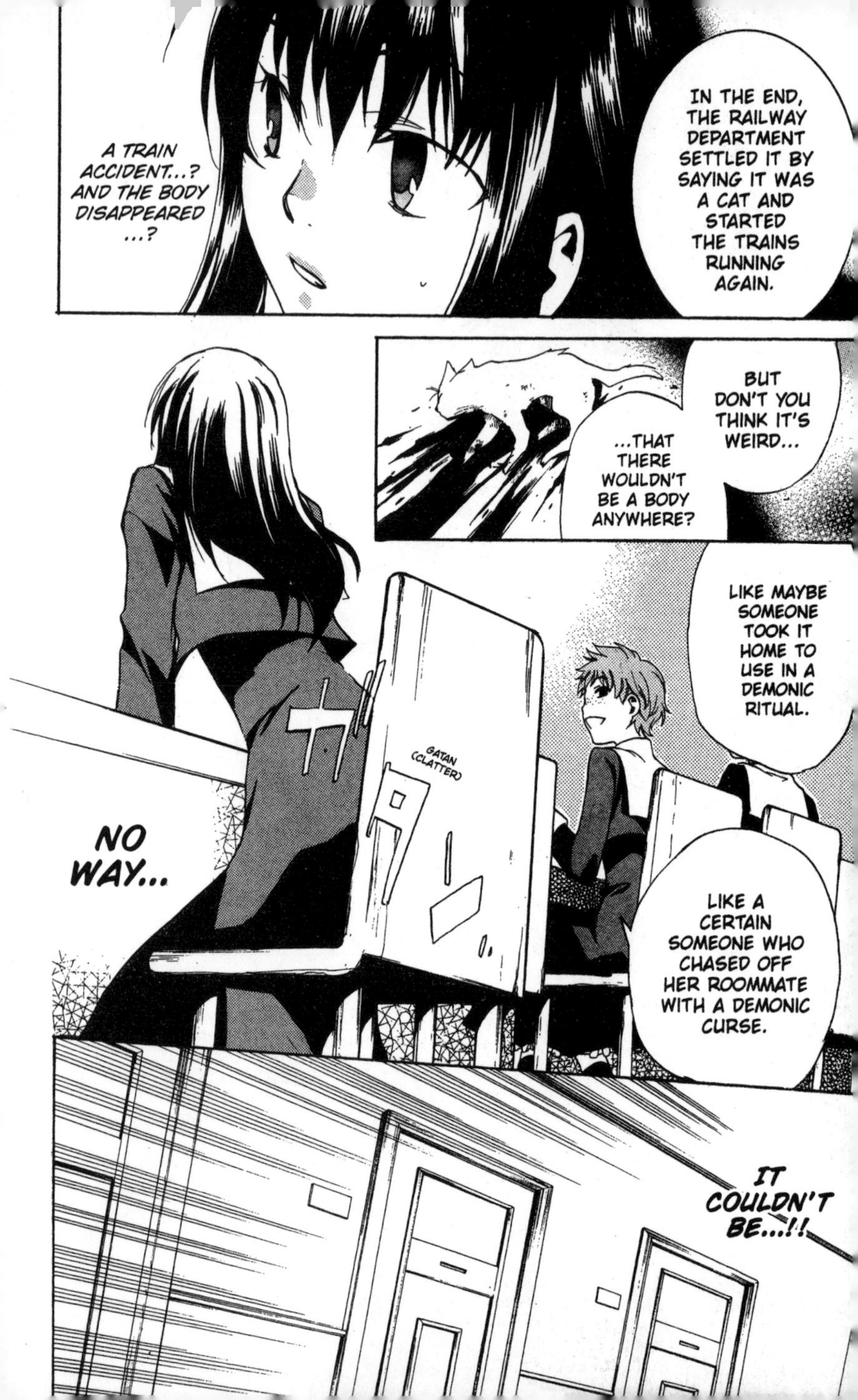
IN THE END, THE RAILWAY DEPARTMENT SETTLED IT BY SAYING IT WAS A CAT AND STARTED THE TRAINS RUNNING AGAIN.
A TRAIN ACCIDENT...? AND THE BODY DISAPPEARED ...?
BUT DON'T YOU THINK IT'S WEIRD...
...THAT THERE WOULDN'T BE A BODY ANYWHERE?
LIKE MAYBE SOMEONE TOOK IT HOME TO USE IN A DEMONIC RITUAL.
GATAN (CLATTER)
LIKE A CERTAIN SOMEONE WHO CHASED OFF HER ROOMMATE WITH A DEMONIC CURSE.
NO WAY...
IT COULDN'T BE...!!

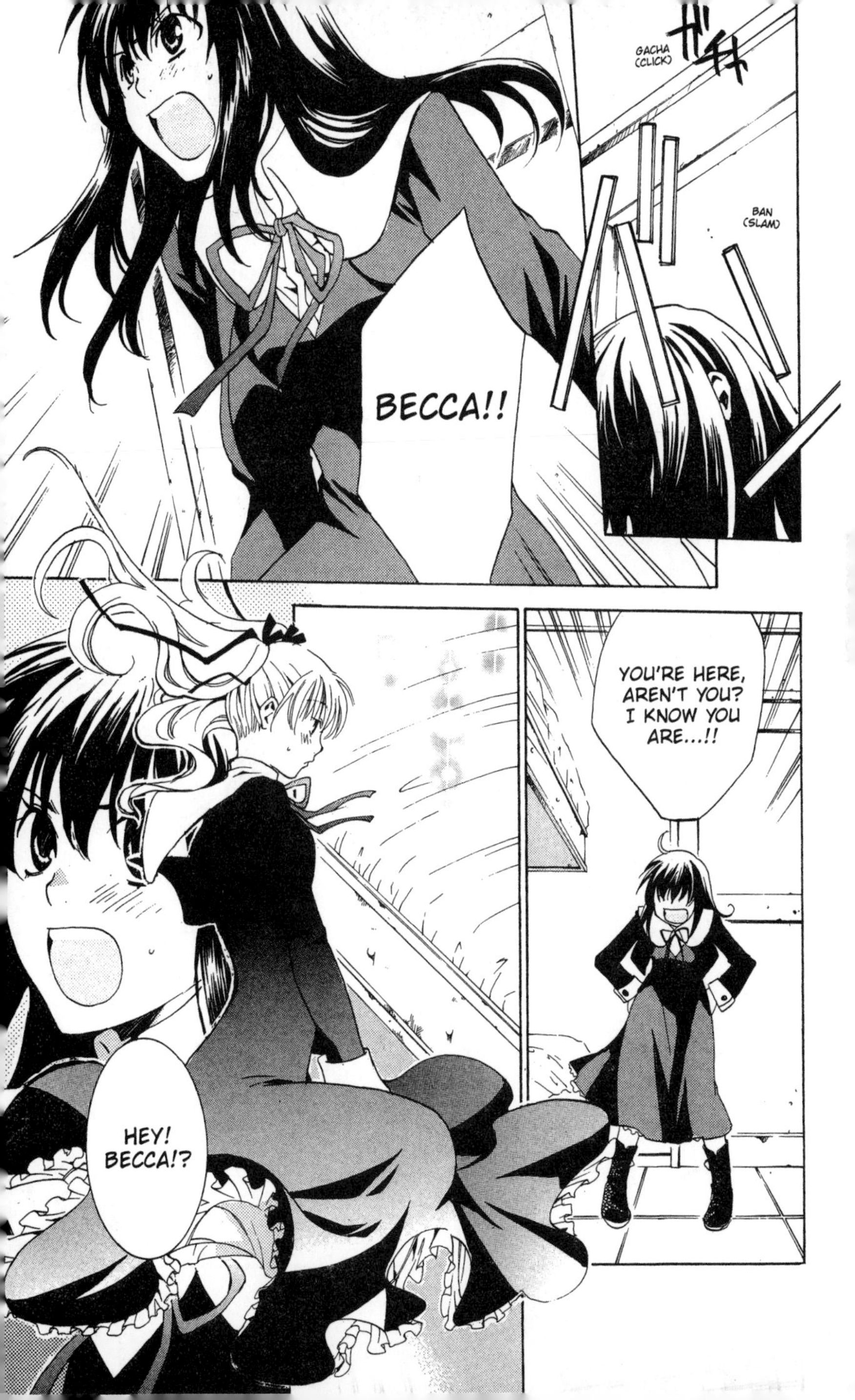
ガチャ
GACHA (CLICK)
BAN (SLAM)
BECCA!!
YOU'RE HERE, AREN'T YOU? I KNOW YOU ARE...!!
HEY! BECCA!?

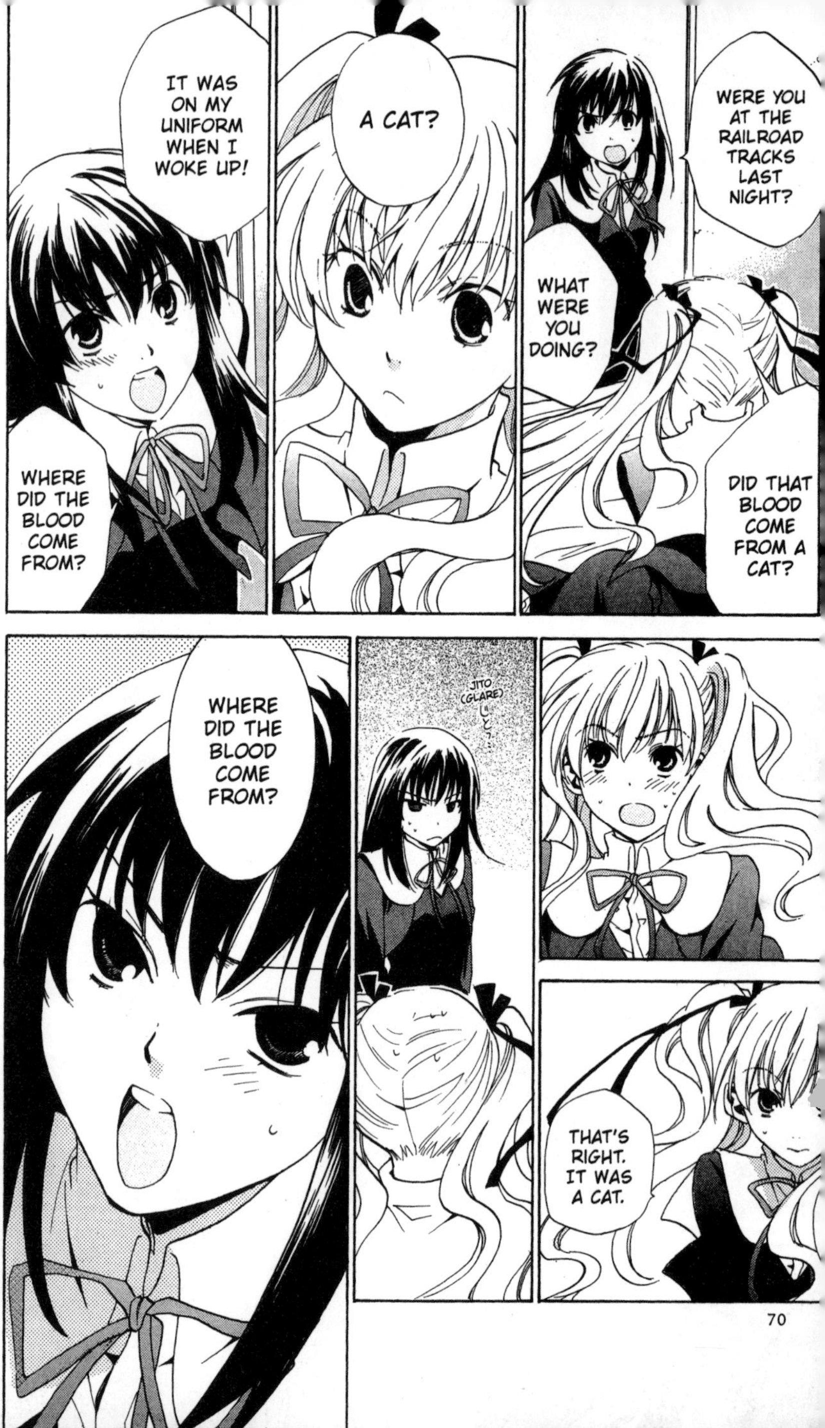
WERE YOU AT THE RAILROAD TRACKS LAST NIGHT?
WHAT WERE YOU DOING?
DID THAT BLOOD COME FROM A CAT?
A CAT?
IT WAS ON MY UNIFORM WHEN I WOKE UP!
WHERE DID THE BLOOD COME FROM?
THAT'S RIGHT. IT WAS A CAT.
JITO (GLARE)
WHERE DID THE BLOOD COME FROM?

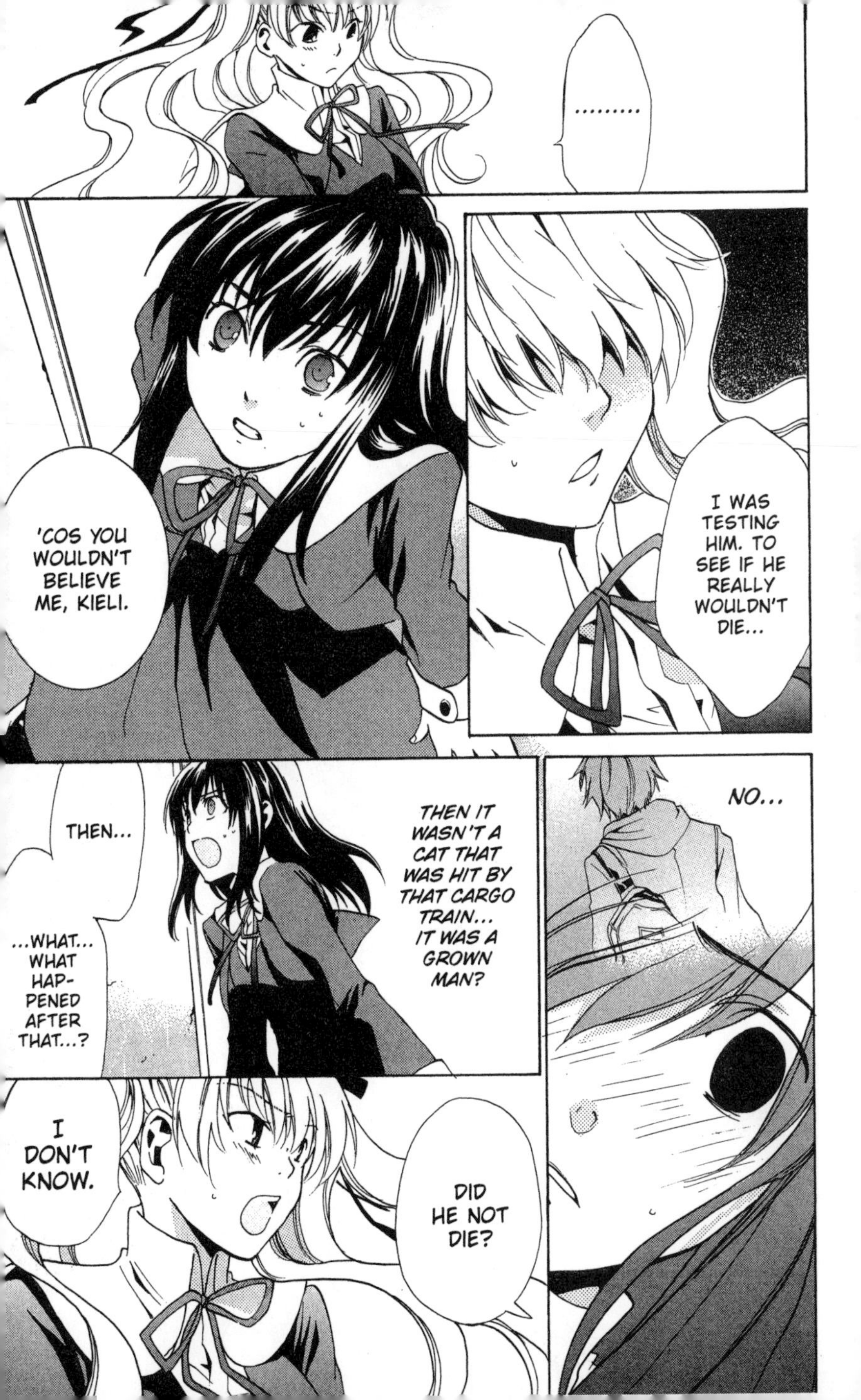
....
I WAS TESTING HIM. TO SEE IF HE REALLY WOULDN'T DIE...
'COS YOU WOULDN'T BELIEVE ME, KIELI.
NO...
THEN IT WASN'T A CAT THAT WAS HIT BY THAT CARGO TRAIN... IT WAS A GROWN MAN?
THEN...
...WHAT... WHAT HAP-PENED AFTER THAT...?
DID HE NOT DIE?
I DON'T KNOW.

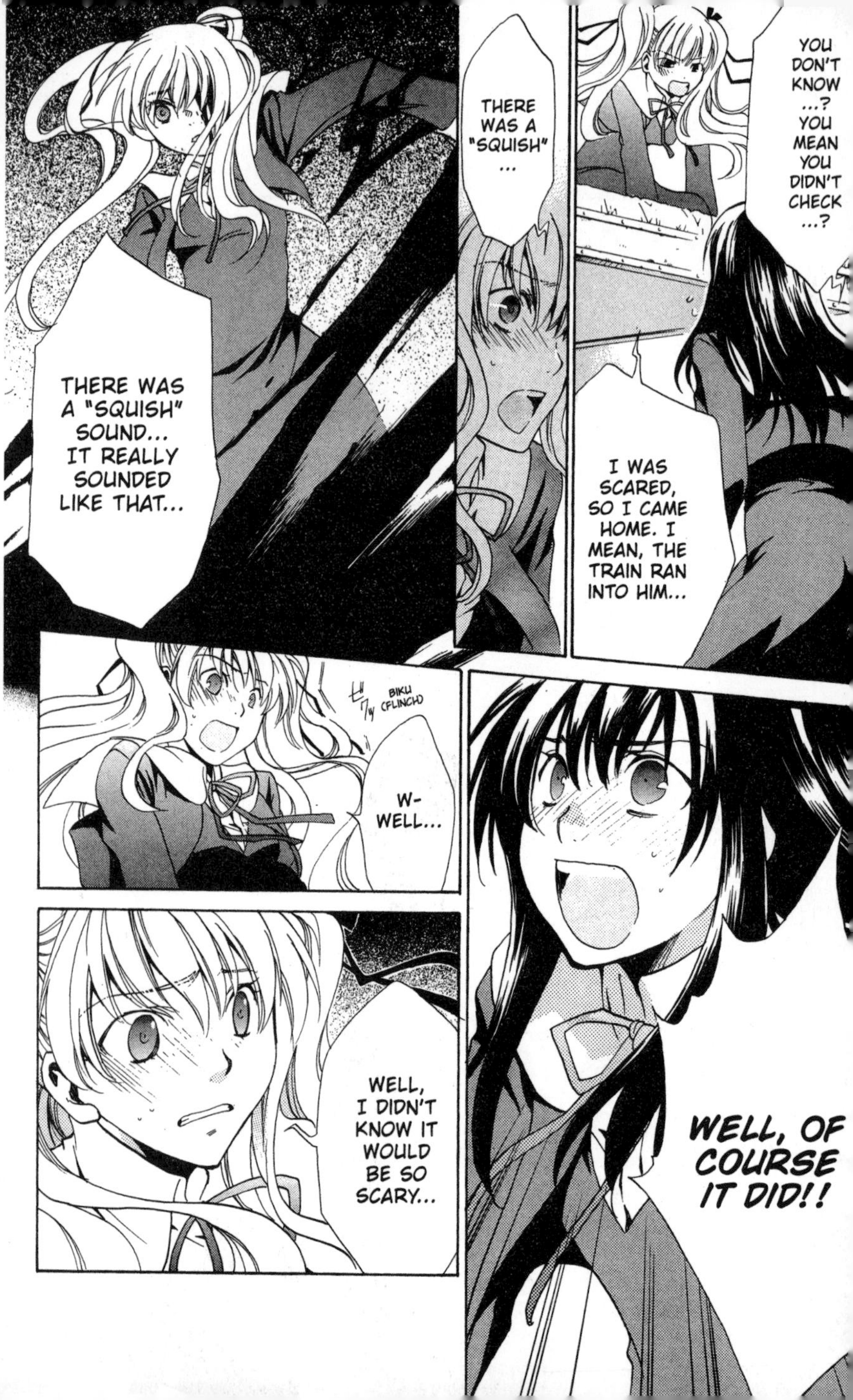
YOU DON'T KNOW ...? YOU MEAN YOU DIDN'T CHECK ...?
I WAS SCARED, SO I CAME HOME. I MEAN, THE TRAIN RAN INTO HIM...
THERE WAS A "SQUISH" ...
THERE WAS A "SQUISH" SOUND... IT REALLY SOUNDED LIKE THAT...
WELL, OF COURSE IT DID!!
BIKU (FLINCH)
W-WELL...
WELL, I DIDN'T KNOW IT WOULD BE SO SCARY...

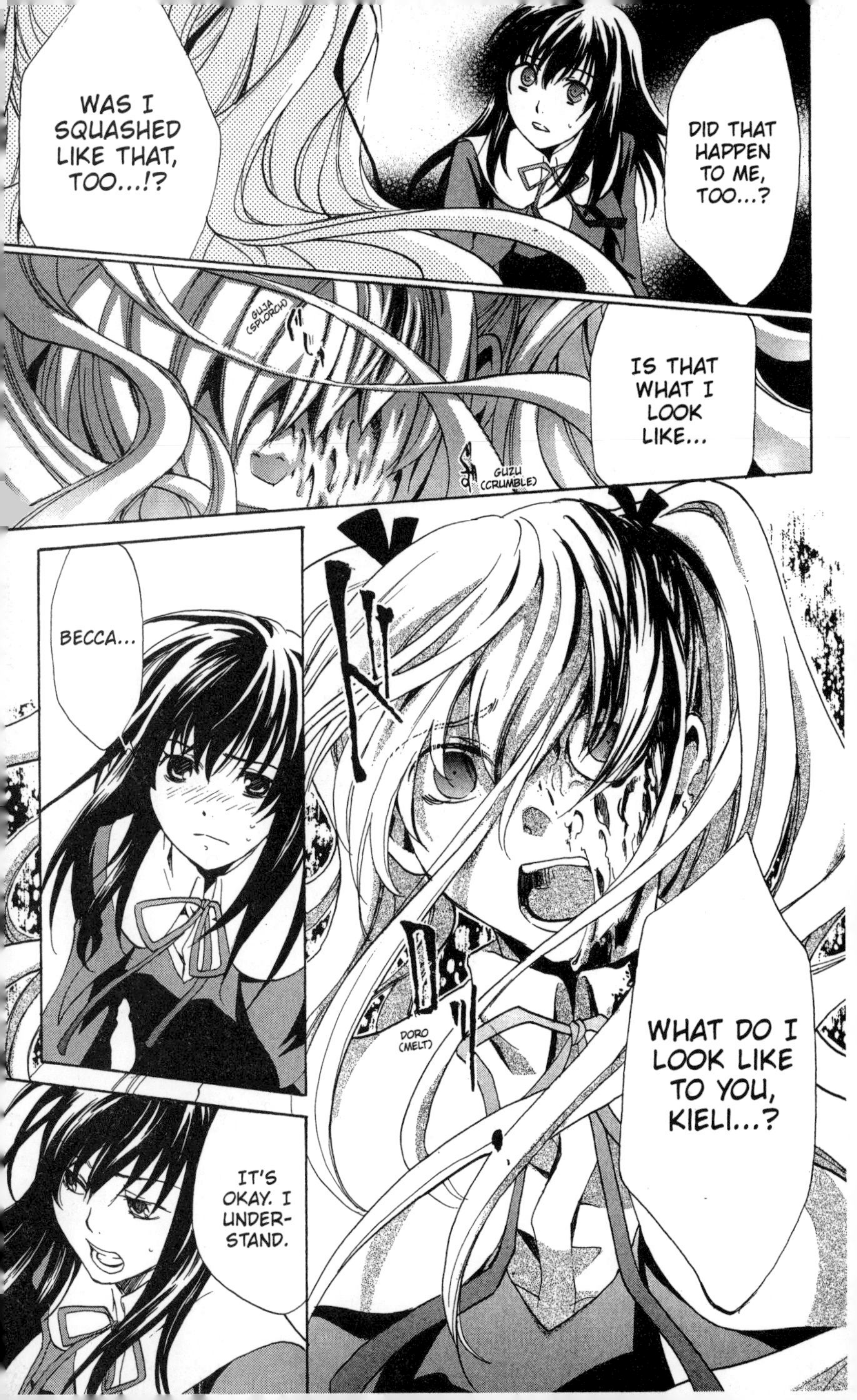
DID THAT HAPPEN TO ME, TOO...?
WAS I SQUASHED LIKE THAT, TOO...!?
IS THAT WHAT I LOOK LIKE...
GUJA (SPLORCH)
GUZU (CRUMBLE)
WHAT DO I LOOK LIKE TO YOU, KIELI...?
DORO (MELT)
BECCA...
IT'S OKAY. I UNDER-STAND.

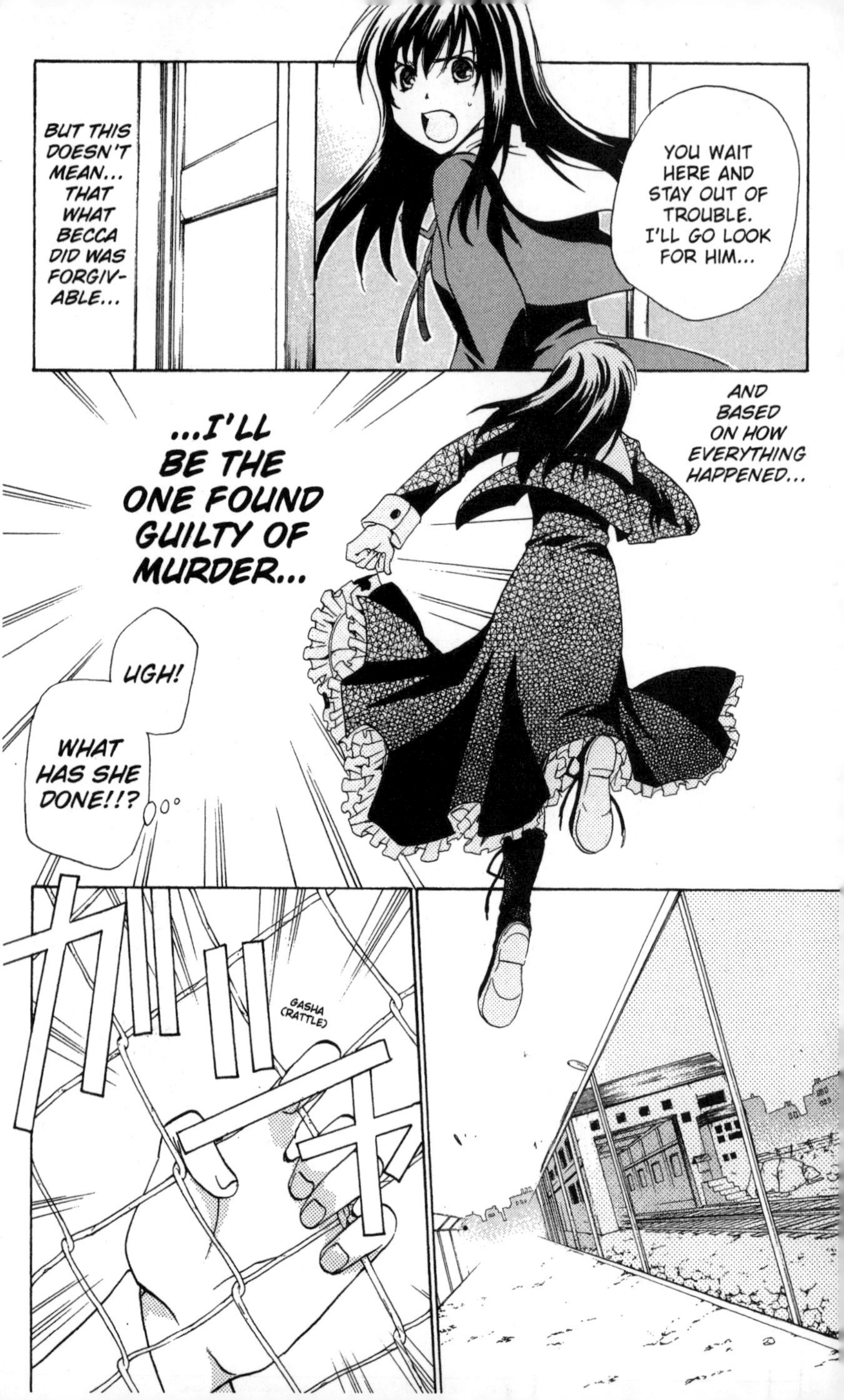
YOU WAIT HERE AND STAY OUT OF TROUBLE. I'LL GO LOOK FOR HIM...
BUT THIS DOESN'T MEAN... THAT WHAT BECCA DID WAS FORGIV-ABLE...
AND BASED ON HOW EVERYTHING HAPPENED...
...I'LL BE THE ONE FOUND GUILTY OF MURDER...
UGH!
WHAT HAS SHE DONE!!?
GASHA (RATTLE)

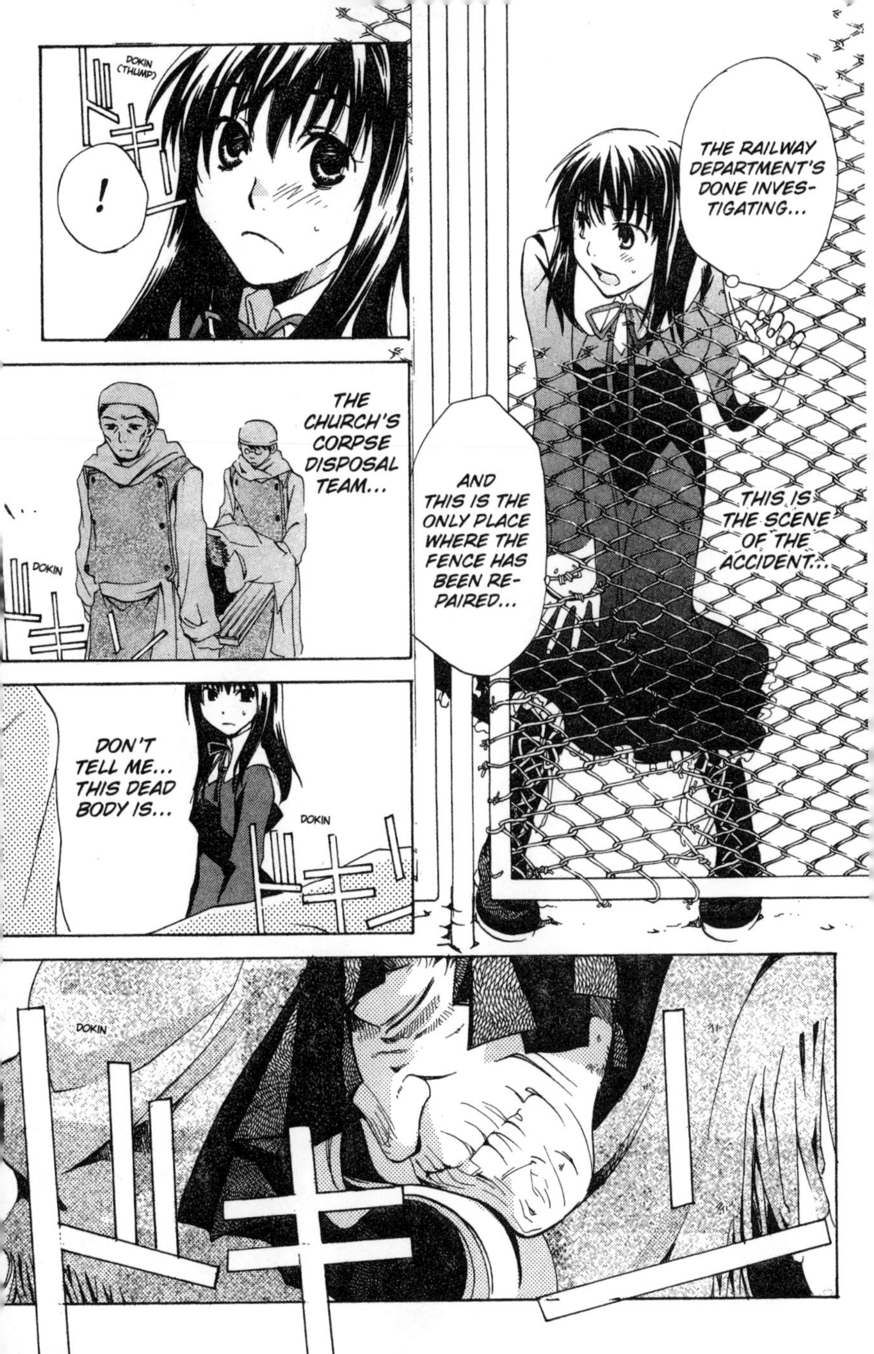
THE RAILWAY DEPARTMENT'S DONE INVES-TIGATING...
THIS IS THE SCENE OF THE ACCIDENT...
AND THIS IS THE ONLY PLACE WHERE THE FENCE HAS BEEN RE-PAIRED...
DOKIN (THUMP)
!
THE CHURCH'S CORPSE DISPOSAL TEAM...
...
DOKIN
DON'T TELL ME... THIS DEAD BODY IS...
DOKIN
DOKIN

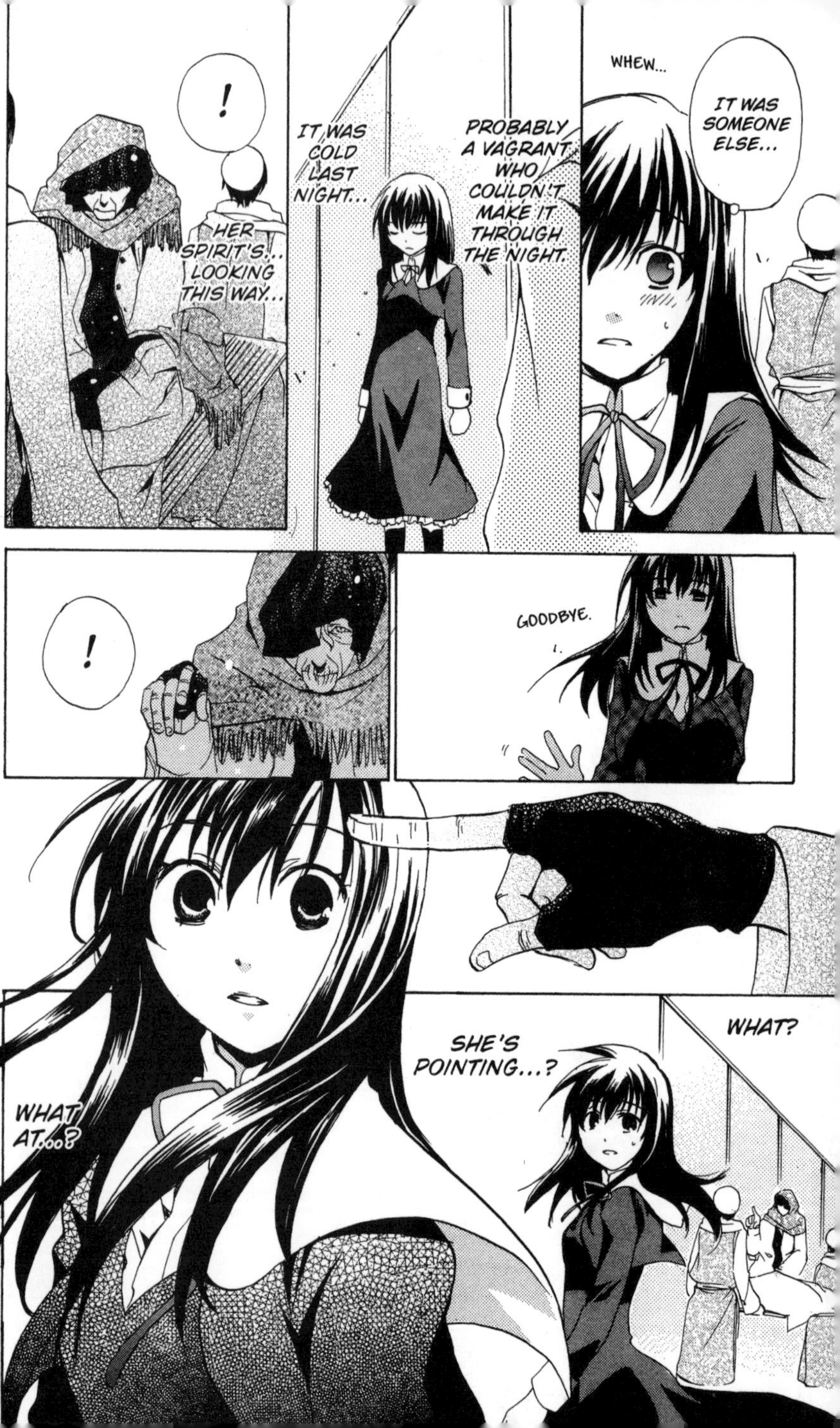
WHEW...
IT WAS SOMEONE ELSE...
PROBABLY A VAGRANT WHO COULDN'T MAKE IT THROUGH THE NIGHT.
IT WAS COLD LAST NIGHT...
!
HER SPIRIT'S... LOOKING THIS WAY...
GOODBYE.
!
WHAT?
SHE'S POINTING...?
WHAT AT...?

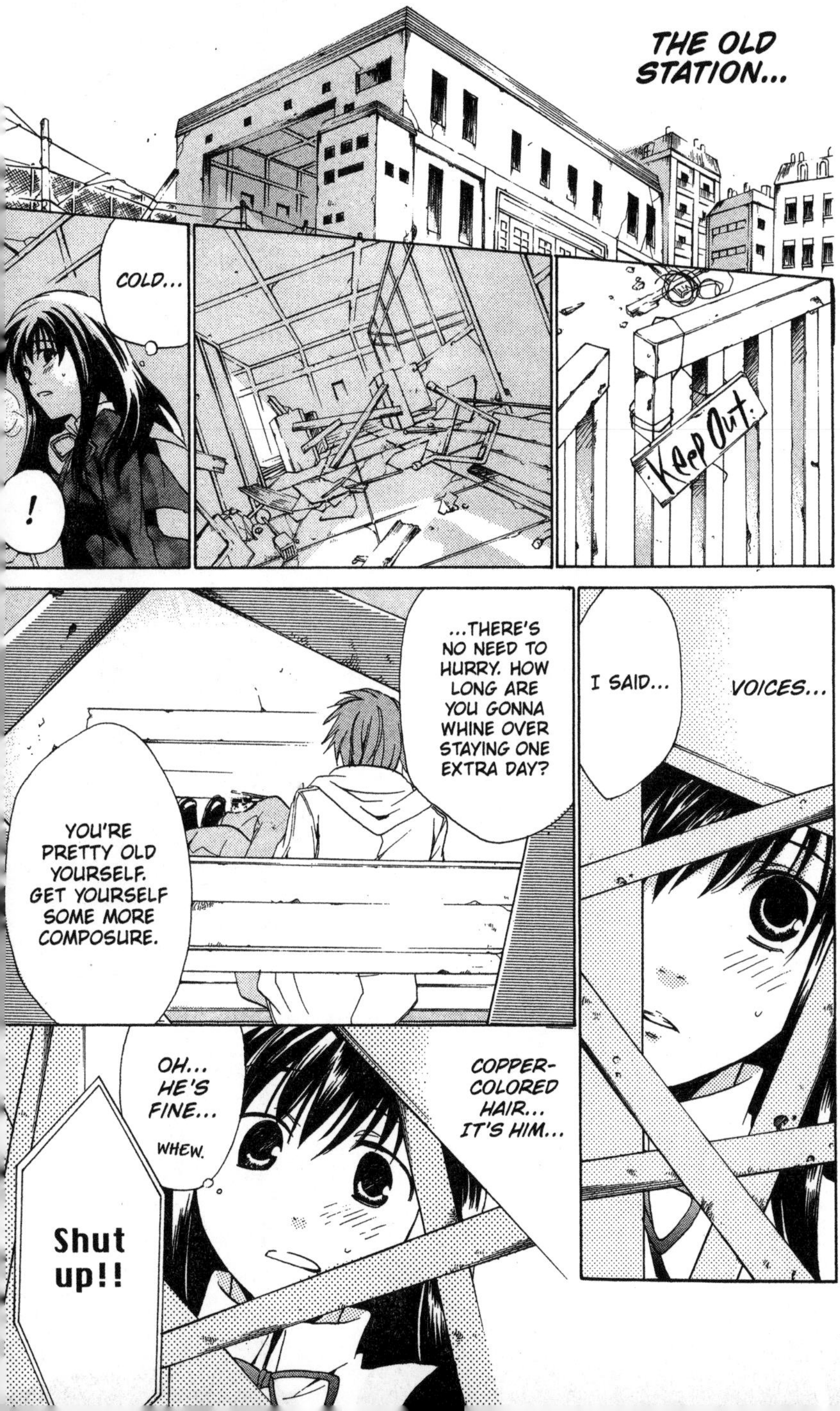
THE OLD STATION...
Keep Out
COLD...
!
VOICES...
I SAID...
...THERE'S NO NEED TO HURRY. HOW LONG ARE YOU GONNA WHINE OVER STAYING ONE EXTRA DAY?
YOU'RE PRETTY OLD YOURSELF. GET YOURSELF SOME MORE COMPOSURE.
COPPER-COLORED HAIR... IT'S HIM...
OH... HE'S FINE...
WHEW.
Shut up!!

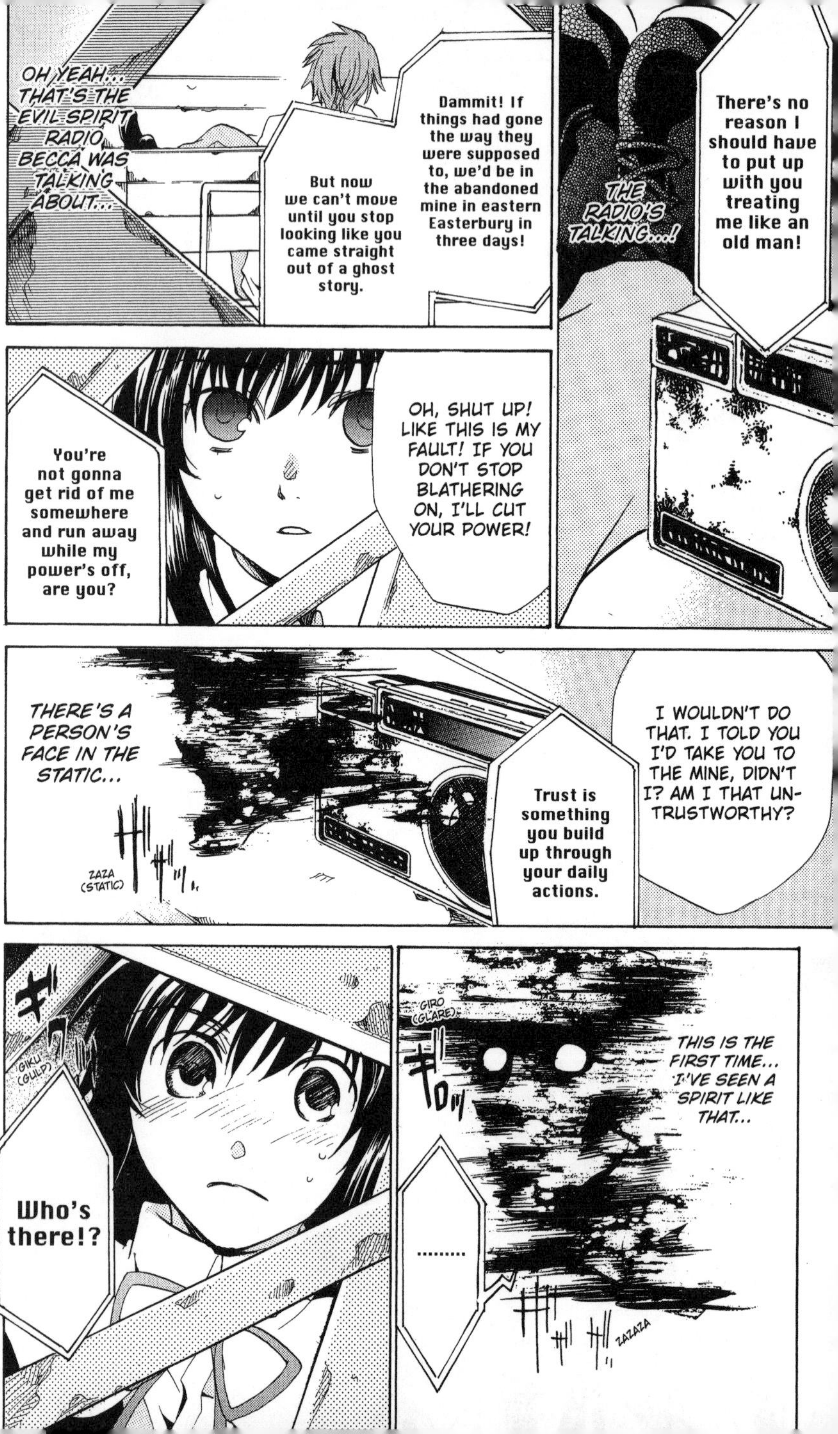
There's no reason I should have to put up with you treating me like an old man!
THE RADIO'S TALKING...!
Dammit! If things had gone the way they were supposed to, we'd be in the abandoned mine in eastern Easterbury in three days!
But now we can't move until you stop looking like you came straight out of a ghost story.
OH YEAH... THAT'S THE EVIL SPIRIT RADIO BECCA WAS TALKING ABOUT...
OH, SHUT UP! LIKE THIS IS MY FAULT! IF YOU DON'T STOP BLATHERING ON, I'LL CUT YOUR POWER!
You're not gonna get rid of me somewhere and run away while my power's off, are you?
I WOULDN'T DO THAT. I TOLD YOU I'D TAKE YOU TO THE MINE, DIDN'T I? AM I THAT UNTRUSTWORTHY?
Trust is something you build up through your daily actions.
THERE'S A PERSON'S FACE IN THE STATIC...
ZAZA (STATIC)
GIRO (GLARE)
THIS IS THE FIRST TIME... I'VE SEEN A SPIRIT LIKE THAT...
....
ZAZAZA
GIKU (GULP)
Who's there!?

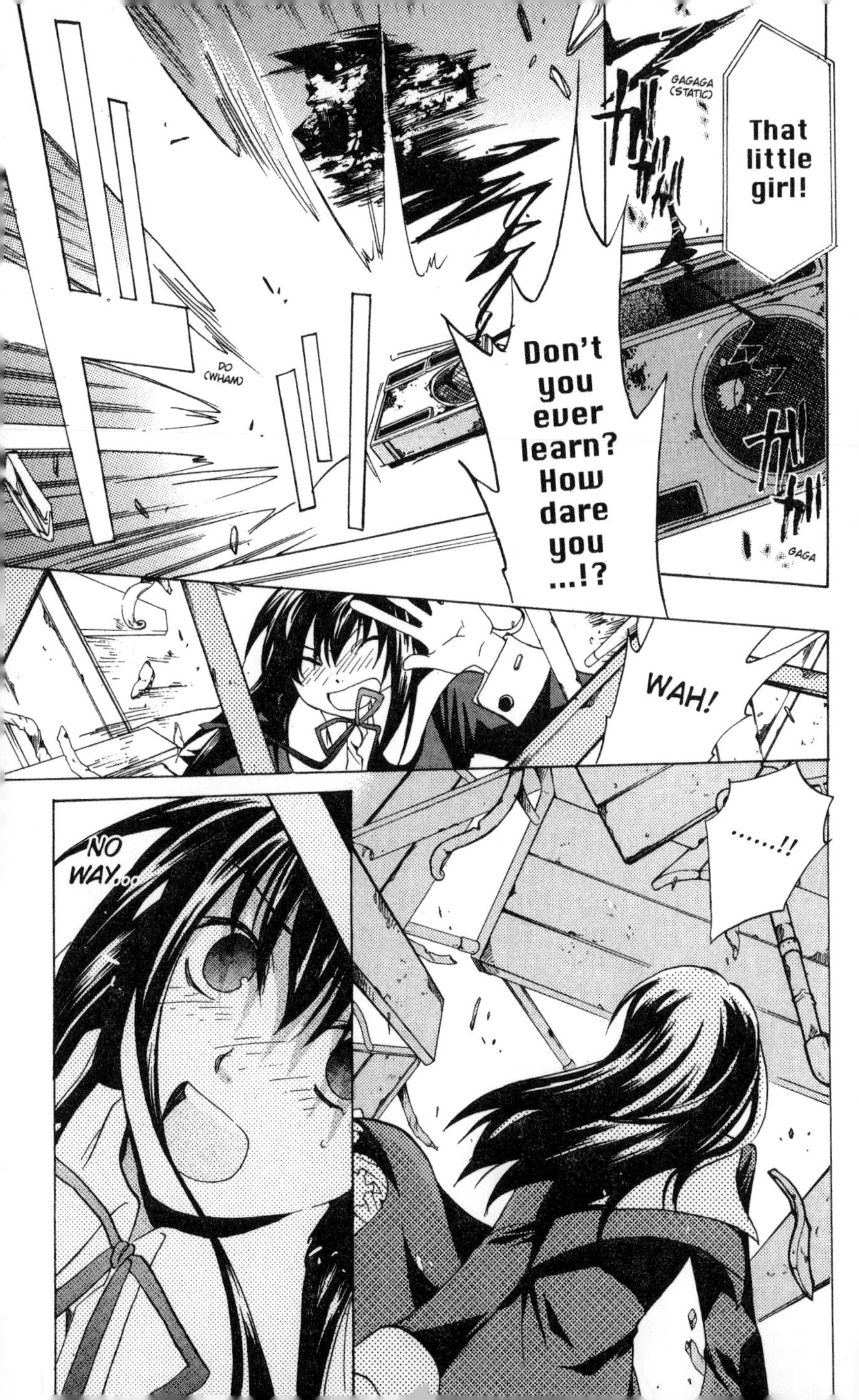

GAGAGA (STATIC)
That little girl!
Don't you ever learn? How dare you ...!?
GAGA
DO (WHAM)
WAH!
......!!
NO WAY...

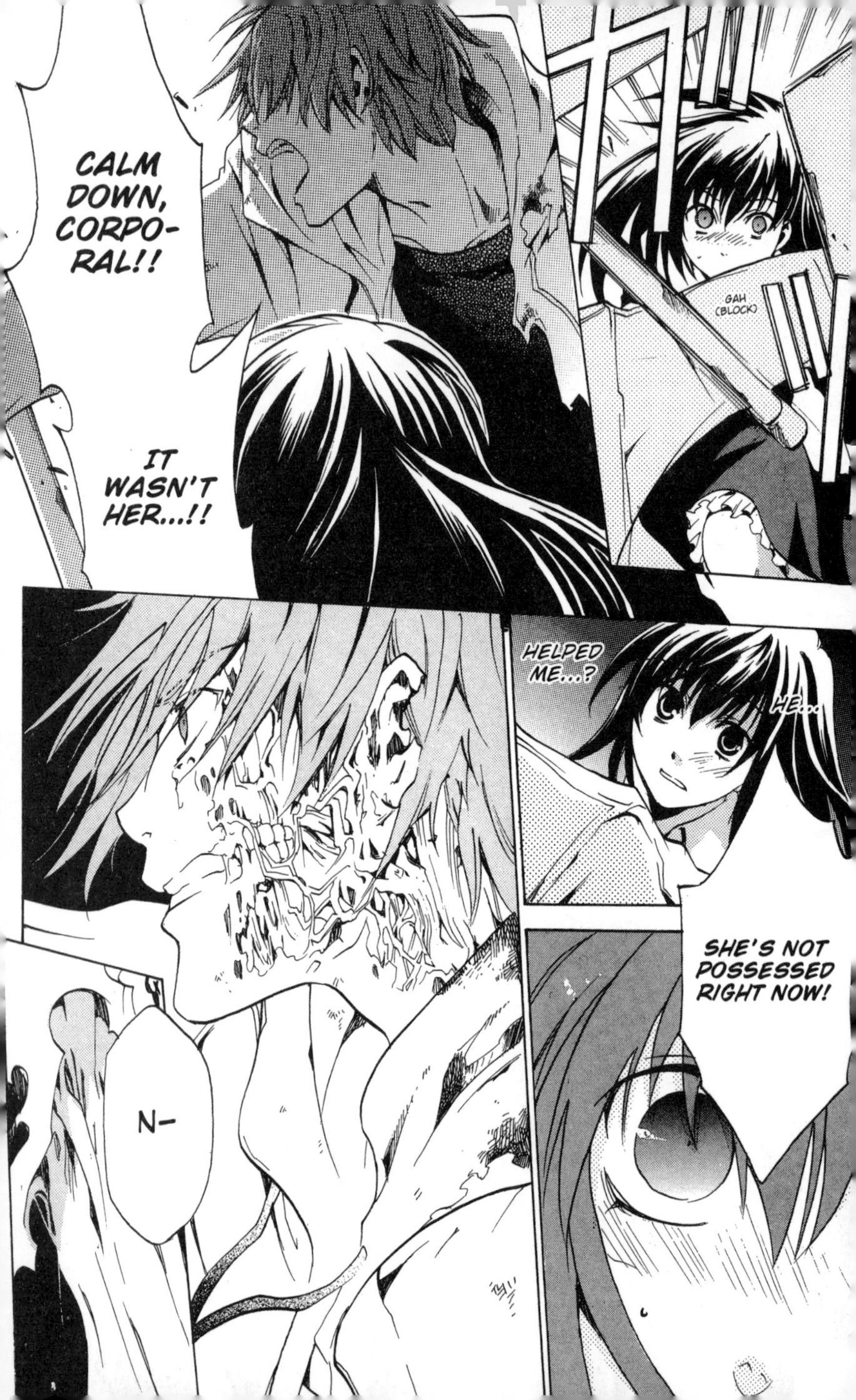
GAH (BLOCK)
CALM DOWN, CORPORAL!!
IT WASN'T HER...!!
HE...
HELPED ME...?
SHE'S NOT POSSESSED RIGHT NOW!
N-

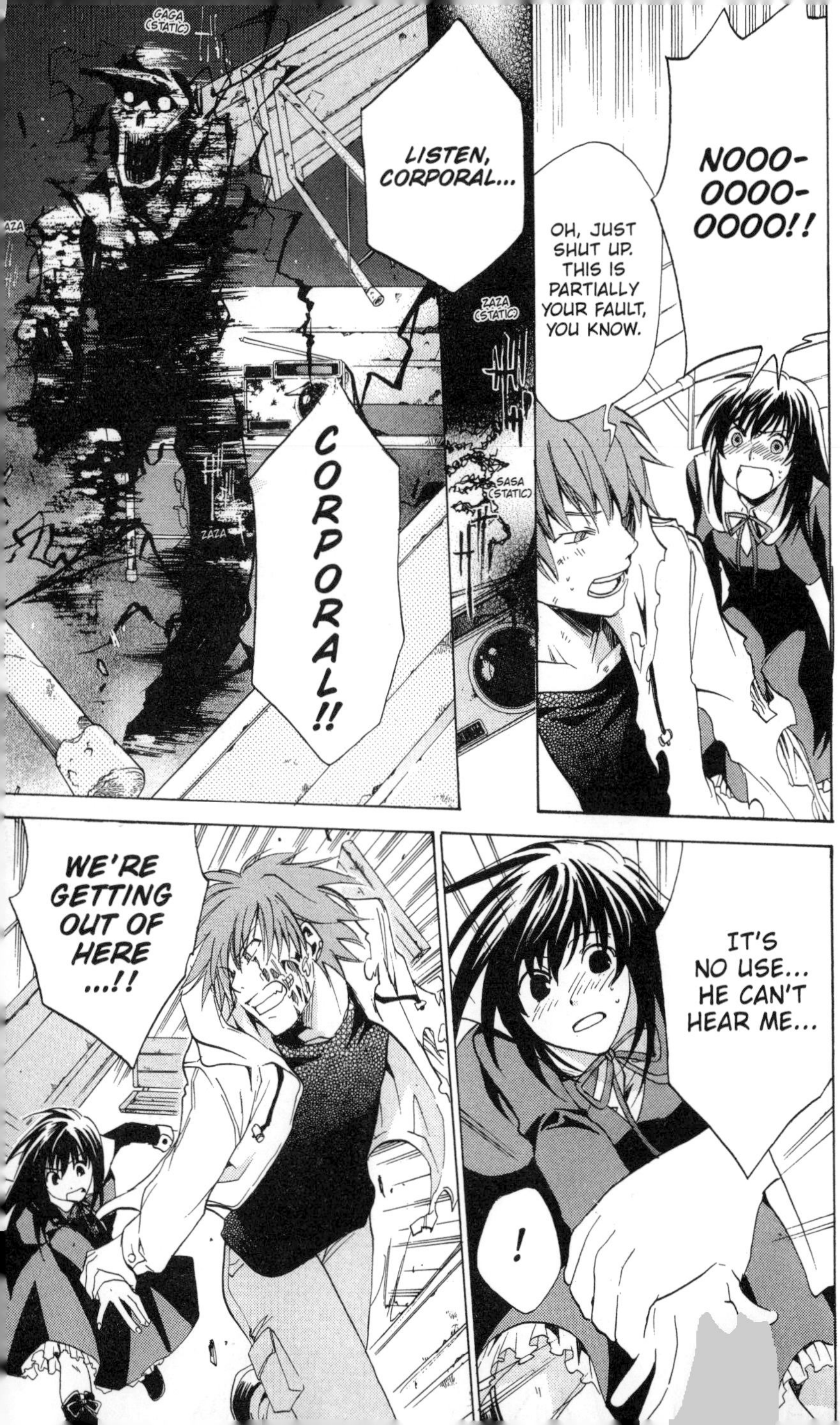
NOOO-
OOOO-
OOOO!!
OH, JUST SHUT UP. THIS IS PARTIALLY YOUR FAULT, YOU KNOW.
ZAZA (STATIC)
SASA (STATIC)
GAGA (STATIC)
LISTEN, CORPORAL...
ZAZA
CORPORAL!!
ZAZA
IT'S NO USE... HE CAN'T HEAR ME...
!
WE'RE GETTING OUT OF HERE ...!!

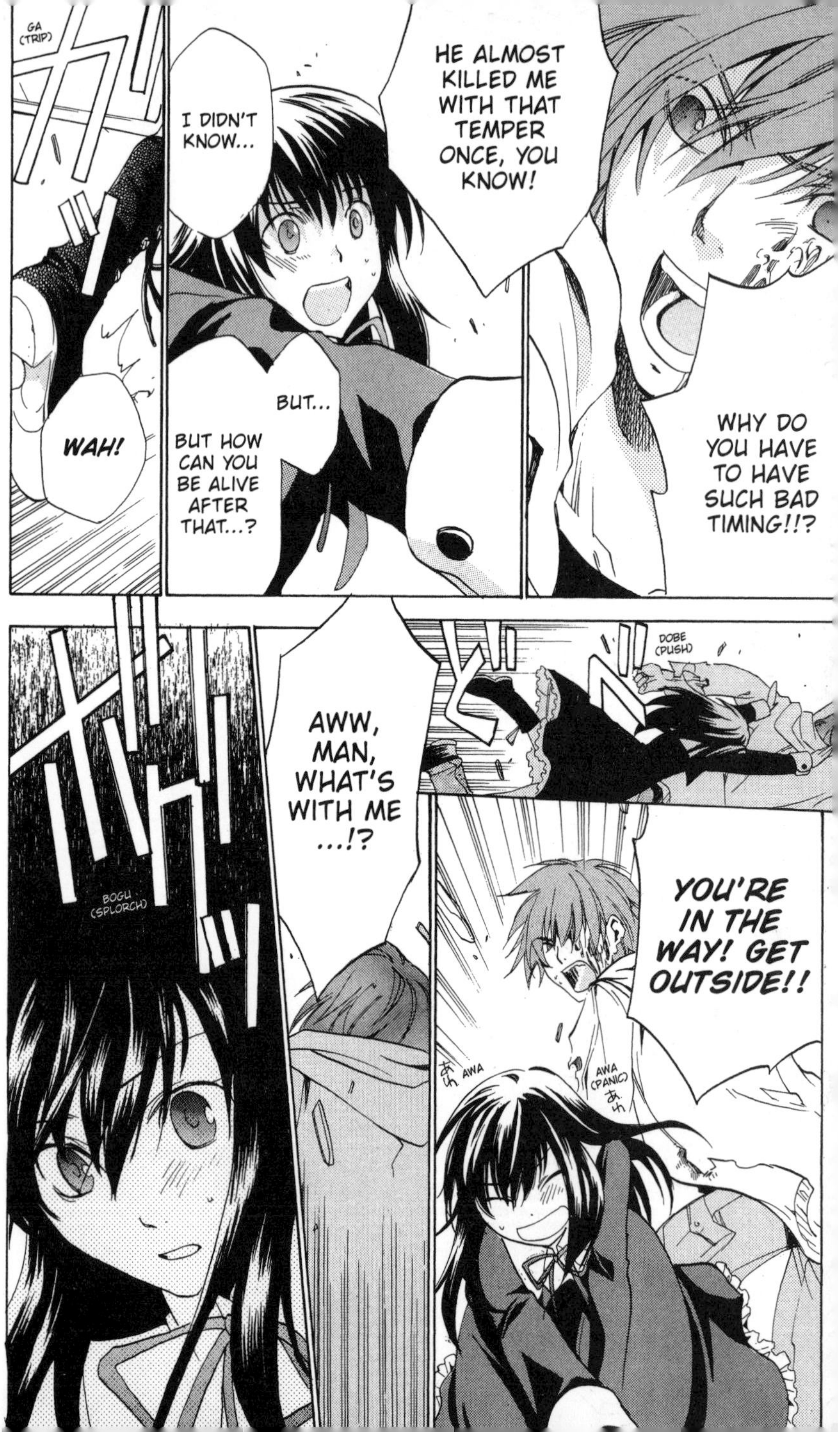
HE ALMOST KILLED ME WITH THAT TEMPER ONCE, YOU KNOW!
WHY DO YOU HAVE TO HAVE SUCH BAD TIMING!!?
I DIDN'T KNOW...
BUT...
BUT HOW CAN YOU BE ALIVE AFTER THAT...?
GA (TRIP)
WAH!
DOBE (PUSH)
YOU'RE IN THE WAY! GET OUTSIDE!!
AWA (PANIC) あわ
あわ AWA
AWW, MAN, WHAT'S WITH ME ...!?
BOGU (SPLORCH)

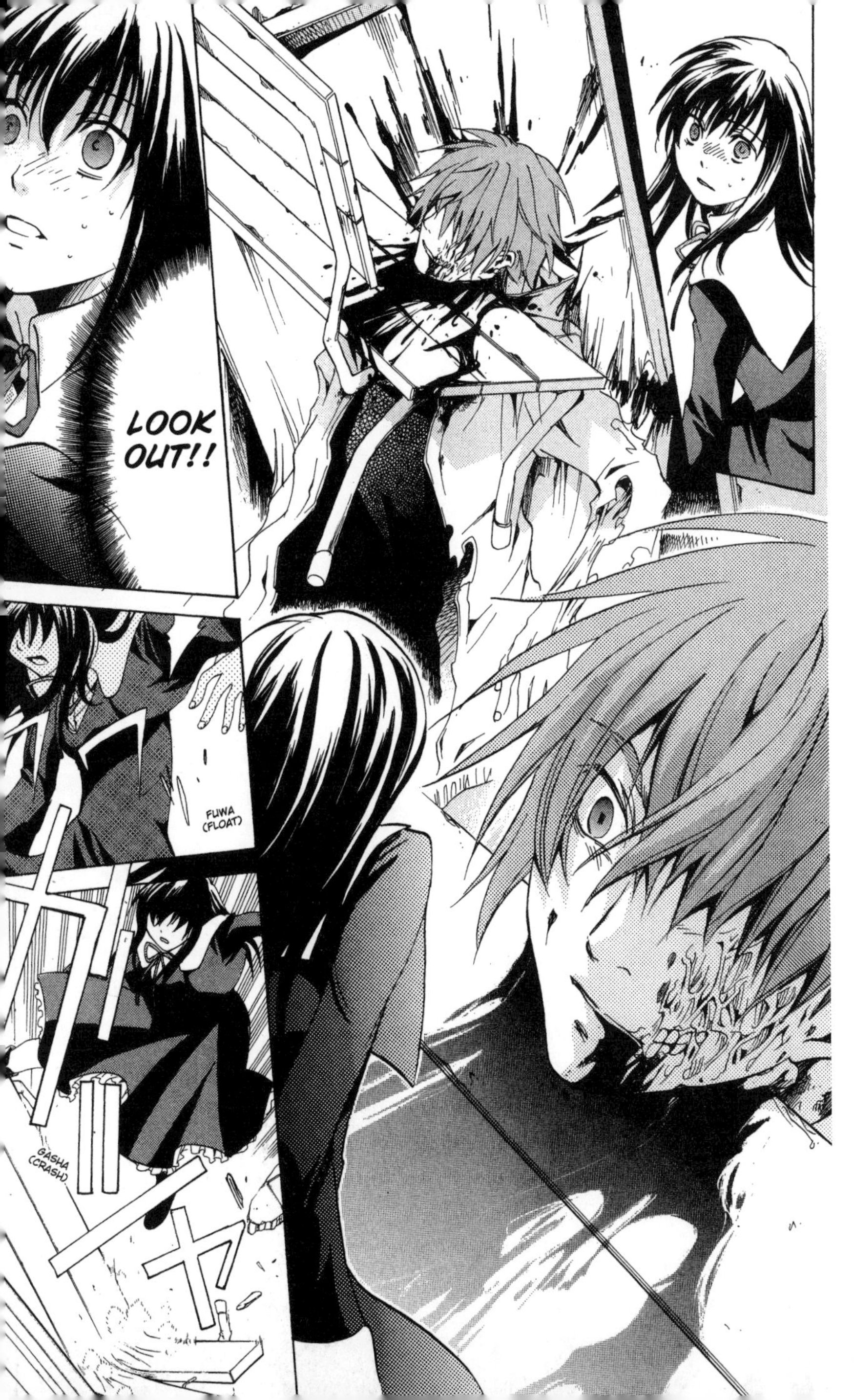
LOOK OUT!!
FUWA (FLOAT)
GASHA (CRASH)

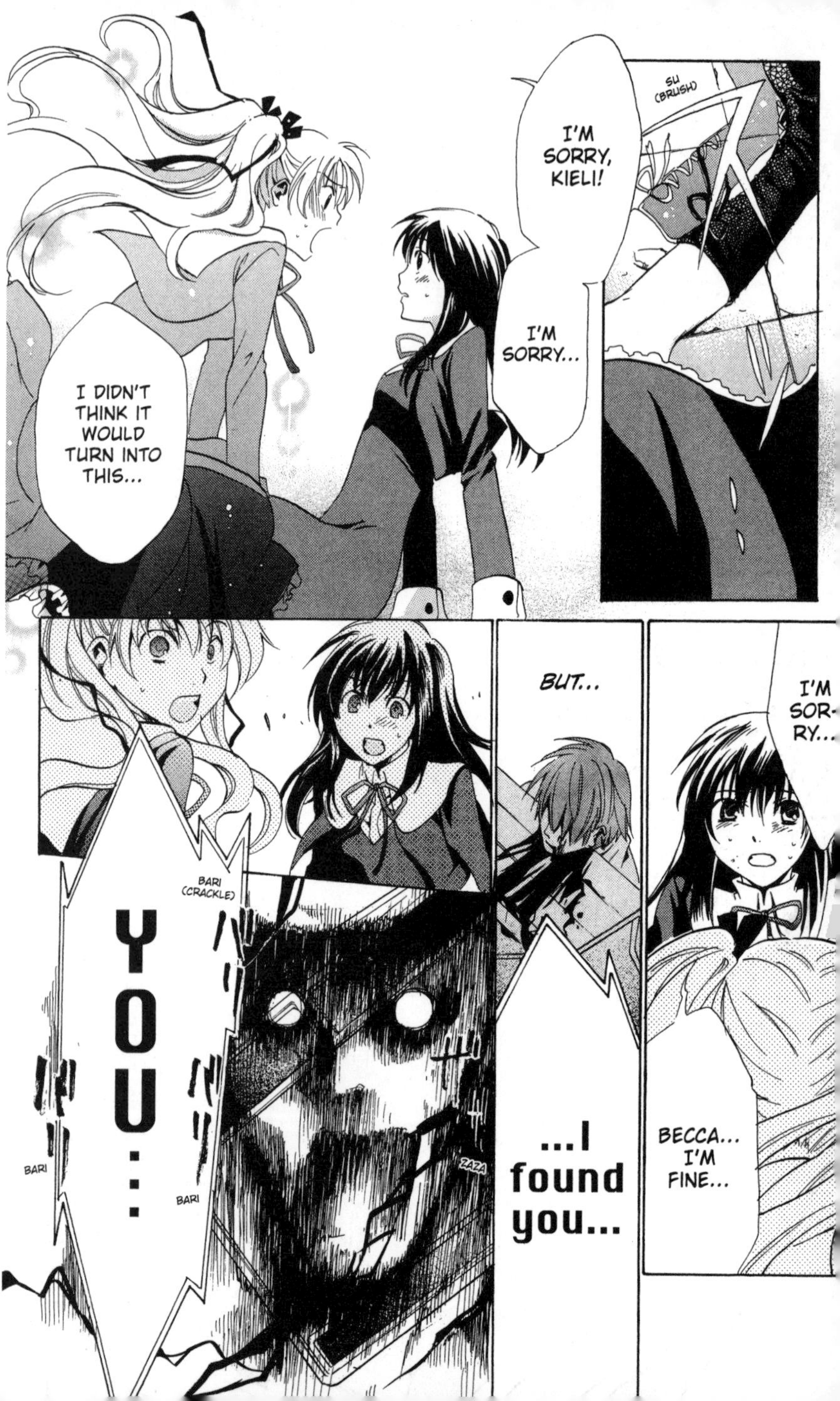
SU (BRUSH)
I'M SORRY, KIELI!
I'M SORRY...
I DIDN'T THINK IT WOULD TURN INTO THIS...
I'M SORRY...
BECCA... I'M FINE...
BUT...
...I found you...
BARI (CRACKLE)
YOU...
ZAZA
BARI
BARI

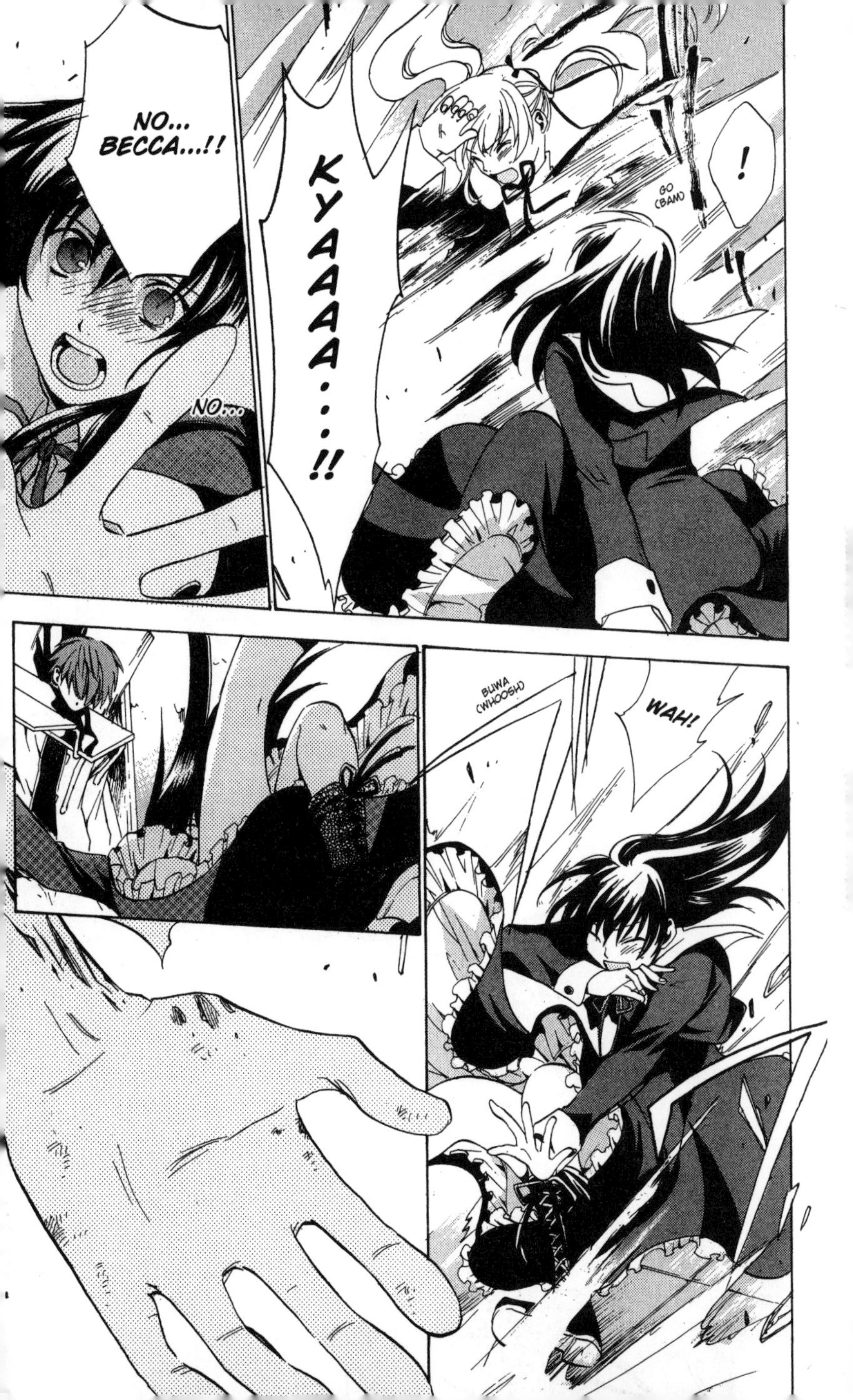
!
GO (BAM)
KYAAAA...!!
NO... BECCA...!!
NO...
WAH!
BUWA (WHOOSH)
!..

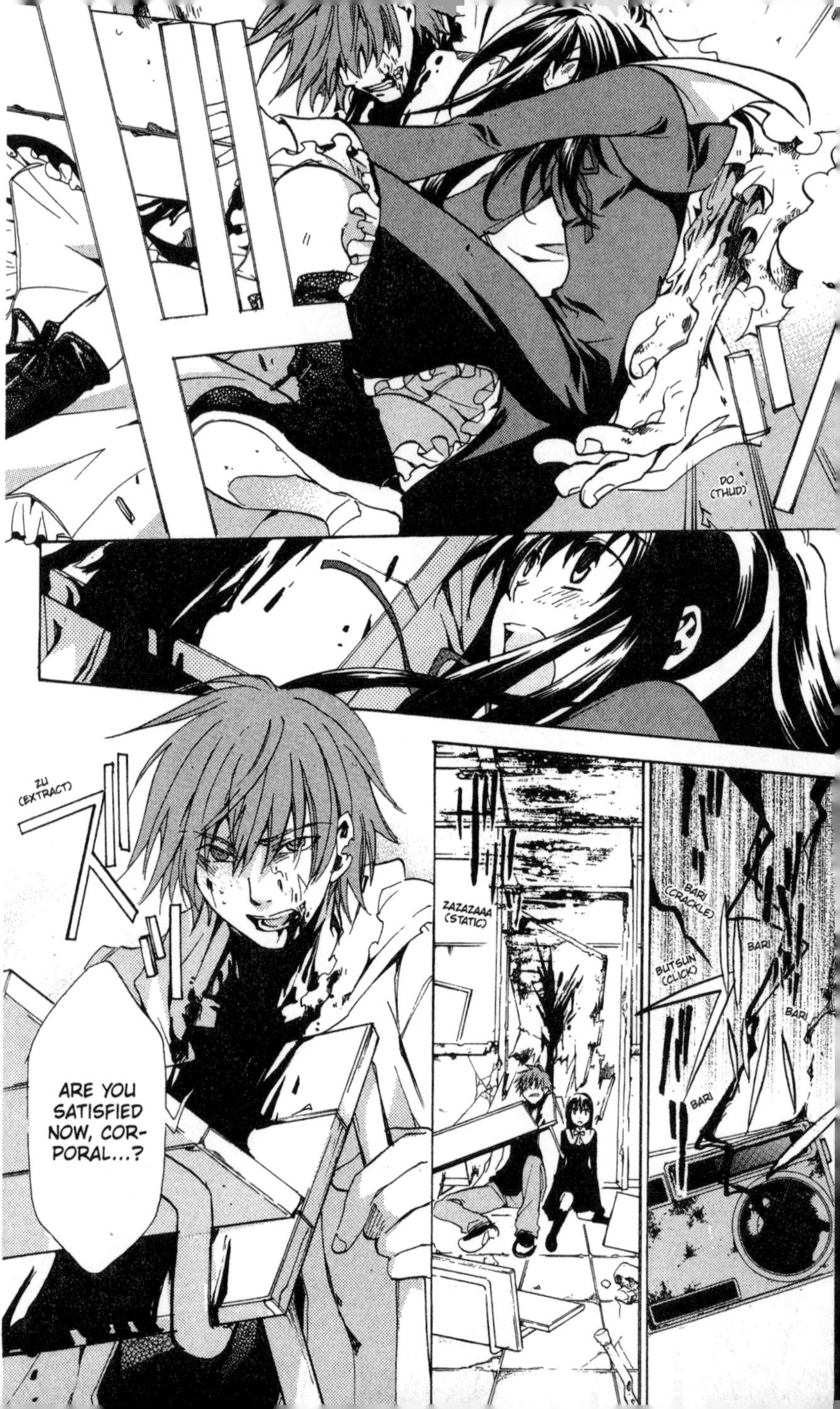
DO (THUD)
BARI (CRACKLE)
BARI
BUTSUN (CLICK)
BARI
BARI
ZAZAZAAA (STATIC)
ZU (EXTRACT)
ARE YOU SATISFIED NOW, COR-PORAL...?

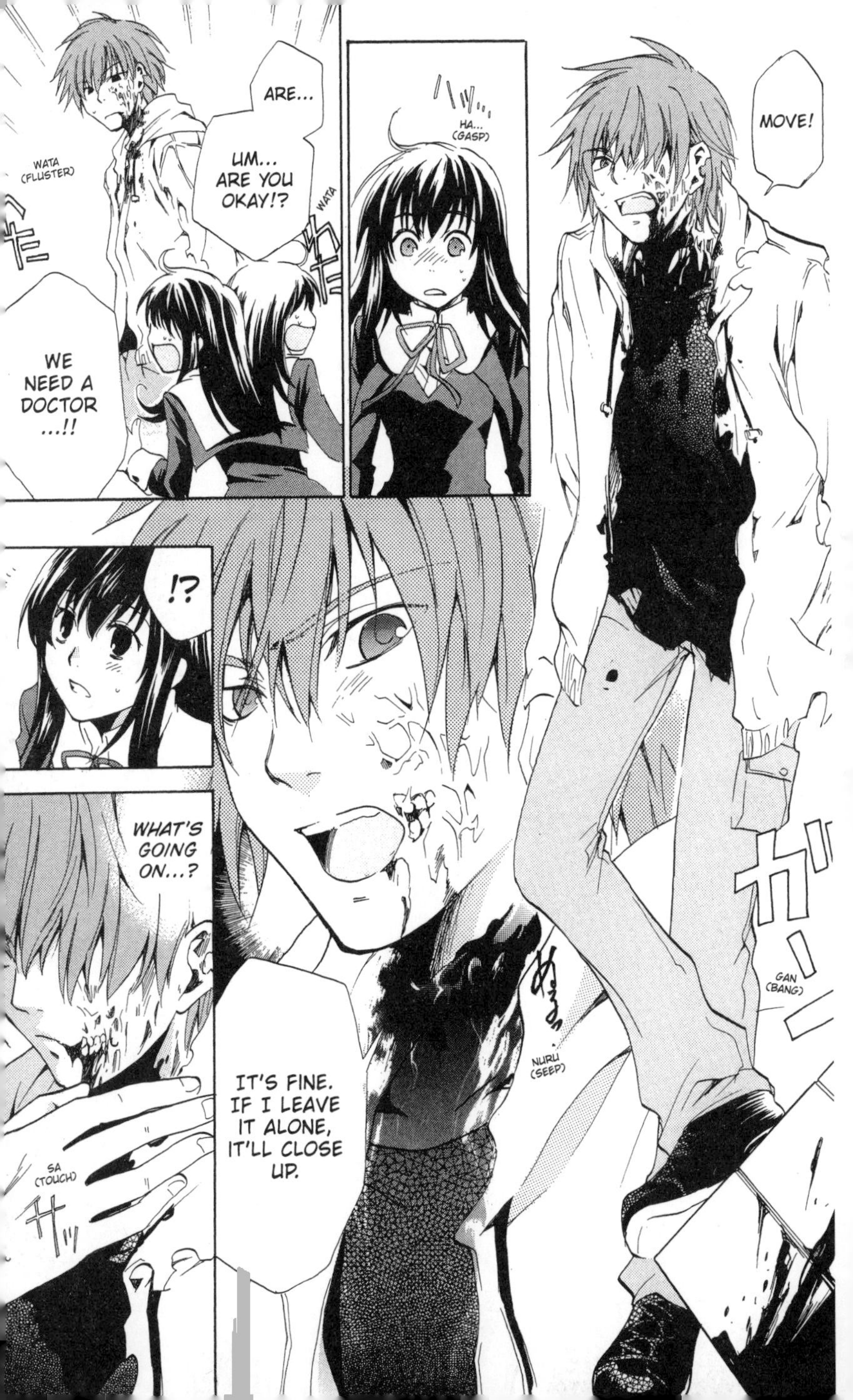

ARE...
UM... ARE YOU OKAY!?
WATA
WATA (FLUSTER)
WE NEED A DOCTOR ...!!
HA... (GASP)
MOVE!
GAN (BANG)
!?
IT'S FINE. IF I LEAVE IT ALONE, IT'LL CLOSE UP.
NURU (SEEP)
WHAT'S GOING ON...?
SA (TOUCH)

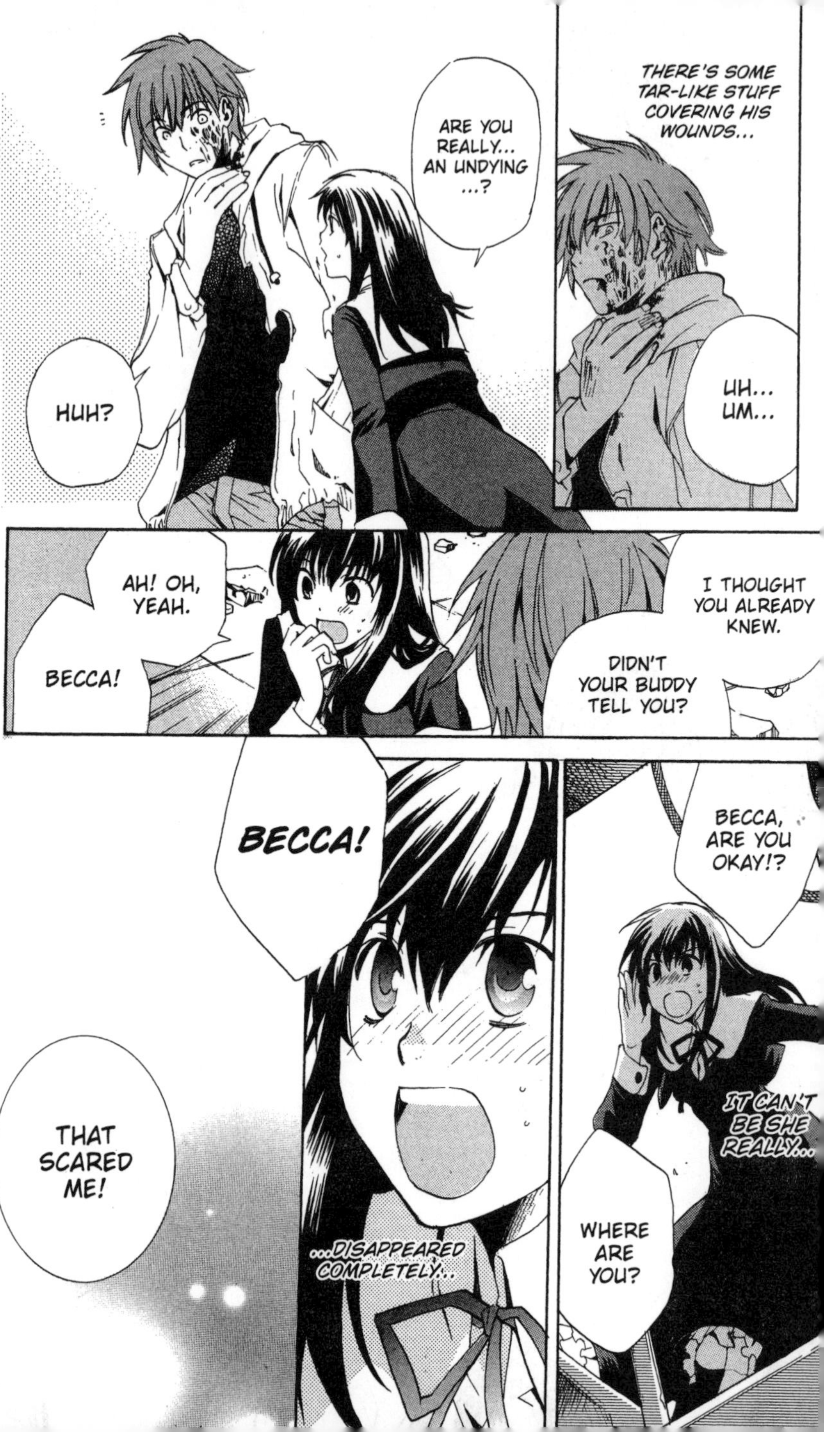
THERE'S SOME TAR-LIKE STUFF COVERING HIS WOUNDS...
UH... UM...
ARE YOU REALLY... AN UNDYING ...?
HUH?
I THOUGHT YOU ALREADY KNEW.
DIDN'T YOUR BUDDY TELL YOU?
AH! OH, YEAH.
BECCA!
BECCA, ARE YOU OKAY!?
IT CAN'T BE SHE REALLY...
WHERE ARE YOU?
BECCA!
...DISAPPEARED COMPLETELY...
THAT SCARED ME!

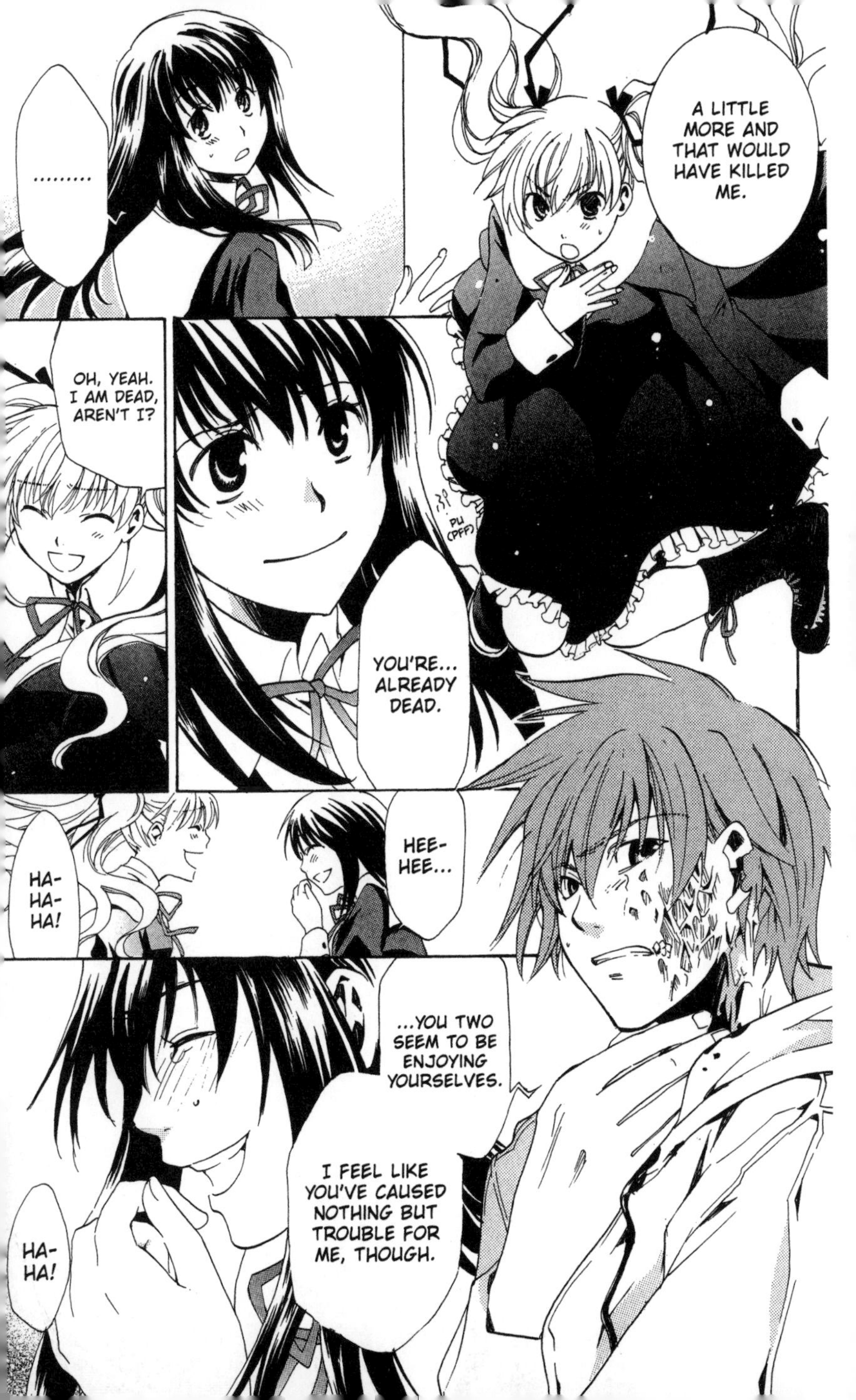
A LITTLE MORE AND THAT WOULD HAVE KILLED ME.
PU (PFF)
....
YOU'RE... ALREADY DEAD.
OH, YEAH. I AM DEAD, AREN'T I?
HEE-HEE...
HA-HA-HA!
...YOU TWO SEEM TO BE ENJOYING YOURSELVES.
I FEEL LIKE YOU'VE CAUSED NOTHING BUT TROUBLE FOR ME, THOUGH.
HA-HA!

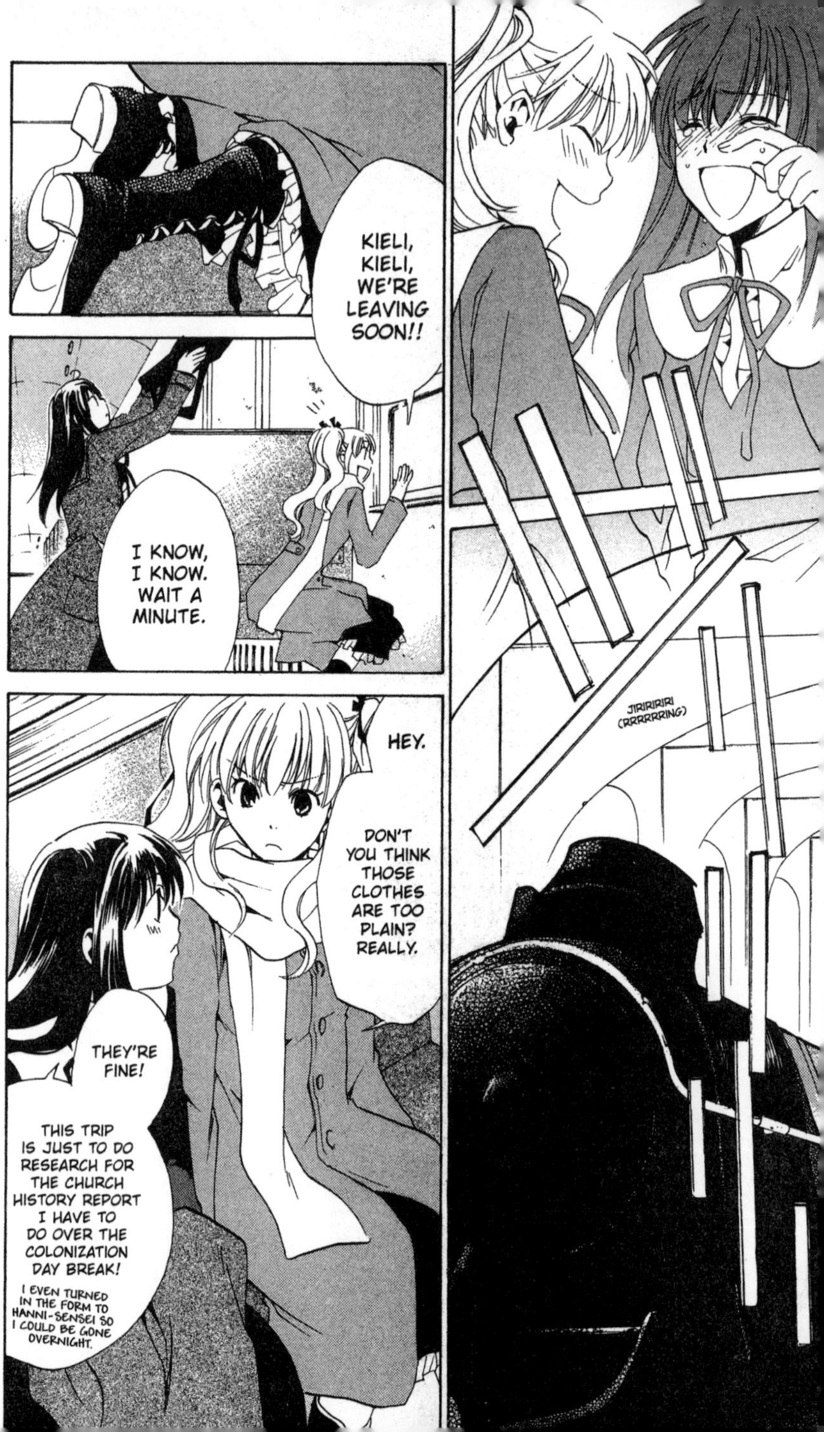
JIRIRIRIRI
(RRRRRRING)
KIELI, KIELI, WE'RE LEAVING SOON!!
I KNOW, I KNOW. WAIT A MINUTE.
HEY.
DON'T YOU THINK THOSE CLOTHES ARE TOO PLAIN? REALLY.
THEY'RE FINE!
THIS TRIP IS JUST TO DO RESEARCH FOR THE CHURCH HISTORY REPORT I HAVE TO DO OVER THE COLONIZATION DAY BREAK!
I EVEN TURNED IN THE FORM TO HANNI-SENSEI SO I COULD BE GONE OVERNIGHT.

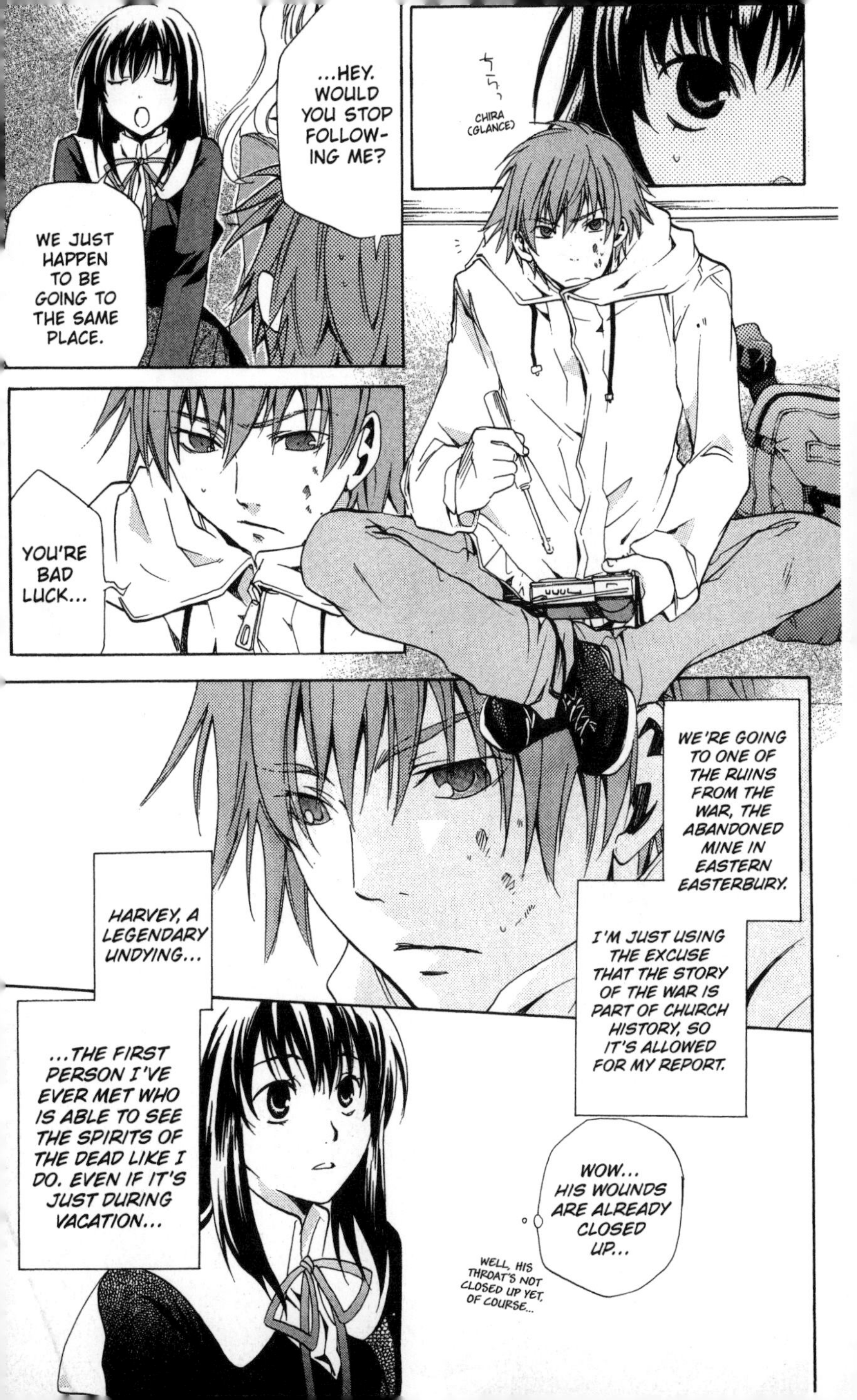

ちらっ
CHIRA (GLANCE)
...HEY. WOULD YOU STOP FOLLOWING ME?
WE JUST HAPPEN TO BE GOING TO THE SAME PLACE.
YOU'RE BAD LUCK...
WE'RE GOING TO ONE OF THE RUINS FROM THE WAR, THE ABANDONED MINE IN EASTERN EASTERBURY.
I'M JUST USING THE EXCUSE THAT THE STORY OF THE WAR IS PART OF CHURCH HISTORY, SO IT'S ALLOWED FOR MY REPORT.
HARVEY, A LEGENDARY UNDYING...
...THE FIRST PERSON I'VE EVER MET WHO IS ABLE TO SEE THE SPIRITS OF THE DEAD LIKE I DO. EVEN IF IT'S JUST DURING VACATION...
WOW... HIS WOUNDS ARE ALREADY CLOSED UP...
WELL, HIS THROAT'S NOT CLOSED UP YET, OF COURSE...

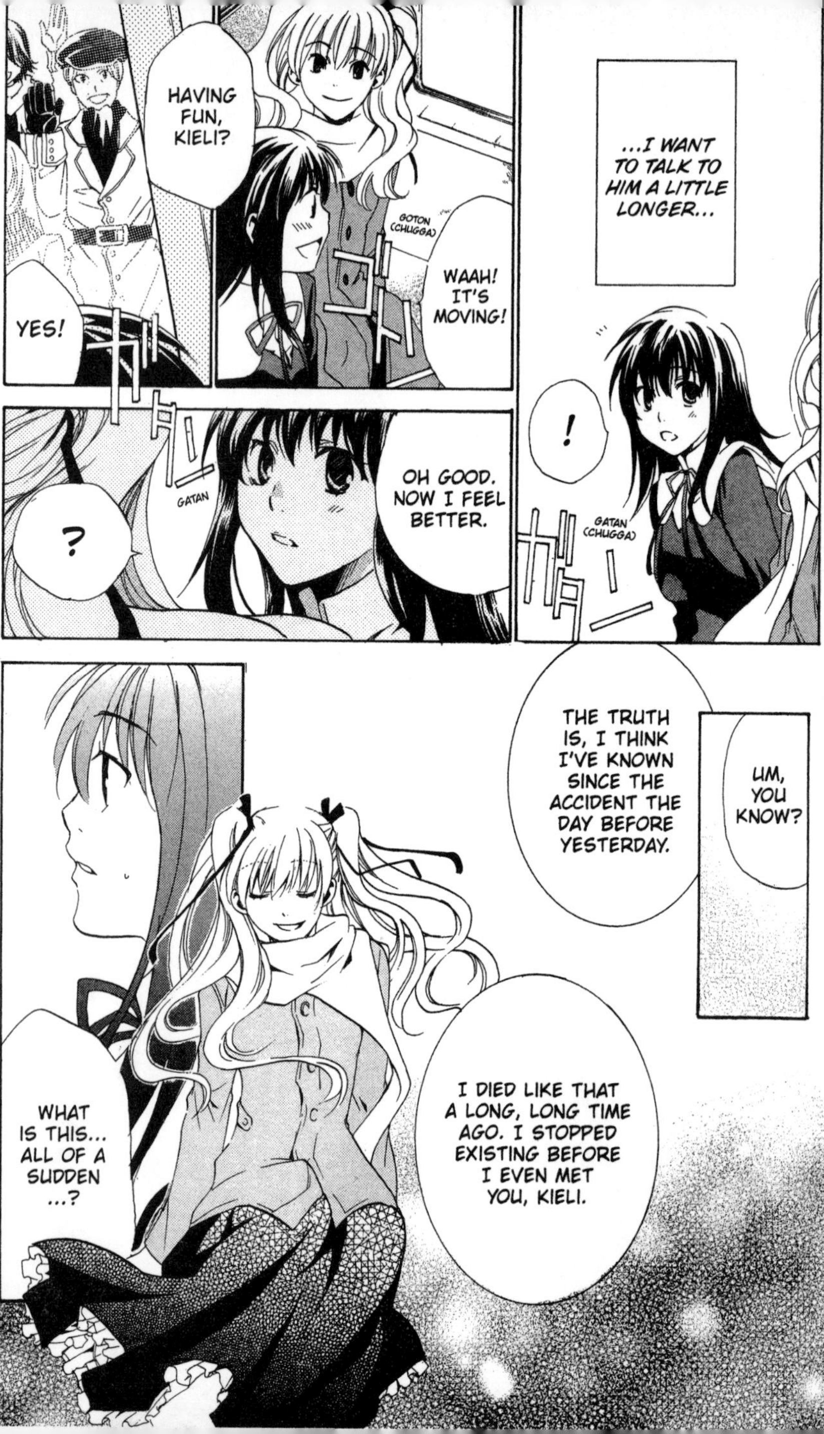
…I WANT TO TALK TO HIM A LITTLE LONGER…
!
GATAN (CHUGGA)
GOTON (CHUGGA)
WAAH! IT'S MOVING!
HAVING FUN, KIELI?
YES!
OH GOOD. NOW I FEEL BETTER.
GATAN
?
UM, YOU KNOW?
THE TRUTH IS, I THINK I'VE KNOWN SINCE THE ACCIDENT THE DAY BEFORE YESTERDAY.
I DIED LIKE THAT A LONG, LONG TIME AGO. I STOPPED EXISTING BEFORE I EVEN MET YOU, KIELI.
WHAT IS THIS… ALL OF A SUDDEN …?

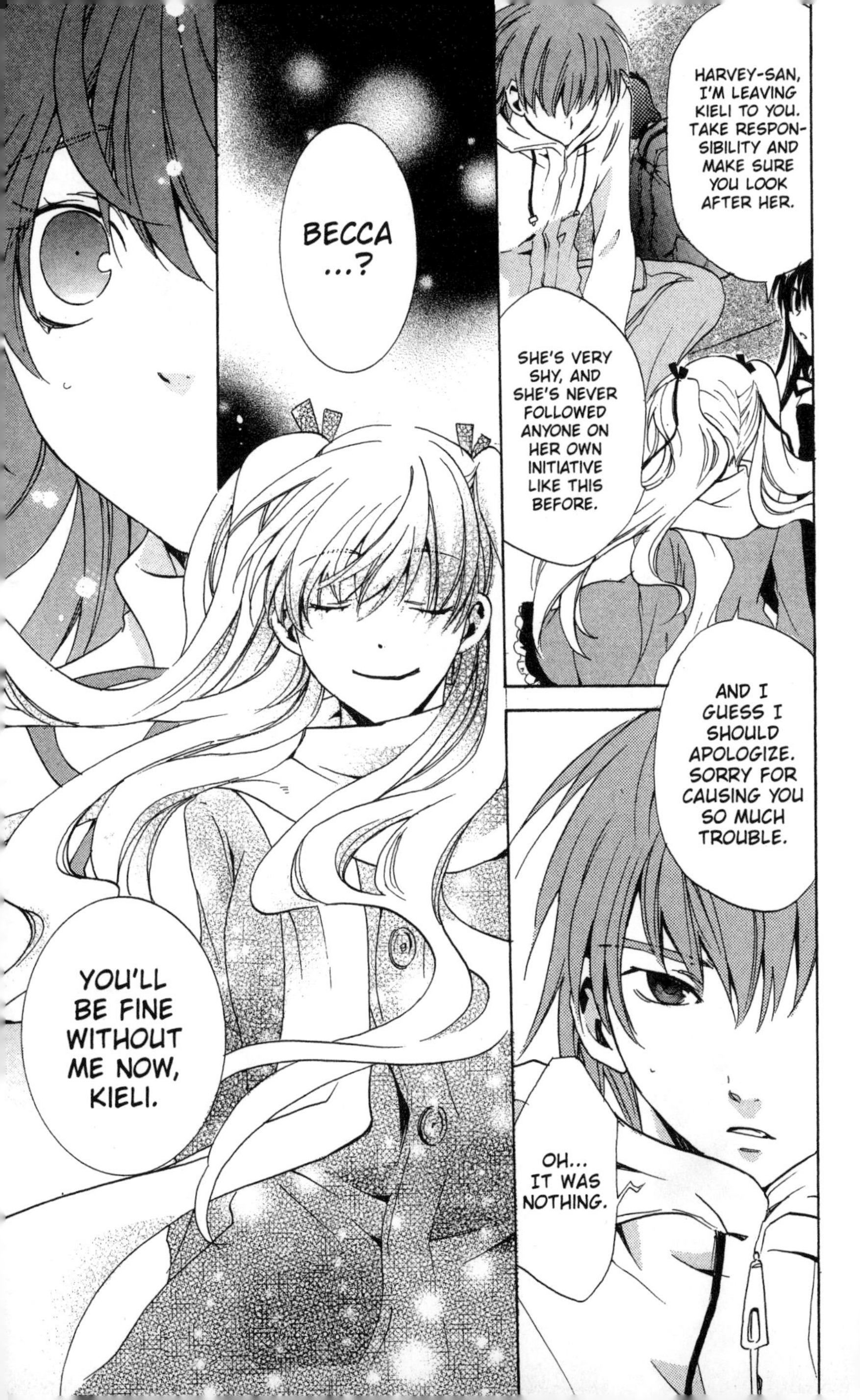
HARVEY-SAN, I'M LEAVING KIELI TO YOU. TAKE RESPON-SIBILITY AND MAKE SURE YOU LOOK AFTER HER.
SHE'S VERY SHY, AND SHE'S NEVER FOLLOWED ANYONE ON HER OWN INITIATIVE LIKE THIS BEFORE.
BECCA ...?
AND I GUESS I SHOULD APOLOGIZE. SORRY FOR CAUSING YOU SO MUCH TROUBLE.
OH... IT WAS NOTHING.
YOU'LL BE FINE WITHOUT ME NOW, KIELI.

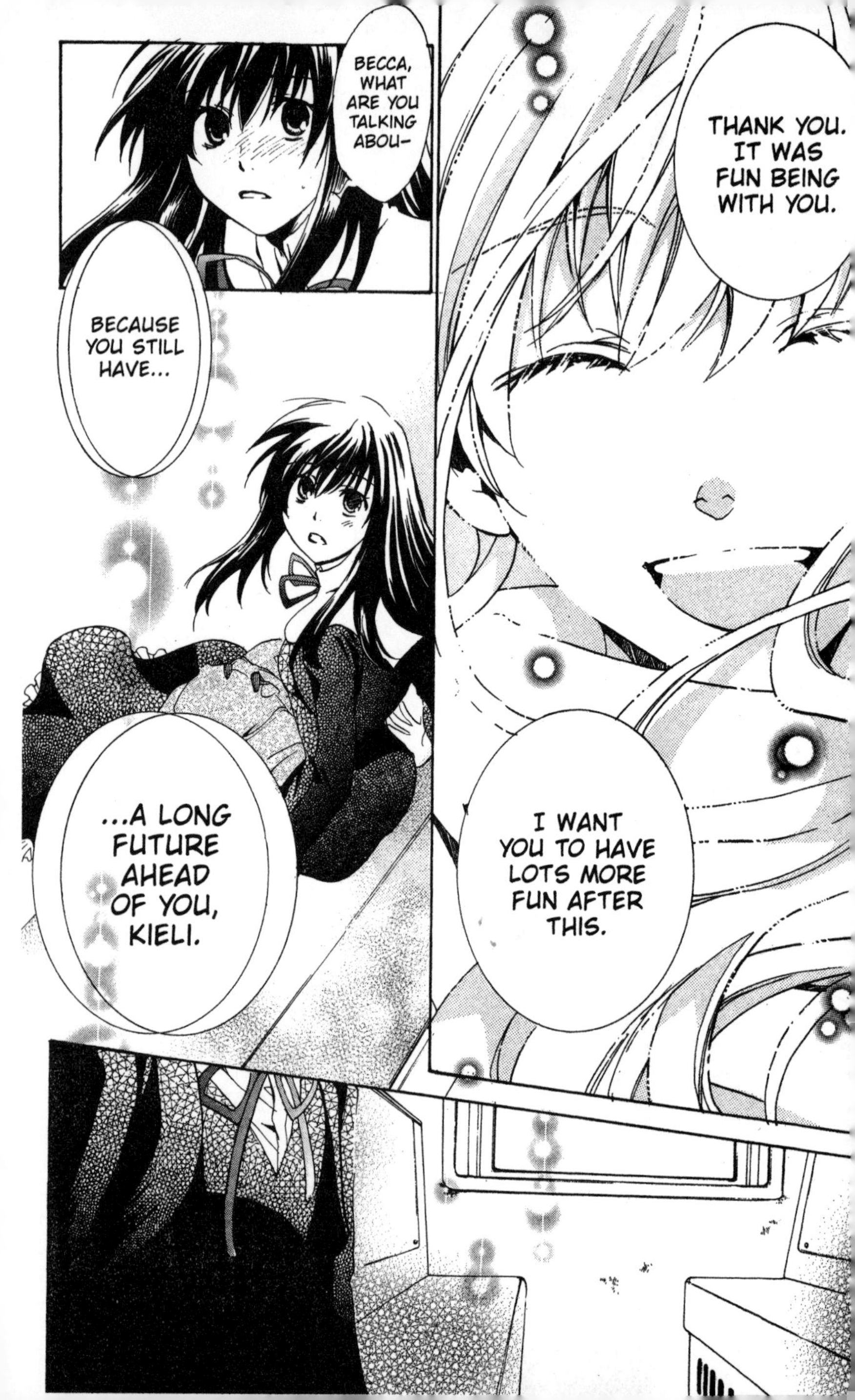
THANK YOU. IT WAS FUN BEING WITH YOU.
I WANT YOU TO HAVE LOTS MORE FUN AFTER THIS.
BECCA, WHAT ARE YOU TALKING ABOU-
BECAUSE YOU STILL HAVE...
...A LONG FUTURE AHEAD OF YOU, KIELI.

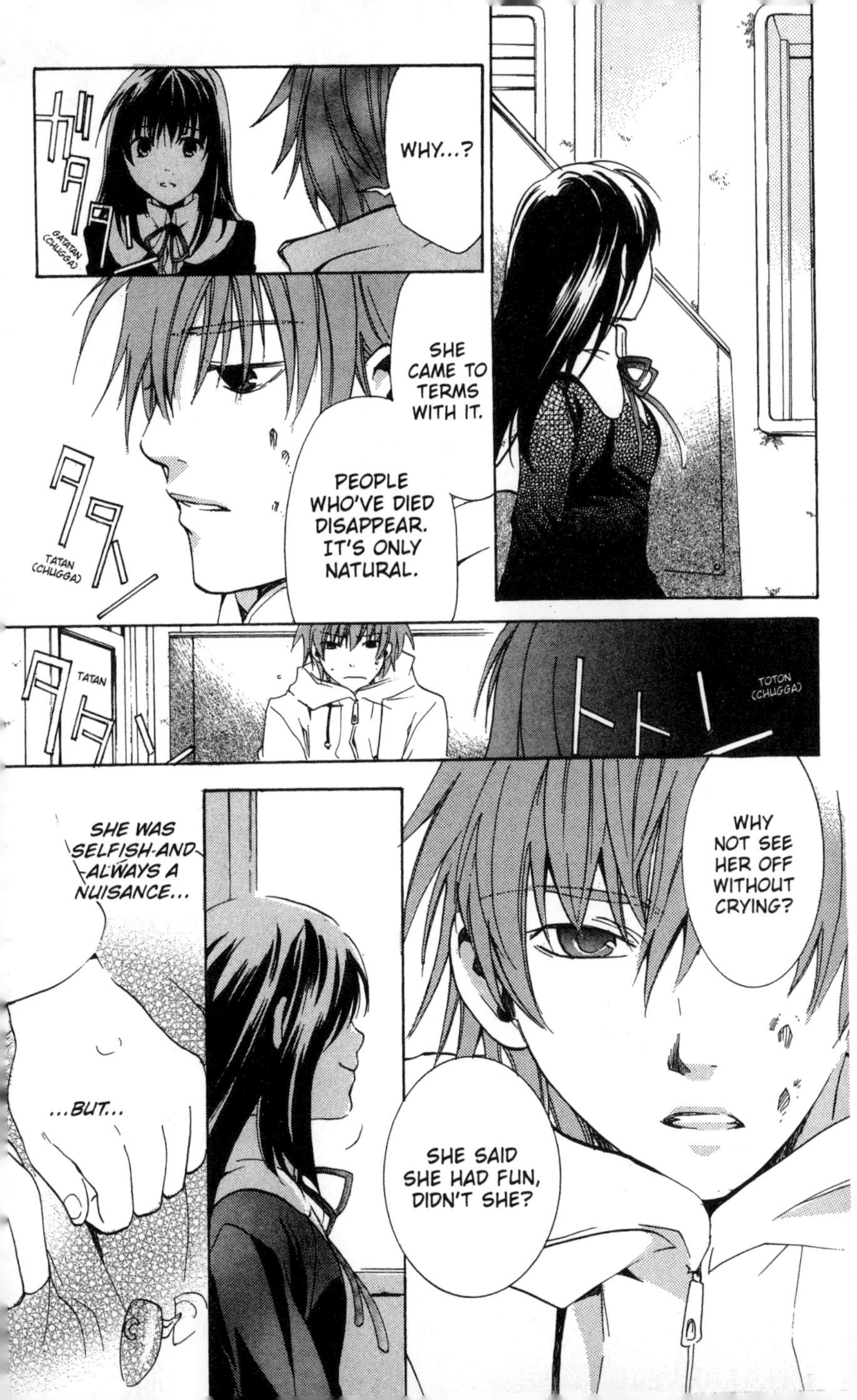
WHY...?
GATATAN (CHUGGA)
SHE CAME TO TERMS WITH IT.
PEOPLE WHO'VE DIED DISAPPEAR. IT'S ONLY NATURAL.
TATAN (CHUGGA)
TOTON (CHUGGA)
TATAN
WHY NOT SEE HER OFF WITHOUT CRYING?
SHE SAID SHE HAD FUN, DIDN'T SHE?
SHE WAS SELFISH AND ALWAYS A NUISANCE...
...BUT...

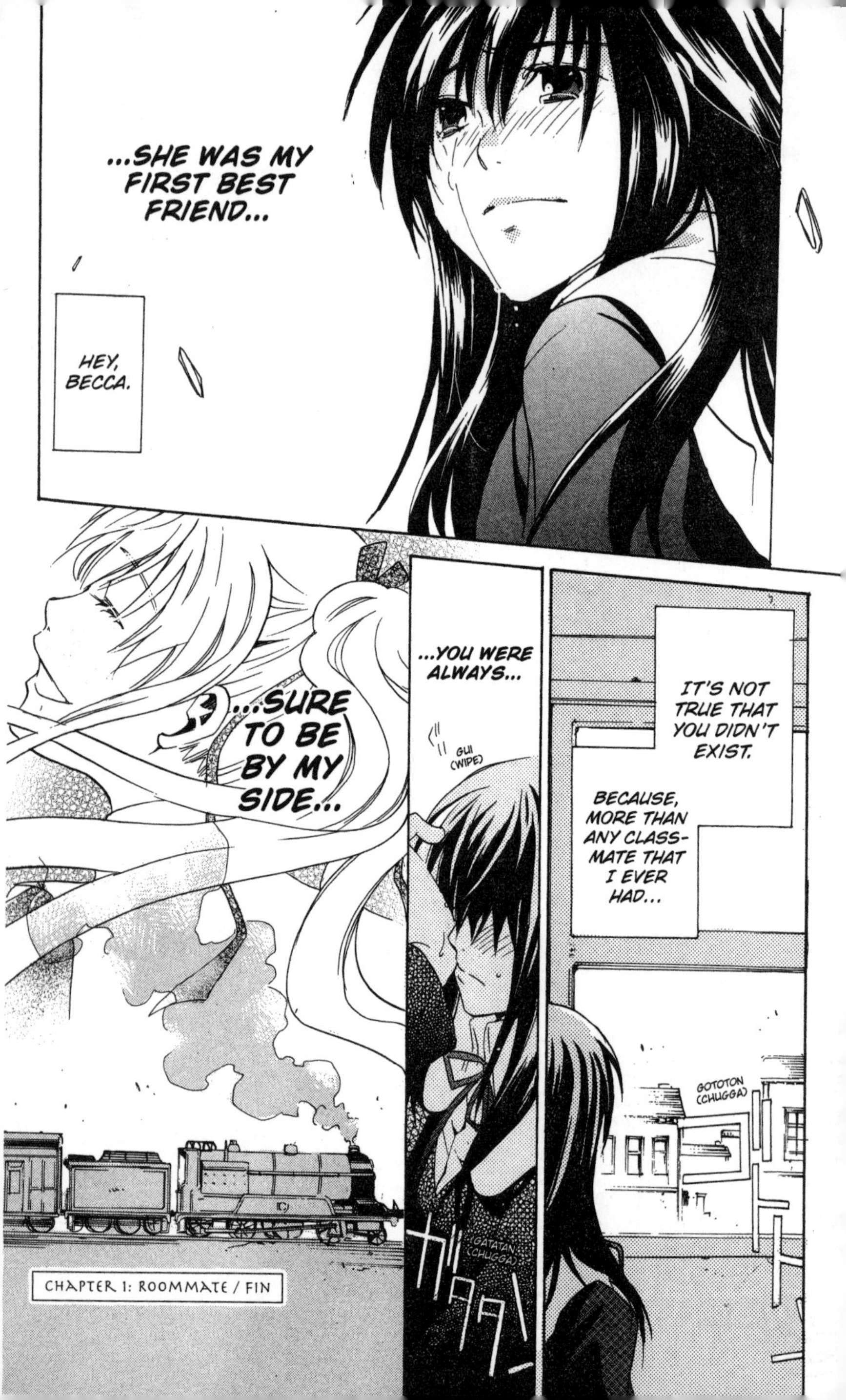
...SHE WAS MY FIRST BEST FRIEND...
HEY, BECCA.
IT'S NOT TRUE THAT YOU DIDN'T EXIST.
BECAUSE, MORE THAN ANY CLASSMATE THAT I EVER HAD...
GOTOTON (CHUGGA)
...YOU WERE ALWAYS...
GUI (WIPE)
GATATAN (CHUGGA)
...SURE TO BE BY MY SIDE...
CHAPTER 1: ROOMMATE / FIN

CHAPTER 2

MAY I SEE YOUR TICKET?

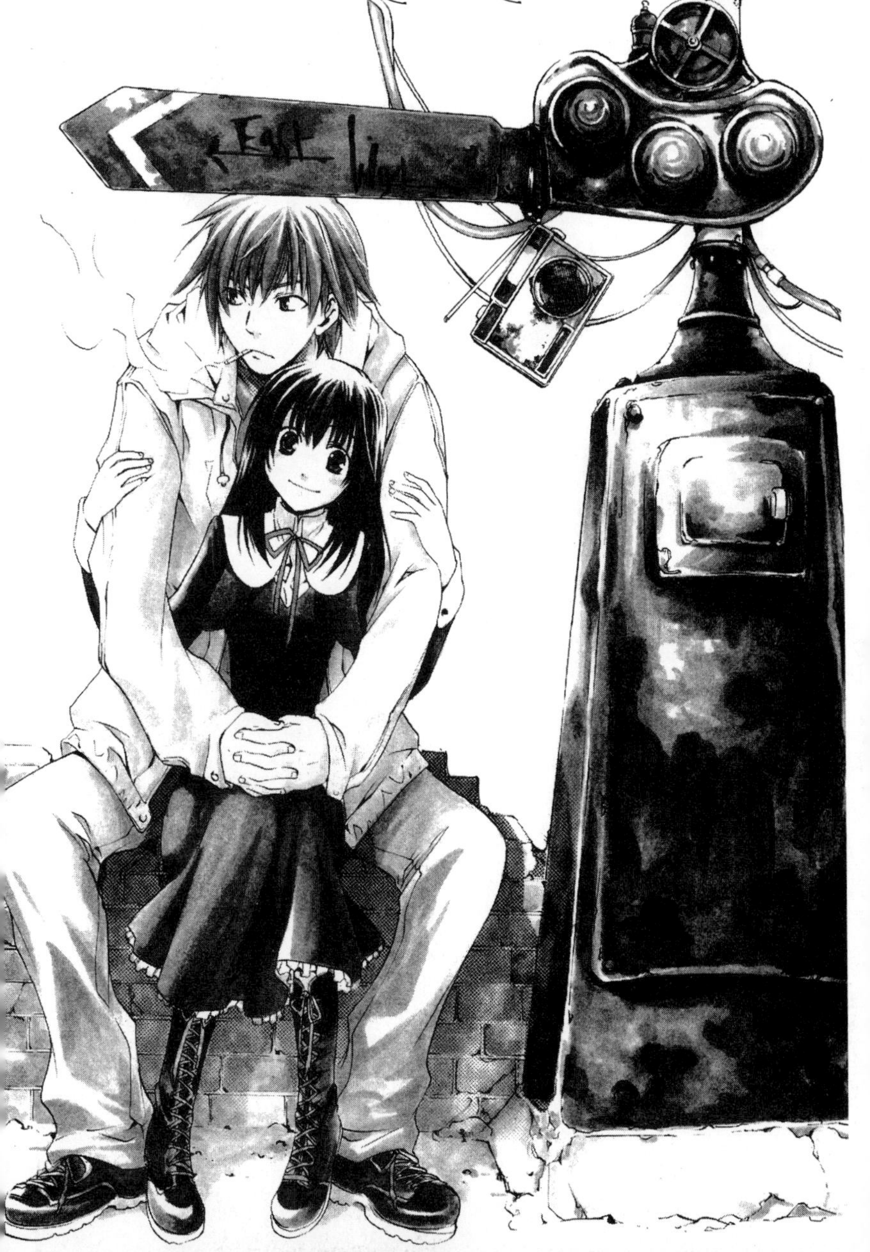
East Way

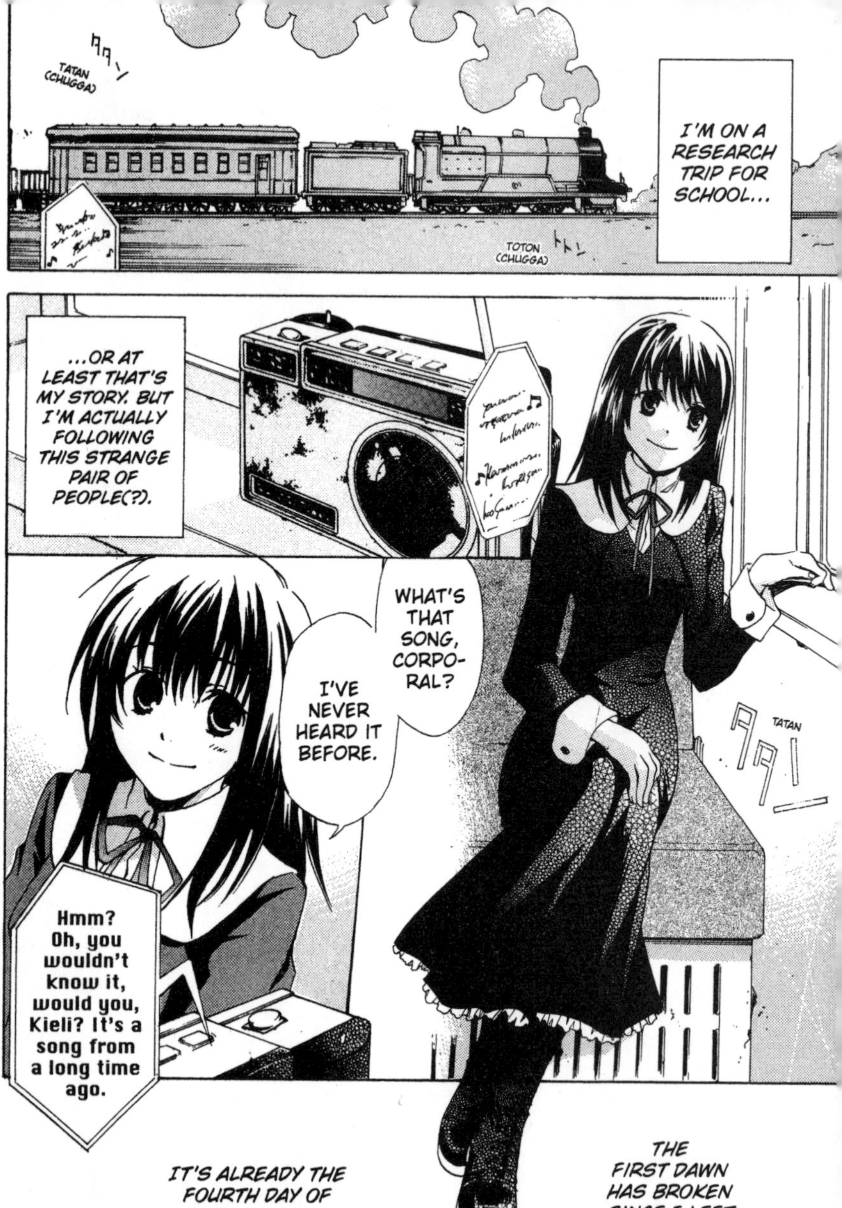
I'M ON A RESEARCH TRIP FOR SCHOOL...
TATAN (CHUGGA)
TOTON (CHUGGA)
...OR AT LEAST THAT'S MY STORY. BUT I'M ACTUALLY FOLLOWING THIS STRANGE PAIR OF PEOPLE(?).
WHAT'S THAT SONG, CORPORAL?
I'VE NEVER HEARD IT BEFORE.
TATAN
Hmm? Oh, you wouldn't know it, would you, Kieli? It's a song from a long time ago.
THE FIRST DAWN HAS BROKEN SINCE I LEFT THE TOWN OF EASTERBURY YESTERDAY.
IT'S ALREADY THE FOURTH DAY OF COLONIZATION.

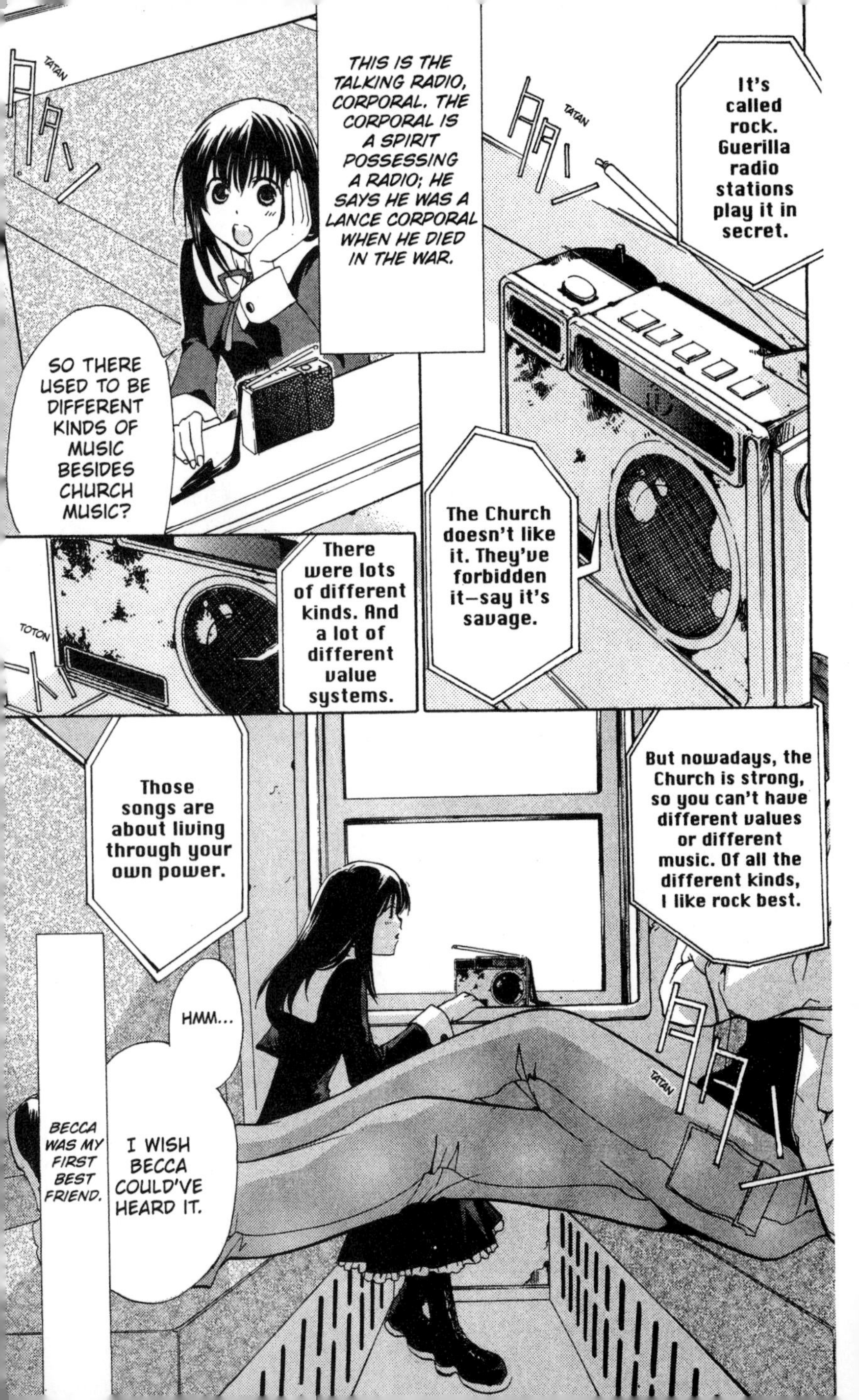
TATAN
It's called rock. Guerilla radio stations play it in secret.
The Church doesn't like it. They've forbidden it—say it's savage.
THIS IS THE TALKING RADIO, CORPORAL. THE CORPORAL IS A SPIRIT POSSESSING A RADIO; HE SAYS HE WAS A LANCE CORPORAL WHEN HE DIED IN THE WAR.
TATAN
SO THERE USED TO BE DIFFERENT KINDS OF MUSIC BESIDES CHURCH MUSIC?
There were lots of different kinds. And a lot of different value systems.
TOTON
But nowadays, the Church is strong, so you can't have different values or different music. Of all the different kinds, I like rock best.
TATAN
Those songs are about living through your own power.
HMM...
I WISH BECCA COULD'VE HEARD IT.
BECCA WAS MY FIRST BEST FRIEND.

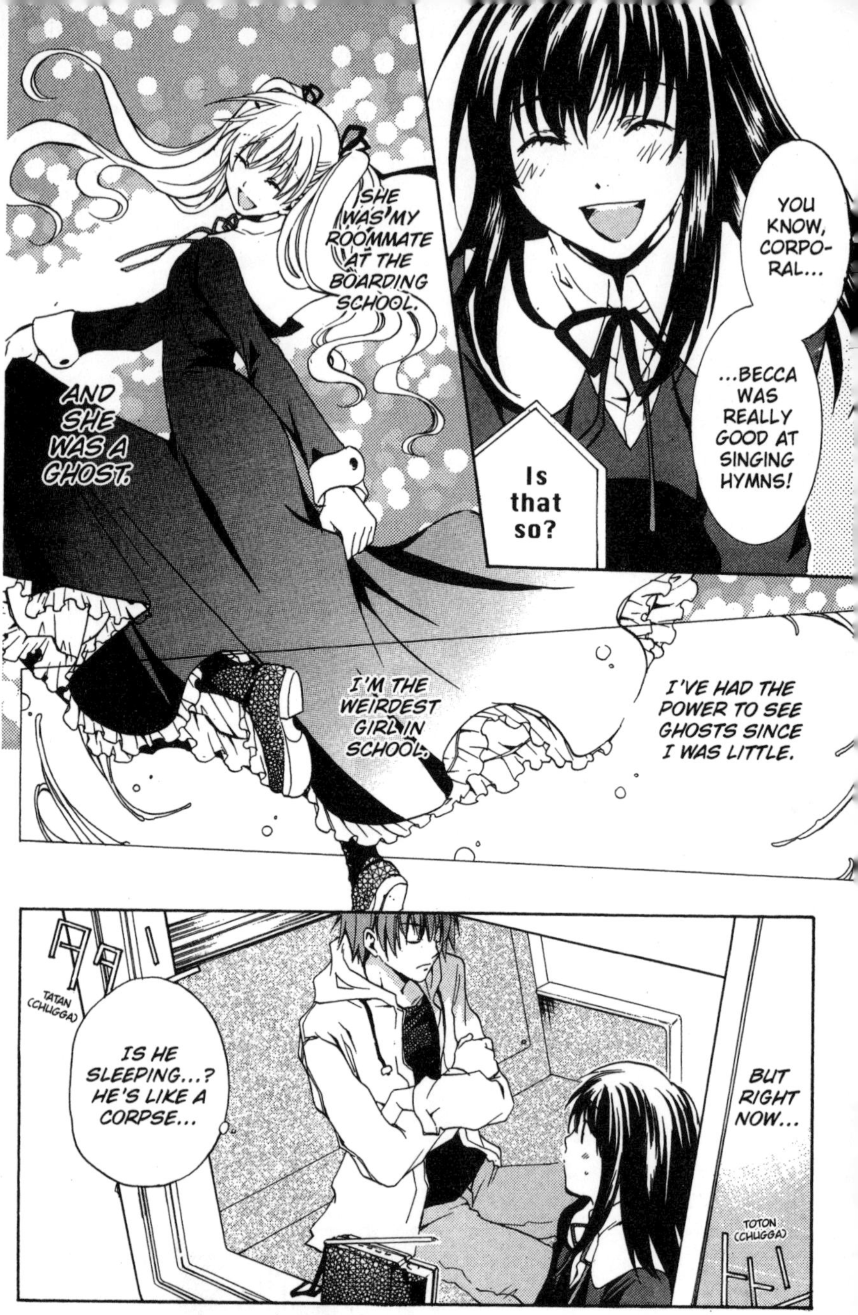
YOU KNOW, CORPORAL...
...BECCA WAS REALLY GOOD AT SINGING HYMNS!
Is that so?
SHE WAS MY ROOMMATE AT THE BOARDING SCHOOL.
AND SHE WAS A GHOST.
I'VE HAD THE POWER TO SEE GHOSTS SINCE I WAS LITTLE.
I'M THE WEIRDEST GIRL IN SCHOOL.
BUT RIGHT NOW...
TOTON (CHUGGA)
IS HE SLEEPING...? HE'S LIKE A CORPSE...
TATAN (CHUGGA)

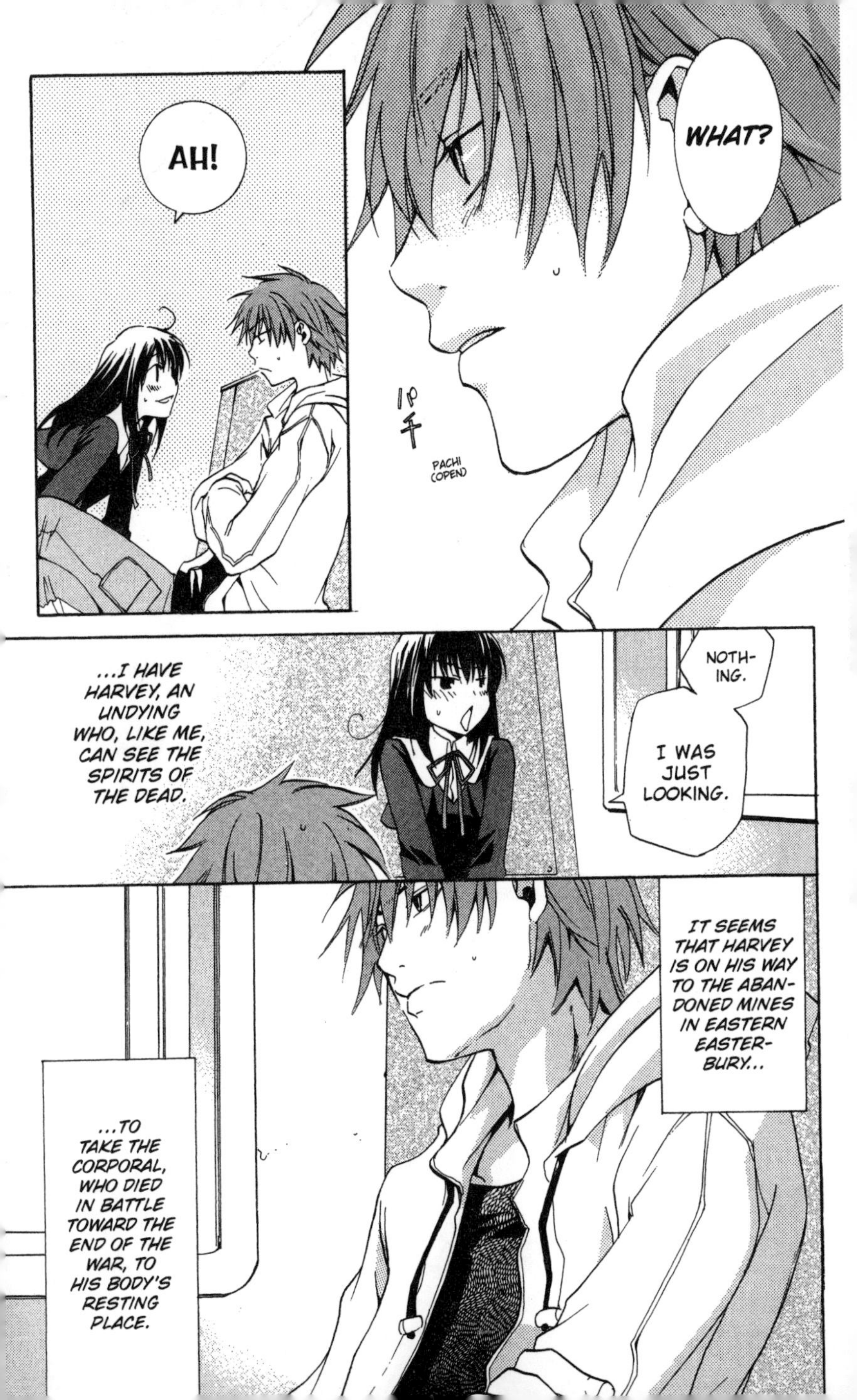
WHAT?
パチ
PACHI (OPEN)
AH!
NOTH-ING.
I WAS JUST LOOKING.
...I HAVE HARVEY, AN UNDYING WHO, LIKE ME, CAN SEE THE SPIRITS OF THE DEAD.
IT SEEMS THAT HARVEY IS ON HIS WAY TO THE ABAN-DONED MINES IN EASTERN EASTER-BURY...
...TO TAKE THE CORPORAL, WHO DIED IN BATTLE TOWARD THE END OF THE WAR, TO HIS BODY'S RESTING PLACE.

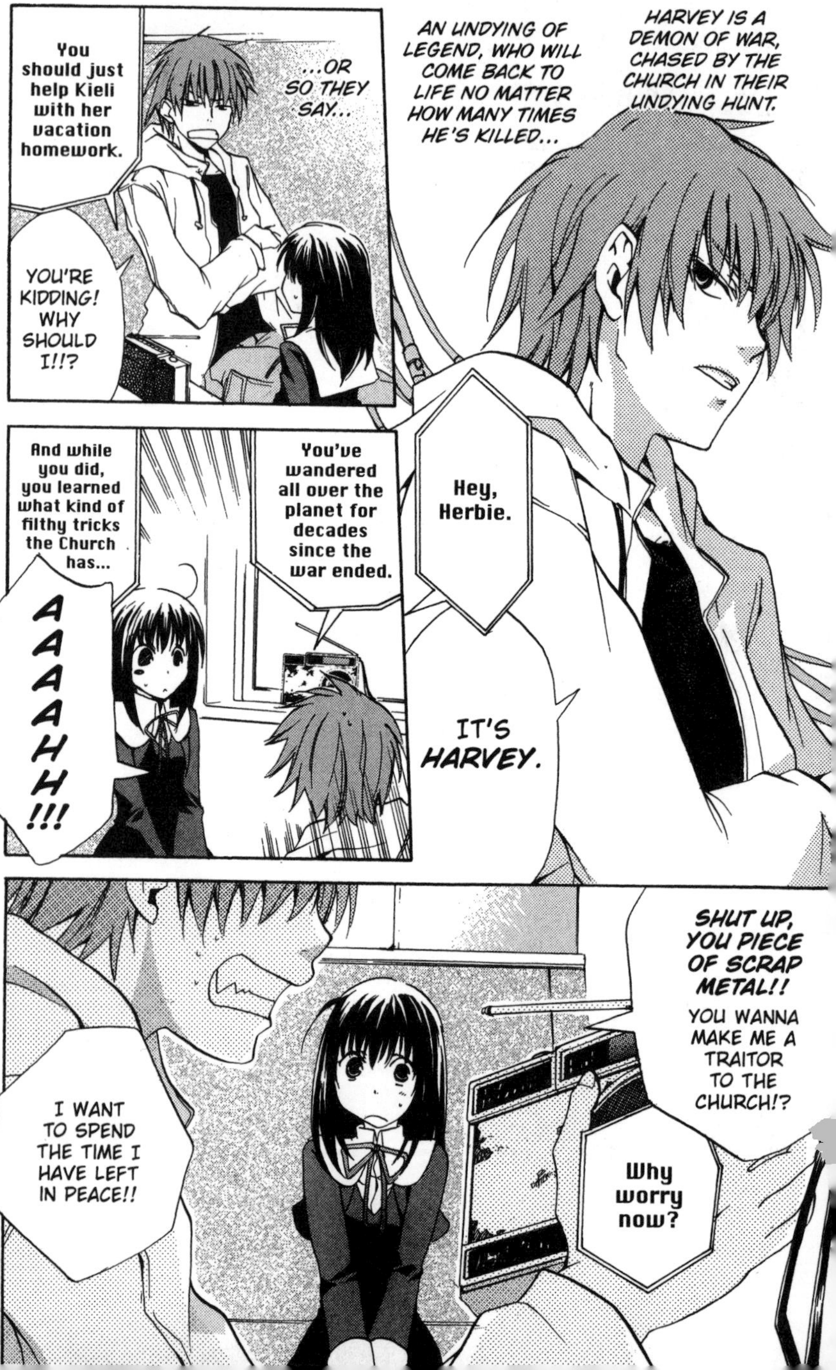

HARVEY IS A DEMON OF WAR, CHASED BY THE CHURCH IN THEIR UNDYING HUNT.
AN UNDYING OF LEGEND, WHO WILL COME BACK TO LIFE NO MATTER HOW MANY TIMES HE'S KILLED...
Hey, Herbie.
IT'S HARVEY.
...OR SO THEY SAY...
You should just help Kieli with her vacation homework.
YOU'RE KIDDING! WHY SHOULD I!!?
You've wandered all over the planet for decades since the war ended.
And while you did, you learned what kind of filthy tricks the Church has...
AAAAAHH!!!
SHUT UP, YOU PIECE OF SCRAP METAL!!
YOU WANNA MAKE ME A TRAITOR TO THE CHURCH!?
Why worry now?
I WANT TO SPEND THE TIME I HAVE LEFT IN PEACE!!

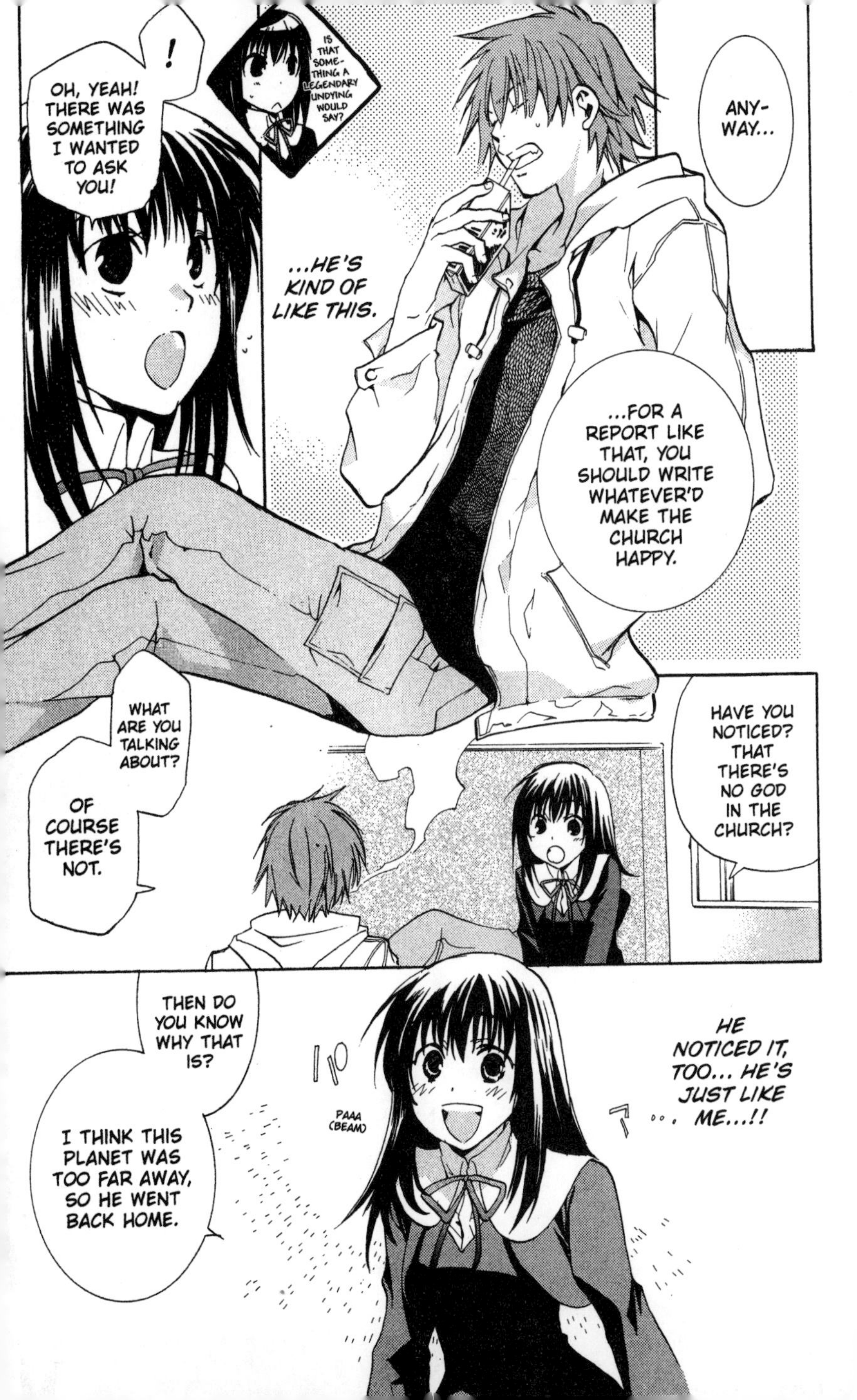
ANY-WAY...
...FOR A REPORT LIKE THAT, YOU SHOULD WRITE WHATEVER'D MAKE THE CHURCH HAPPY.
...HE'S KIND OF LIKE THIS.
IS THAT SOMETHING A LEGENDARY UNDYING WOULD SAY?
!
OH, YEAH! THERE WAS SOMETHING I WANTED TO ASK YOU!
HAVE YOU NOTICED? THAT THERE'S NO GOD IN THE CHURCH?
WHAT ARE YOU TALKING ABOUT?
OF COURSE THERE'S NOT.
HE NOTICED IT, TOO... HE'S JUST LIKE ME...!!
PAAA (BEAM)
THEN DO YOU KNOW WHY THAT IS?
I THINK THIS PLANET WAS TOO FAR AWAY, SO HE WENT BACK HOME.

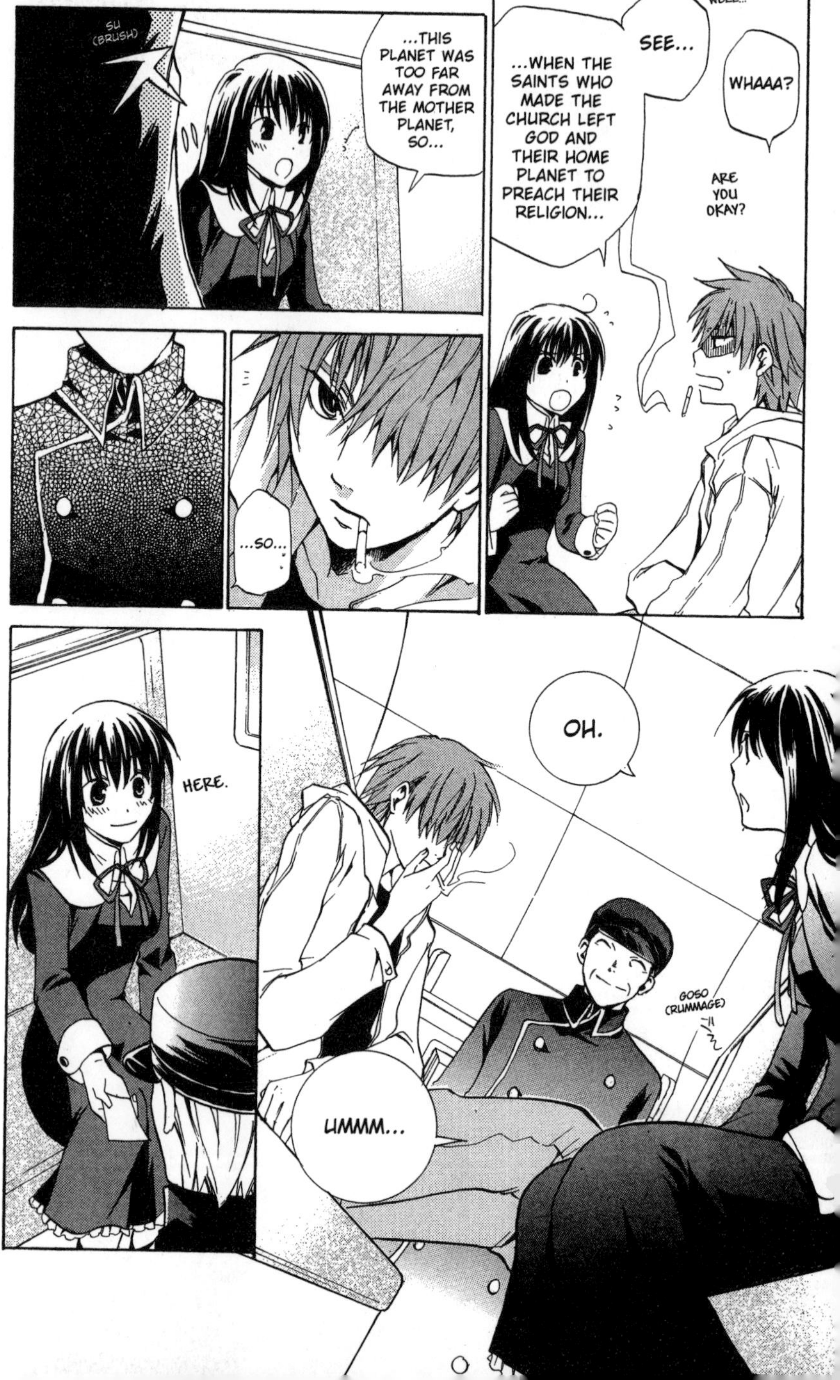
UM, WELL...
WHAAA?
SEE...
...WHEN THE SAINTS WHO MADE THE CHURCH LEFT GOD AND THEIR HOME PLANET TO PREACH THEIR RELIGION...
ARE YOU OKAY?
...THIS PLANET WAS TOO FAR AWAY FROM THE MOTHER PLANET, SO...
SU (BRUSH)
...SO...
OH.
GOSO (RUMMAGE)
UMMM...
HERE.

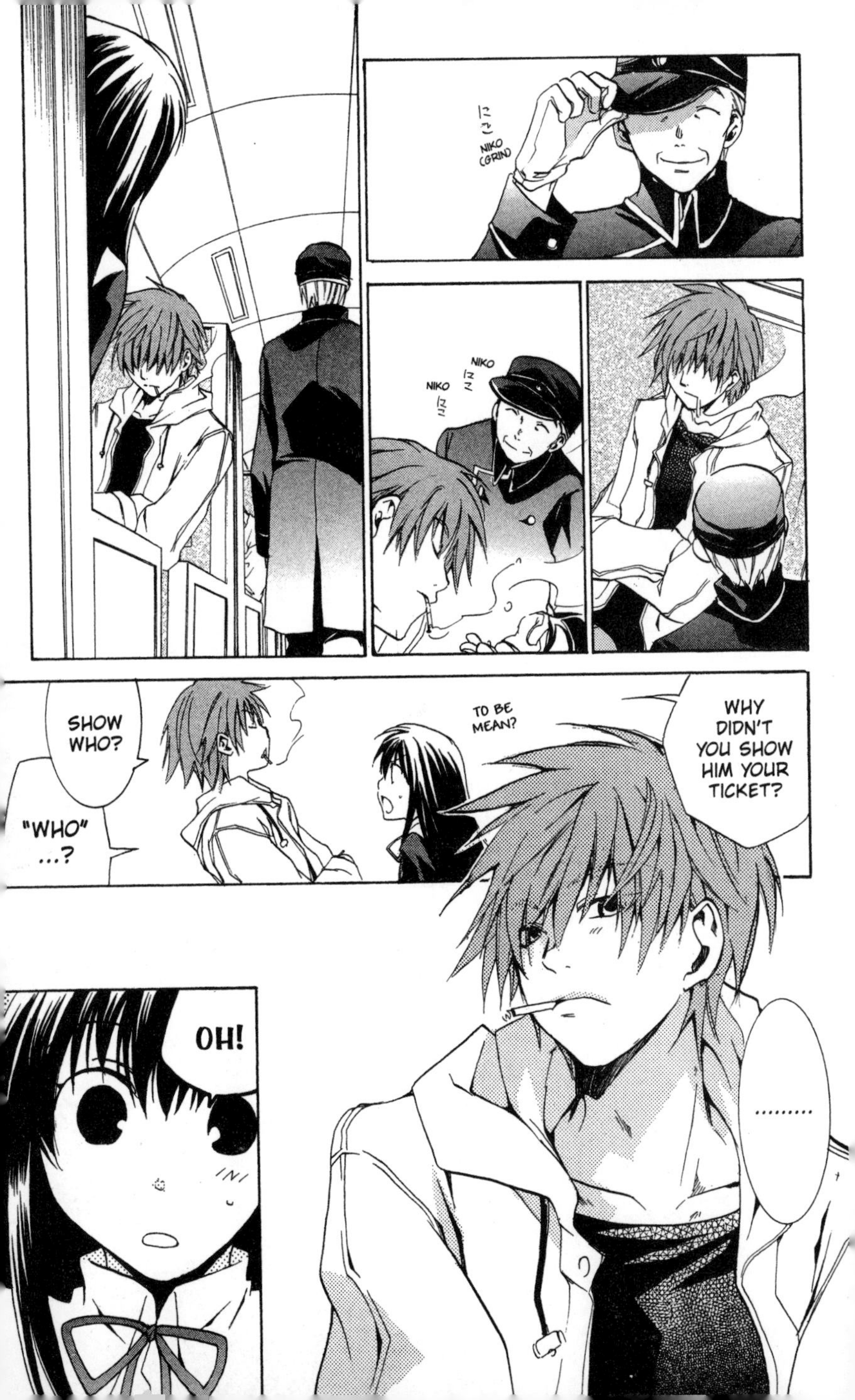
にこ
NIKO (GRIN)
にこ
NIKO
にこ
NIKO
WHY DIDN'T YOU SHOW HIM YOUR TICKET?
TO BE MEAN?
SHOW WHO?
"WHO" ...?
....
OH!

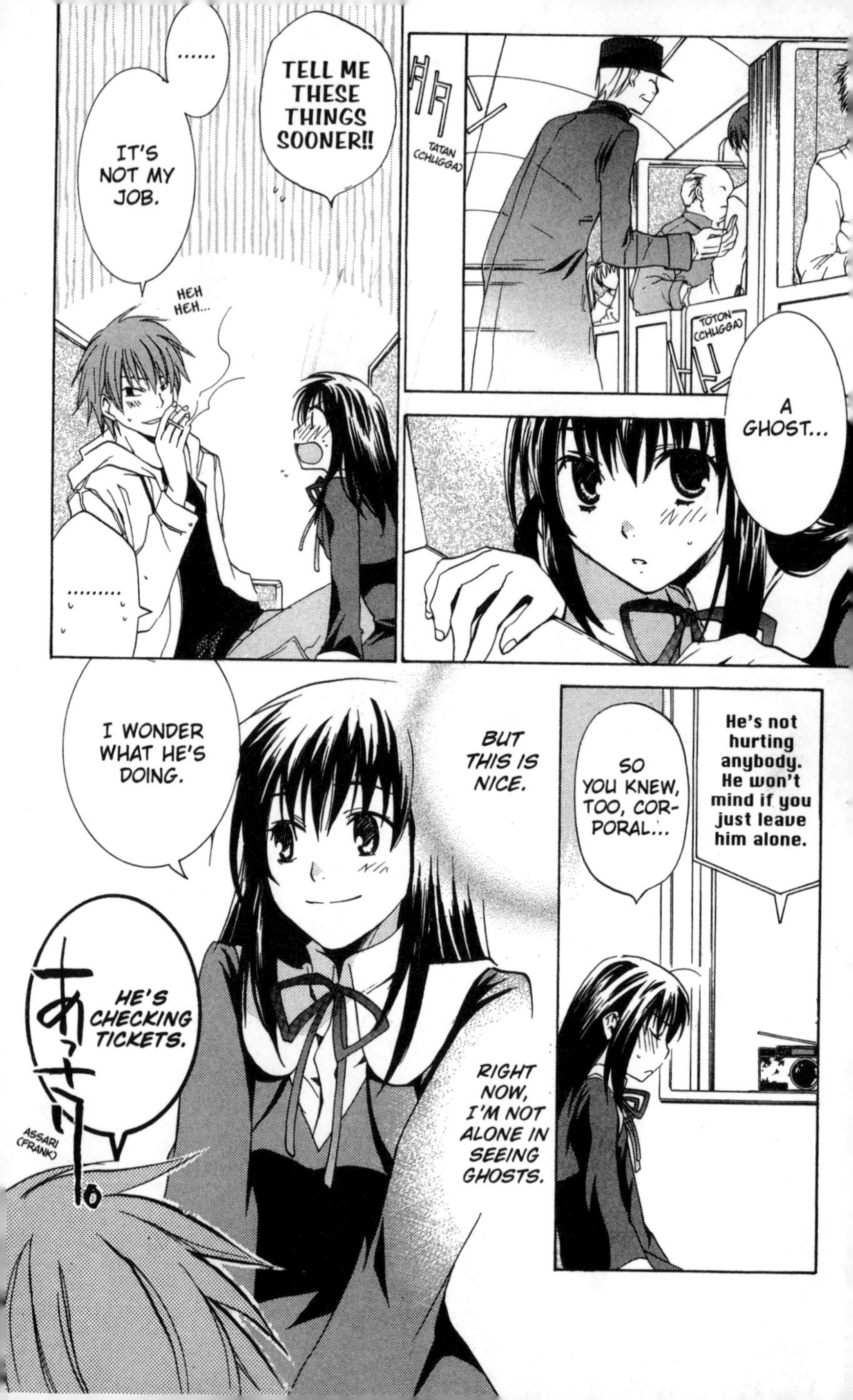
TATAN (CHUGGA)
TOTON (CHUGGA)
A GHOST...
TELL ME THESE THINGS SOONER!!
......
IT'S NOT MY JOB.
HEH HEH...
....
He's not hurting anybody. He won't mind if you just leave him alone.
SO YOU KNEW, TOO, CORPORAL...
BUT THIS IS NICE.
RIGHT NOW, I'M NOT ALONE IN SEEING GHOSTS.
I WONDER WHAT HE'S DOING.
HE'S CHECKING TICKETS.
あっさり
ASSARI (FRANK)

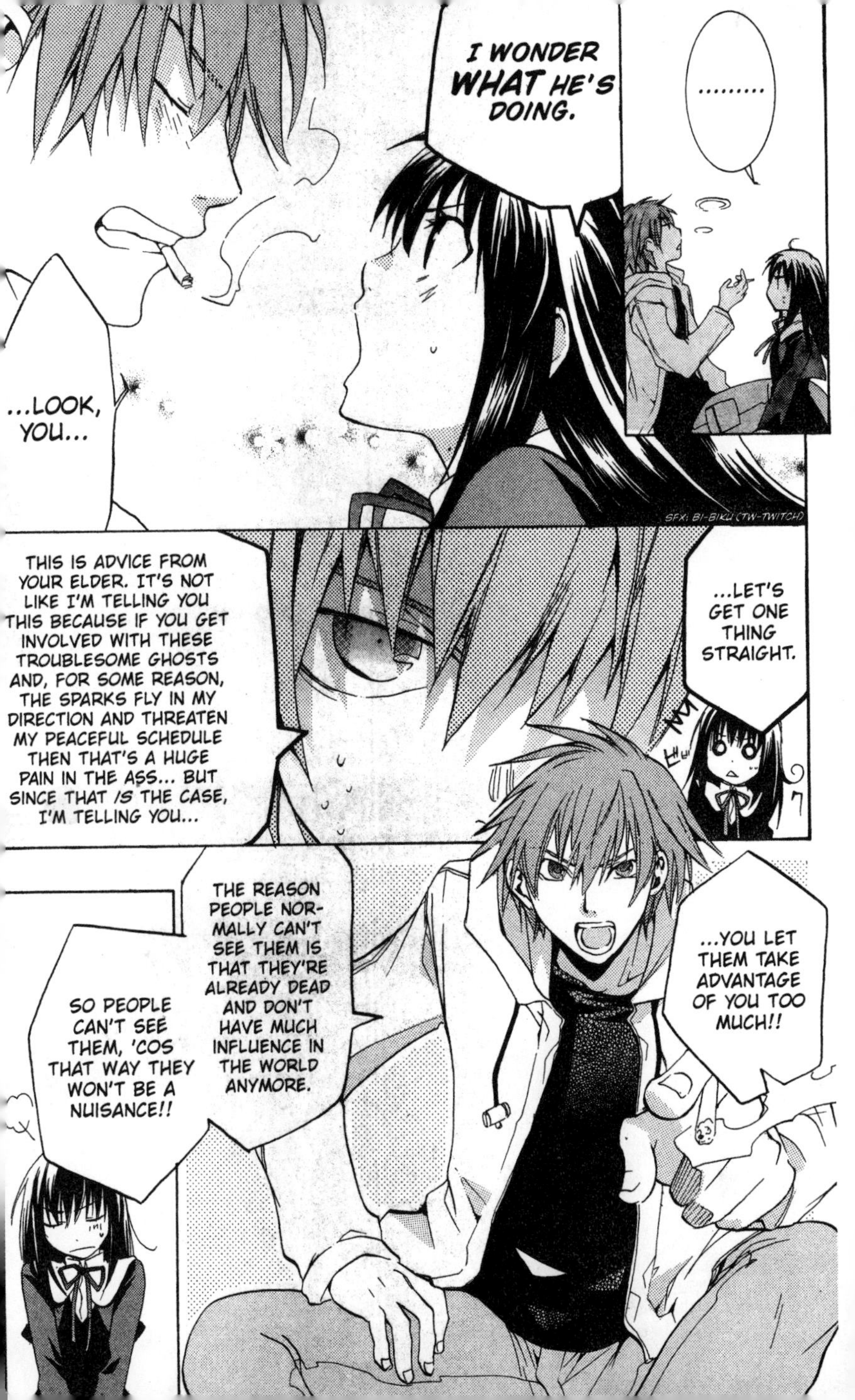
....
I WONDER WHAT HE'S DOING.
SFX: BI-BIKU (TW-TWITCH)
...LOOK, YOU...
...LET'S GET ONE THING STRAIGHT.
THIS IS ADVICE FROM YOUR ELDER. IT'S NOT LIKE I'M TELLING YOU THIS BECAUSE IF YOU GET INVOLVED WITH THESE TROUBLESOME GHOSTS AND, FOR SOME REASON, THE SPARKS FLY IN MY DIRECTION AND THREATEN MY PEACEFUL SCHEDULE THEN THAT'S A HUGE PAIN IN THE ASS... BUT SINCE THAT IS THE CASE, I'M TELLING YOU...
...YOU LET THEM TAKE ADVANTAGE OF YOU TOO MUCH!!
THE REASON PEOPLE NOR-MALLY CAN'T SEE THEM IS THAT THEY'RE ALREADY DEAD AND DON'T HAVE MUCH INFLUENCE IN THE WORLD ANYMORE.
SO PEOPLE CAN'T SEE THEM, 'COS THAT WAY THEY WON'T BE A NUISANCE!!

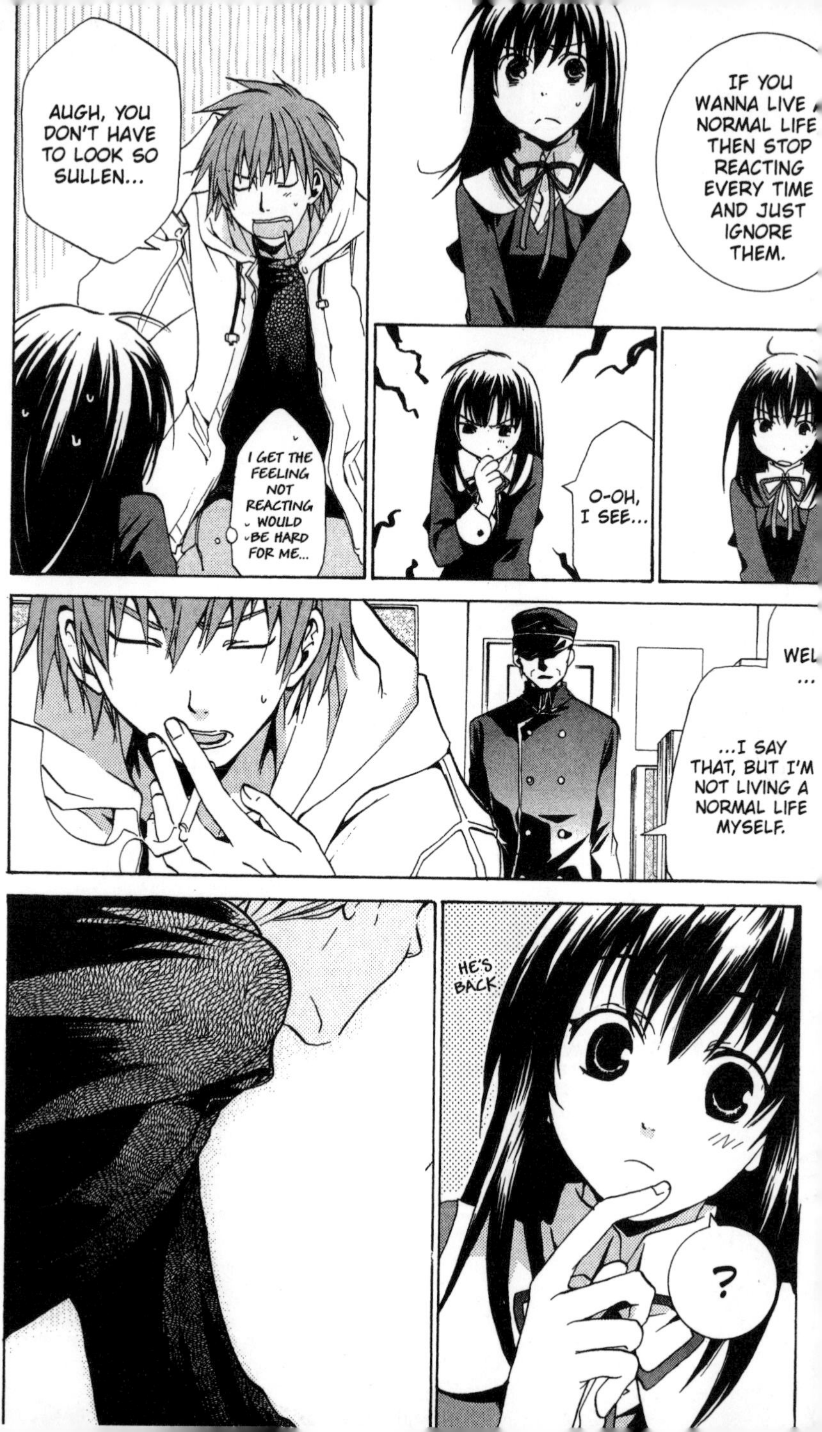
IF YOU WANNA LIVE A NORMAL LIFE THEN STOP REACTING EVERY TIME AND JUST IGNORE THEM.
O-OH, I SEE...
AUGH, YOU DON'T HAVE TO LOOK SO SULLEN...
I GET THE FEELING NOT REACTING WOULD BE HARD FOR ME...
WEL ...
...I SAY THAT, BUT I'M NOT LIVING A NORMAL LIFE MYSELF.
HE'S BACK
?

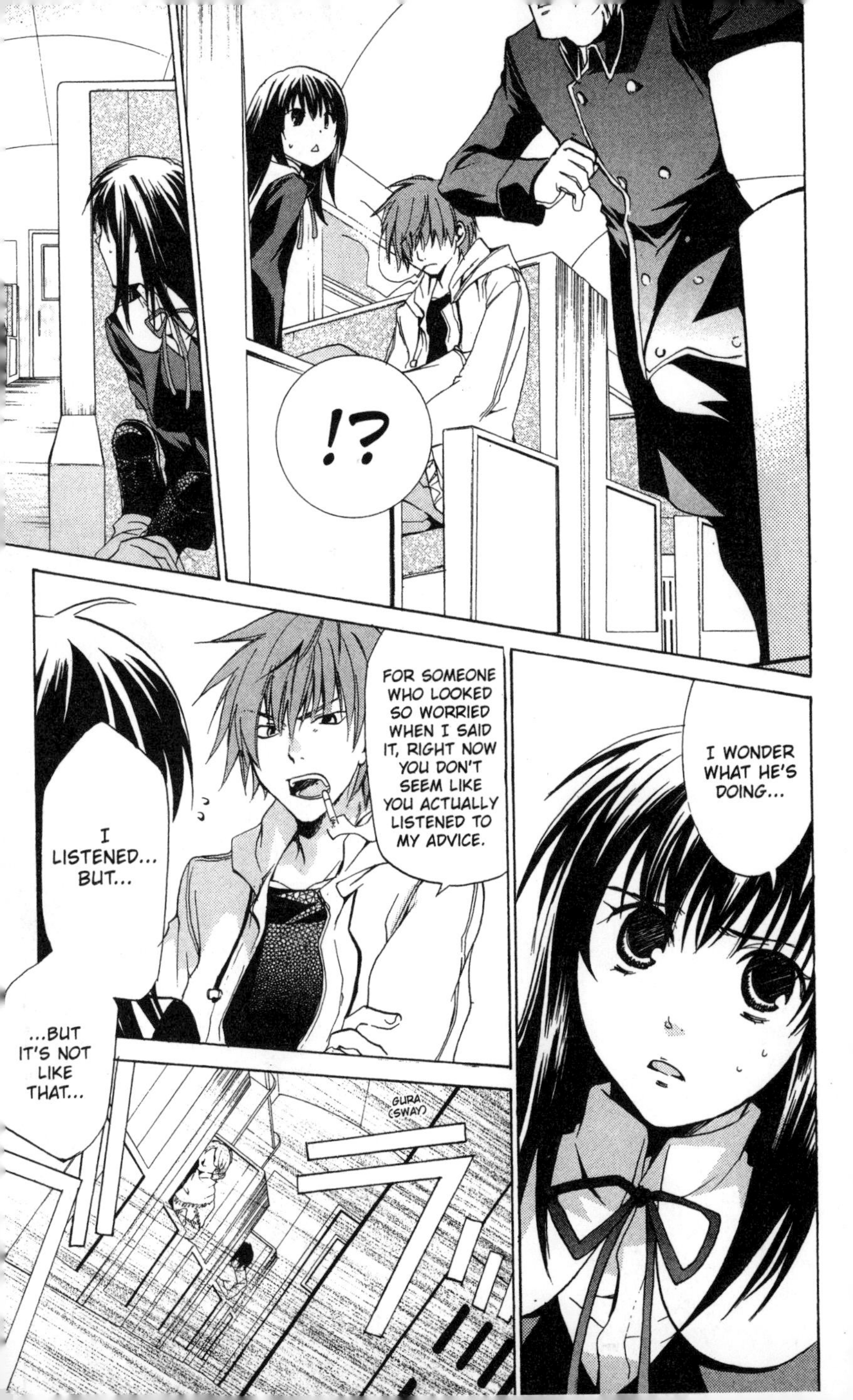
!?
I WONDER WHAT HE'S DOING...
FOR SOMEONE WHO LOOKED SO WORRIED WHEN I SAID IT, RIGHT NOW YOU DON'T SEEM LIKE YOU ACTUALLY LISTENED TO MY ADVICE.
I LISTENED... BUT...
...BUT IT'S NOT LIKE THAT...
GURA (SWAY)

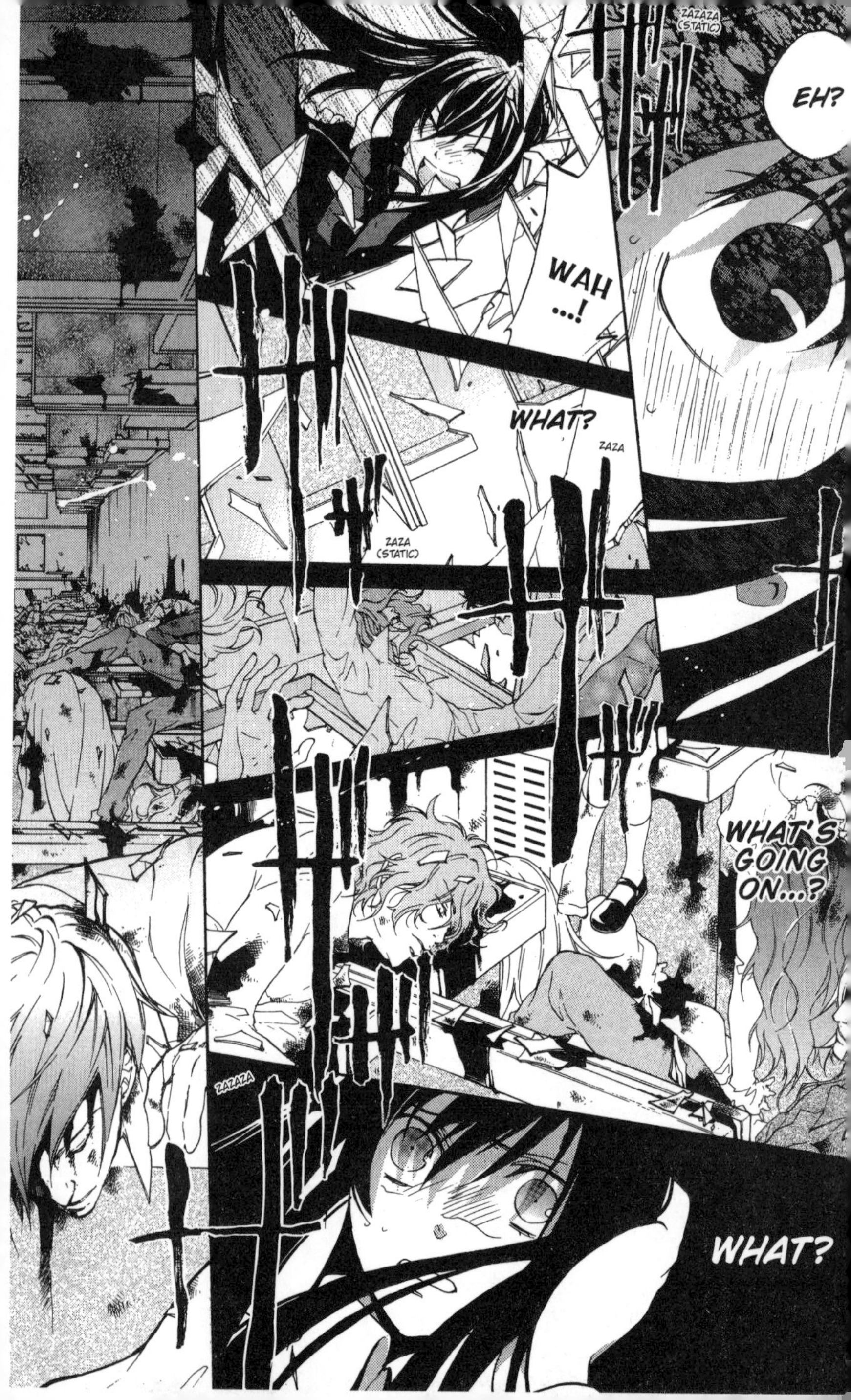
EH?
ZAZAZA (STATIC)
WAH ...!
WHAT?
ZAZA
ZAZA (STATIC)
WHAT'S GOING ON...?
ZAZAZA
WHAT?

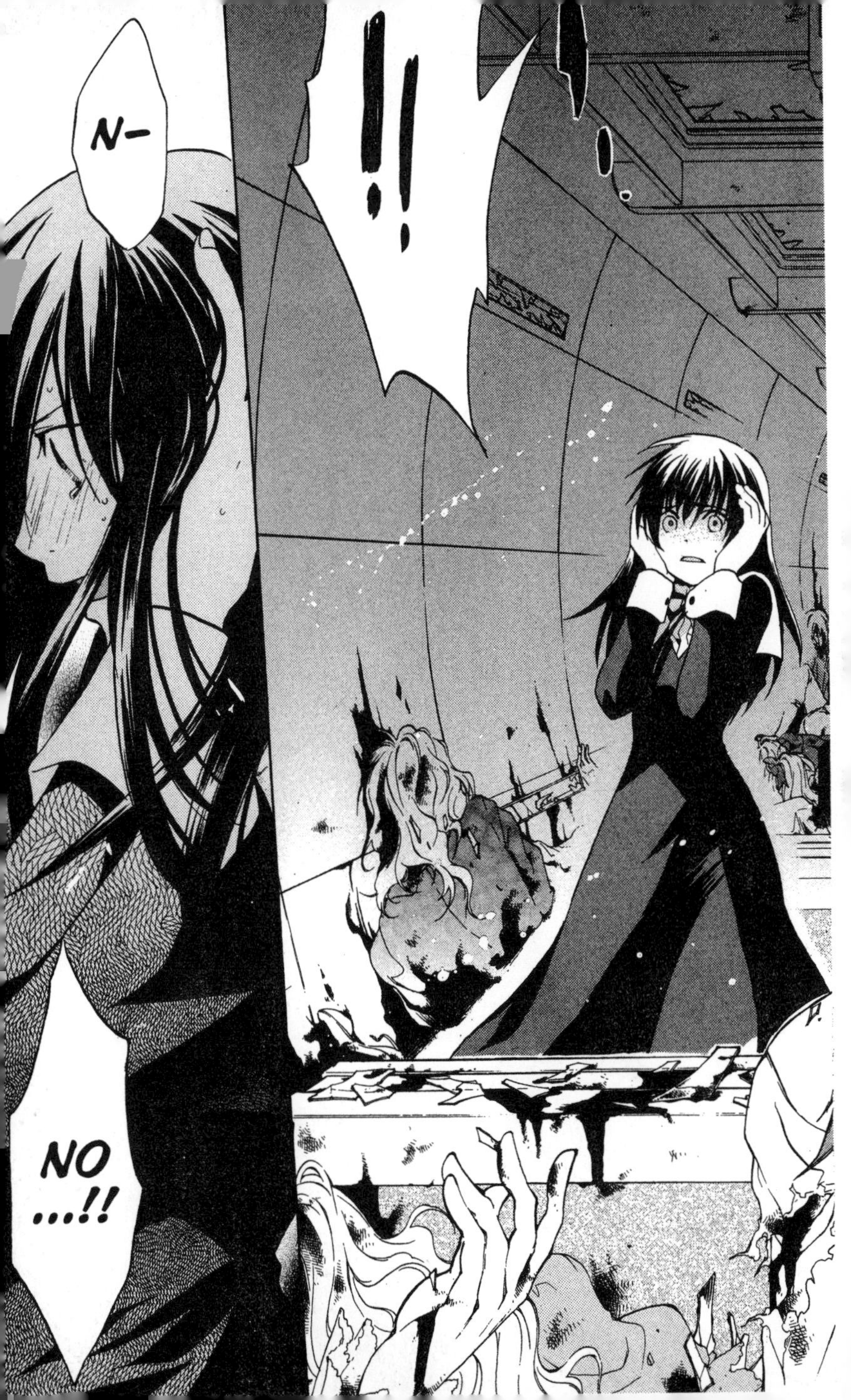
!!
N–
NO ...!!

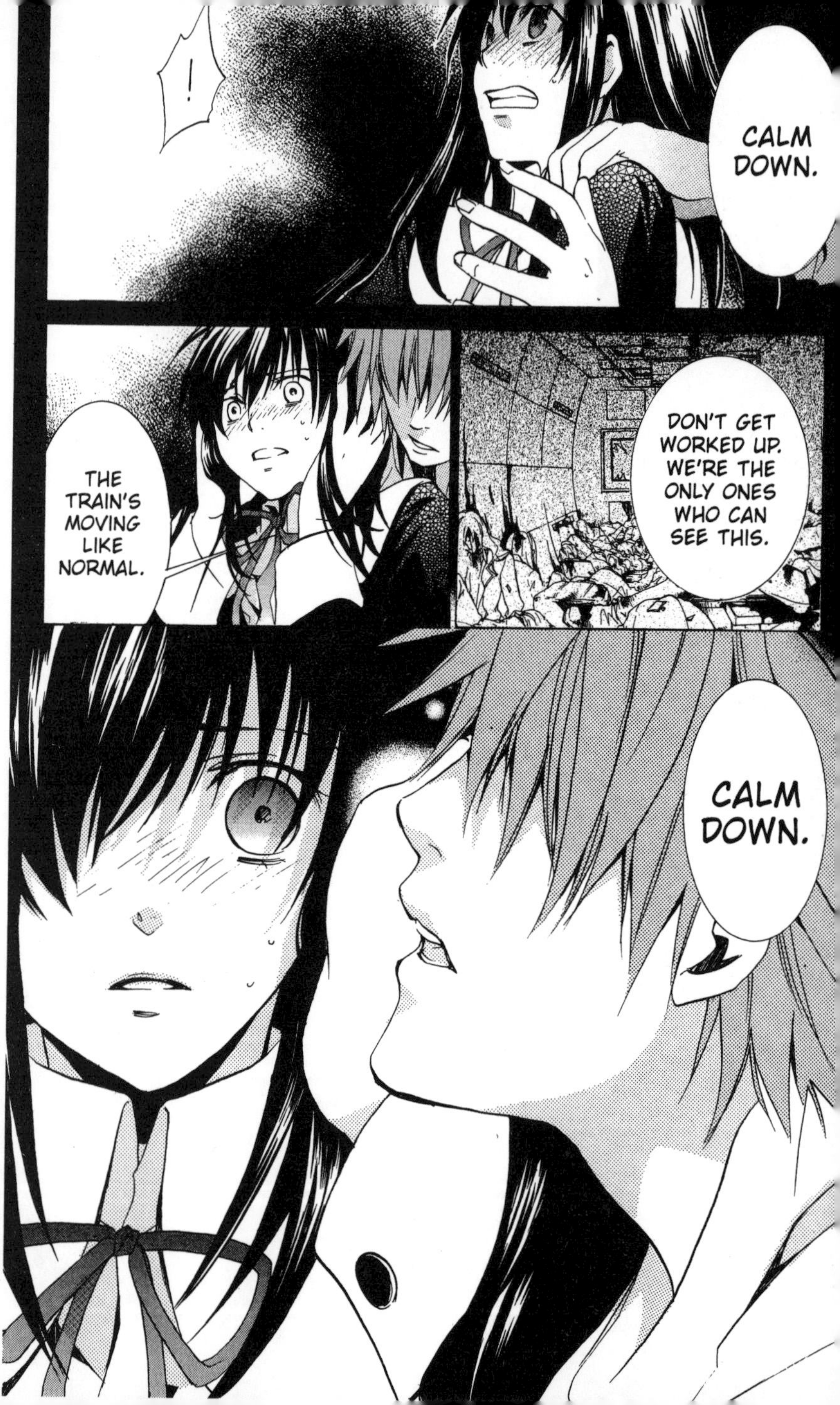
CALM DOWN.
!
DON'T GET WORKED UP. WE'RE THE ONLY ONES WHO CAN SEE THIS.
THE TRAIN'S MOVING LIKE NORMAL.
CALM DOWN.

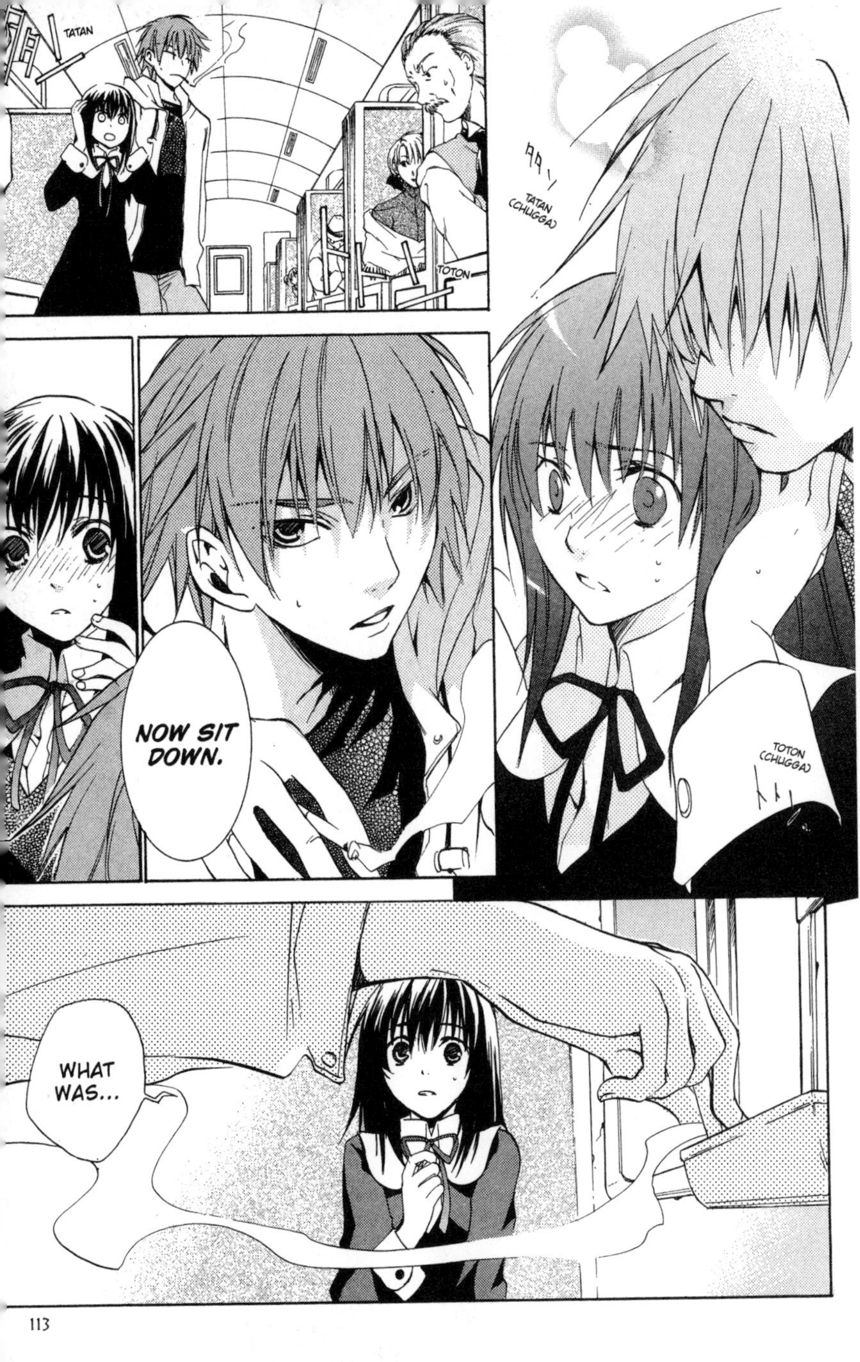
TATAN (CHUGGA)
TATAN
TOTON
TOTON (CHUGGA)
NOW SIT DOWN.
WHAT WAS...

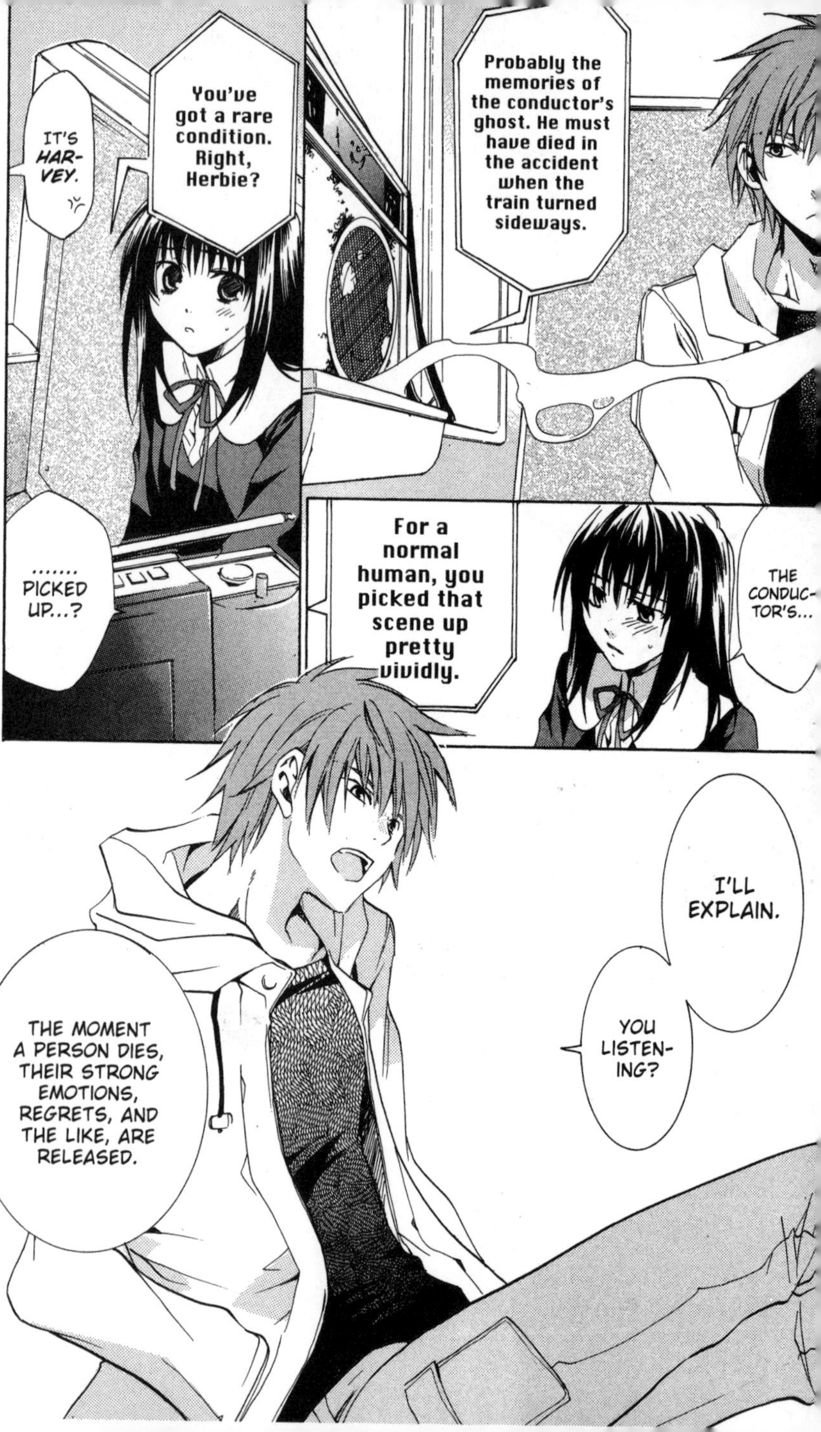
Probably the memories of the conductor's ghost. He must have died in the accident when the train turned sideways.
THE CONDUCTOR'S...
For a normal human, you picked that scene up pretty vividly.
.... PICKED UP...?
You've got a rare condition. Right, Herbie?
IT'S HARVEY.
I'LL EXPLAIN.
YOU LISTENING?
THE MOMENT A PERSON DIES, THEIR STRONG EMOTIONS, REGRETS, AND THE LIKE, ARE RELEASED.

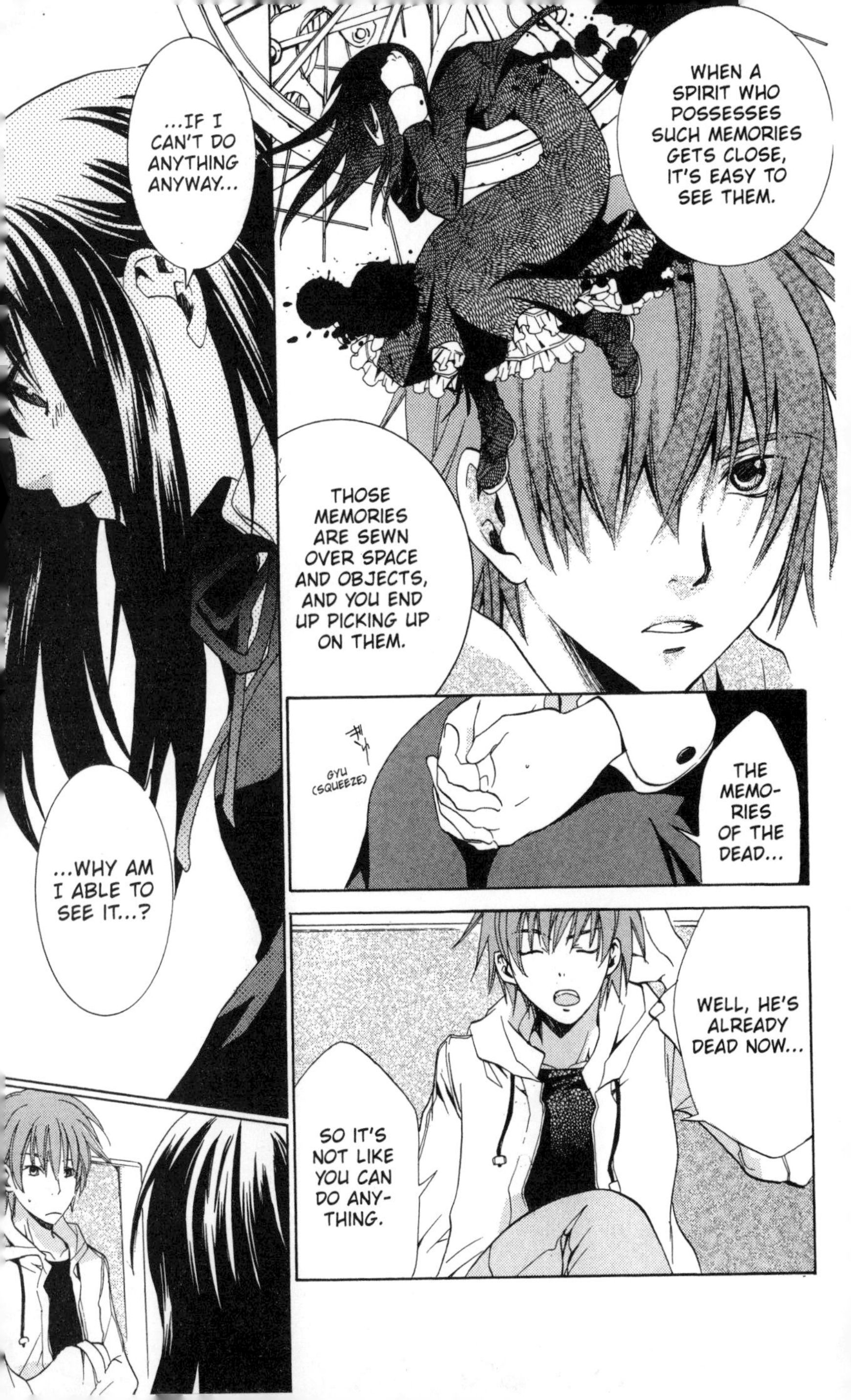

WHEN A SPIRIT WHO POSSESSES SUCH MEMORIES GETS CLOSE, IT'S EASY TO SEE THEM.
THOSE MEMORIES ARE SEWN OVER SPACE AND OBJECTS, AND YOU END UP PICKING UP ON THEM.
THE MEMORIES OF THE DEAD...
GYU (SQUEEZE)
WELL, HE'S ALREADY DEAD NOW...
SO IT'S NOT LIKE YOU CAN DO ANYTHING.
...IF I CAN'T DO ANYTHING ANYWAY...
...WHY AM I ABLE TO SEE IT...?

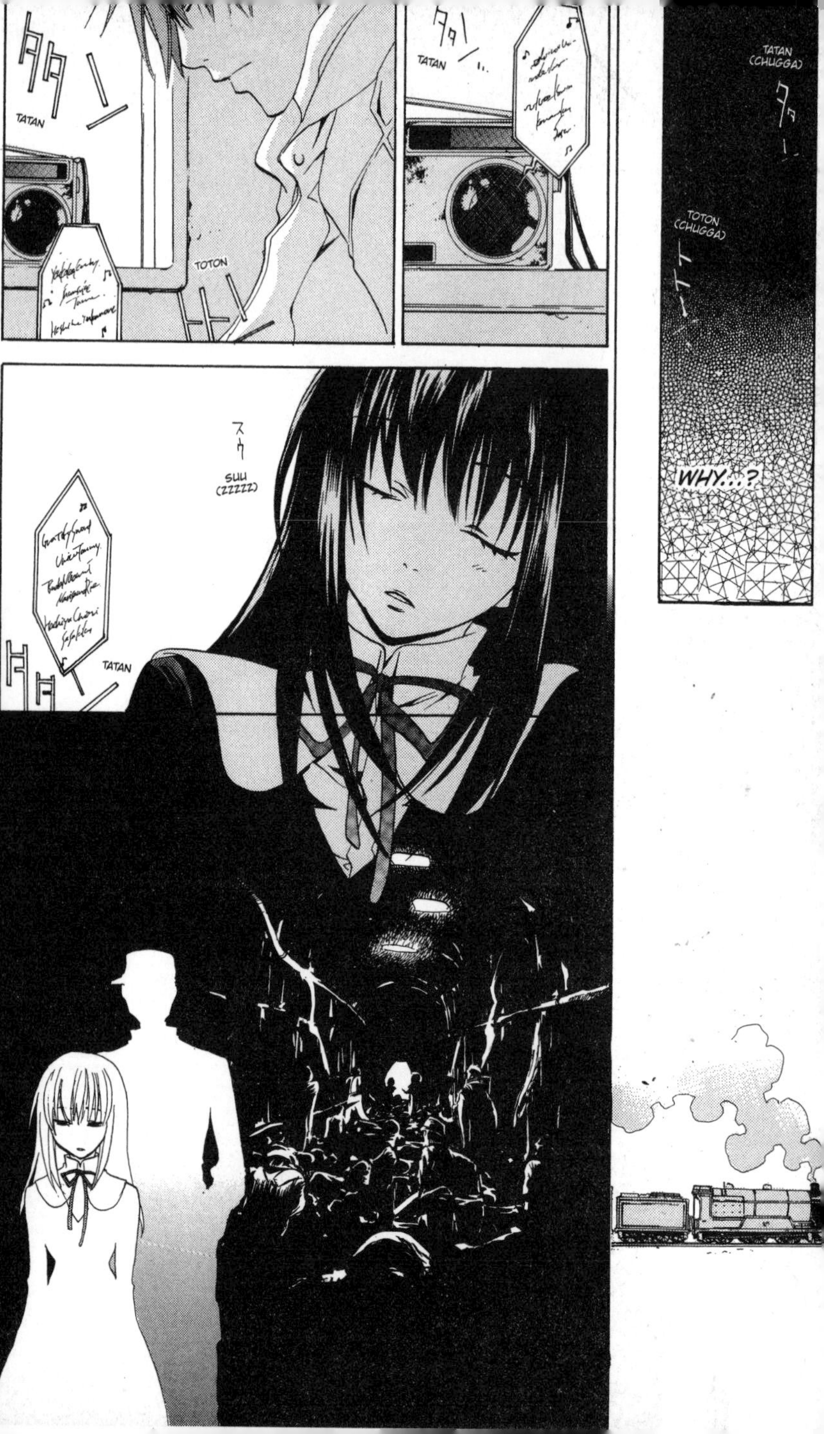

TATAN (CHUGGA)
TOTON (CHUGGA)
WHY...?
TATAN
TATAN
TOTON
SUU (ZZZZZ)
TATAN

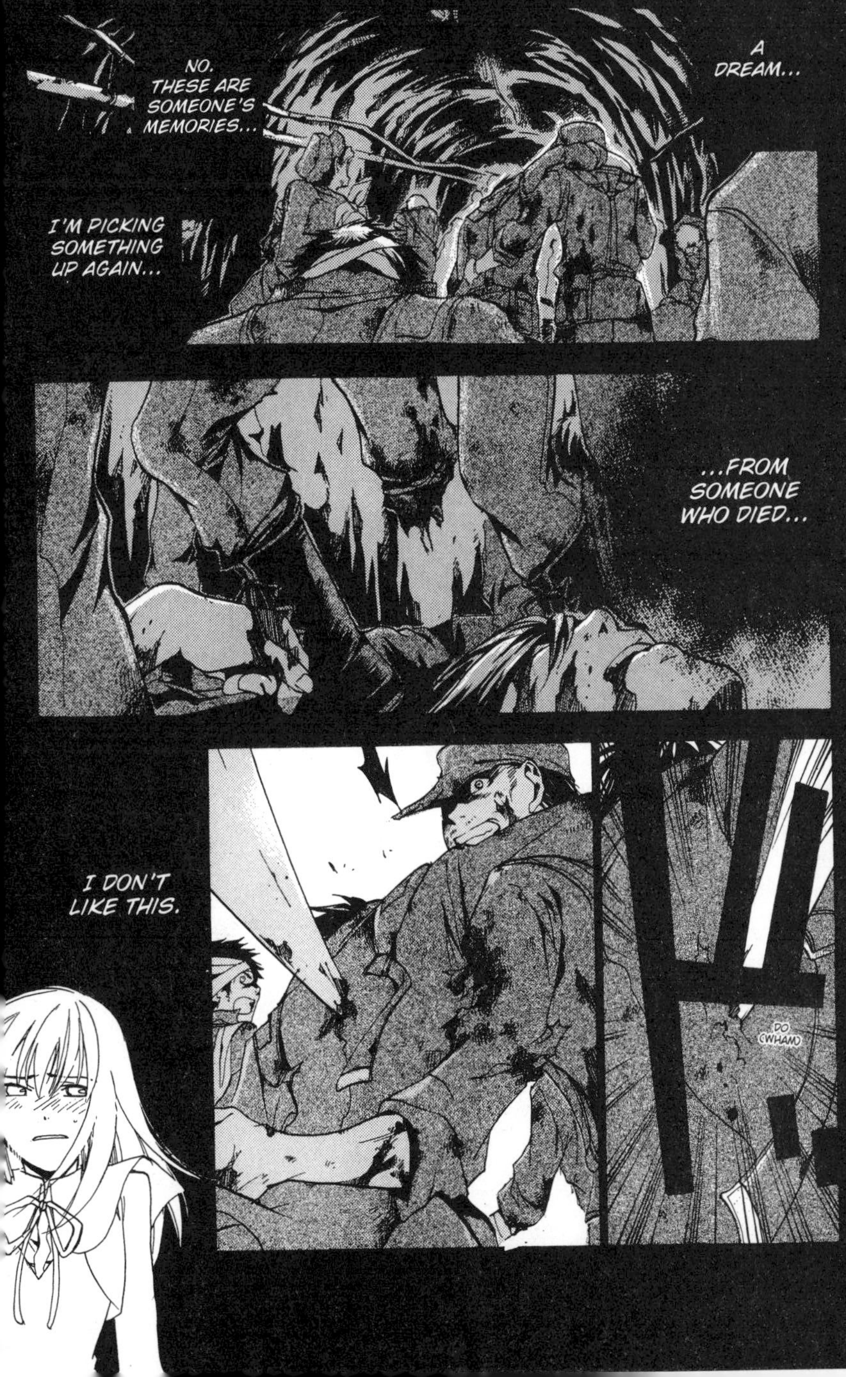
A DREAM...
NO. THESE ARE SOMEONE'S MEMORIES...
I'M PICKING SOMETHING UP AGAIN...
...FROM SOMEONE WHO DIED...
DO (WHAM)
I DON'T LIKE THIS.

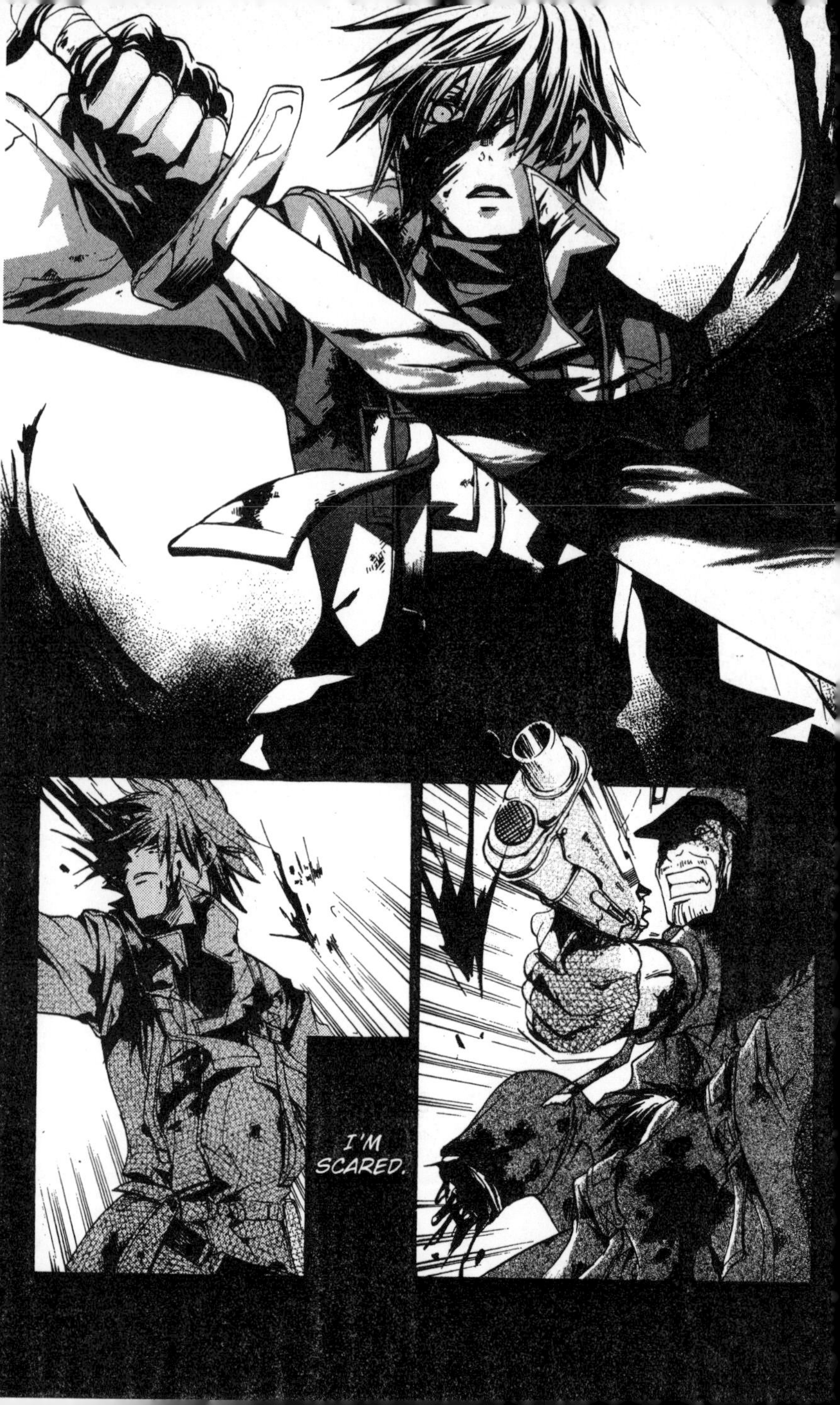
I'M SCARED.

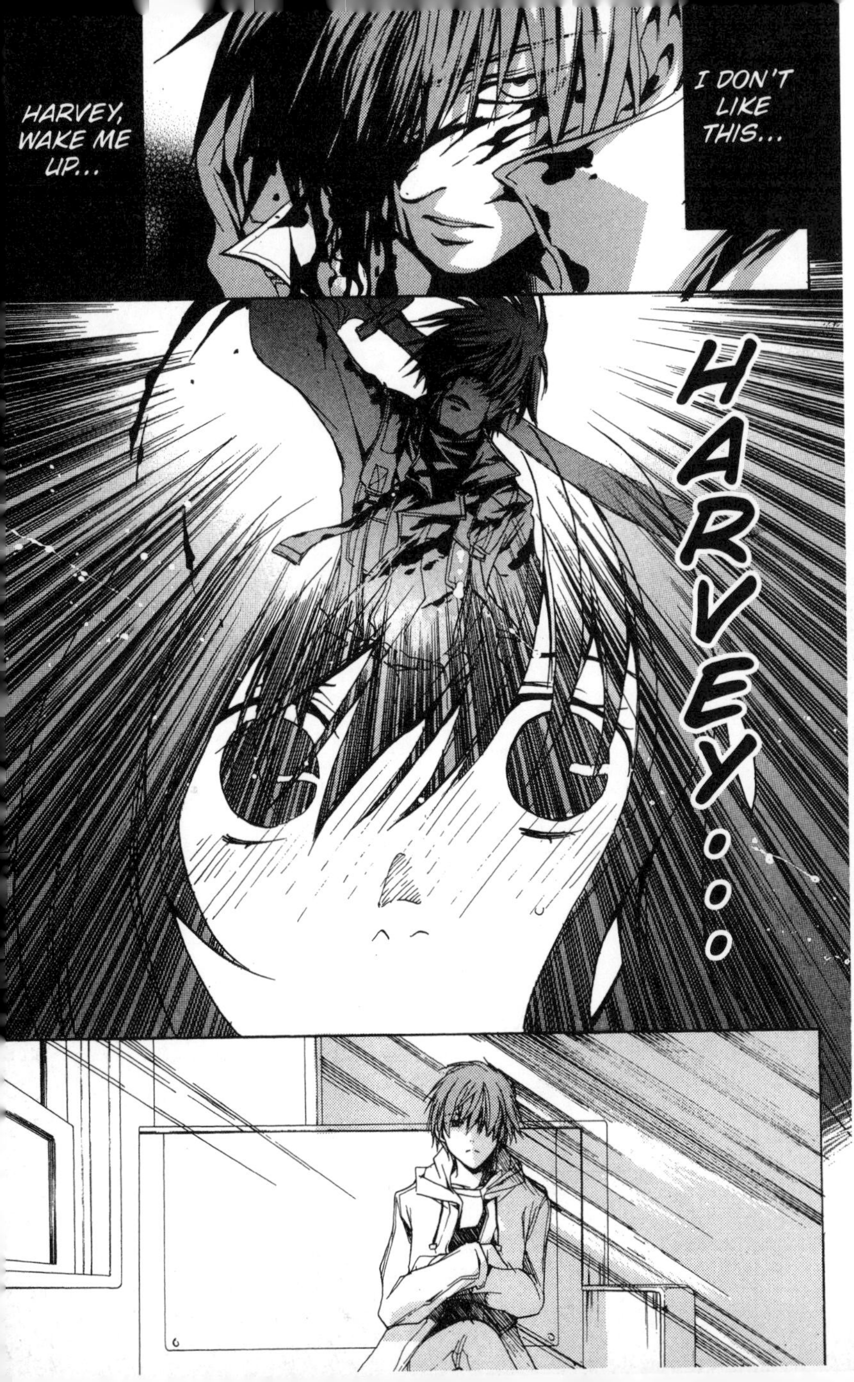
I DON'T LIKE THIS...
HARVEY, WAKE ME UP...
HARVEY...

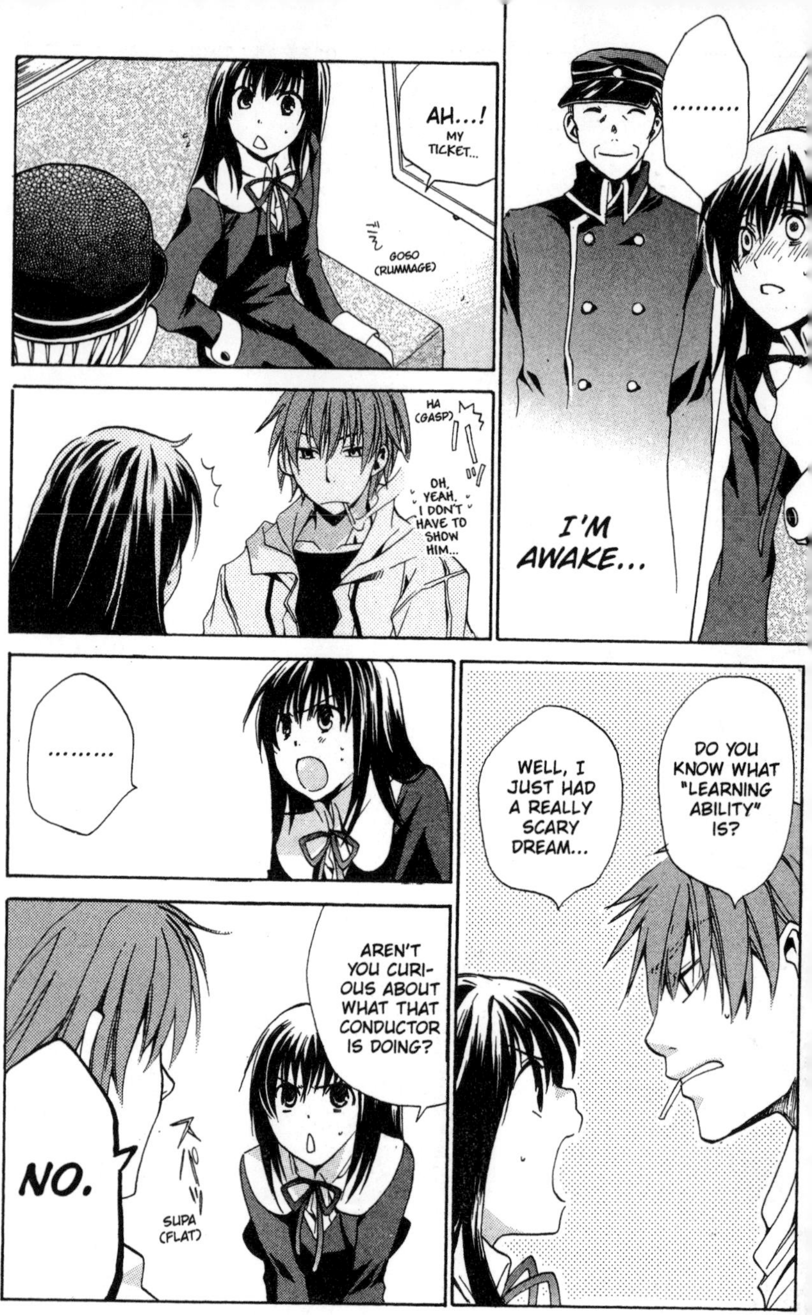
....
I'M AWAKE...
AH...! MY TICKET...
GOSO (RUMMAGE)
HA (GASP)
OH, YEAH. I DON'T HAVE TO SHOW HIM...
DO YOU KNOW WHAT "LEARNING ABILITY" IS?
WELL, I JUST HAD A REALLY SCARY DREAM...
....
AREN'T YOU CURI-OUS ABOUT WHAT THAT CONDUCTOR IS DOING?
NO.
SUPA (FLAT)

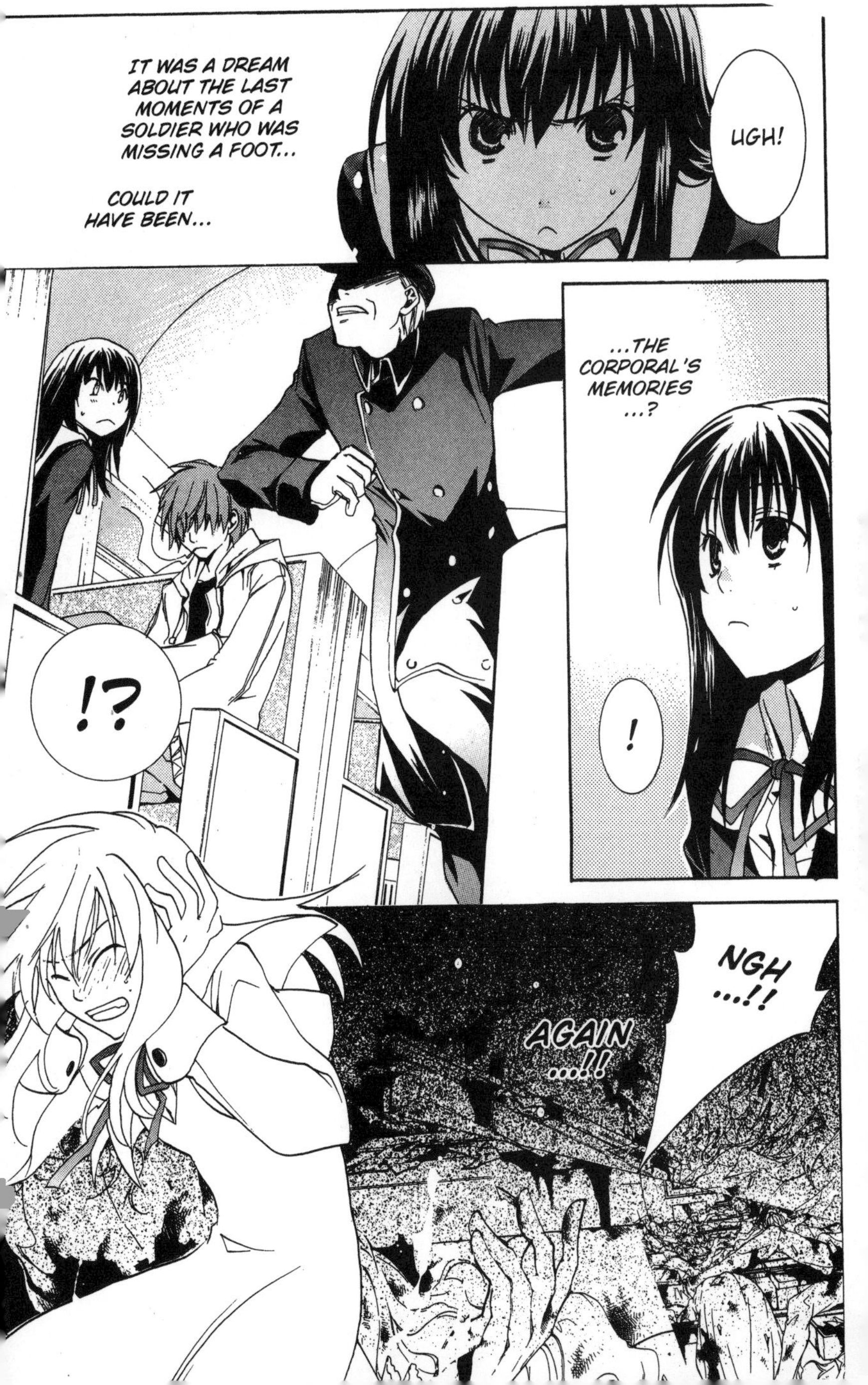
UGH!
IT WAS A DREAM ABOUT THE LAST MOMENTS OF A SOLDIER WHO WAS MISSING A FOOT...
COULD IT HAVE BEEN...
...THE CORPORAL'S MEMORIES ...?
!
!?
NGH ...!!
AGAIN ...!!

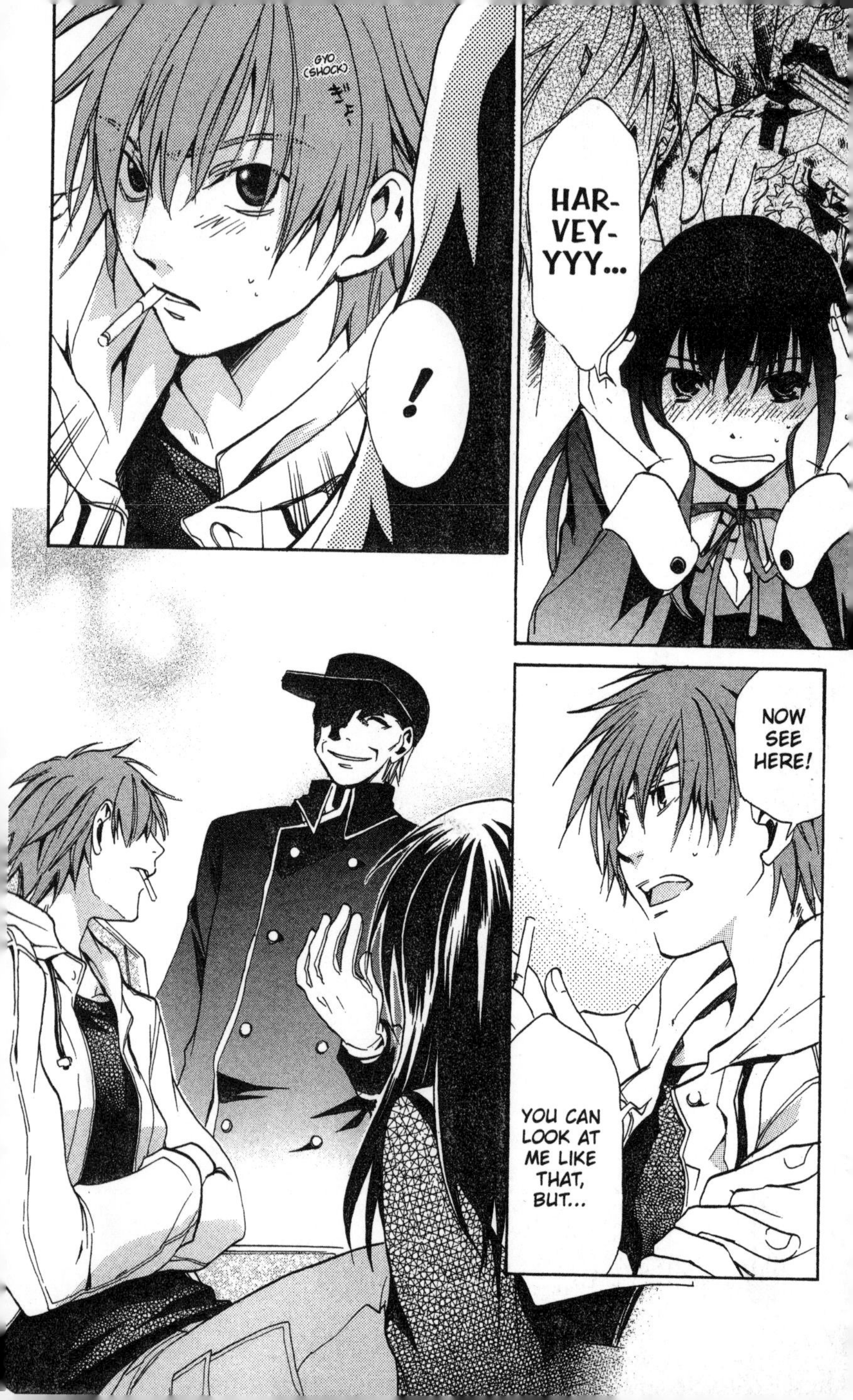
HAR-VEY-YYY...
GYO (SHOCK)
ギョ
!
NOW SEE HERE!
YOU CAN LOOK AT ME LIKE THAT, BUT...

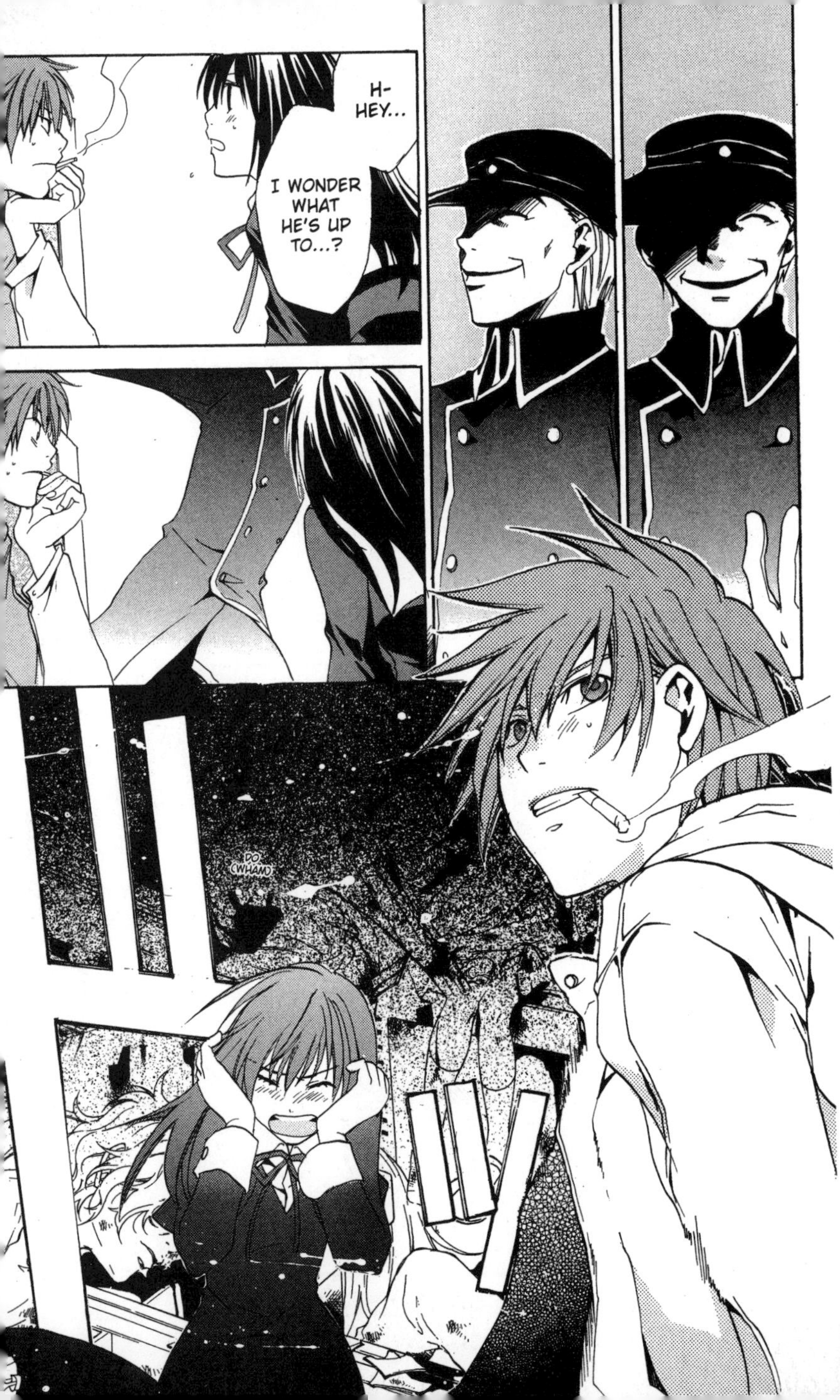
H-
HEY...
I WONDER WHAT HE'S UP TO...?
DO
(WHAM)

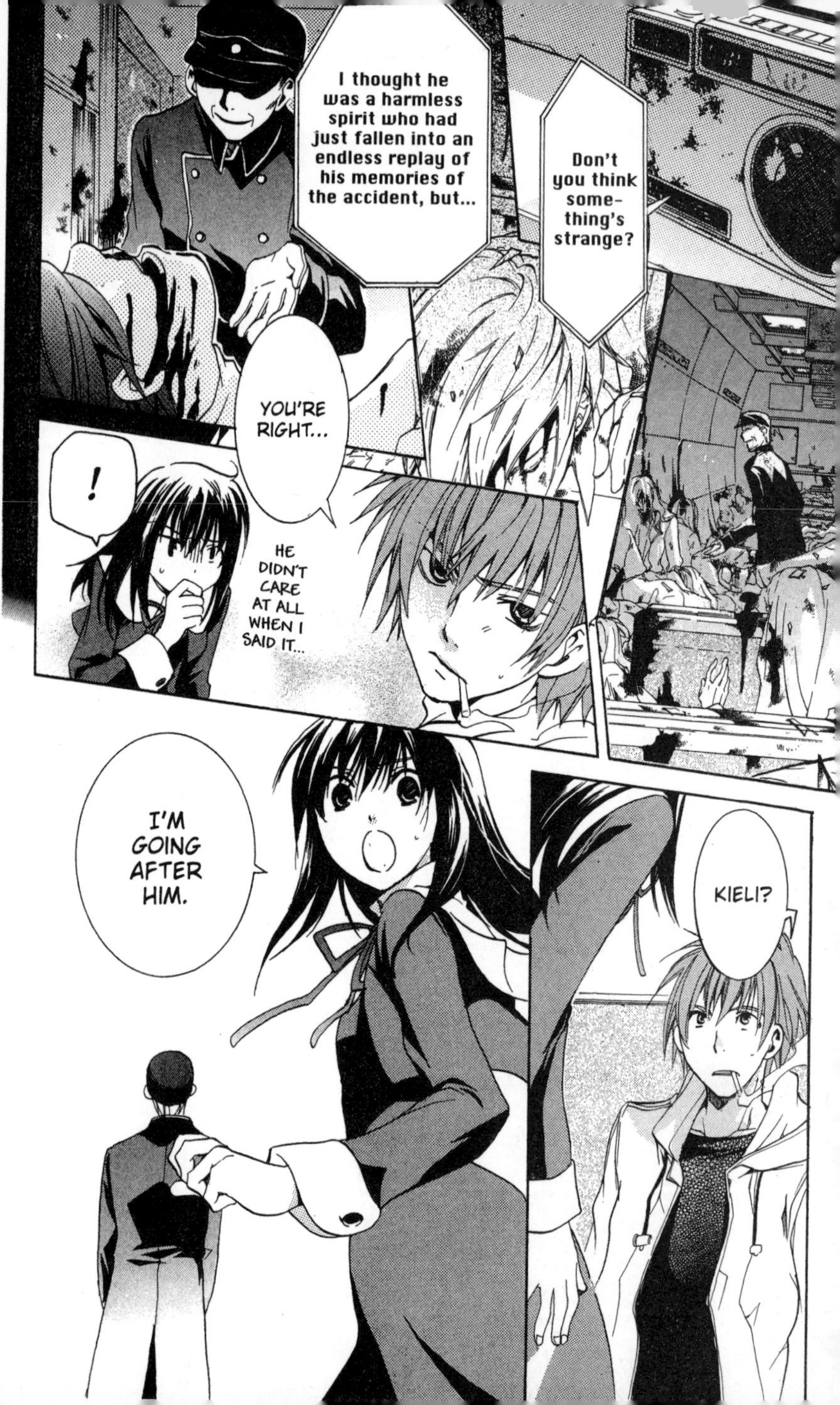

I thought he was a harmless spirit who had just fallen into an endless replay of his memories of the accident, but...
Don't you think something's strange?
YOU'RE RIGHT...
!
HE DIDN'T CARE AT ALL WHEN I SAID IT...
KIELI?
I'M GOING AFTER HIM.

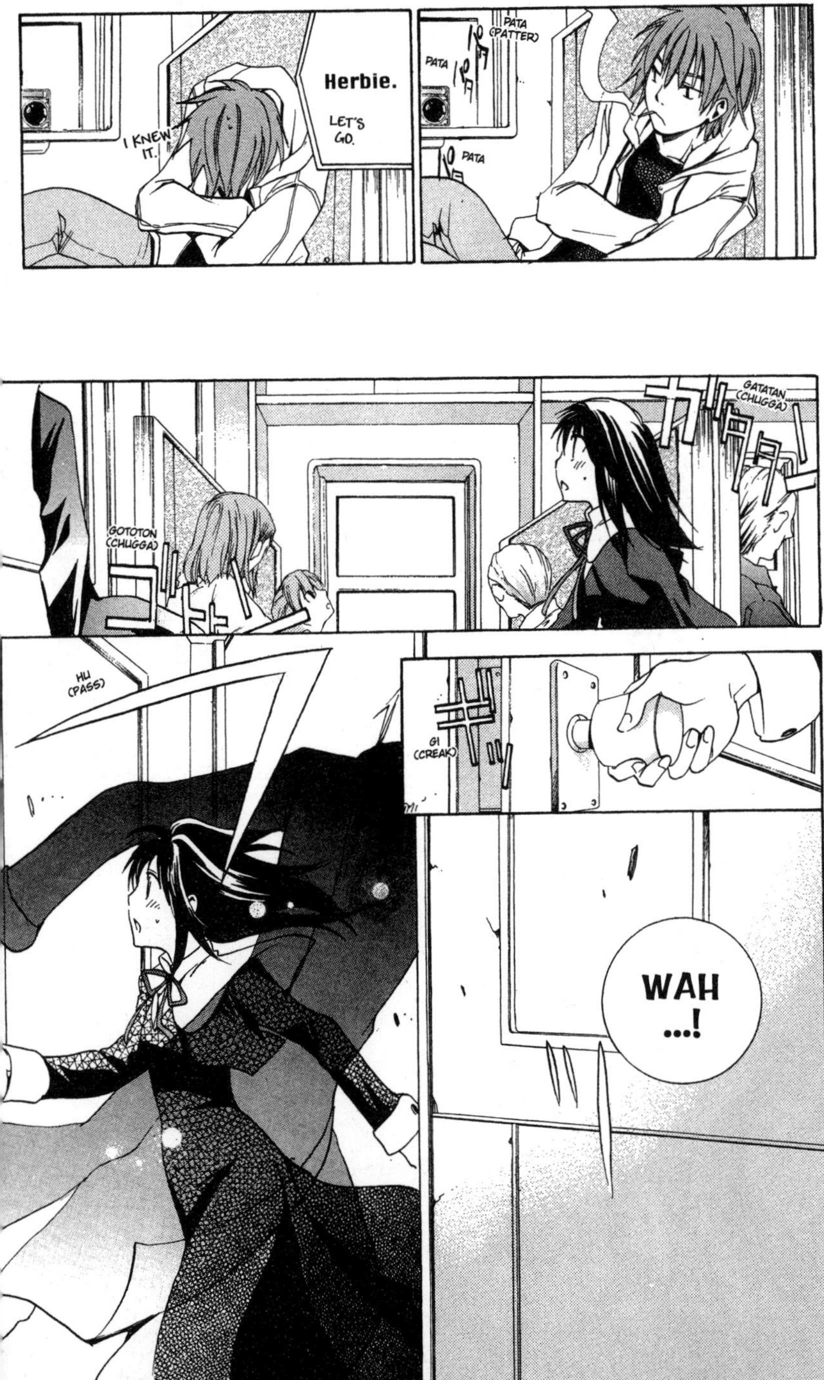

PATA (PATTER)
PATA
...
PATA
Herbie.
LET'S GO.
I KNEW IT.
GATATAN (CHUGGA)
GOTOTON (CHUGGA)
GI (CREAK)
WAH ...!
HU (PASS)
...

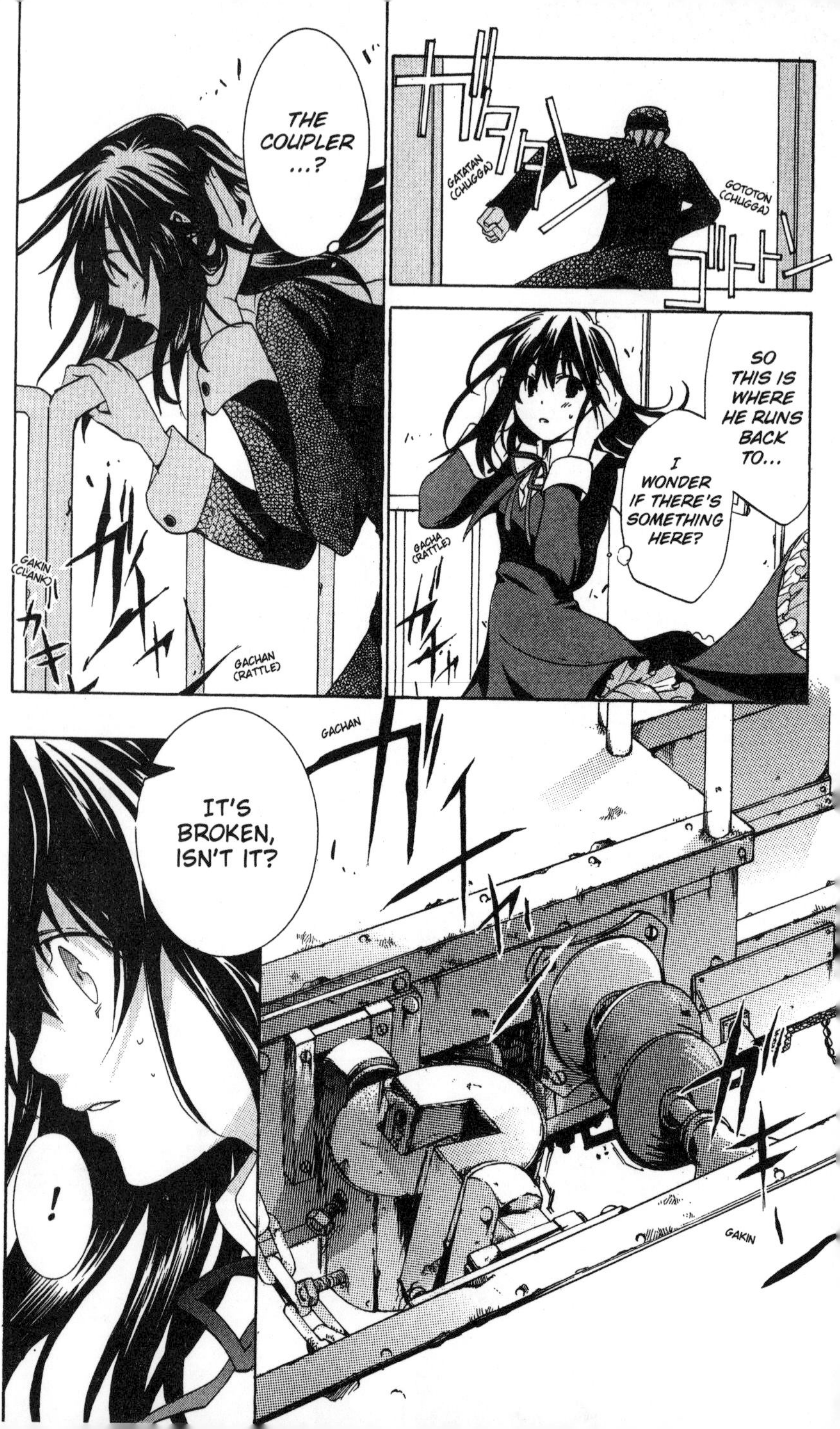
GATATAN (CHUGGA)
GOTOTON (CHUGGA)
SO THIS IS WHERE HE RUNS BACK TO...
I WONDER IF THERE'S SOMETHING HERE?
GACHA (RATTLE)
THE COUPLER ...?
GAKIN (CLANK)
GACHAN (RATTLE)
GACHAN
IT'S BROKEN, ISN'T IT?
GAKIN
!

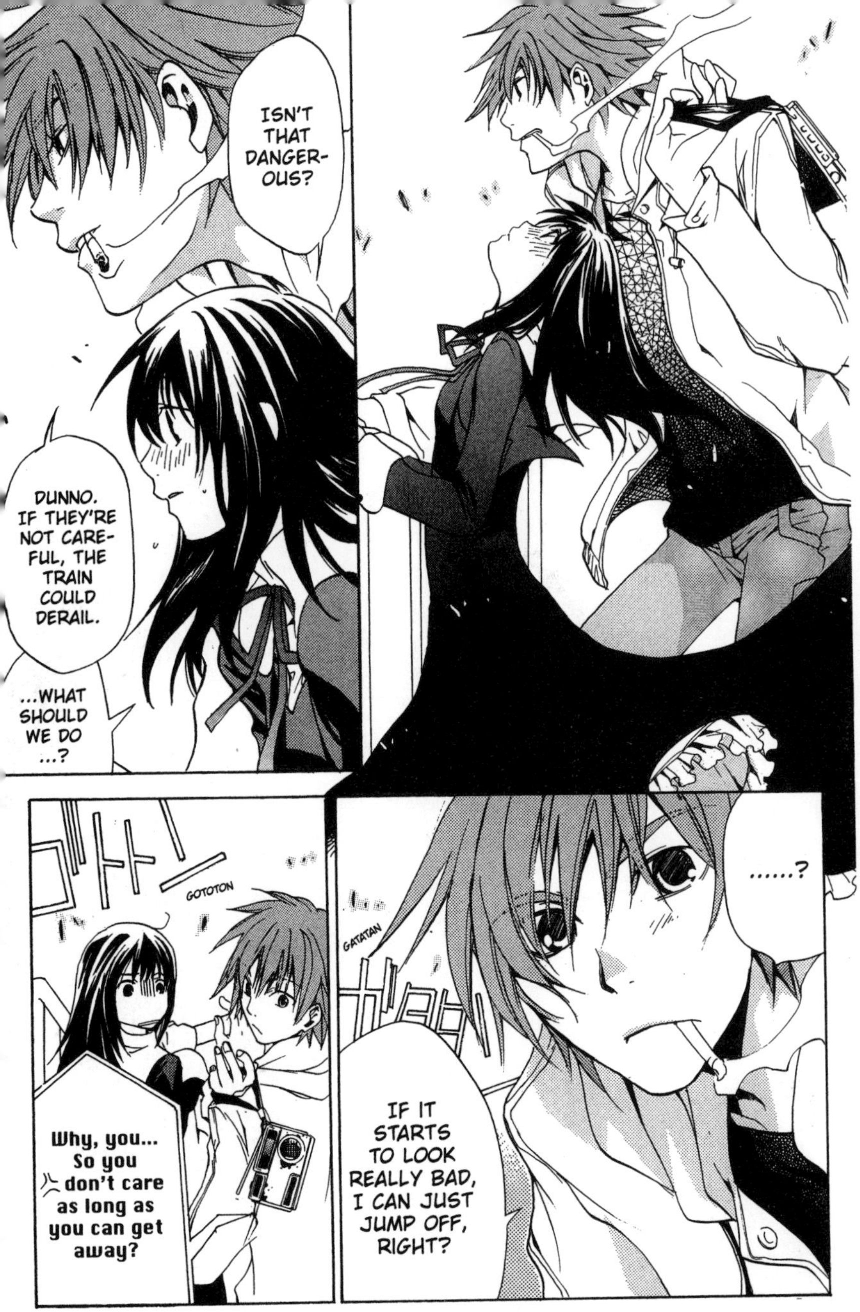
ISN'T THAT DANGER-OUS?
DUNNO. IF THEY'RE NOT CARE-FUL, THE TRAIN COULD DERAIL.
...WHAT SHOULD WE DO ...?
......?
GATATAN
IF IT STARTS TO LOOK REALLY BAD, I CAN JUST JUMP OFF, RIGHT?
GOTOTON
Why, you... So you don't care as long as you can get away?

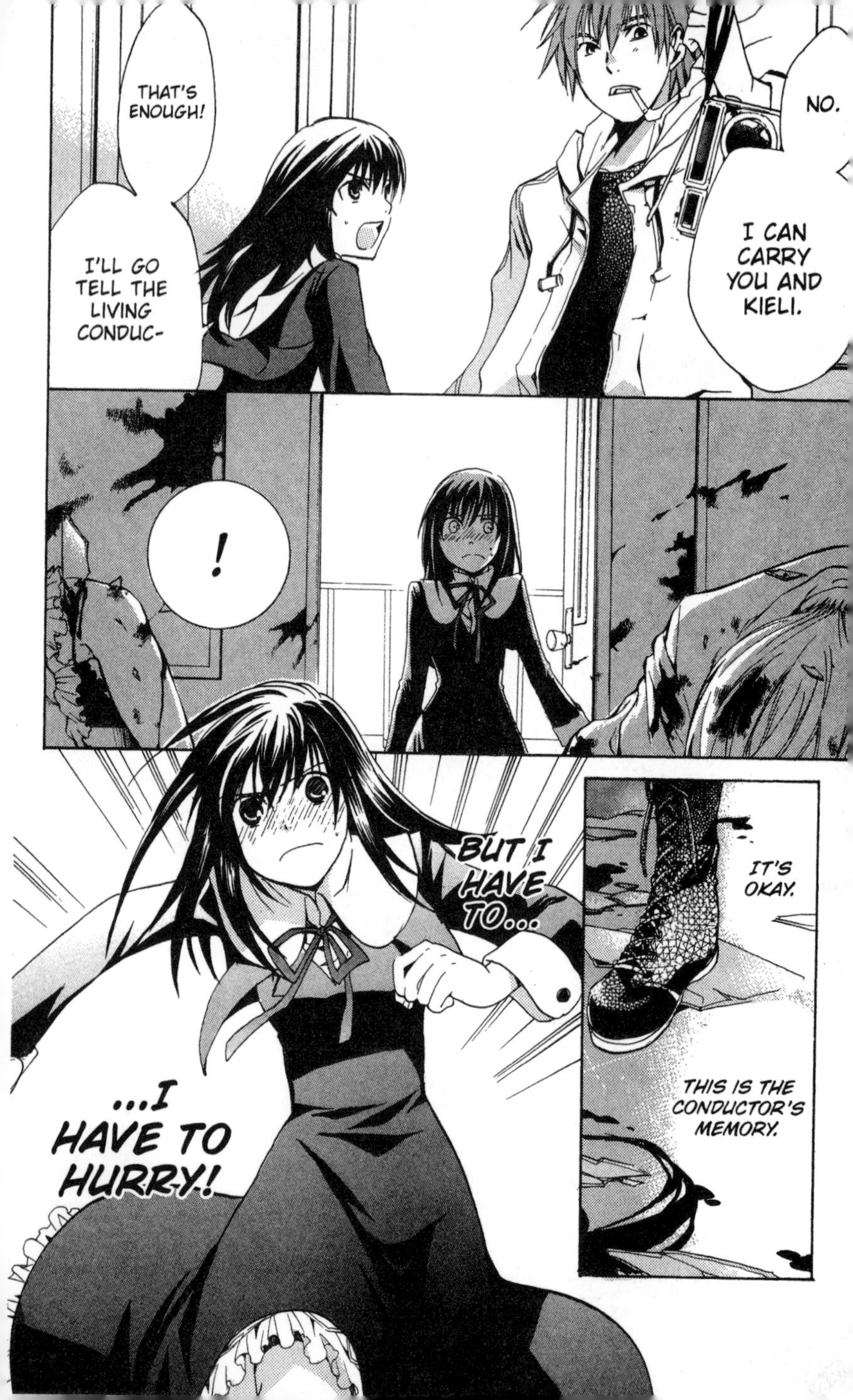
THAT'S ENOUGH!
I'LL GO TELL THE LIVING CONDUC-
NO.
I CAN CARRY YOU AND KIELI.
!
IT'S OKAY.
THIS IS THE CONDUCTOR'S MEMORY.
BUT I HAVE TO...
...I HAVE TO HURRY!

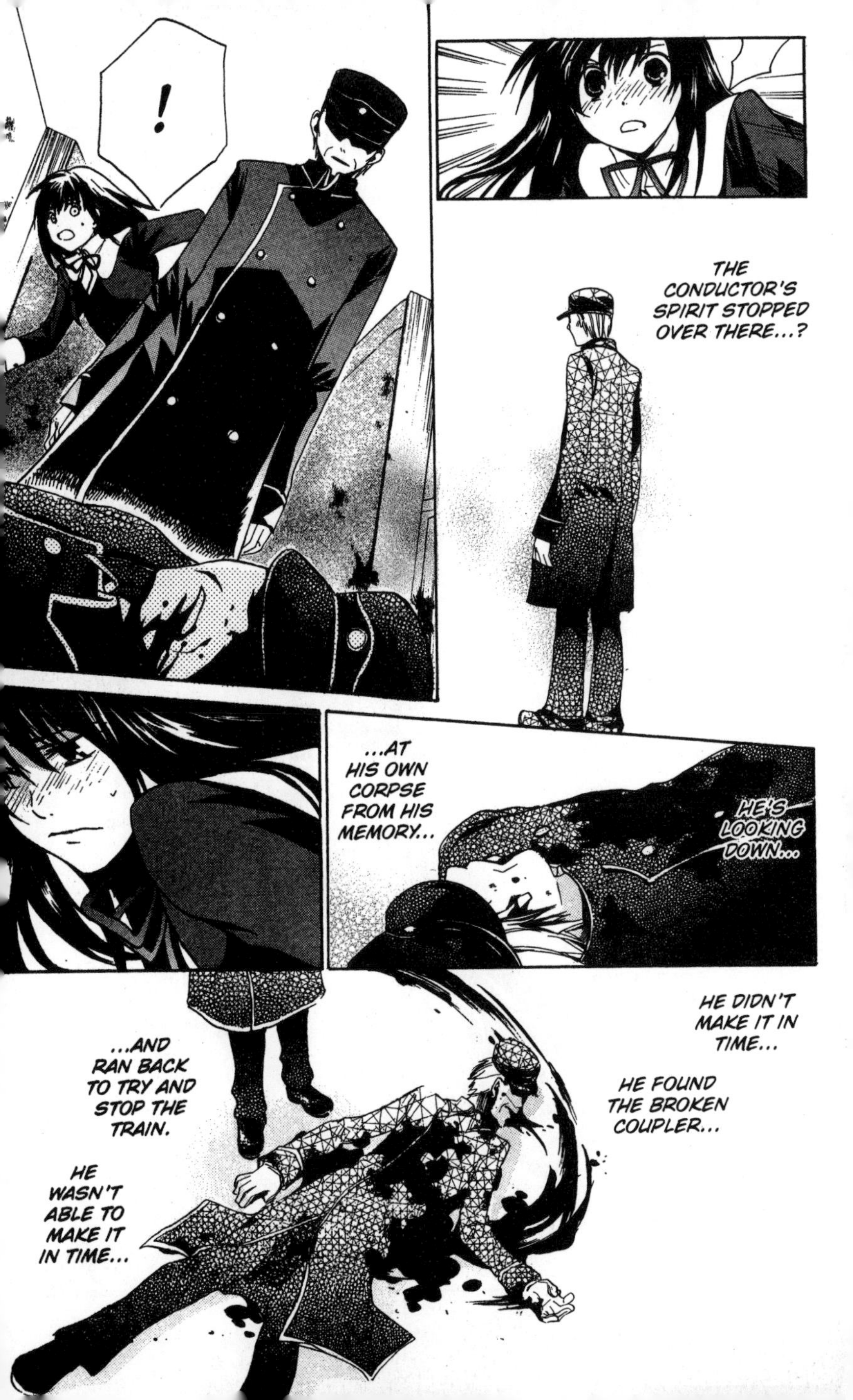
THE CONDUCTOR'S SPIRIT STOPPED OVER THERE...?
!
HE'S LOOKING DOWN...
...AT HIS OWN CORPSE FROM HIS MEMORY...
HE DIDN'T MAKE IT IN TIME...
HE FOUND THE BROKEN COUPLER...
...AND RAN BACK TO TRY AND STOP THE TRAIN.
HE WASN'T ABLE TO MAKE IT IN TIME...

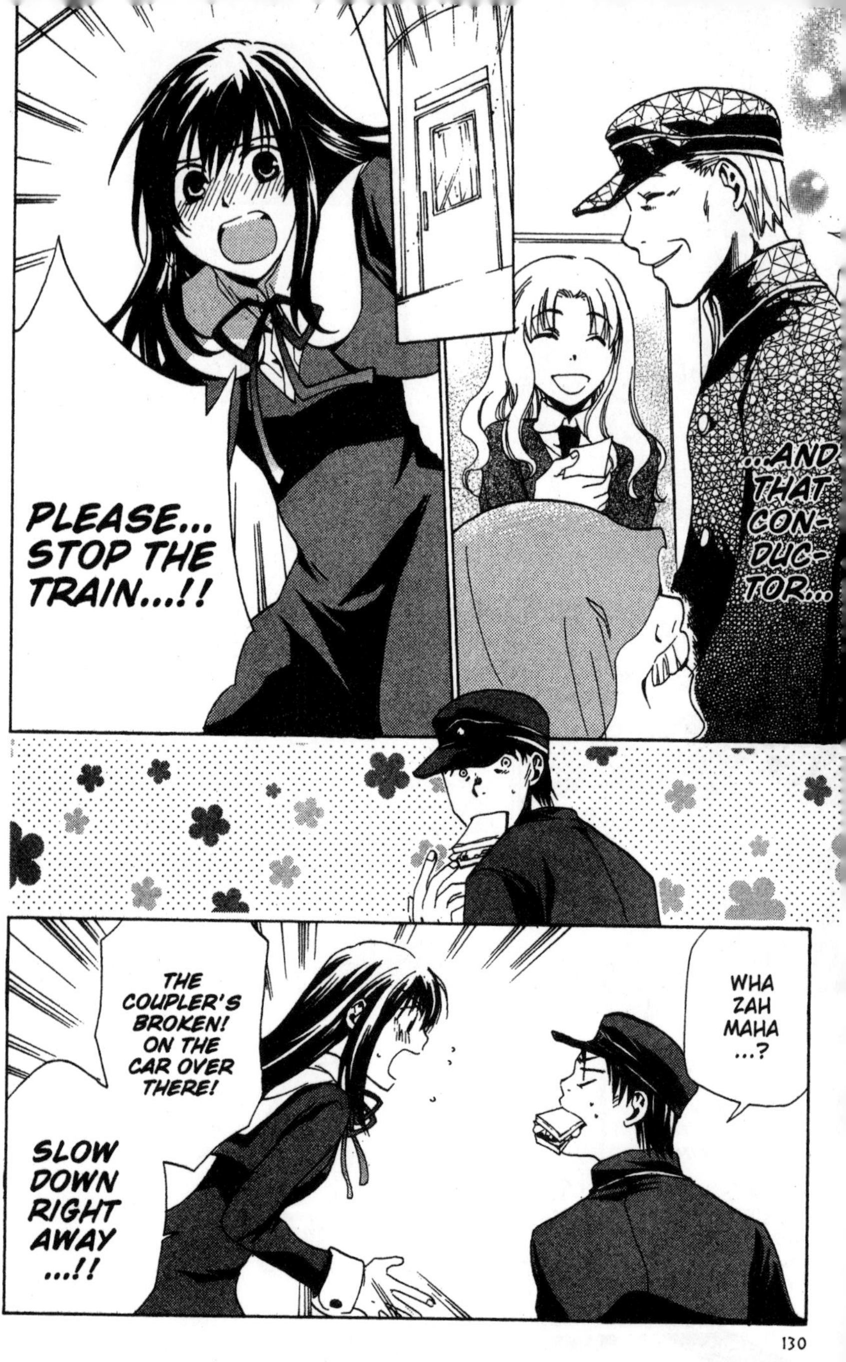
...AND THAT CONDUCTOR...
PLEASE... STOP THE TRAIN...!!
WHA ZAH MAHA ...?
THE COUPLER'S BROKEN! ON THE CAR OVER THERE!
SLOW DOWN RIGHT AWAY ...!!

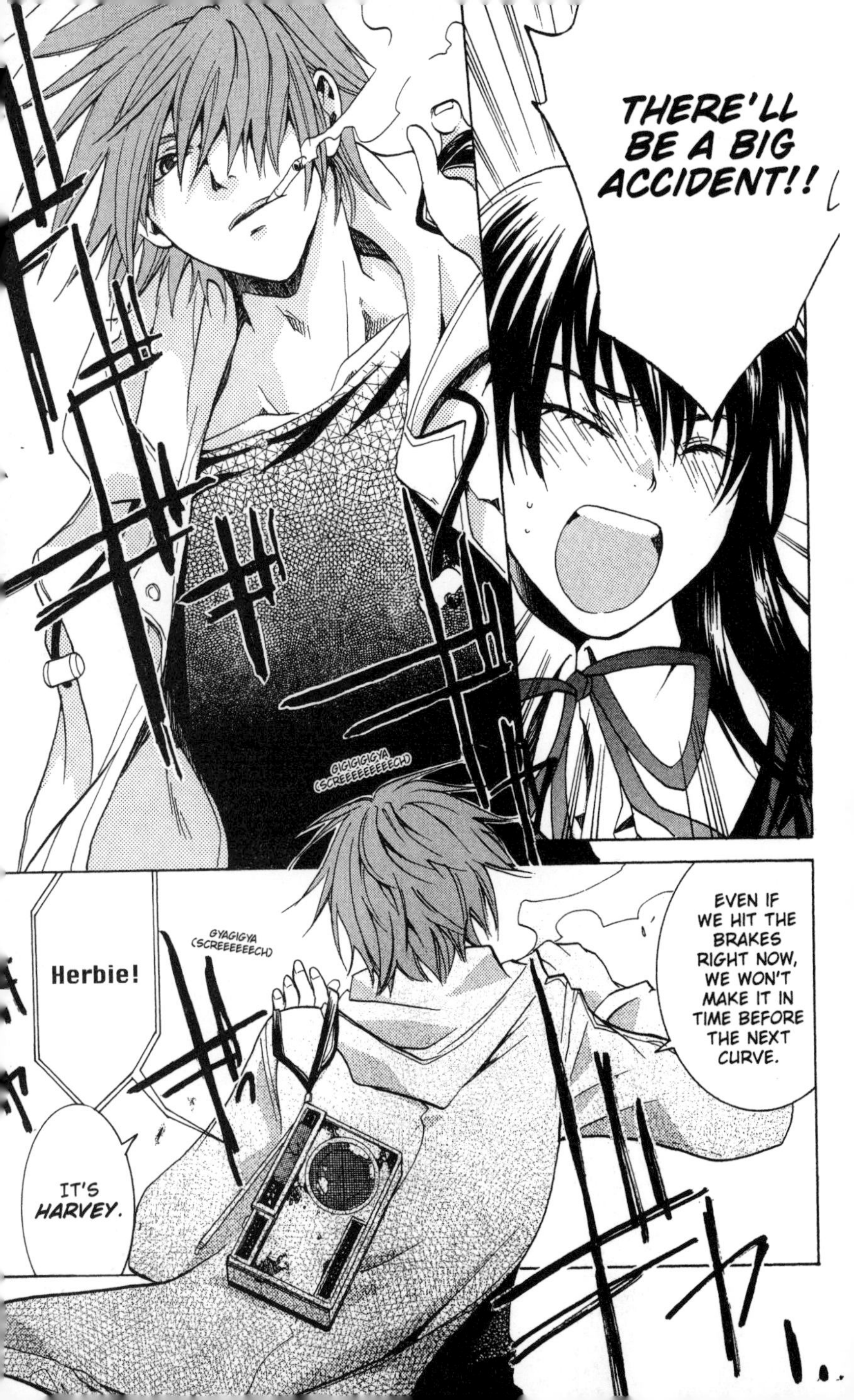
THERE'LL BE A BIG ACCIDENT!!
GIGIGIGIGYA (SCREEEEEEEEEECH)
EVEN IF WE HIT THE BRAKES RIGHT NOW, WE WON'T MAKE IT IN TIME BEFORE THE NEXT CURVE.
GYAGIGYA (SCREEEEEECH)
Herbie!
IT'S HARVEY.

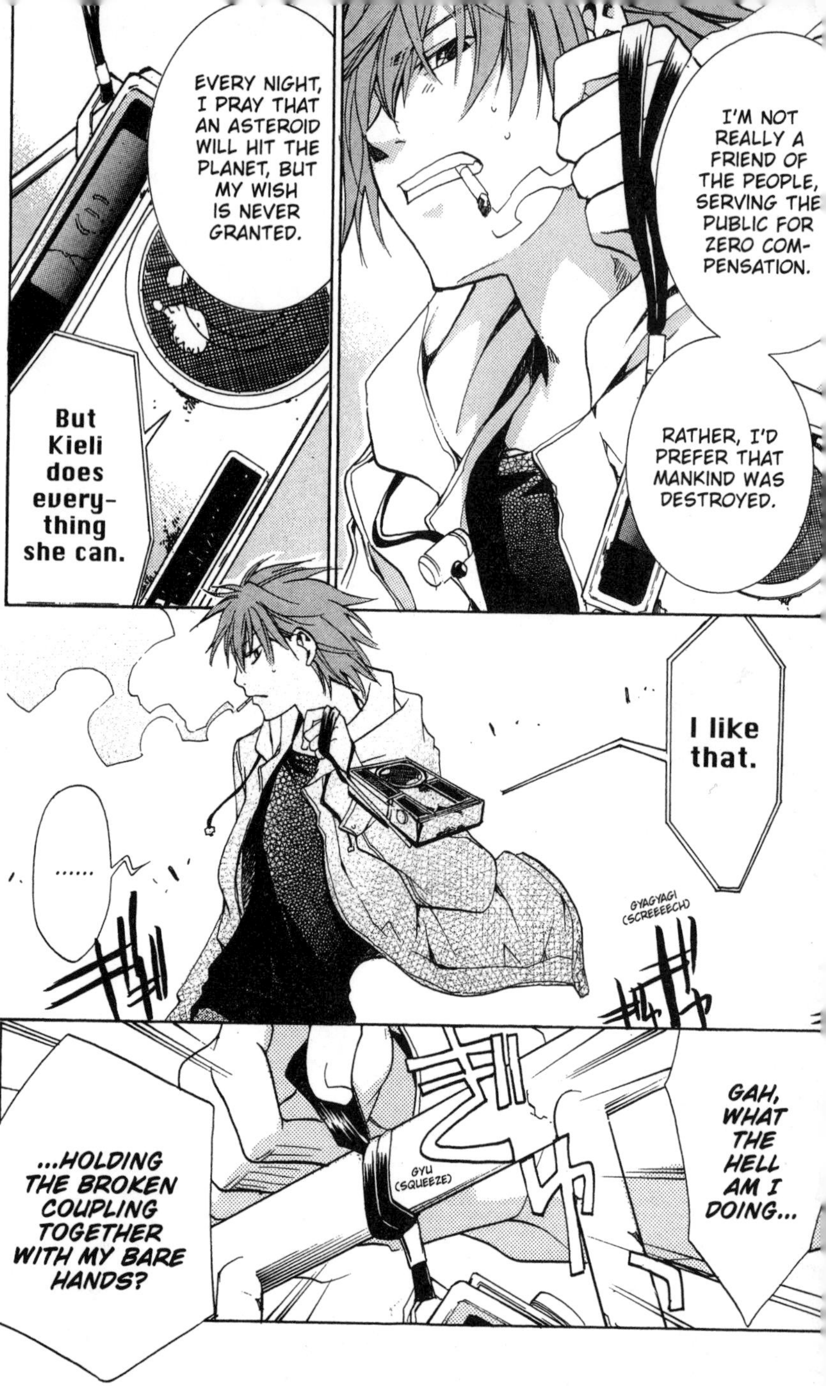
I'M NOT REALLY A FRIEND OF THE PEOPLE, SERVING THE PUBLIC FOR ZERO COMPENSATION.
RATHER, I'D PREFER THAT MANKIND WAS DESTROYED.
EVERY NIGHT, I PRAY THAT AN ASTEROID WILL HIT THE PLANET, BUT MY WISH IS NEVER GRANTED.
But Kieli does everything she can.
I like that.
......
GYAGYAGI (SCREEEECH)
GAH, WHAT THE HELL AM I DOING...
...HOLDING THE BROKEN COUPLING TOGETHER WITH MY BARE HANDS?
GYU (SQUEEZE)

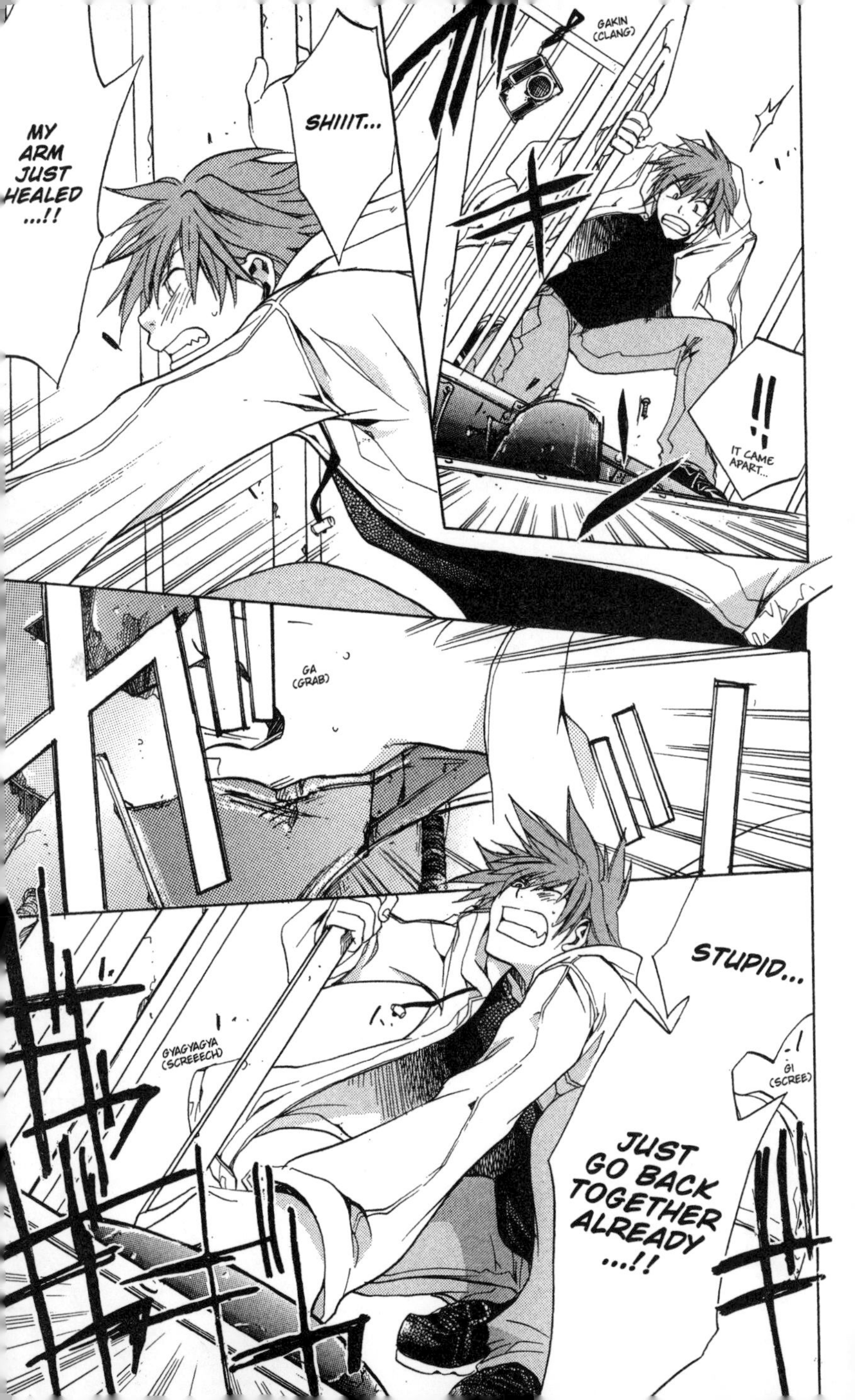
GAKIN (CLANG)
!!
IT CAME APART...
SHIIIT...
MY ARM JUST HEALED ...!!
GA (GRAB)
STUPID...
GI (SCREE)
JUST GO BACK TOGETHER ALREADY ...!!
GYAGYAGYA (SCREEECH)

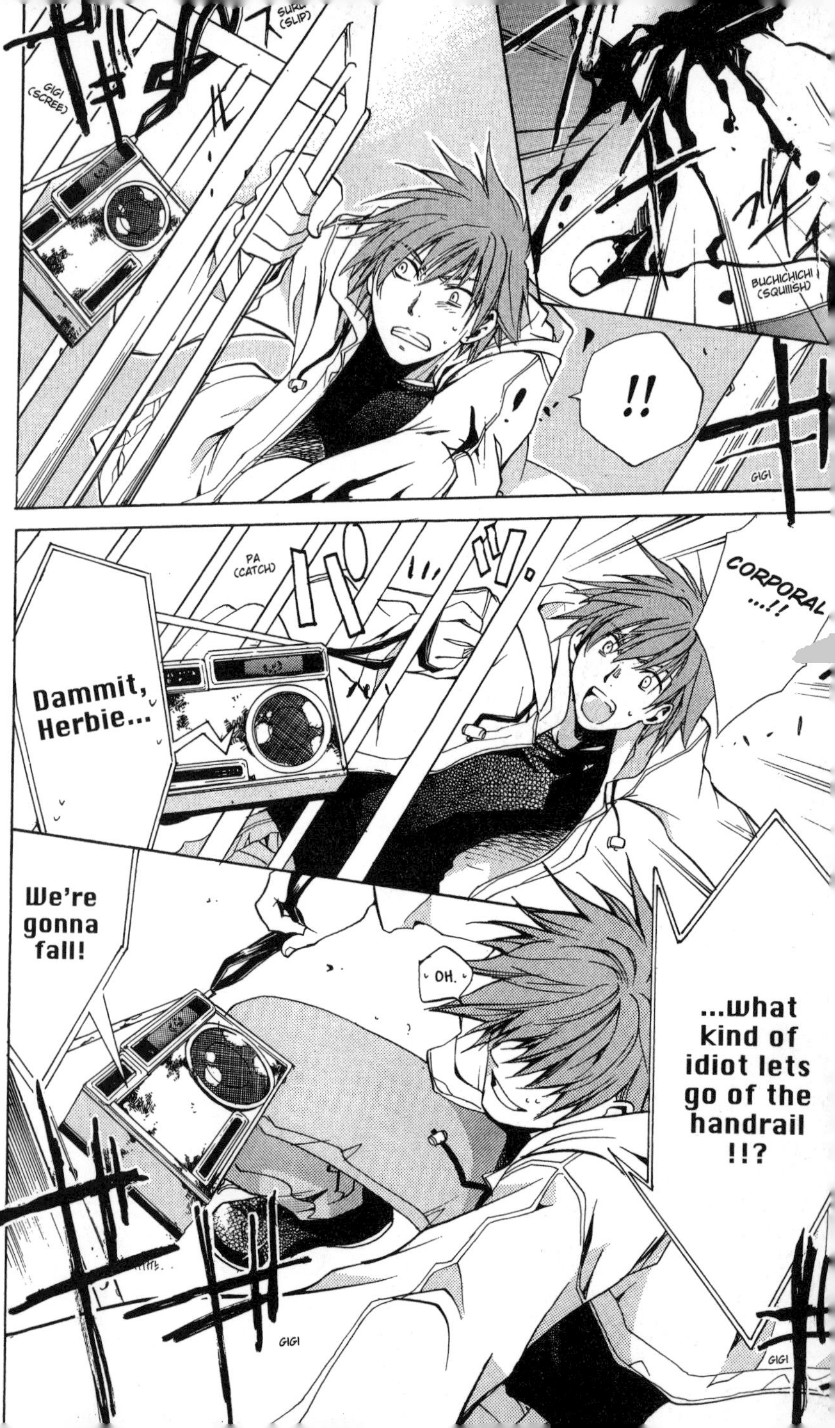
BUCHICHICHI (SQUIIISH)
GIGI
!!
SUR (SLIP)
GIGI (SCREE)
CORPORAL ...!!
PA (CATCH)
Dammit, Herbie...
...what kind of idiot lets go of the handrail !!?
OH.
We're gonna fall!
GIGI
GIGI

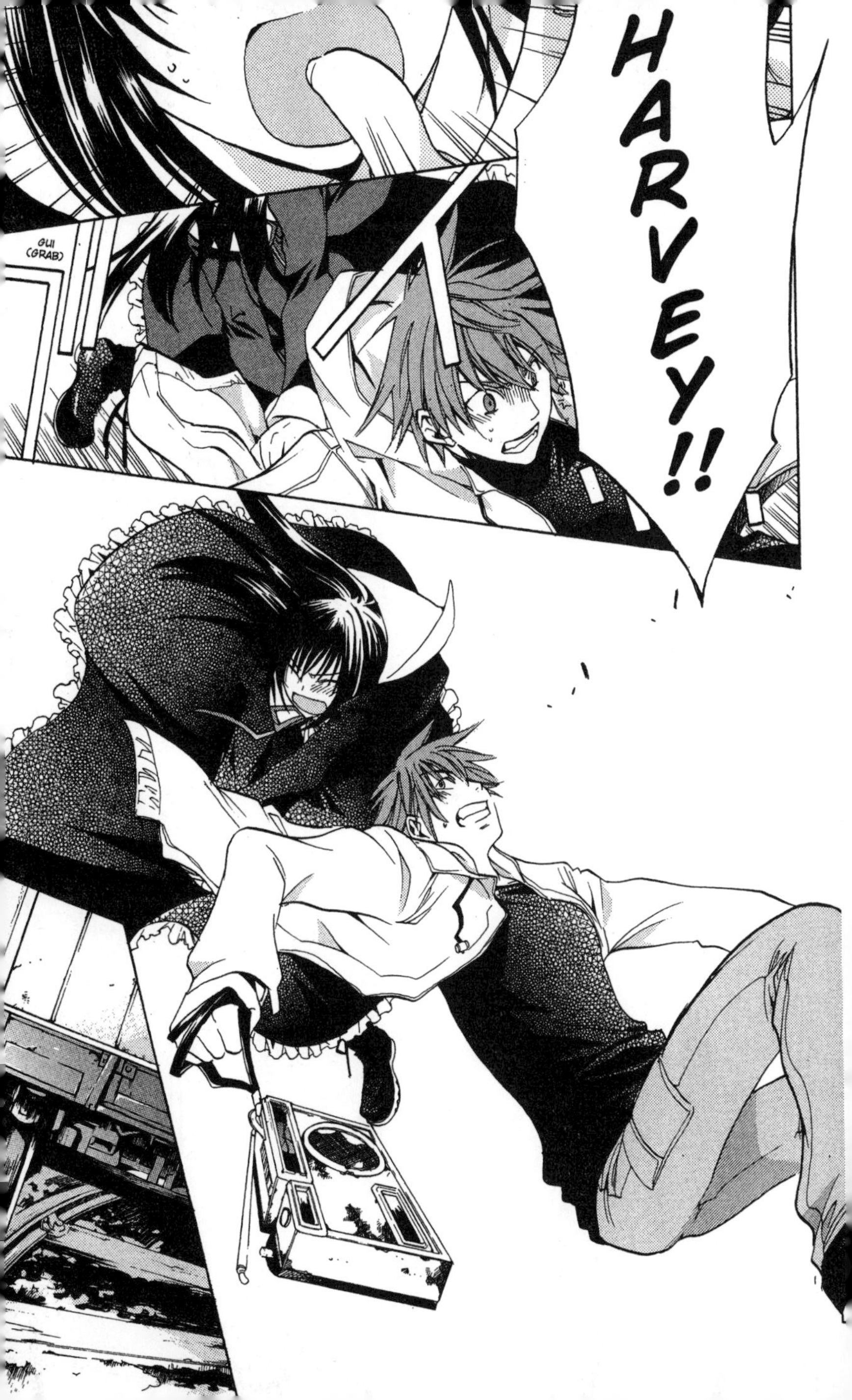
HARVEY!!
GUI (GRAB)

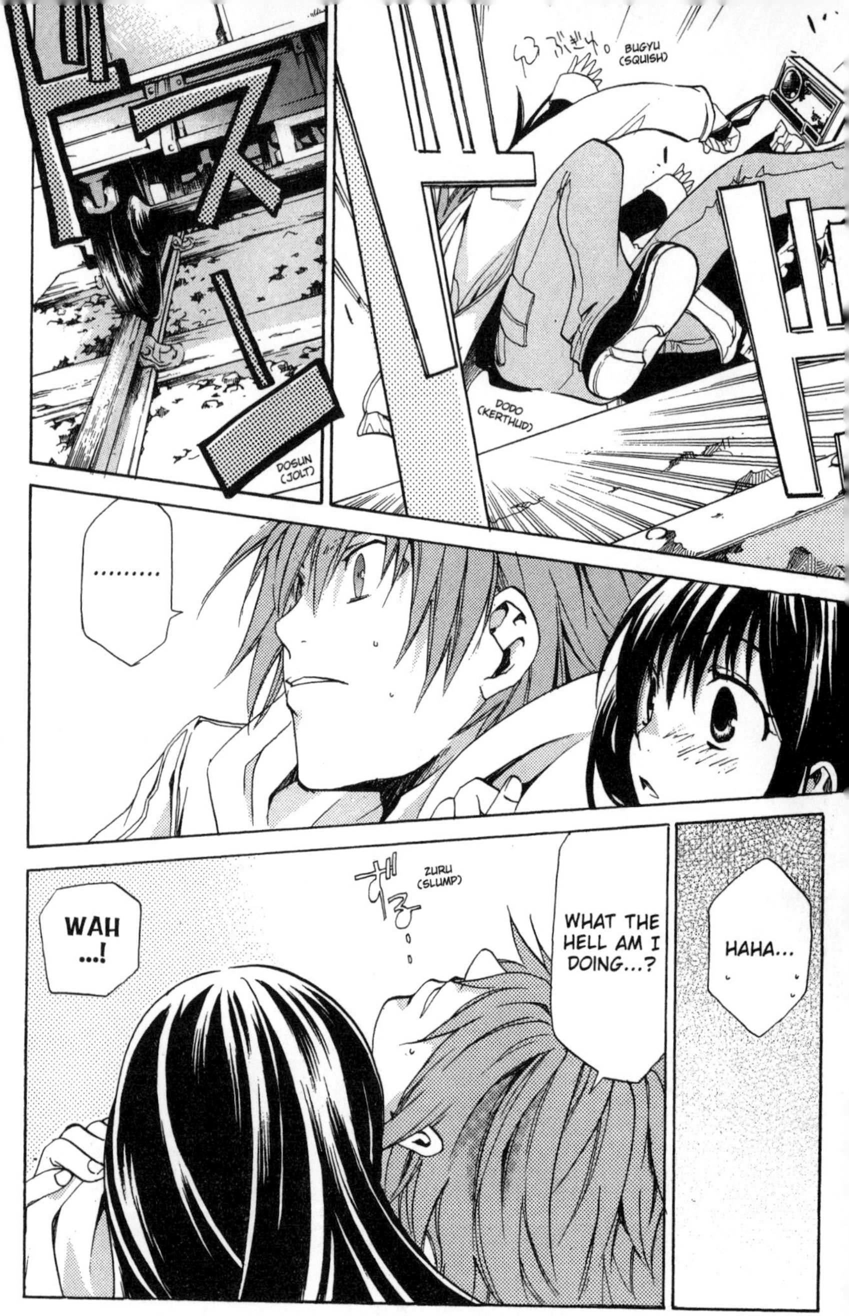
BUGYU (SQUISH)
DODO (KERTHUD)
DOSUN (JOLT)
....
HAHA...
WHAT THE HELL AM I DOING...?
ZURU (SLUMP)
WAH ...!

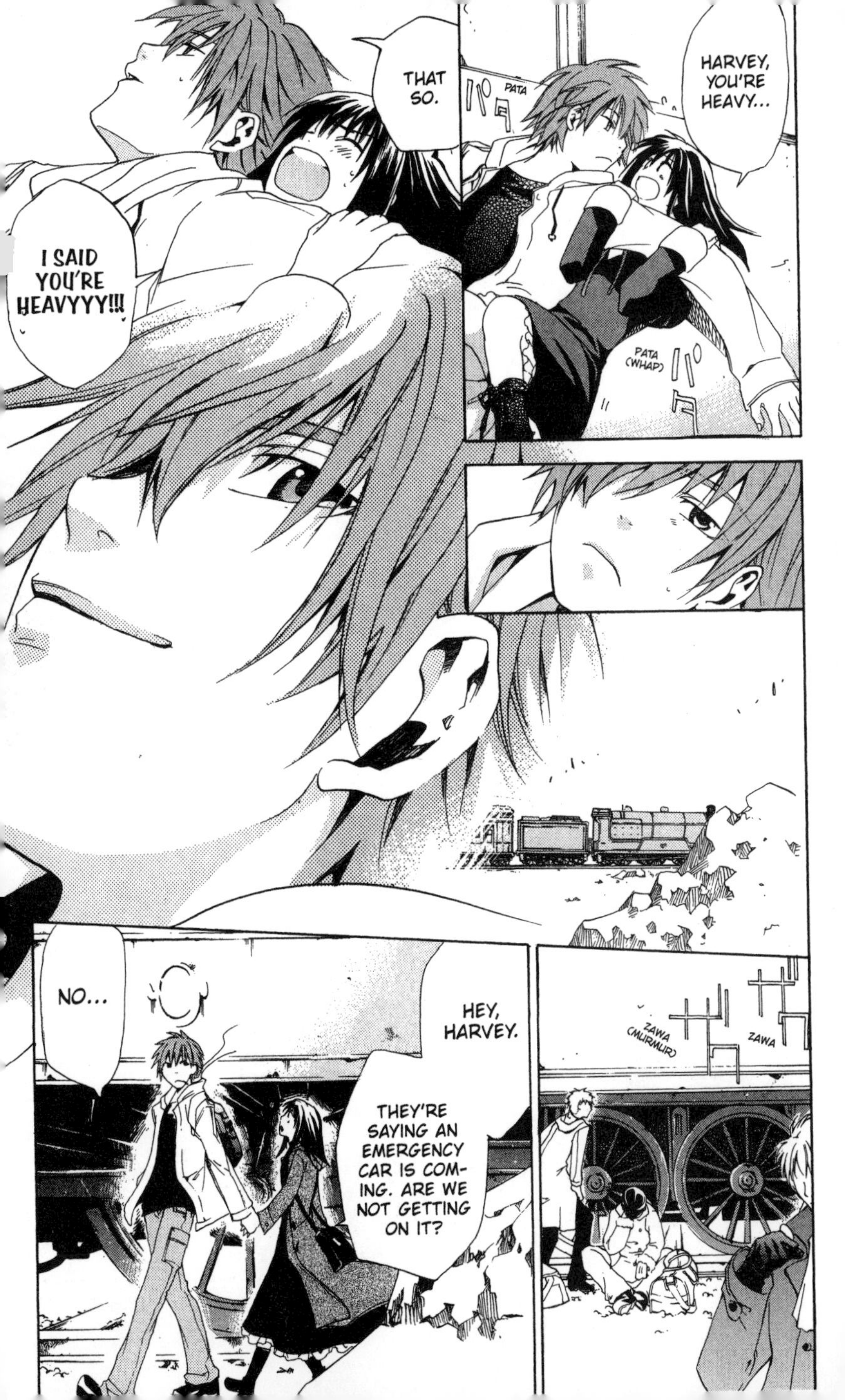
HARVEY, YOU'RE HEAVY...
PATA
PATA (WHAP)
THAT SO.
I SAID YOU'RE HEAVYYY!!!
ZAWA
ZAWA (MURMUR)
HEY, HARVEY.
THEY'RE SAYING AN EMERGENCY CAR IS COMING. ARE WE NOT GETTING ON IT?
NO...

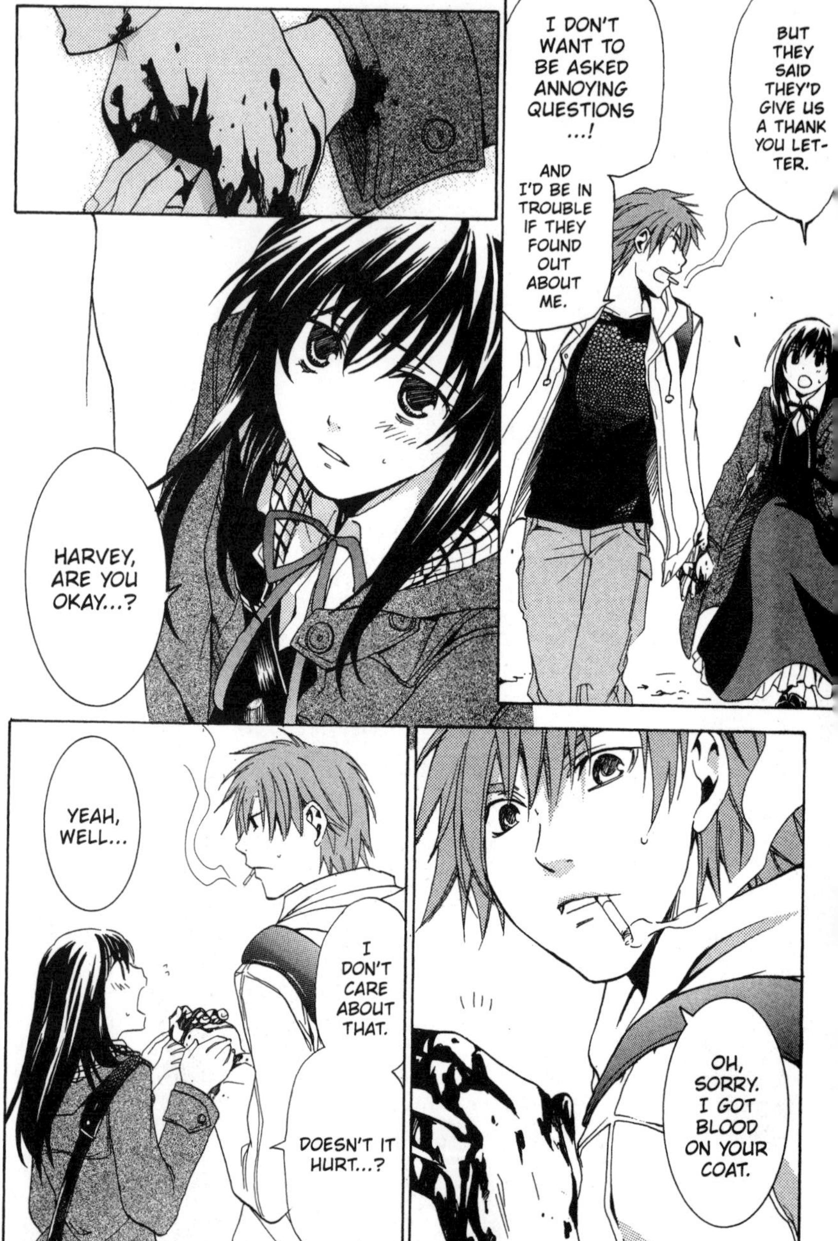
BUT THEY SAID THEY'D GIVE US A THANK YOU LET-TER.
I DON'T WANT TO BE ASKED ANNOYING QUESTIONS ...!
AND I'D BE IN TROUBLE IF THEY FOUND OUT ABOUT ME.
HARVEY, ARE YOU OKAY...?
OH, SORRY. I GOT BLOOD ON YOUR COAT.
YEAH, WELL...
I DON'T CARE ABOUT THAT.
DOESN'T IT HURT...?

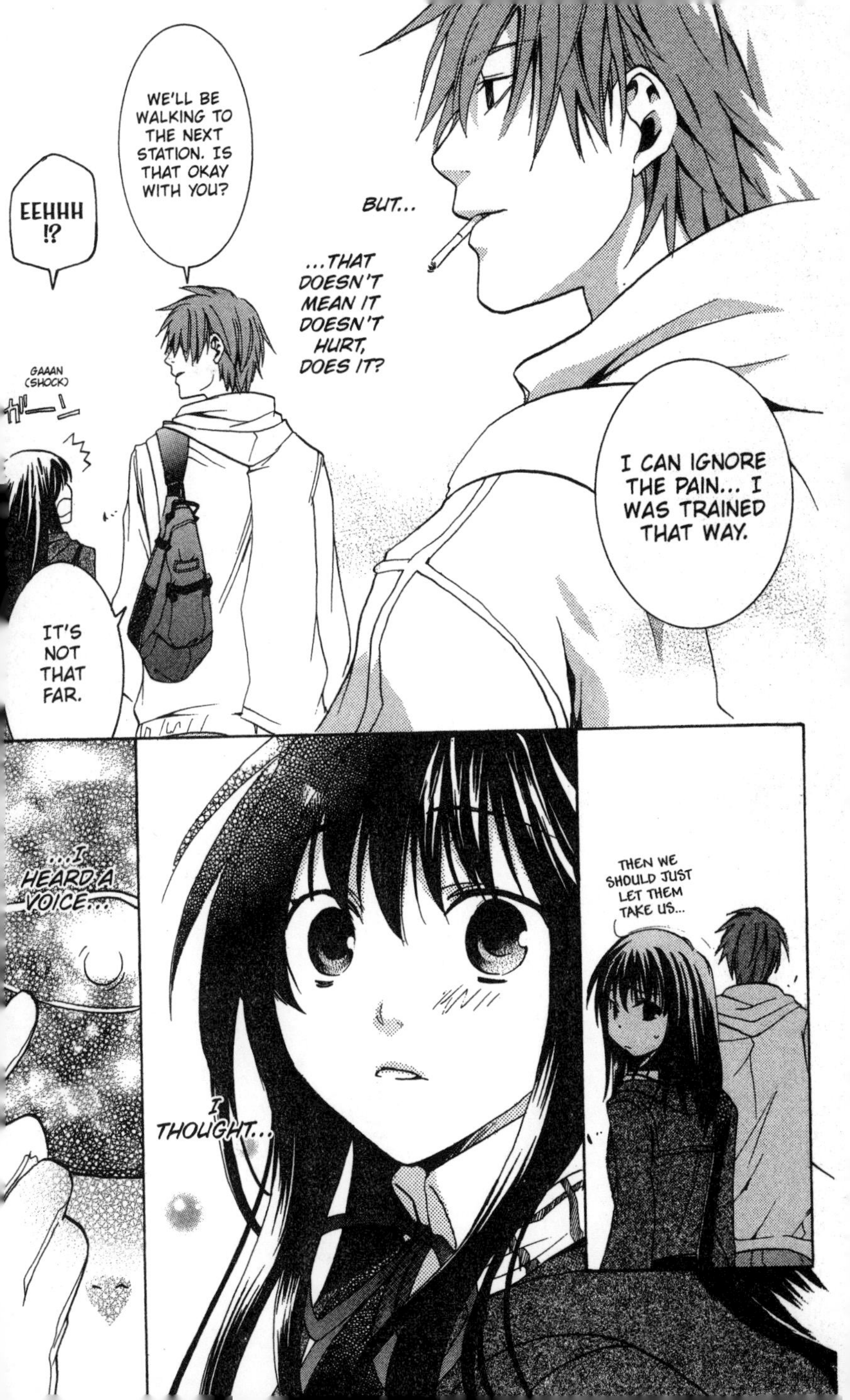
I CAN IGNORE THE PAIN... I WAS TRAINED THAT WAY.
BUT...
...THAT DOESN'T MEAN IT DOESN'T HURT, DOES IT?
WE'LL BE WALKING TO THE NEXT STATION. IS THAT OKAY WITH YOU?
EEHHH!?
GAAAN (SHOCK)
IT'S NOT THAT FAR.
THEN WE SHOULD JUST LET THEM TAKE US...
I THOUGHT...
...I HEARD A VOICE...

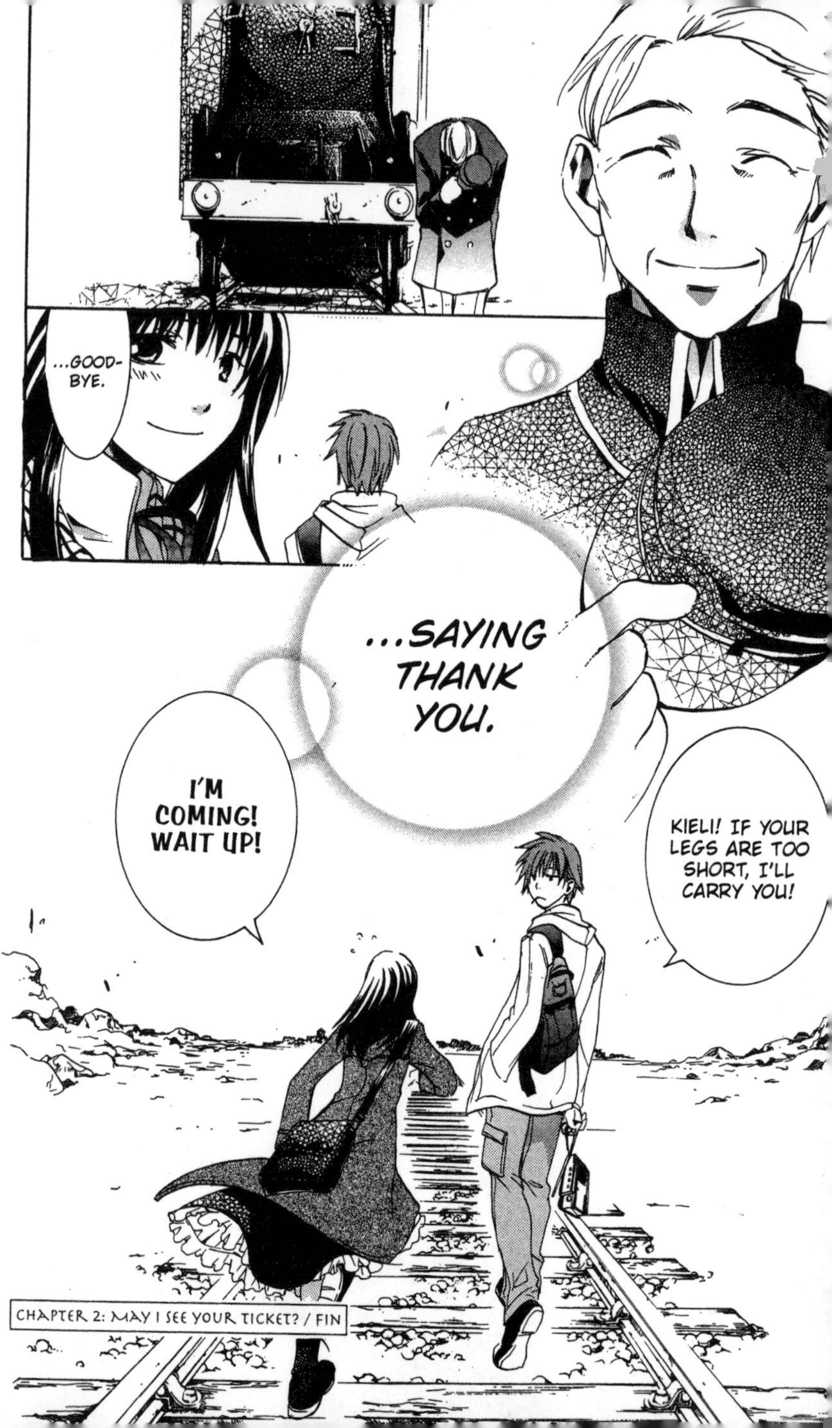
...GOOD-BYE.
...SAYING THANK YOU.
KIELI! IF YOUR LEGS ARE TOO SHORT, I'LL CARRY YOU!
I'M COMING! WAIT UP!
CHAPTER 2: MAY I SEE YOUR TICKET? / FIN

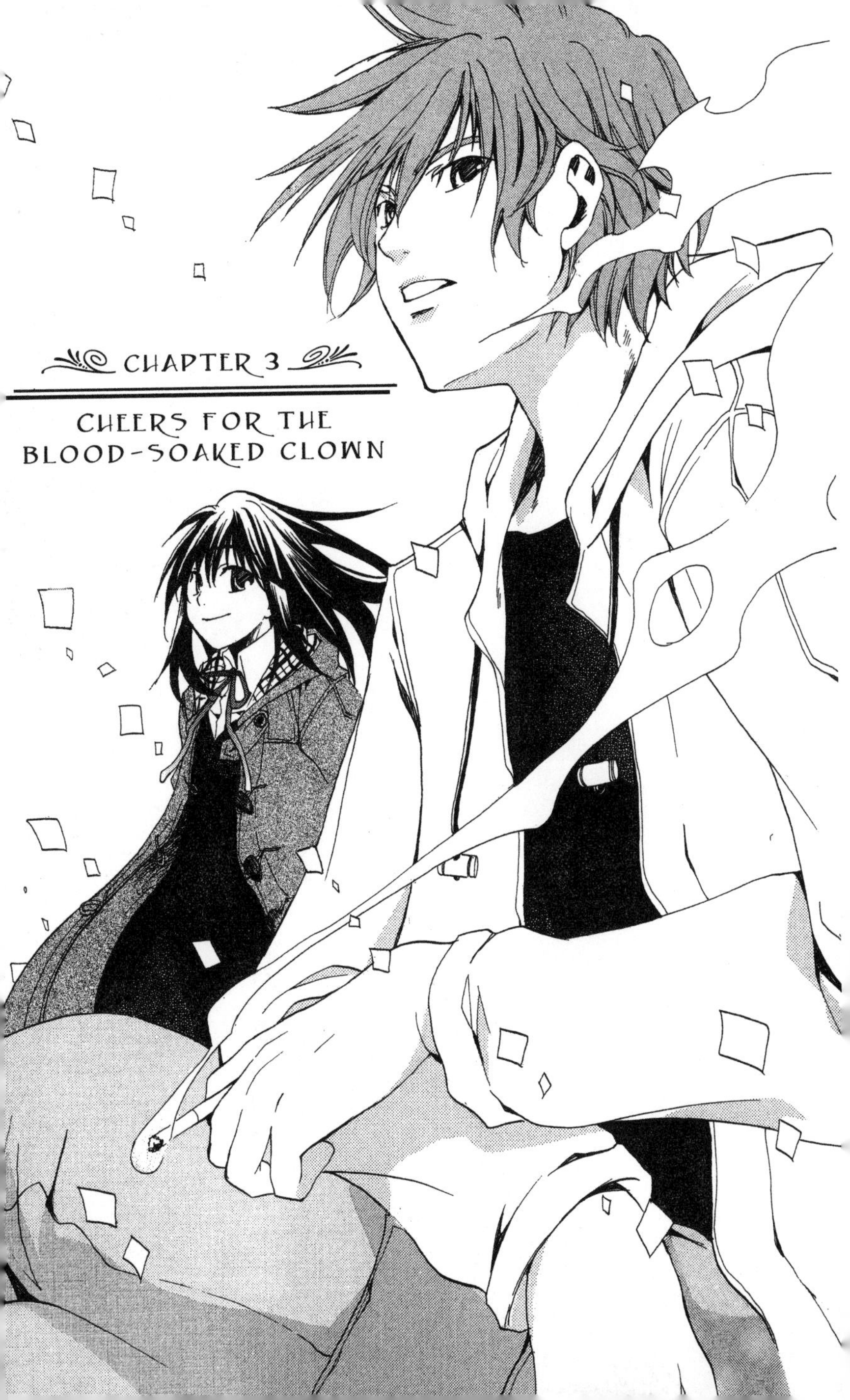
CHAPTER 3
CHEERS FOR THE BLOOD-SOAKED CLOWN

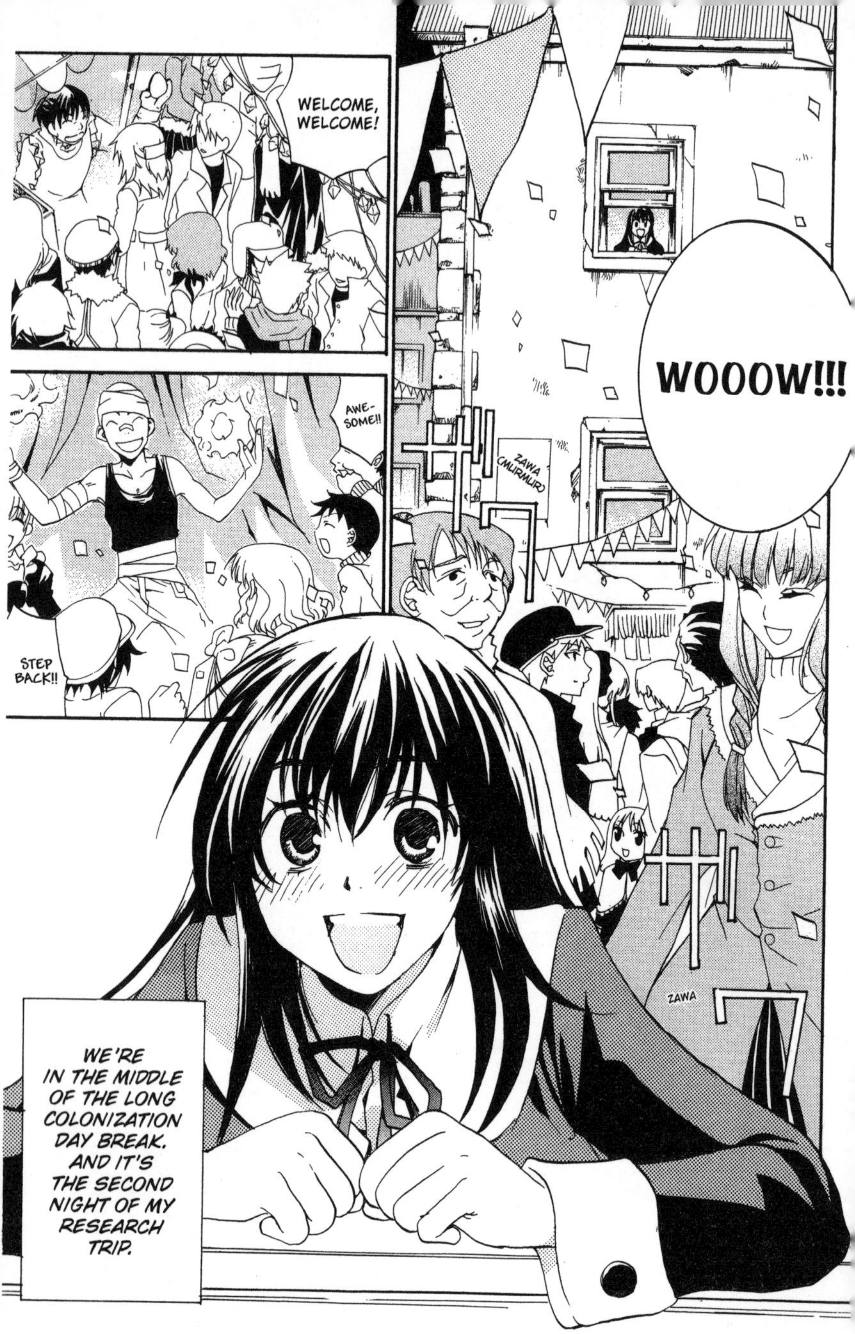

WOOOW!!!
ZAWA (MURMUR)
ZAWA
WE'RE IN THE MIDDLE OF THE LONG COLONIZATION DAY BREAK. AND IT'S THE SECOND NIGHT OF MY RESEARCH TRIP.
WELCOME, WELCOME!
AWE-SOME!!
STEP BACK!!

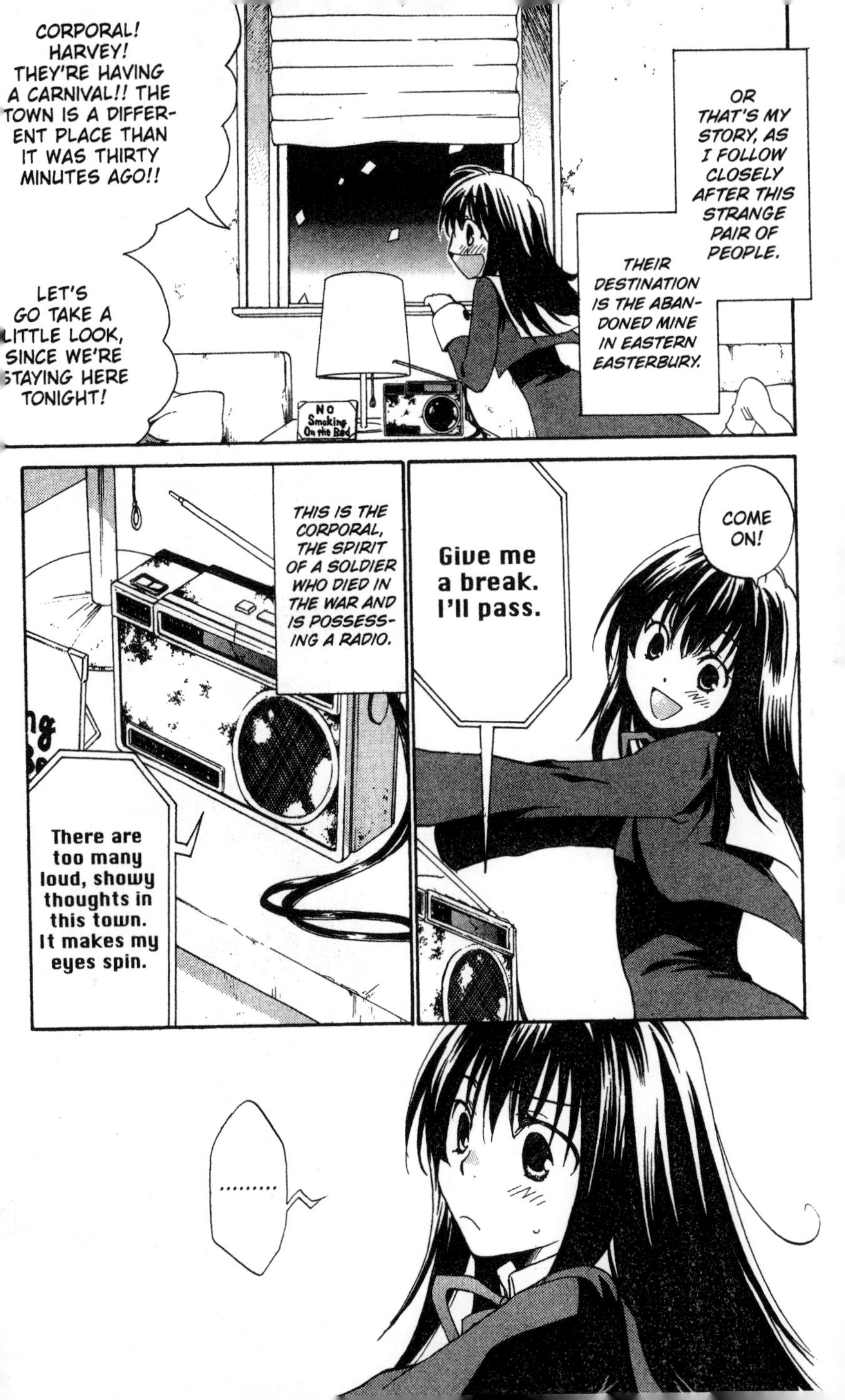
OR THAT'S MY STORY, AS I FOLLOW CLOSELY AFTER THIS STRANGE PAIR OF PEOPLE.
THEIR DESTINATION IS THE ABANDONED MINE IN EASTERN EASTERBURY.
CORPORAL! HARVEY! THEY'RE HAVING A CARNIVAL!! THE TOWN IS A DIFFERENT PLACE THAN IT WAS THIRTY MINUTES AGO!!
LET'S GO TAKE A LITTLE LOOK, SINCE WE'RE STAYING HERE TONIGHT!
No Smoking On the Bed
COME ON!
Give me a break. I'll pass.
THIS IS THE CORPORAL, THE SPIRIT OF A SOLDIER WHO DIED IN THE WAR AND IS POSSESSING A RADIO.
There are too many loud, showy thoughts in this town. It makes my eyes spin.
....

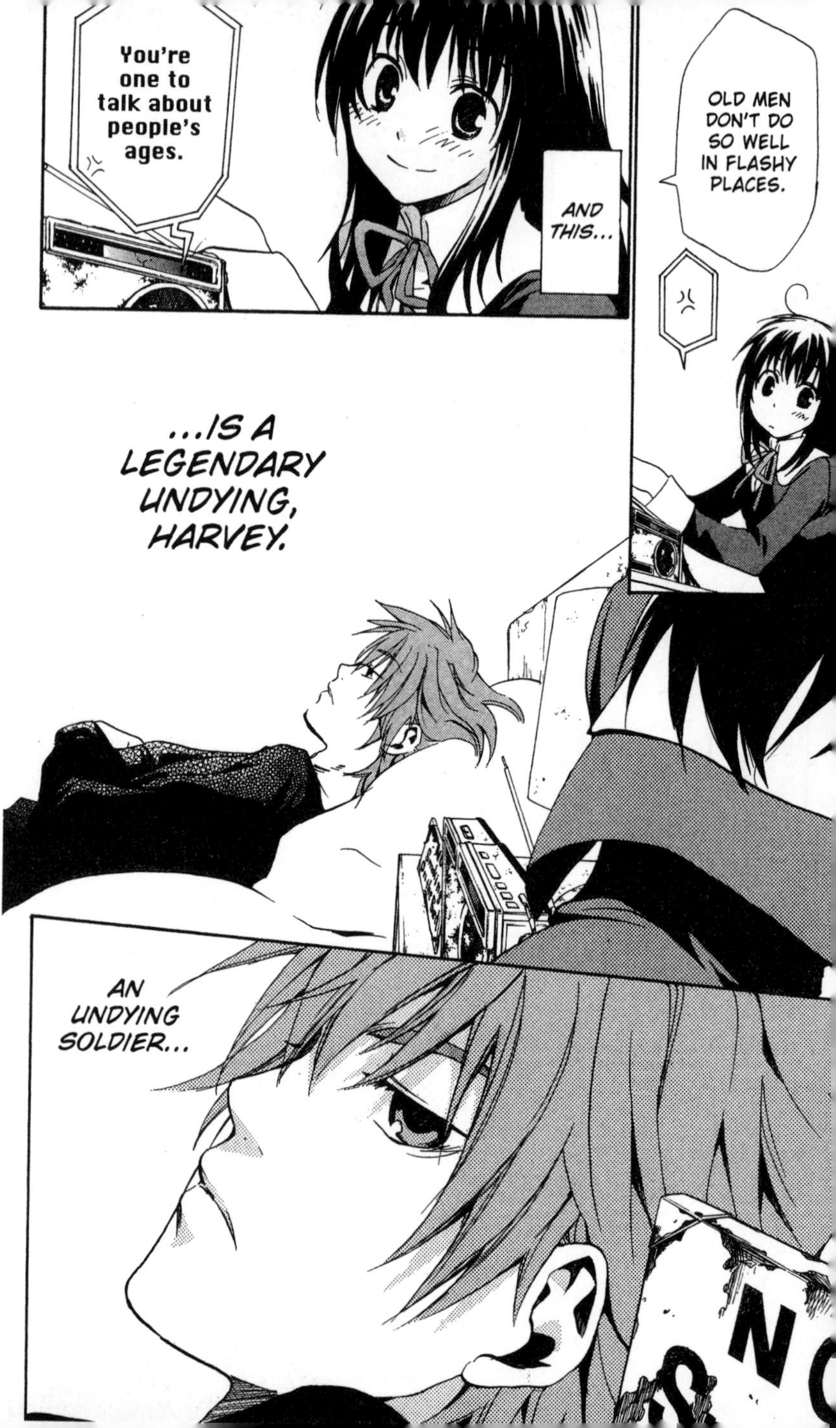
OLD MEN DON'T DO SO WELL IN FLASHY PLACES.
You're one to talk about people's ages.
AND THIS...
...IS A LEGENDARY UNDYING, HARVEY.
AN UNDYING SOLDIER...

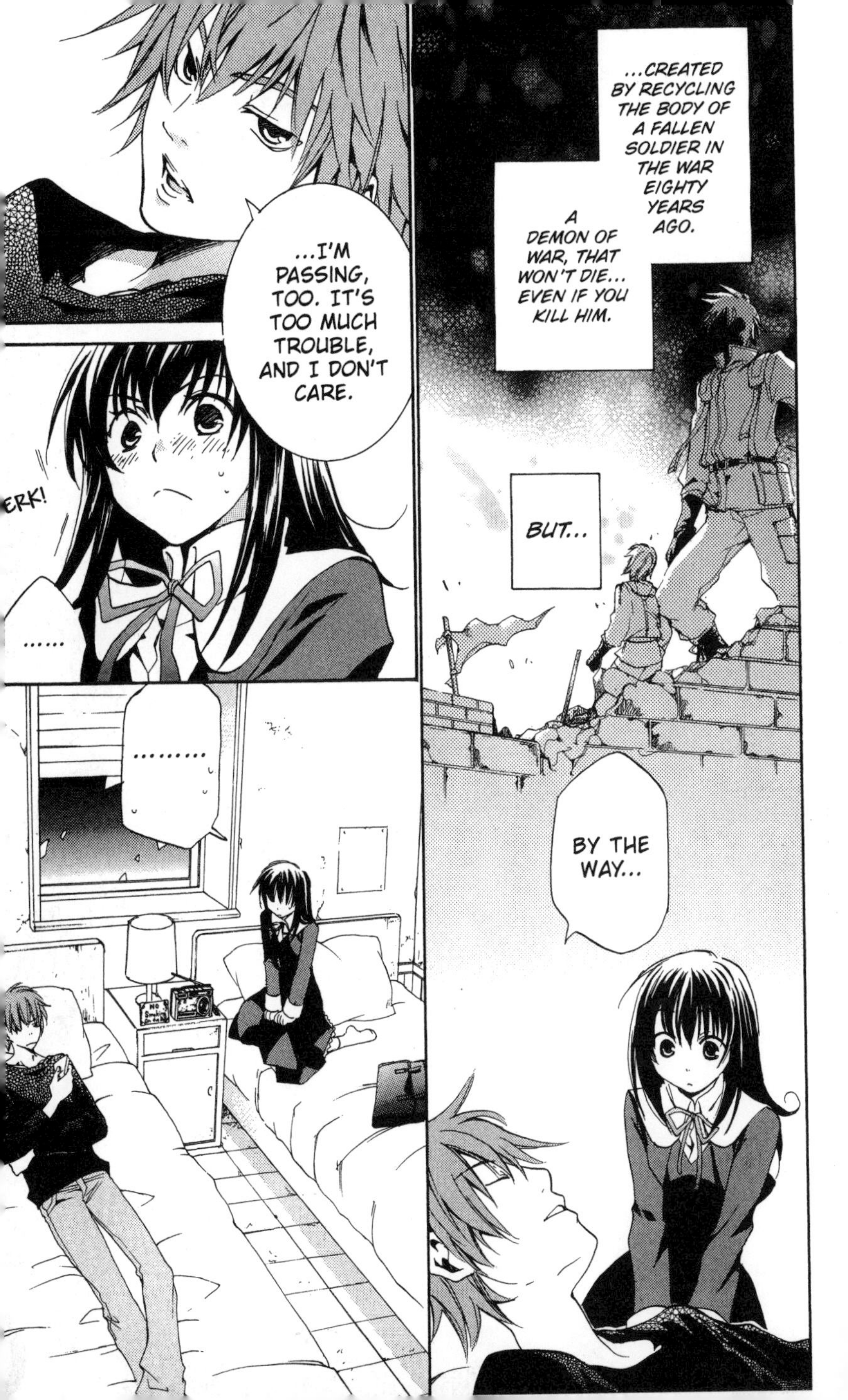
...CREATED BY RECYCLING THE BODY OF A FALLEN SOLDIER IN THE WAR EIGHTY YEARS AGO.
A DEMON OF WAR, THAT WON'T DIE... EVEN IF YOU KILL HIM.
BUT...
BY THE WAY...
...I'M PASSING, TOO. IT'S TOO MUCH TROUBLE, AND I DON'T CARE.
ERK!
......
....

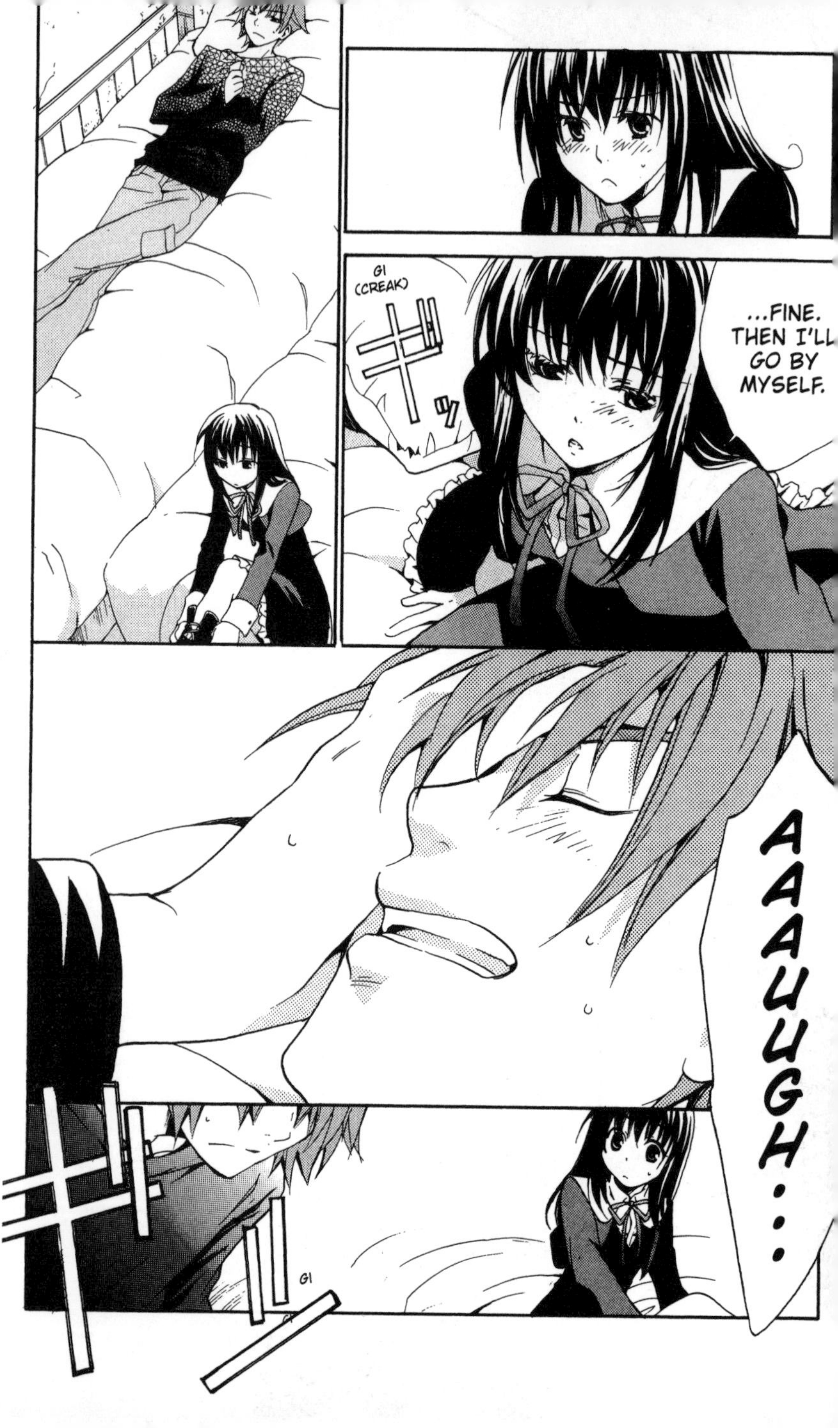
GI
(CREAK)
...FINE. THEN I'LL GO BY MYSELF.
AAAUUGH...
GI

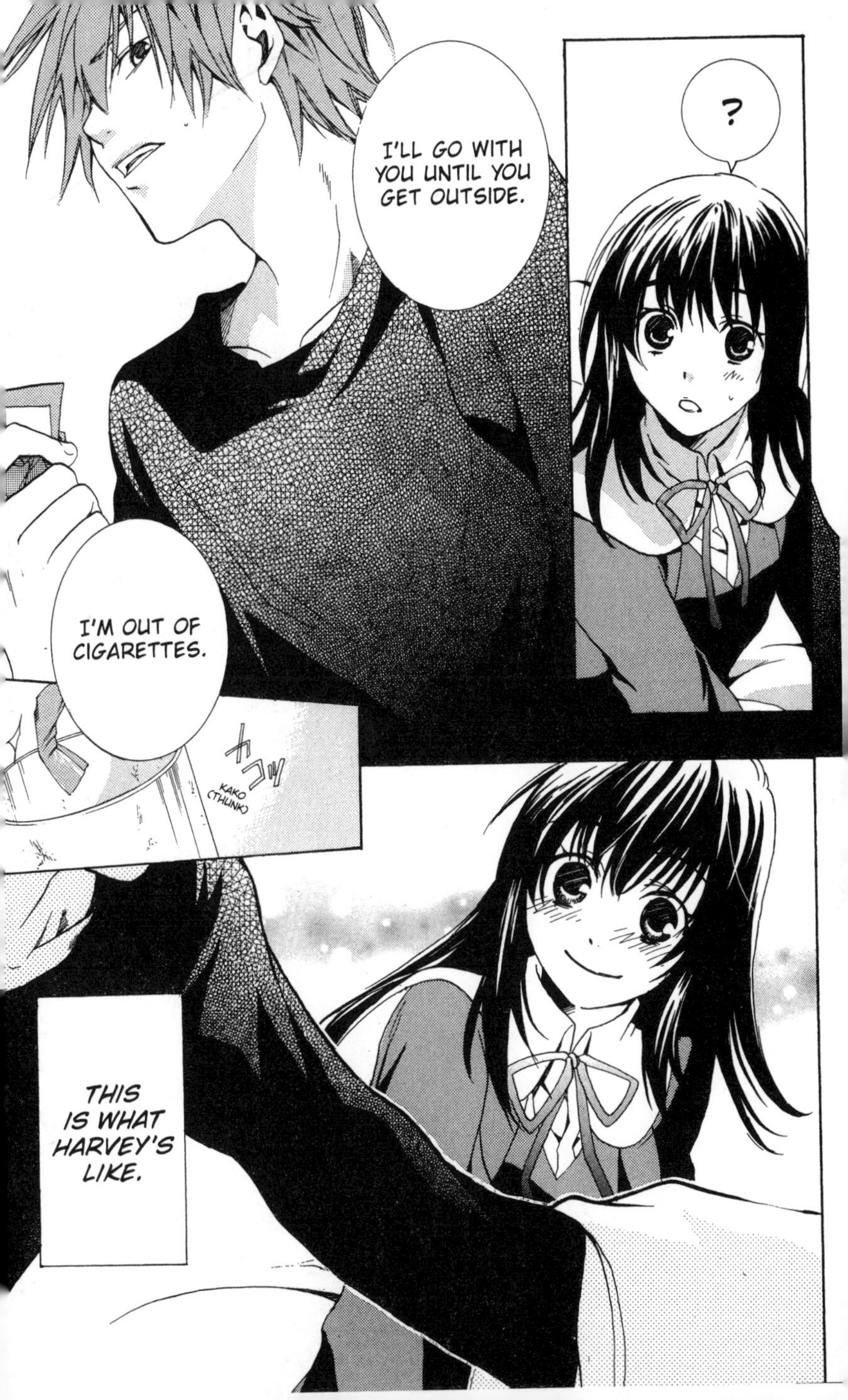
?
I'LL GO WITH YOU UNTIL YOU GET OUTSIDE.
I'M OUT OF CIGARETTES.
カコッ
KAKO (THUNK)
THIS IS WHAT HARVEY'S LIKE.

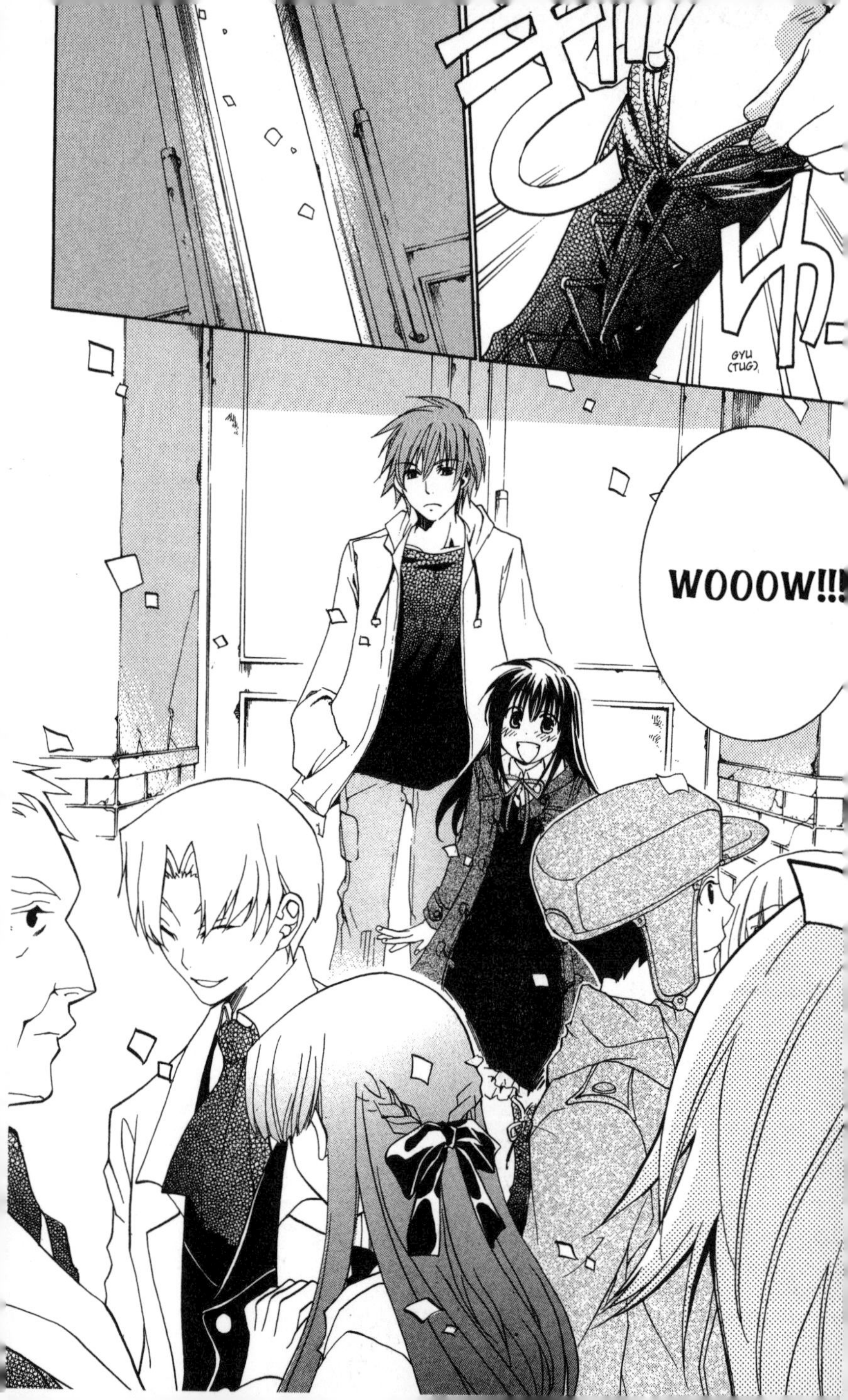
GYU (TUG)
WOOOW!!!

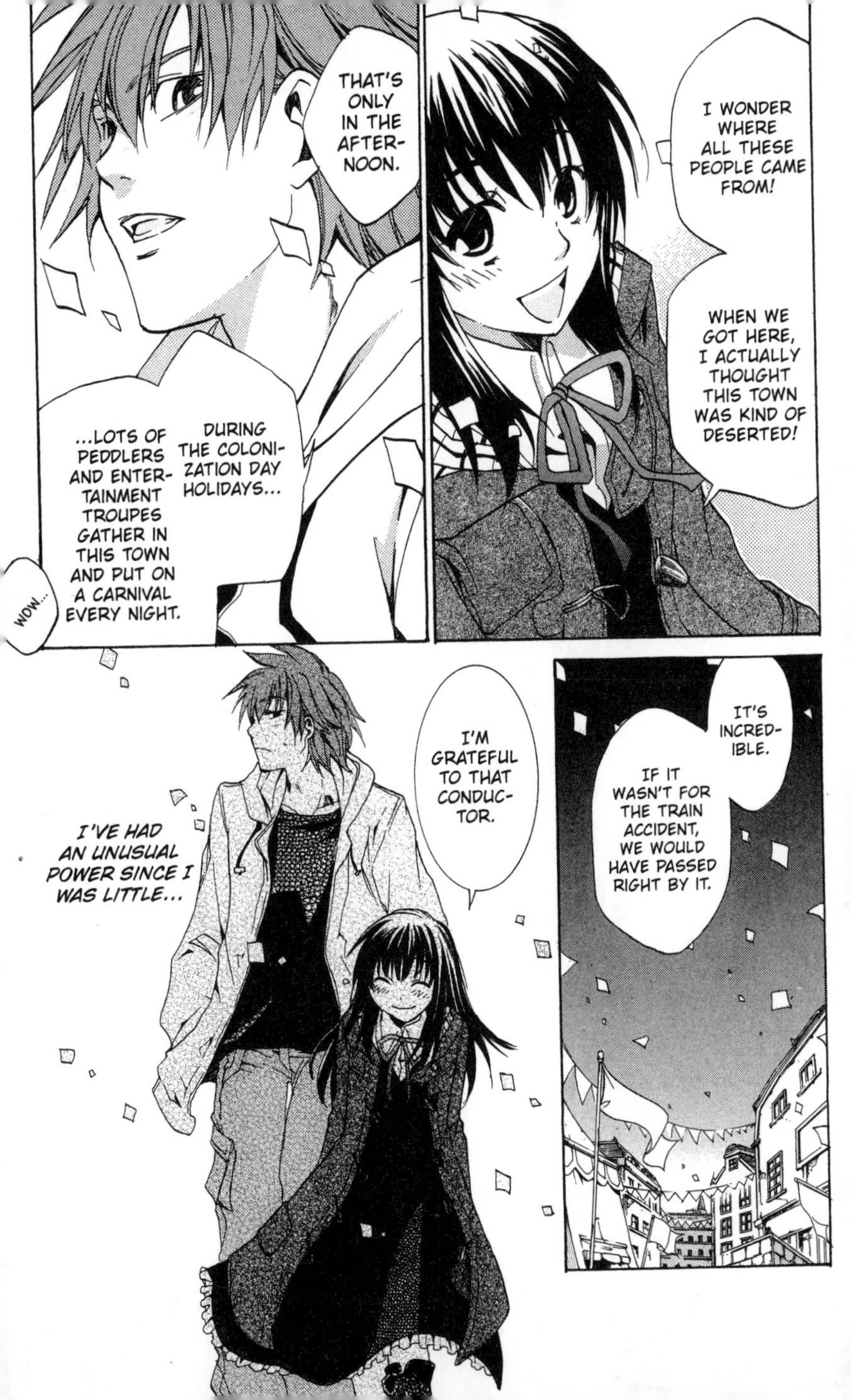
I WONDER WHERE ALL THESE PEOPLE CAME FROM!
WHEN WE GOT HERE, I ACTUALLY THOUGHT THIS TOWN WAS KIND OF DESERTED!
THAT'S ONLY IN THE AFTER-NOON.
DURING THE COLONI-ZATION DAY HOLIDAYS...
...LOTS OF PEDDLERS AND ENTER-TAINMENT TROUPES GATHER IN THIS TOWN AND PUT ON A CARNIVAL EVERY NIGHT.
WOW...
IT'S INCRED-IBLE.
IF IT WASN'T FOR THE TRAIN ACCIDENT, WE WOULD HAVE PASSED RIGHT BY IT.
I'M GRATEFUL TO THAT CONDUC-TOR.
I'VE HAD AN UNUSUAL POWER SINCE I WAS LITTLE...

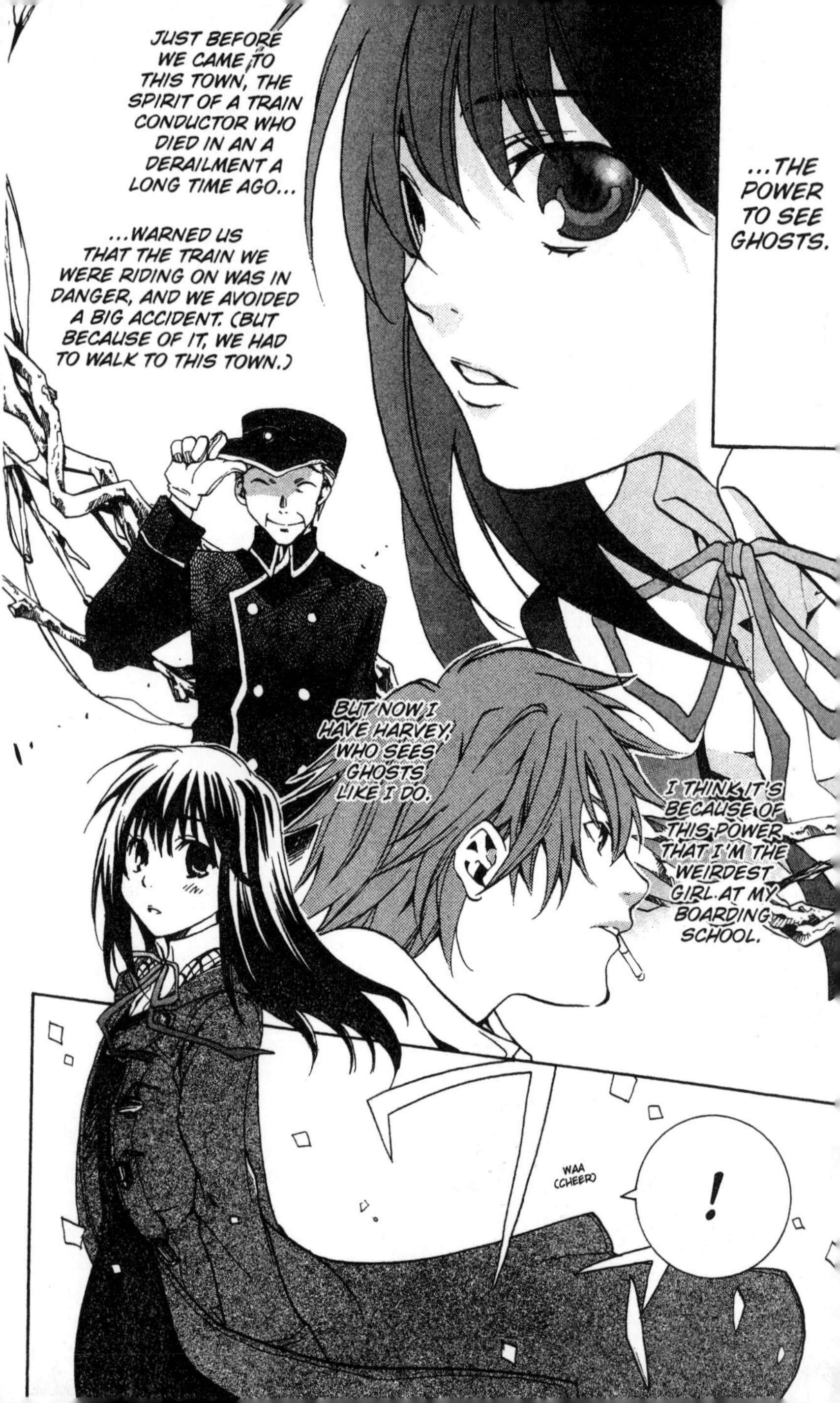
...THE POWER TO SEE GHOSTS.
JUST BEFORE WE CAME TO THIS TOWN, THE SPIRIT OF A TRAIN CONDUCTOR WHO DIED IN AN A DERAILMENT A LONG TIME AGO...
...WARNED US THAT THE TRAIN WE WERE RIDING ON WAS IN DANGER, AND WE AVOIDED A BIG ACCIDENT. (BUT BECAUSE OF IT, WE HAD TO WALK TO THIS TOWN.)
I THINK IT'S BECAUSE OF THIS POWER THAT I'M THE WEIRDEST GIRL AT MY BOARDING SCHOOL.
BUT NOW I HAVE HARVEY, WHO SEES GHOSTS LIKE I DO.
!
WAA (CHEER)

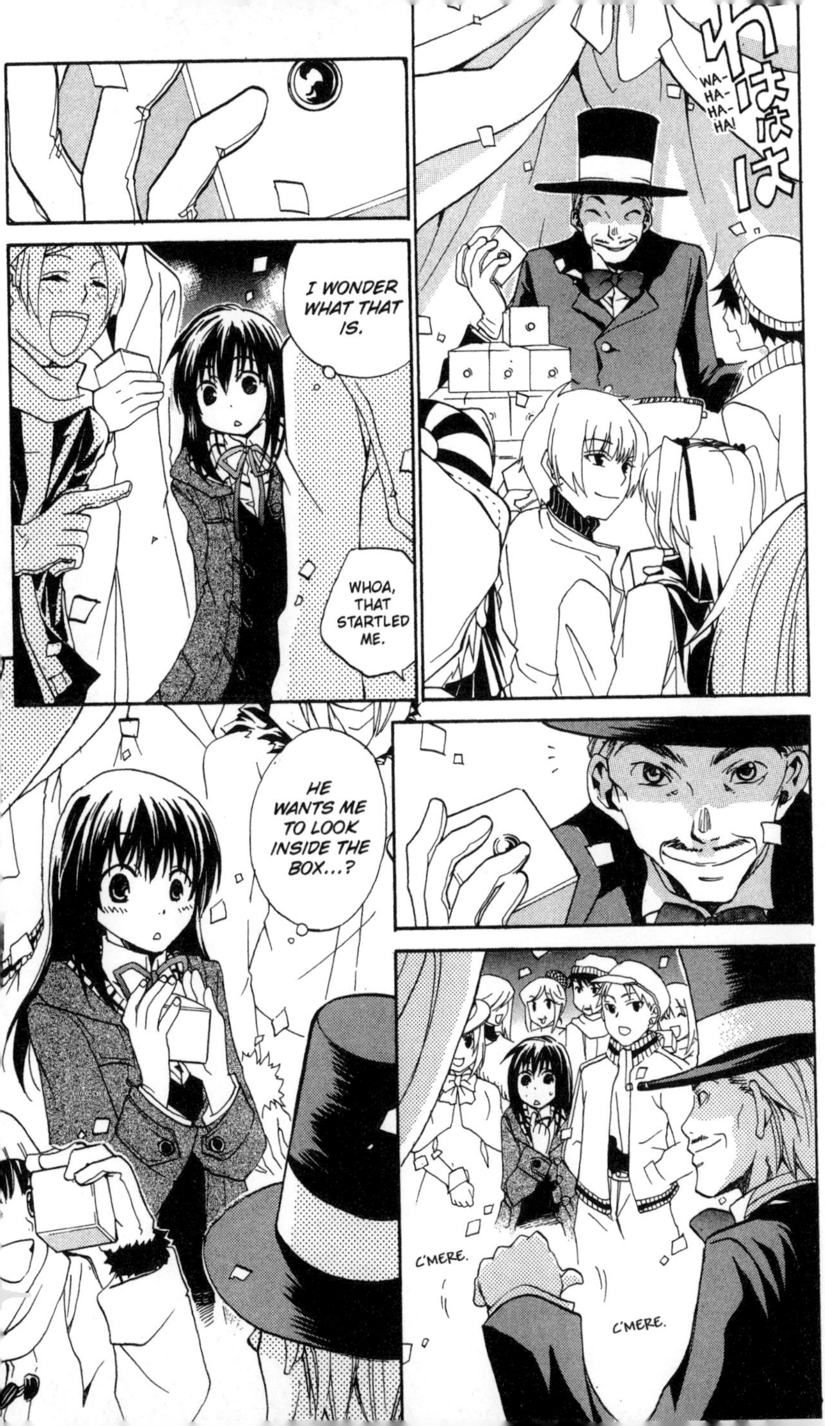
わははは
WA-HA-HA-HA!
I WONDER WHAT THAT IS.
WHOA, THAT STARTLED ME.
C'MERE.
C'MERE.
HE WANTS ME TO LOOK INSIDE THE BOX...?

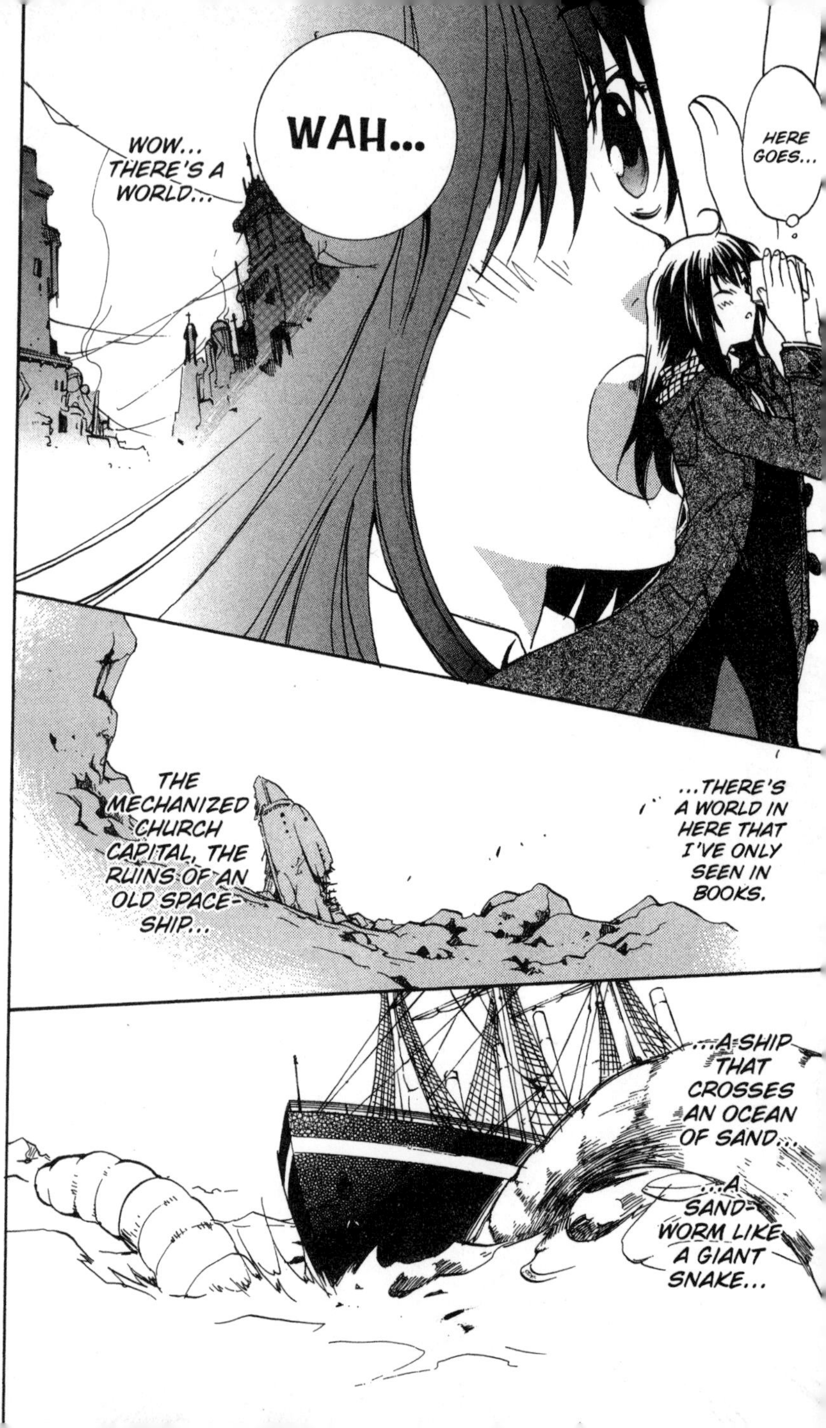
HERE GOES...
WAH...
WOW... THERE'S A WORLD...
...THERE'S A WORLD IN HERE THAT I'VE ONLY SEEN IN BOOKS.
THE MECHANIZED CHURCH CAPITAL, THE RUINS OF AN OLD SPACE-SHIP...
...A SHIP THAT CROSSES AN OCEAN OF SAND...
...A SAND-WORM LIKE A GIANT SNAKE...

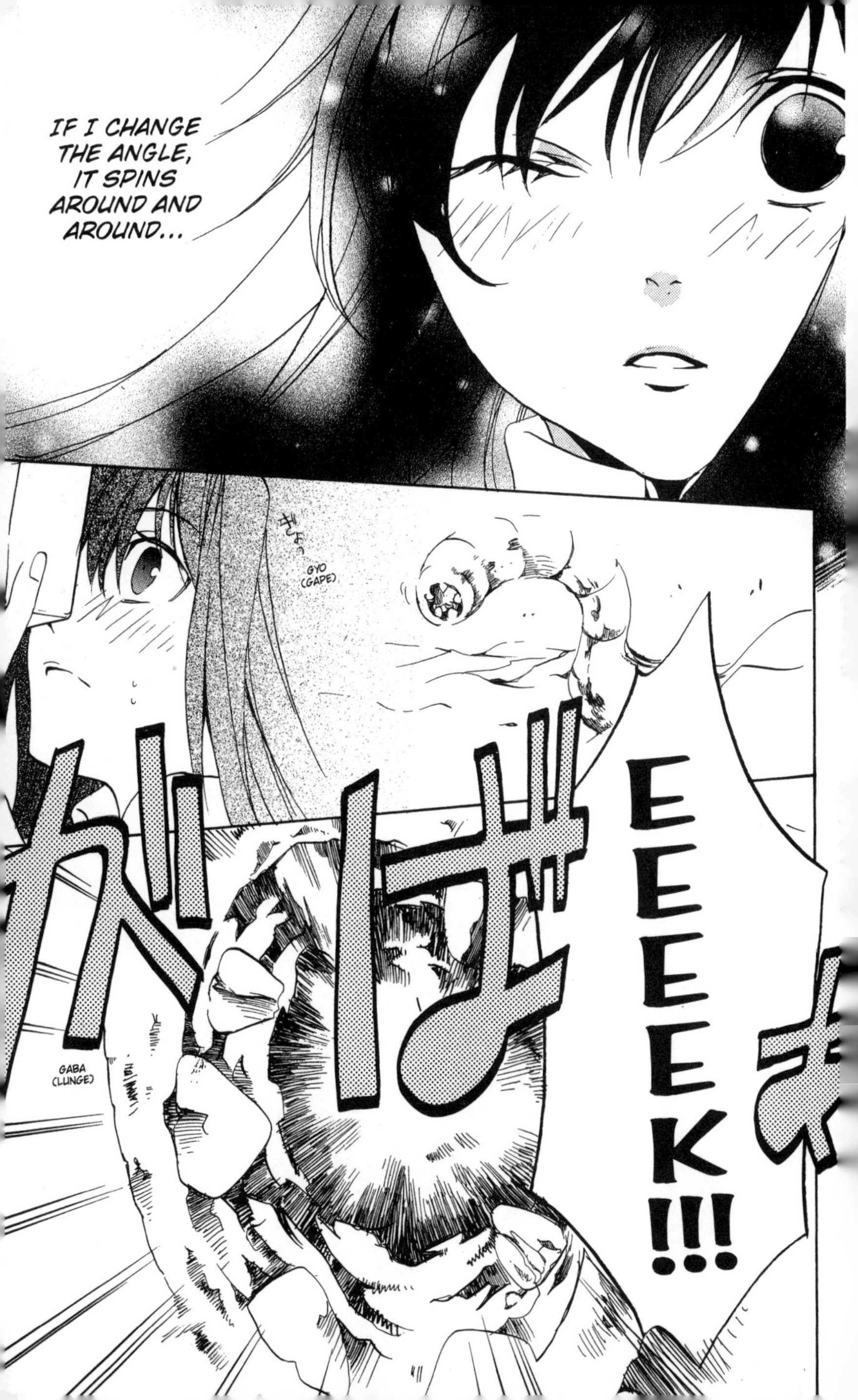
IF I CHANGE THE ANGLE, IT SPINS AROUND AND AROUND...
GYO (GAPE)
EEEEEK!!!
GABA (LUNGE)

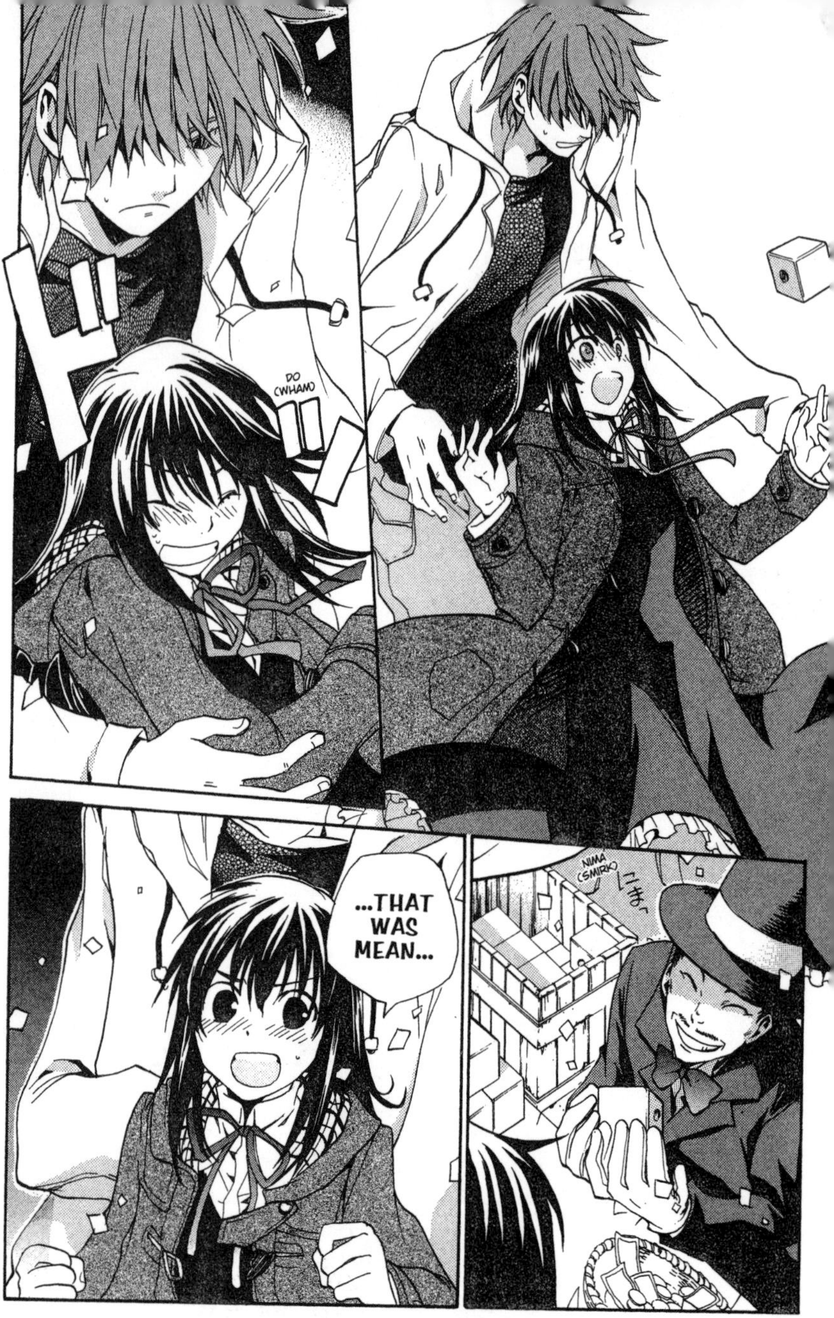
DO (WHAM)
NIMA (SMIRK)
にまっ
...THAT WAS MEAN...

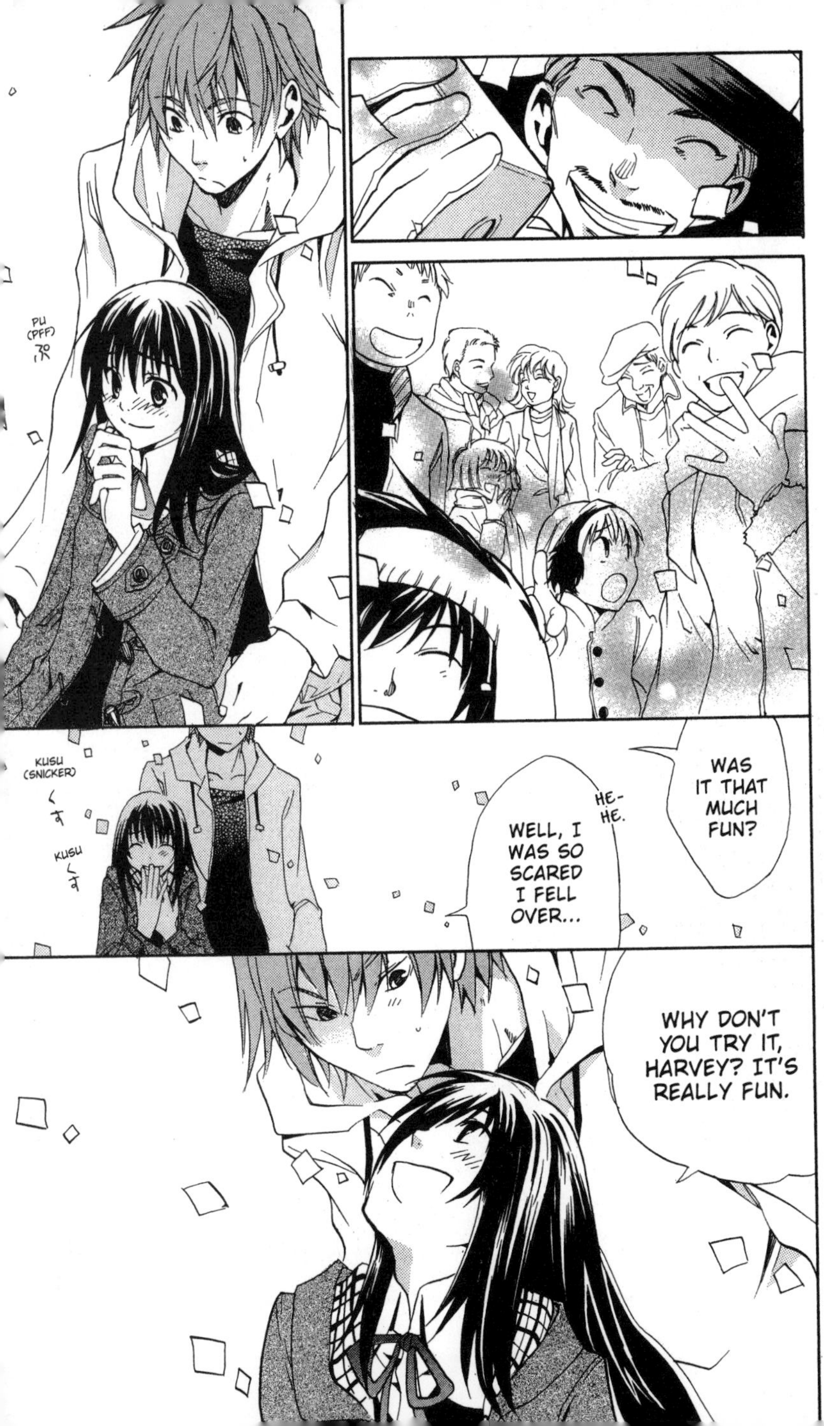
PU (PFF)
ぷ
WAS IT THAT MUCH FUN?
HE-HE.
WELL, I WAS SO SCARED I FELL OVER...
KUSU (SNICKER)
くす
KUSU
くす
WHY DON'T YOU TRY IT, HARVEY? IT'S REALLY FUN.

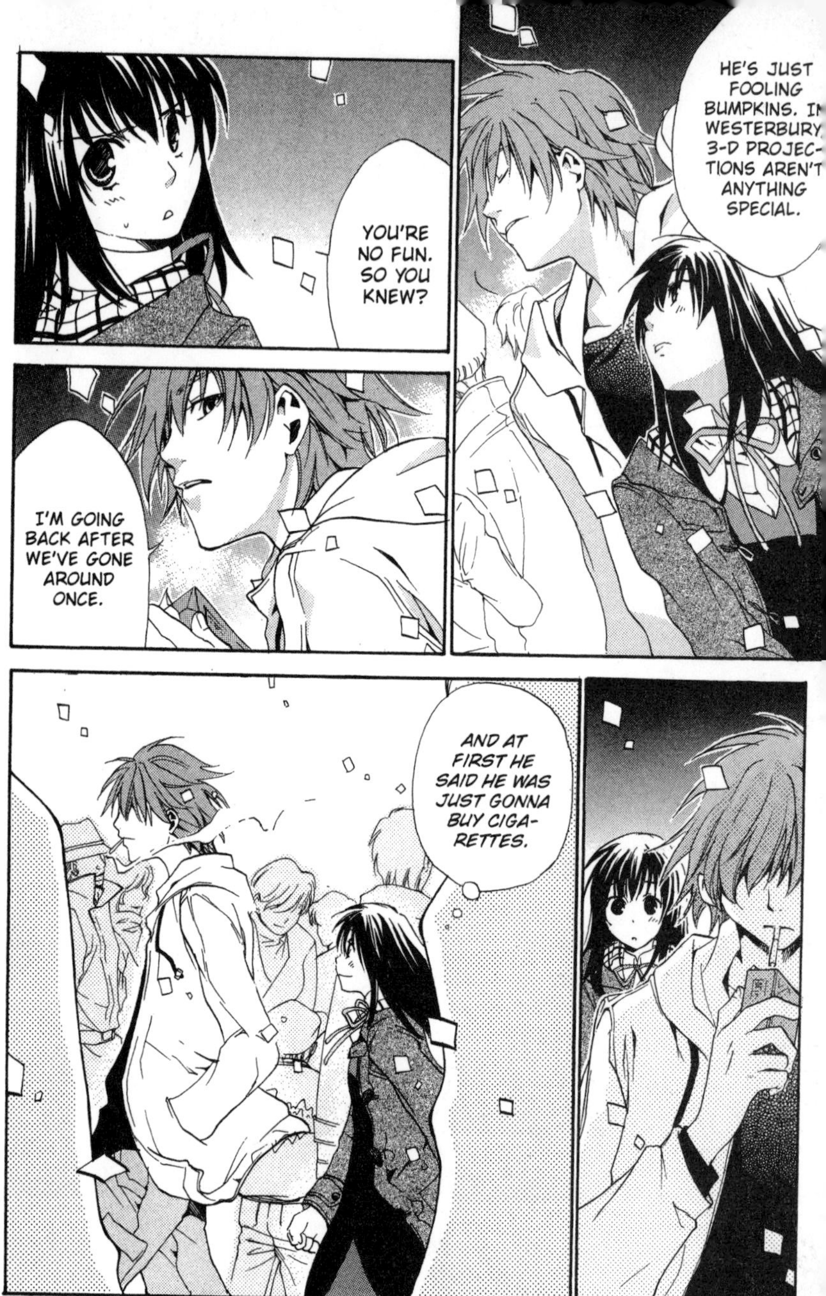
HE'S JUST FOOLING BUMPKINS. IN WESTERBURY, 3-D PROJECTIONS AREN'T ANYTHING SPECIAL.
YOU'RE NO FUN. SO YOU KNEW?
I'M GOING BACK AFTER WE'VE GONE AROUND ONCE.
AND AT FIRST HE SAID HE WAS JUST GONNA BUY CIGARETTES.

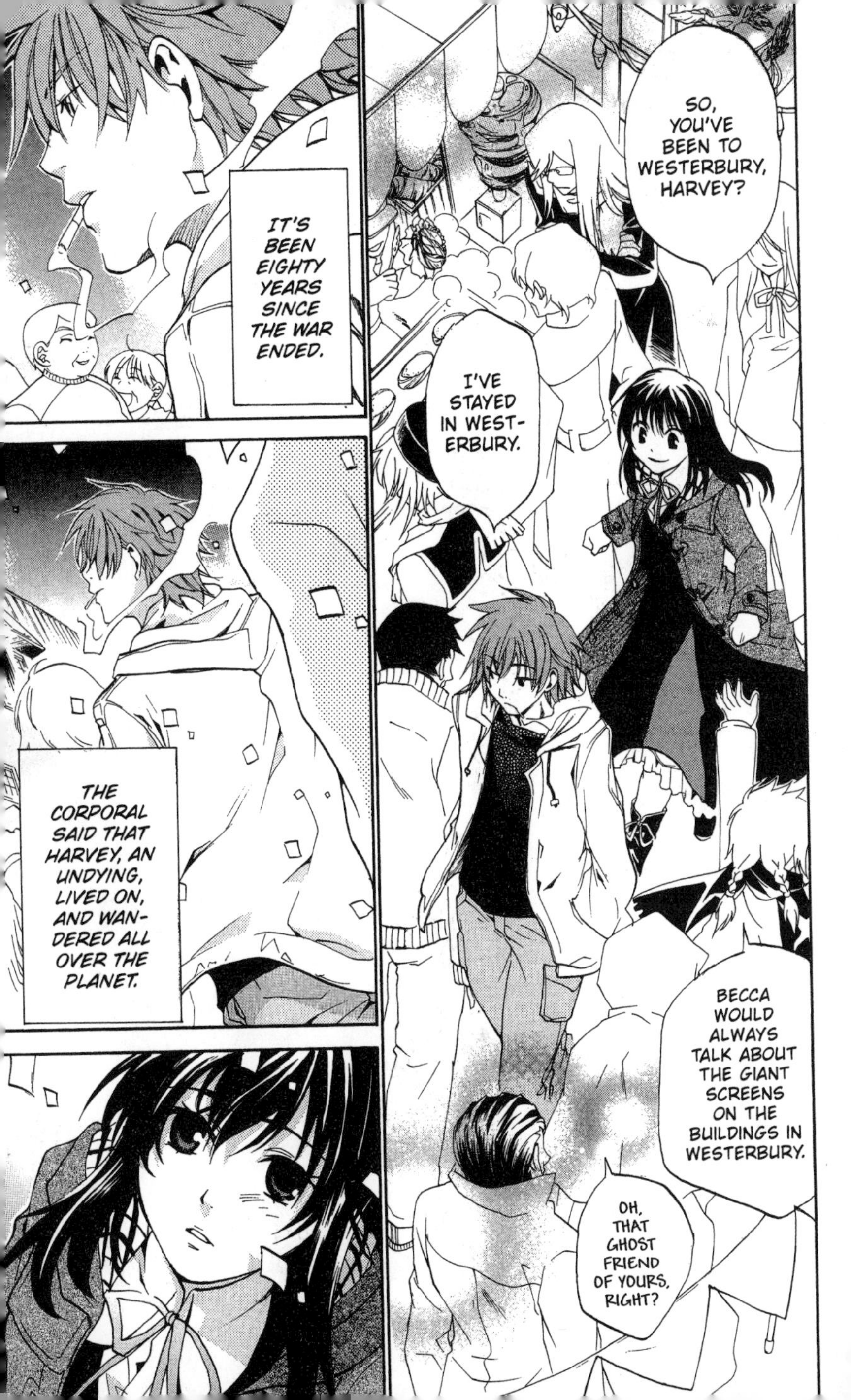
SO, YOU'VE BEEN TO WESTERBURY, HARVEY?
I'VE STAYED IN WEST-ERBURY.
BECCA WOULD ALWAYS TALK ABOUT THE GIANT SCREENS ON THE BUILDINGS IN WESTERBURY.
OH, THAT GHOST FRIEND OF YOURS, RIGHT?
IT'S BEEN EIGHTY YEARS SINCE THE WAR ENDED.
THE CORPORAL SAID THAT HARVEY, AN UNDYING, LIVED ON, AND WAN-DERED ALL OVER THE PLANET.

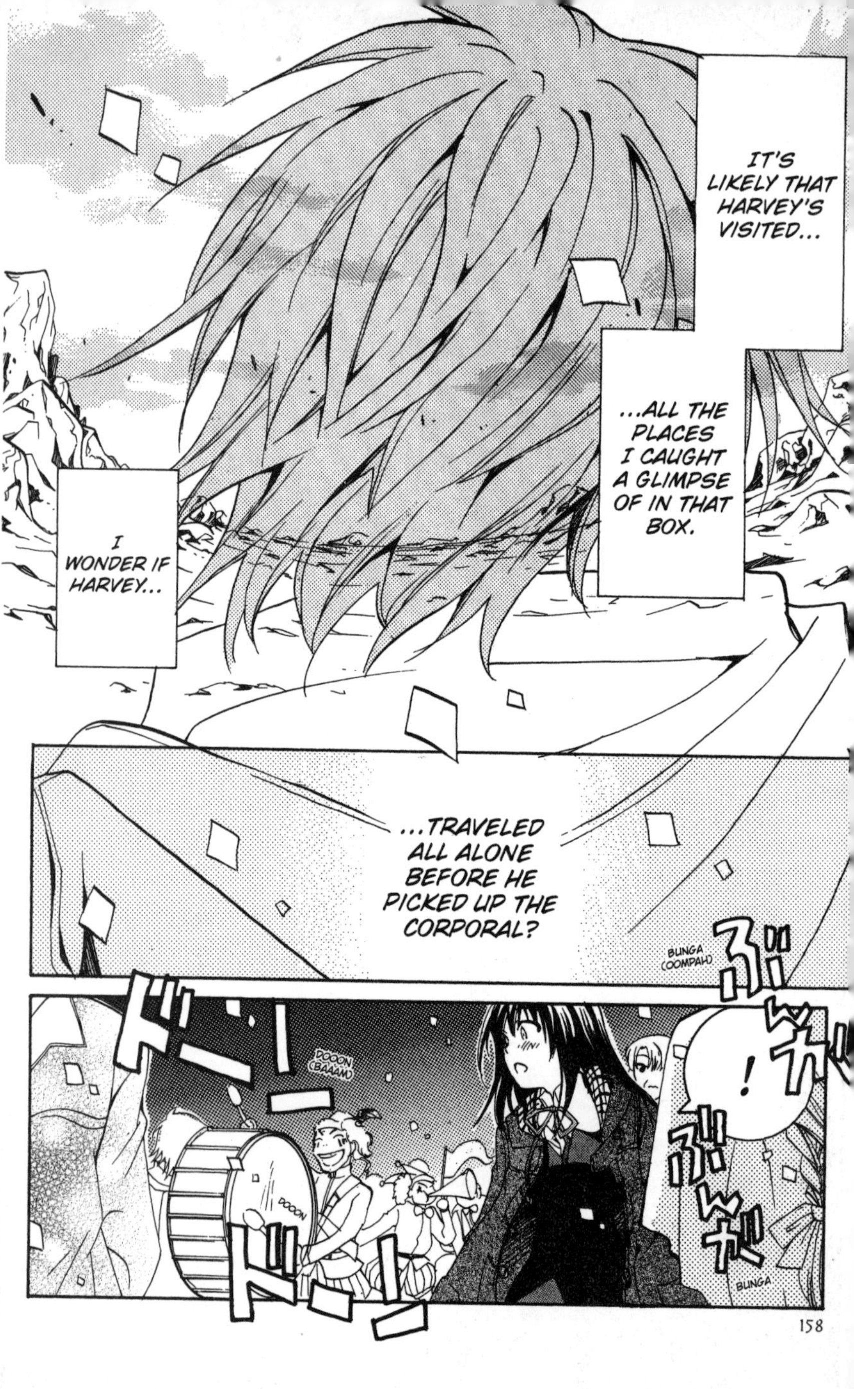
IT'S LIKELY THAT HARVEY'S VISITED...
...ALL THE PLACES I CAUGHT A GLIMPSE OF IN THAT BOX.
I WONDER IF HARVEY...
...TRAVELED ALL ALONE BEFORE HE PICKED UP THE CORPORAL?
BUNGA (OOMPAH)
!
BUNGA
DOOON (BAAAM)
DOOON

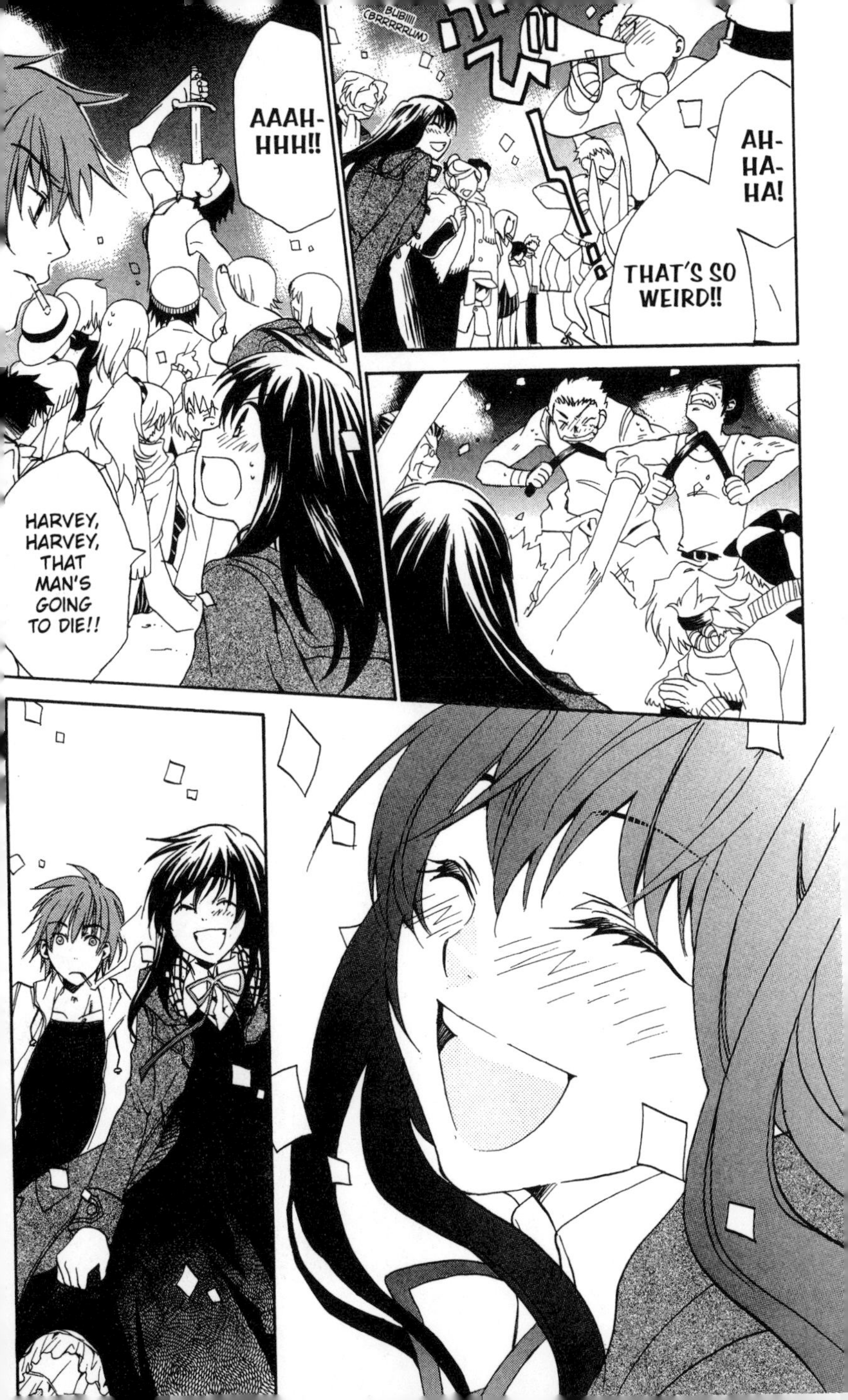
BUBIIIII (BRRRRRRUM)
AH-HA-HA!
THAT'S SO WEIRD!!
AAAH-HHH!!
HARVEY, HARVEY, THAT MAN'S GOING TO DIE!!

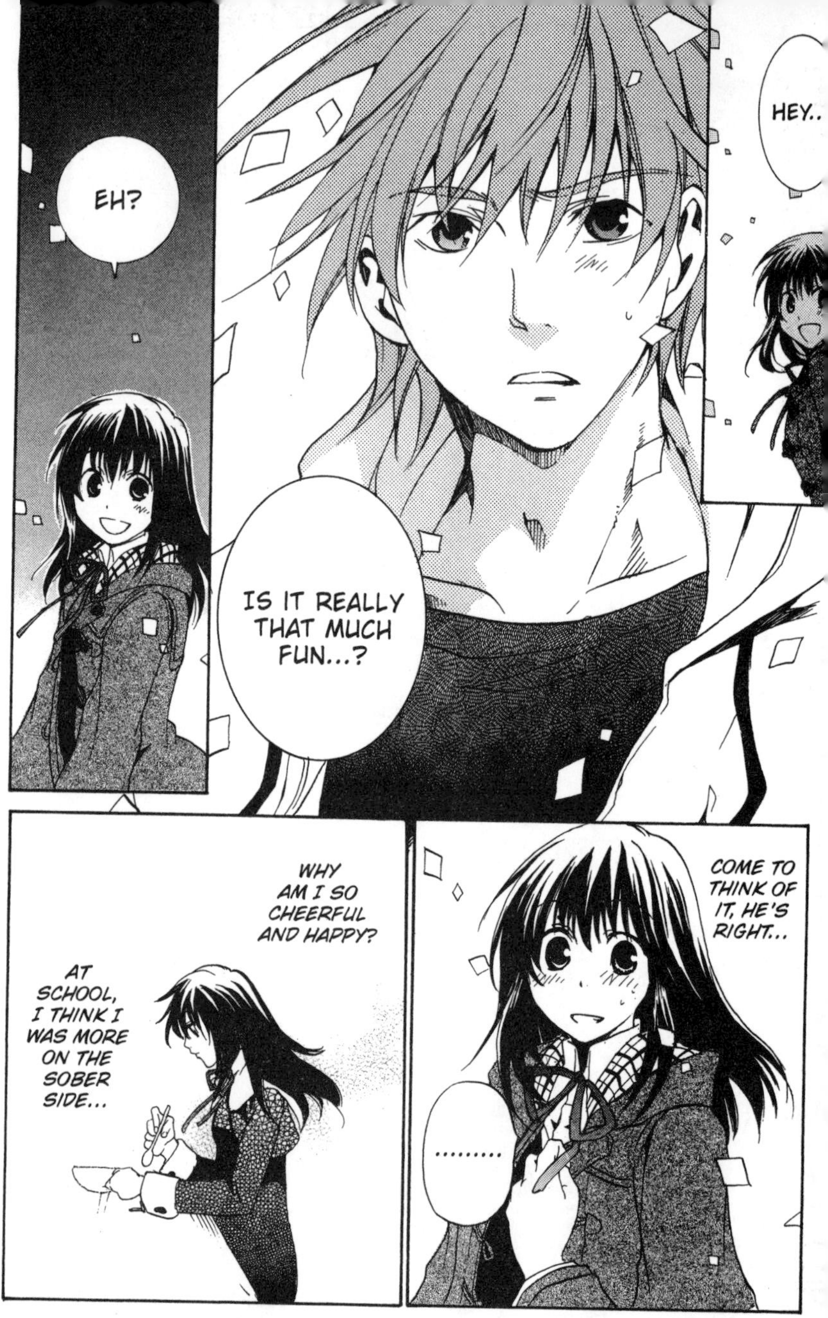
HEY..
IS IT REALLY THAT MUCH FUN...?
EH?
COME TO THINK OF IT, HE'S RIGHT...
....
WHY AM I SO CHEERFUL AND HAPPY?
AT SCHOOL, I THINK I WAS MORE ON THE SOBER SIDE...

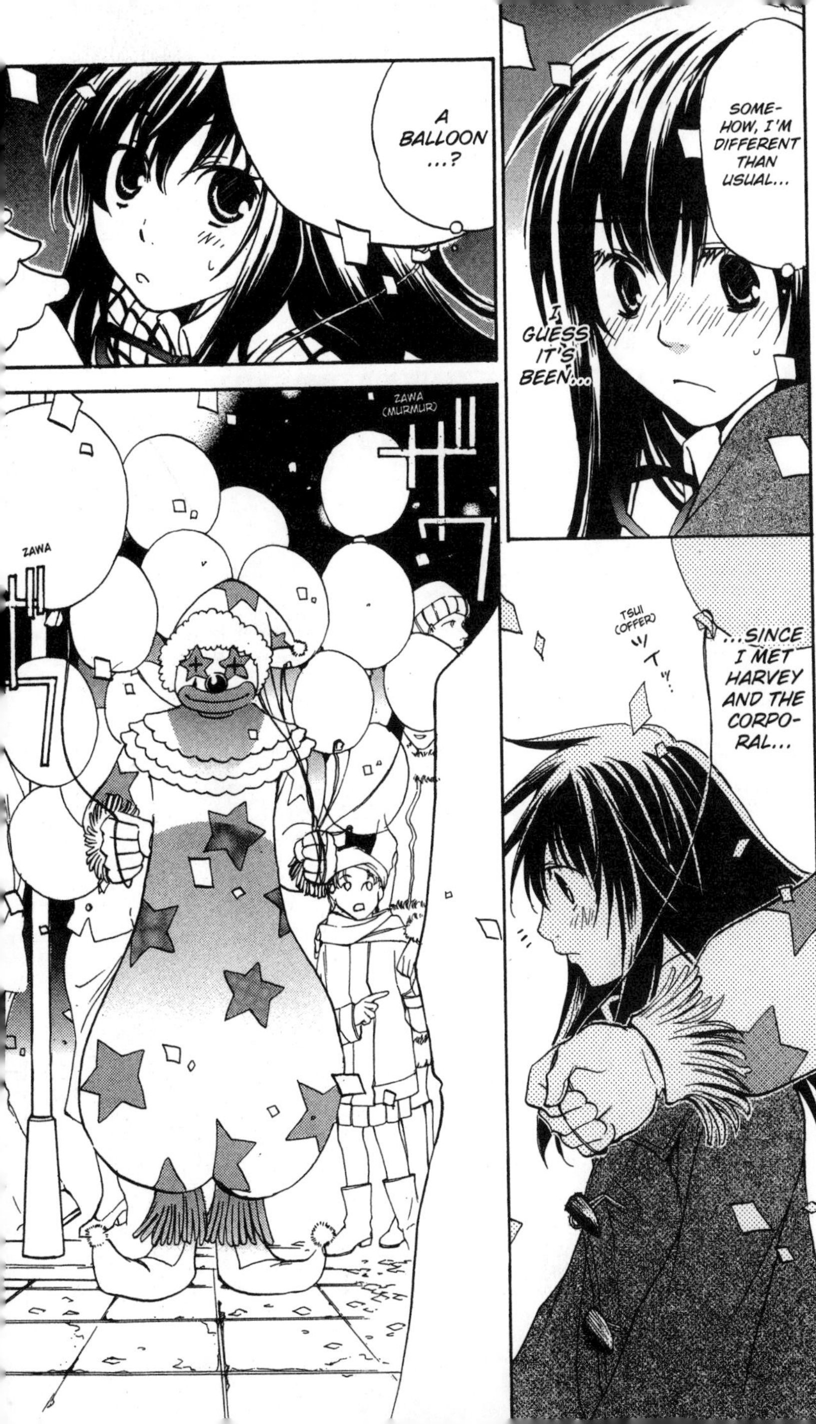
SOME-HOW, I'M DIFFERENT THAN USUAL...
I GUESS IT'S BEEN...
A BALLOON ...?
ZAWA (MURMUR)
ZAWA
TSUI (OFFER)
...SINCE I MET HARVEY AND THE CORPORAL...

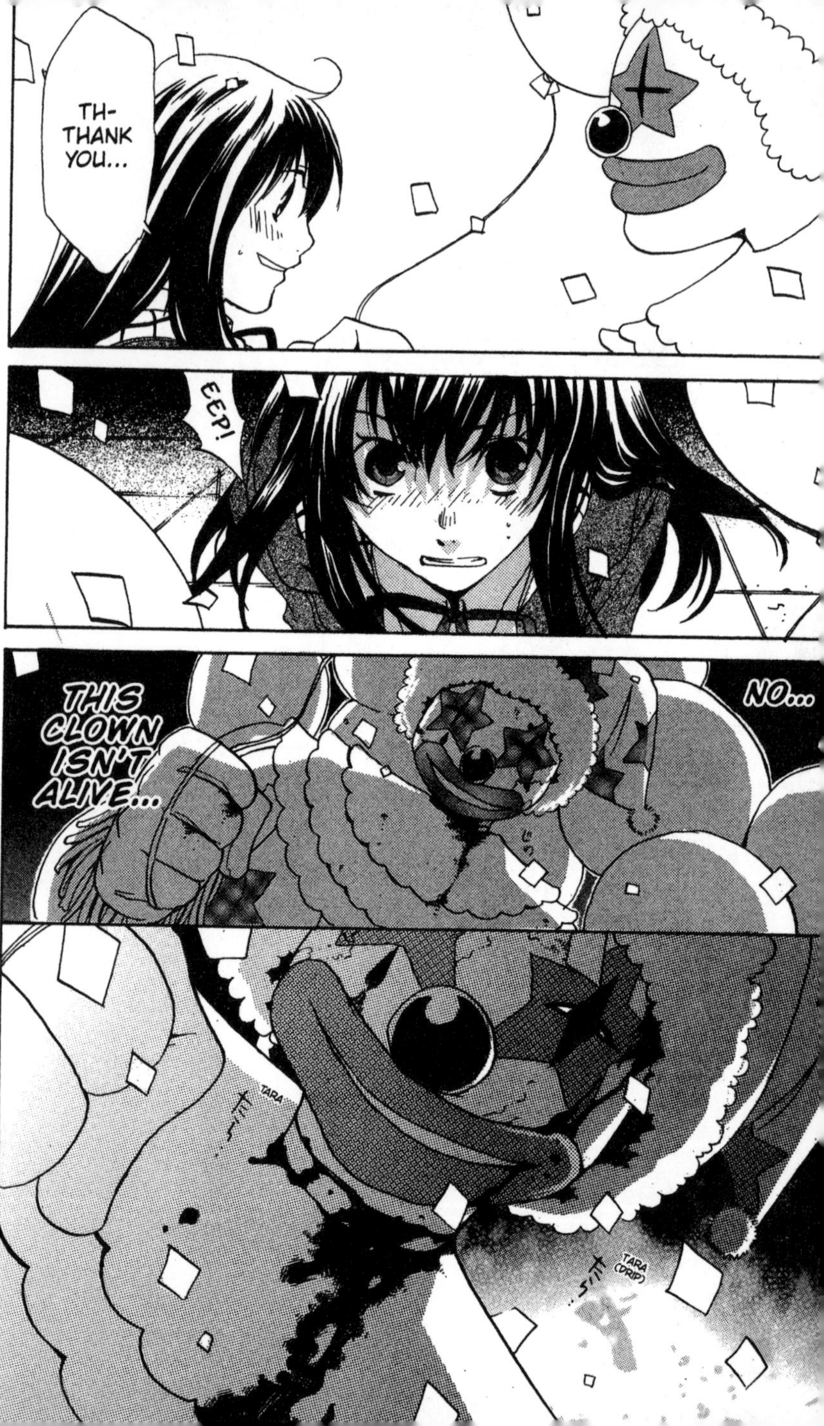
TH- THANK YOU...
EEP!
NO...
THIS CLOWN ISN'T ALIVE...
TARA
TARA (DRIP)

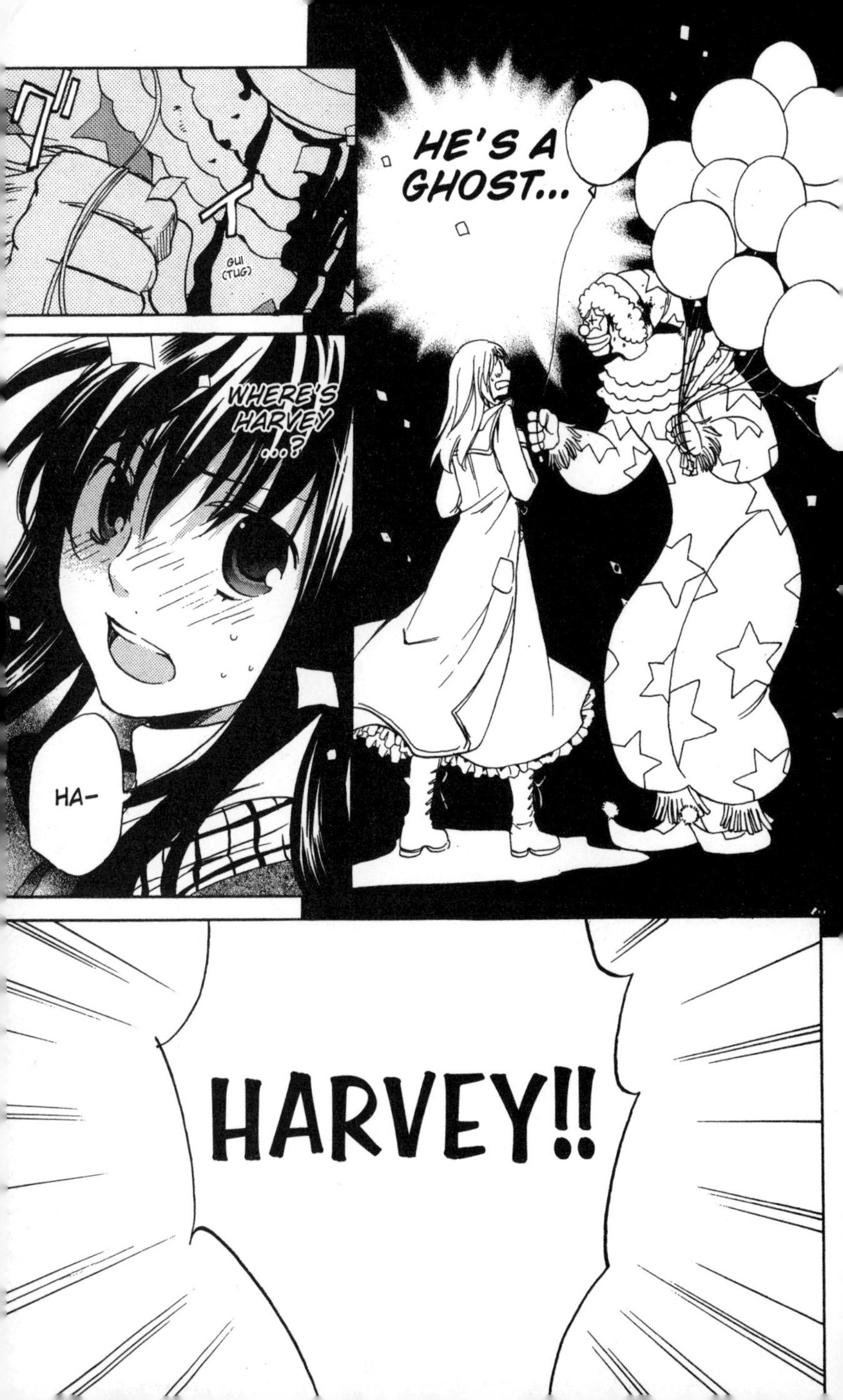
HE'S A GHOST...
GUI (TUG)
WHERE'S HARVEY ...?
HA-
HARVEY!!

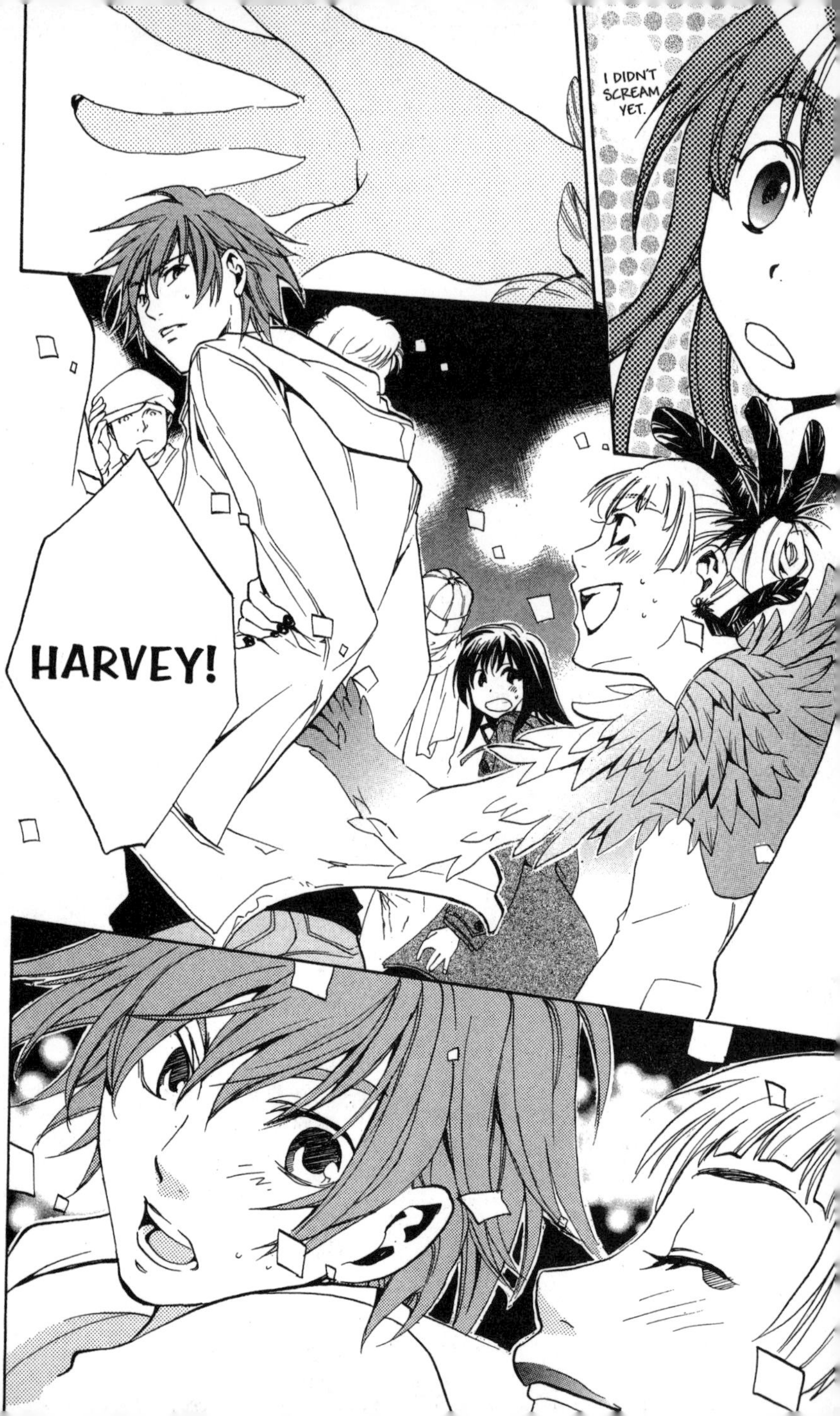
I DIDN'T SCREAM YET.
HARVEY!

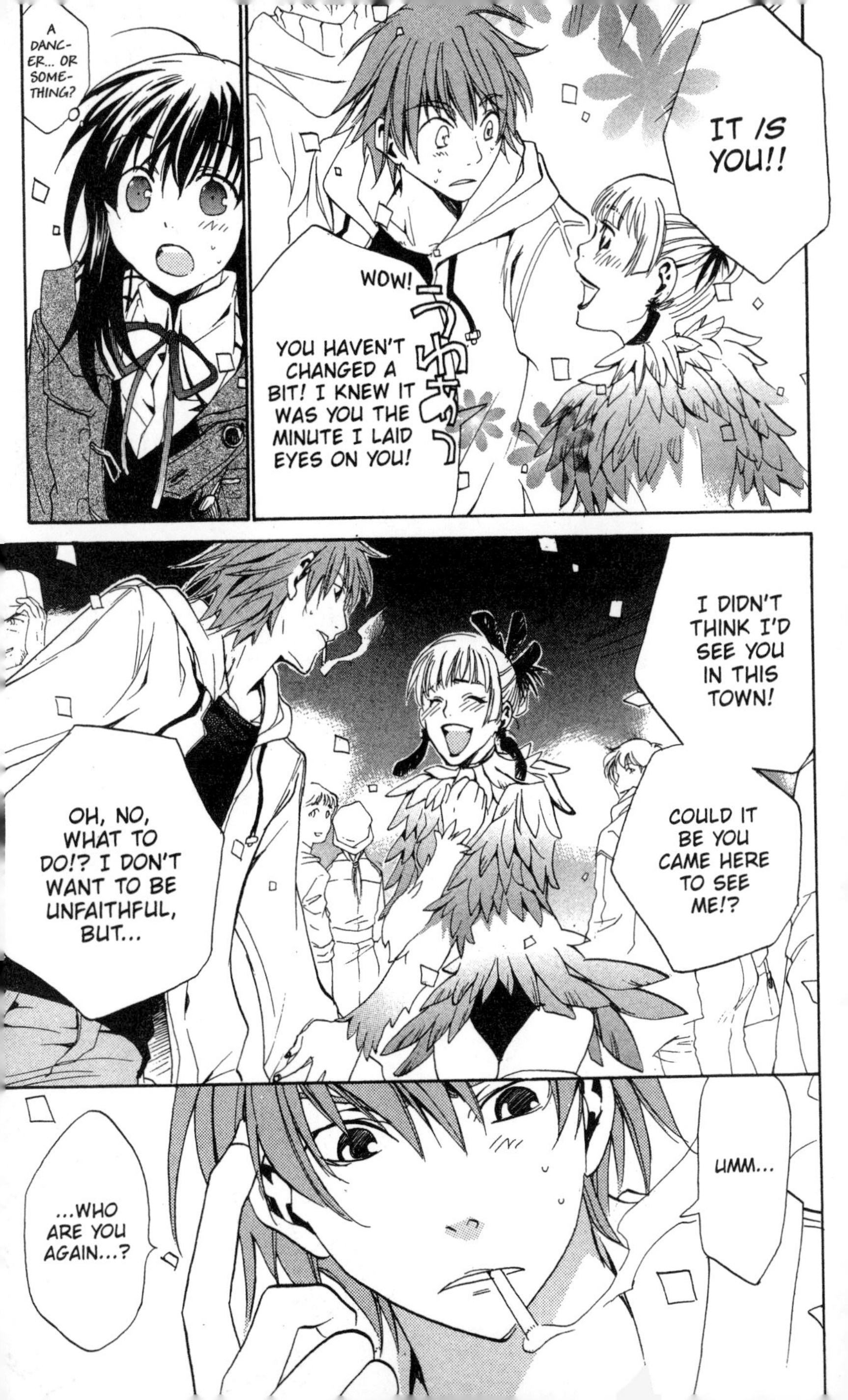
IT IS YOU!!
WOW!
YOU HAVEN'T CHANGED A BIT! I KNEW IT WAS YOU THE MINUTE I LAID EYES ON YOU!
A DANCER... OR SOMETHING?
I DIDN'T THINK I'D SEE YOU IN THIS TOWN!
COULD IT BE YOU CAME HERE TO SEE ME!?
OH, NO, WHAT TO DO!? I DON'T WANT TO BE UNFAITHFUL, BUT...
UMM...
...WHO ARE YOU AGAIN...?

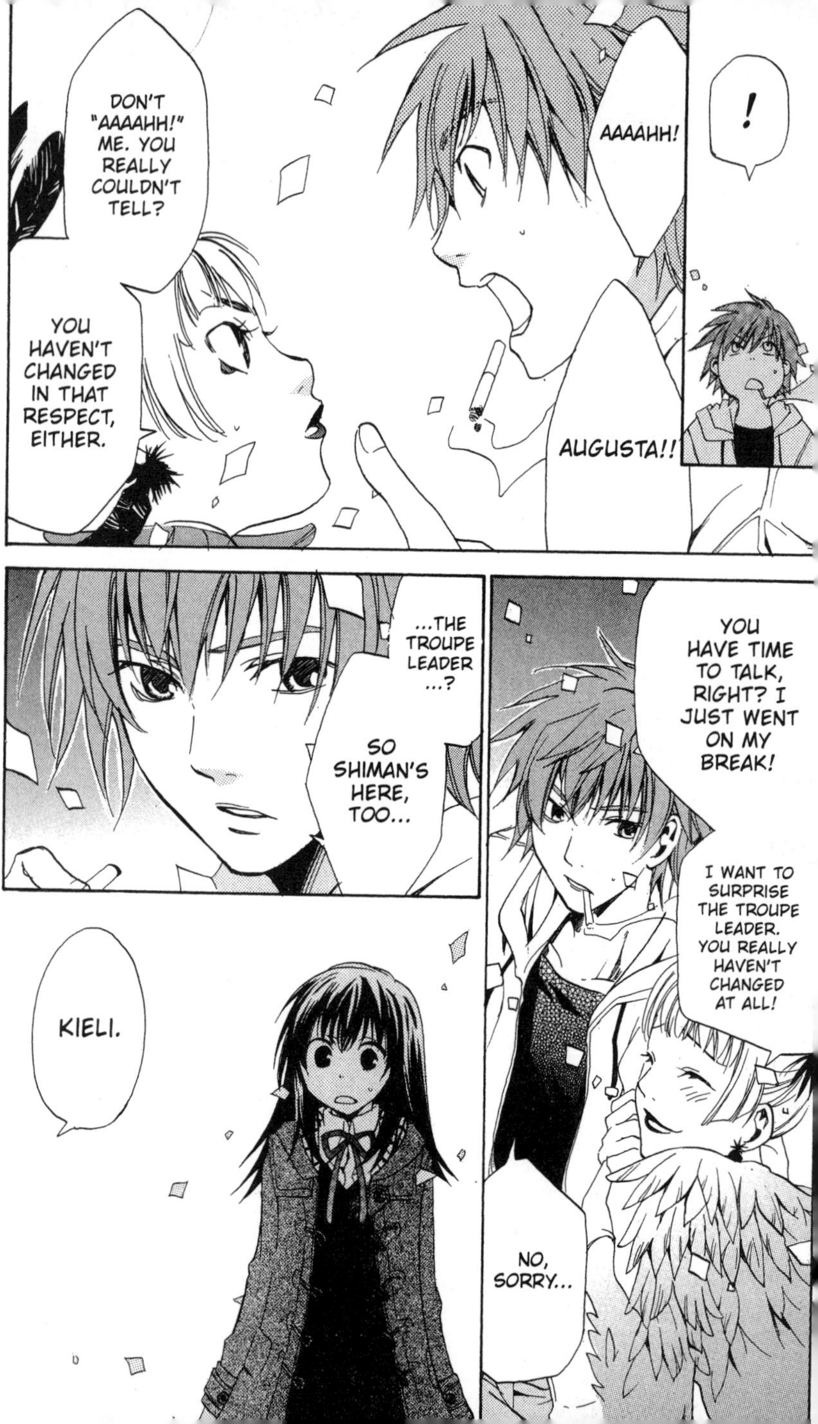
!
AAAAHH!
AUGUSTA!!
DON'T "AAAAHH!" ME. YOU REALLY COULDN'T TELL?
YOU HAVEN'T CHANGED IN THAT RESPECT, EITHER.
YOU HAVE TIME TO TALK, RIGHT? I JUST WENT ON MY BREAK!
I WANT TO SURPRISE THE TROUPE LEADER. YOU REALLY HAVEN'T CHANGED AT ALL!
NO, SORRY...
...THE TROUPE LEADER ...?
SO SHIMAN'S HERE, TOO...
KIELI.

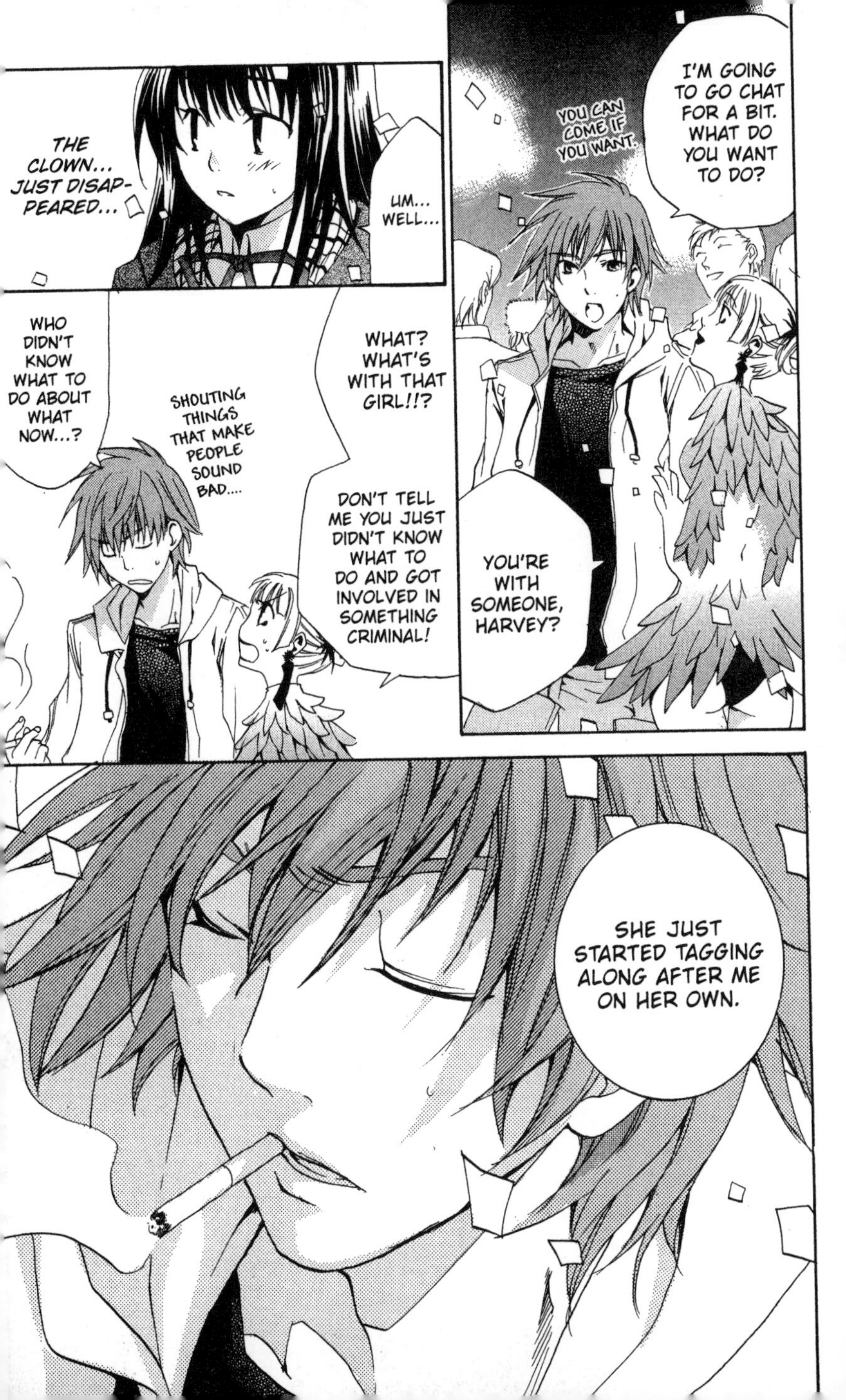
I'M GOING TO GO CHAT FOR A BIT. WHAT DO YOU WANT TO DO?
YOU CAN COME IF YOU WANT.
YOU'RE WITH SOMEONE, HARVEY?
UM... WELL...
THE CLOWN... JUST DISAP-PEARED...
WHAT? WHAT'S WITH THAT GIRL!!?
DON'T TELL ME YOU JUST DIDN'T KNOW WHAT TO DO AND GOT INVOLVED IN SOMETHING CRIMINAL!
SHOUTING THINGS THAT MAKE PEOPLE SOUND BAD....
WHO DIDN'T KNOW WHAT TO DO ABOUT WHAT NOW...?
SHE JUST STARTED TAGGING ALONG AFTER ME ON HER OWN.

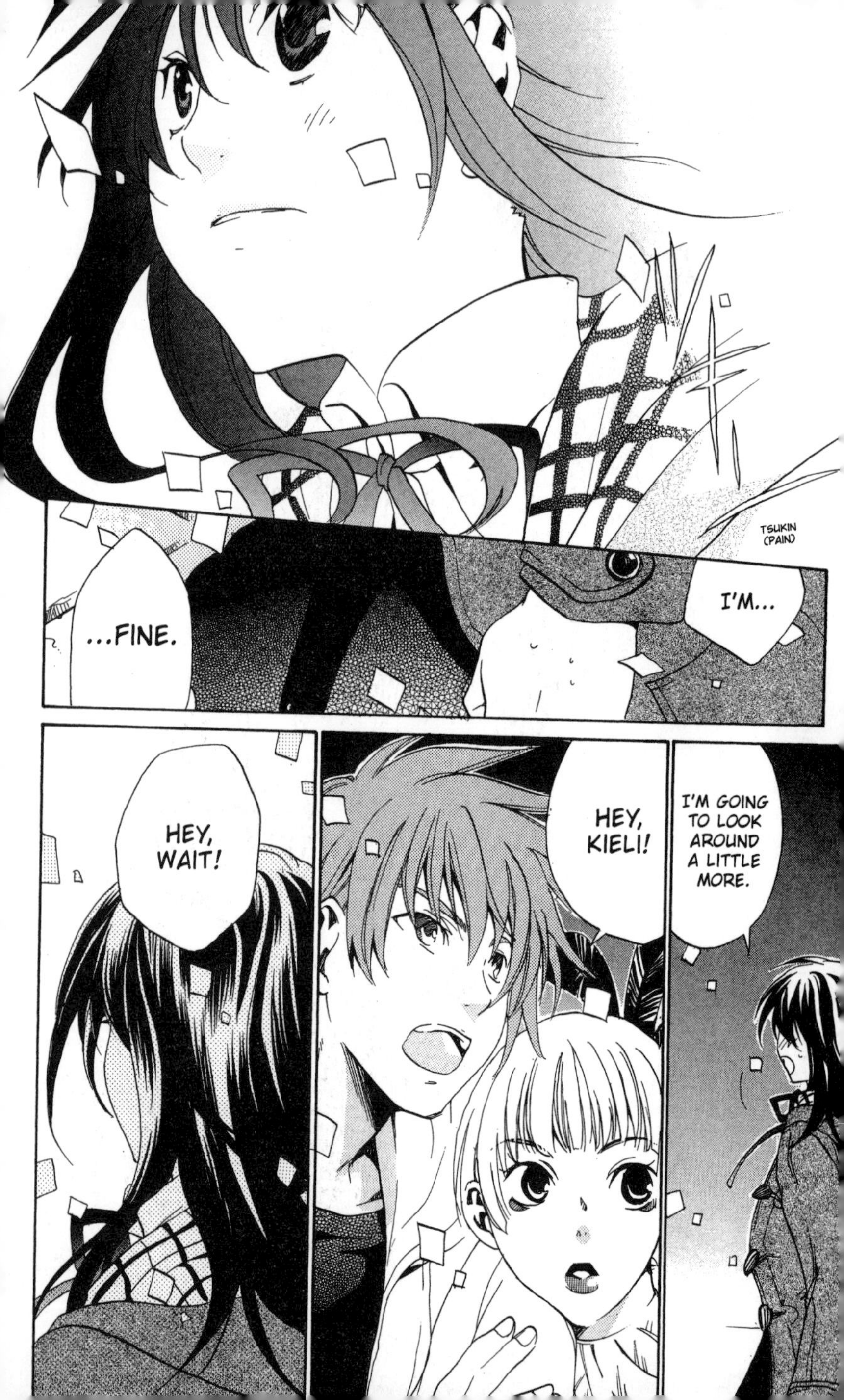
TSUKIN (PAIN)
I'M...
...FINE.
I'M GOING TO LOOK AROUND A LITTLE MORE.
HEY, KIELI!
HEY, WAIT!

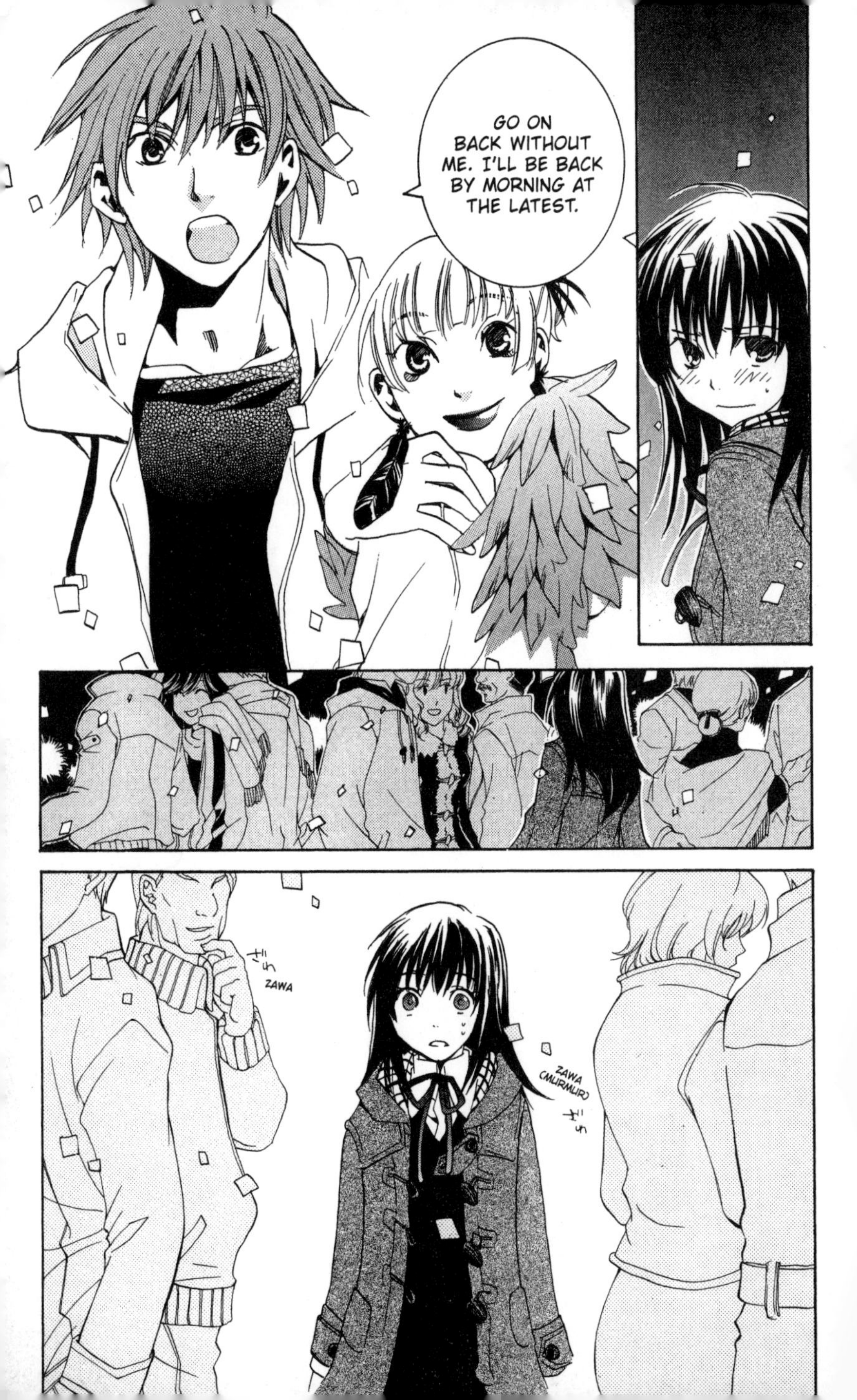
GO ON BACK WITHOUT ME. I'LL BE BACK BY MORNING AT THE LATEST.
ZAWA (MURMUR)
ZAWA

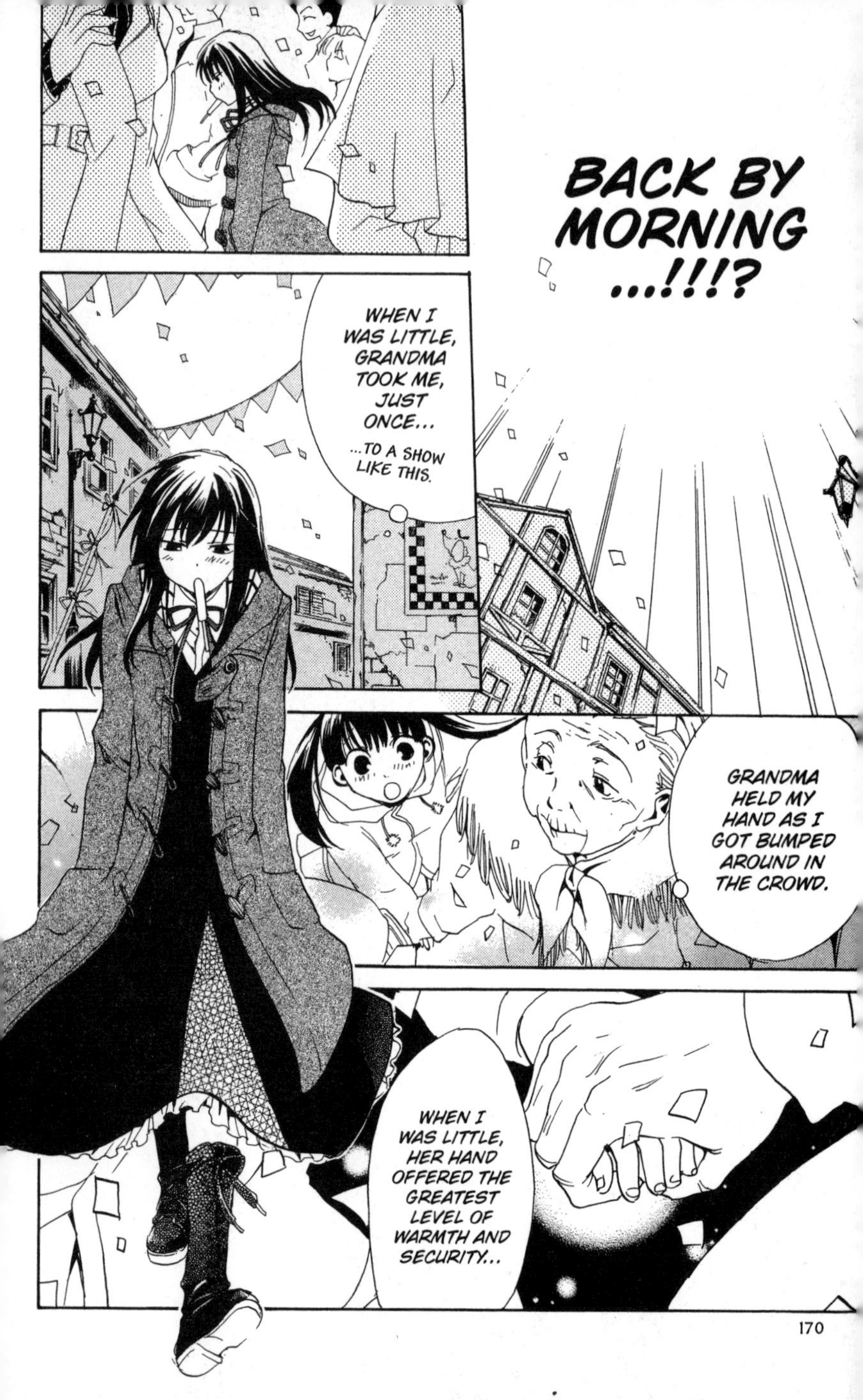
BACK BY MORNING ...!!!?
WHEN I WAS LITTLE, GRANDMA TOOK ME, JUST ONCE...
...TO A SHOW LIKE THIS.
GRANDMA HELD MY HAND AS I GOT BUMPED AROUND IN THE CROWD.
WHEN I WAS LITTLE, HER HAND OFFERED THE GREATEST LEVEL OF WARMTH AND SECURITY...

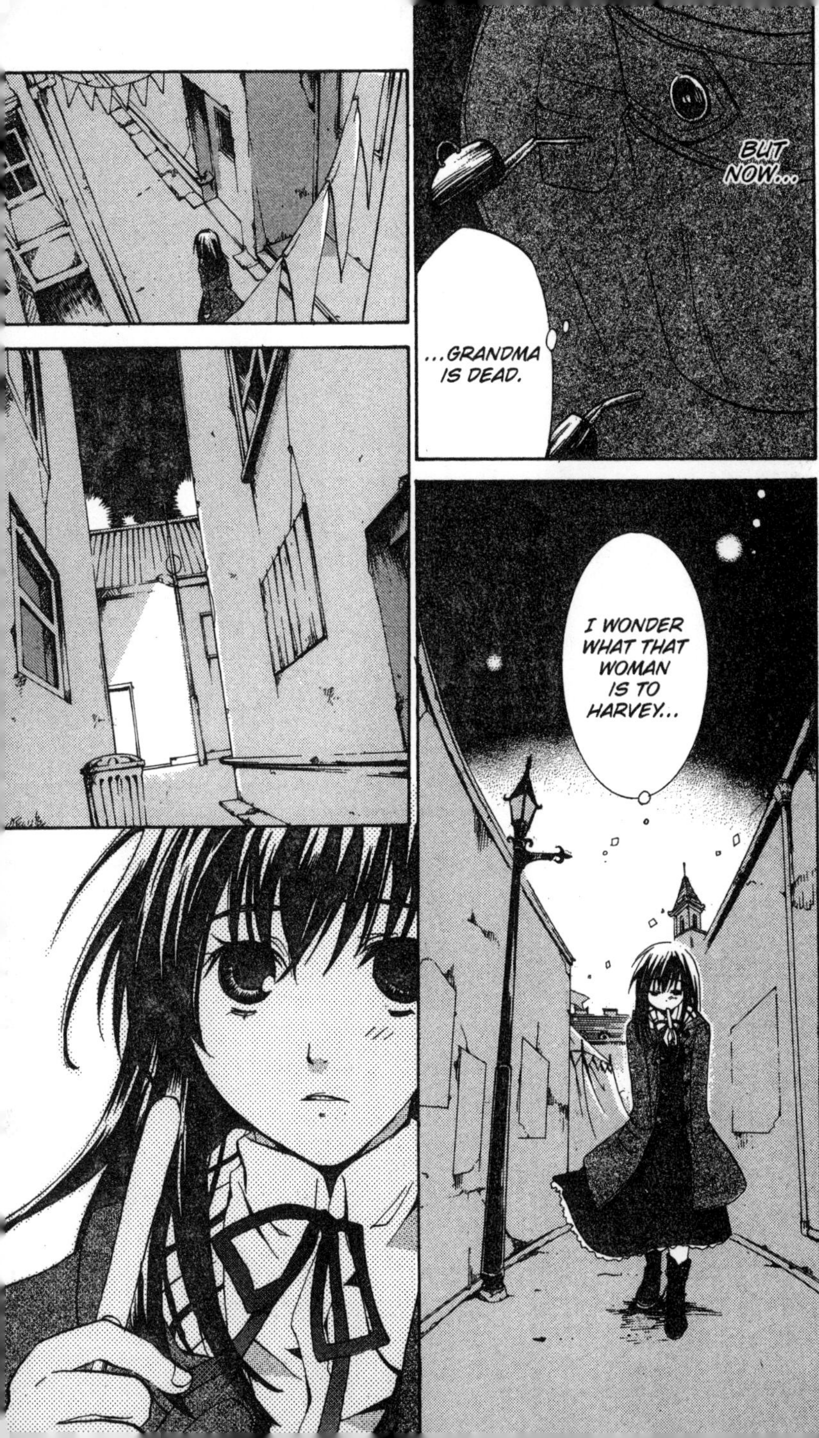
BUT NOW...
...GRANDMA IS DEAD.
I WONDER WHAT THAT WOMAN IS TO HARVEY...

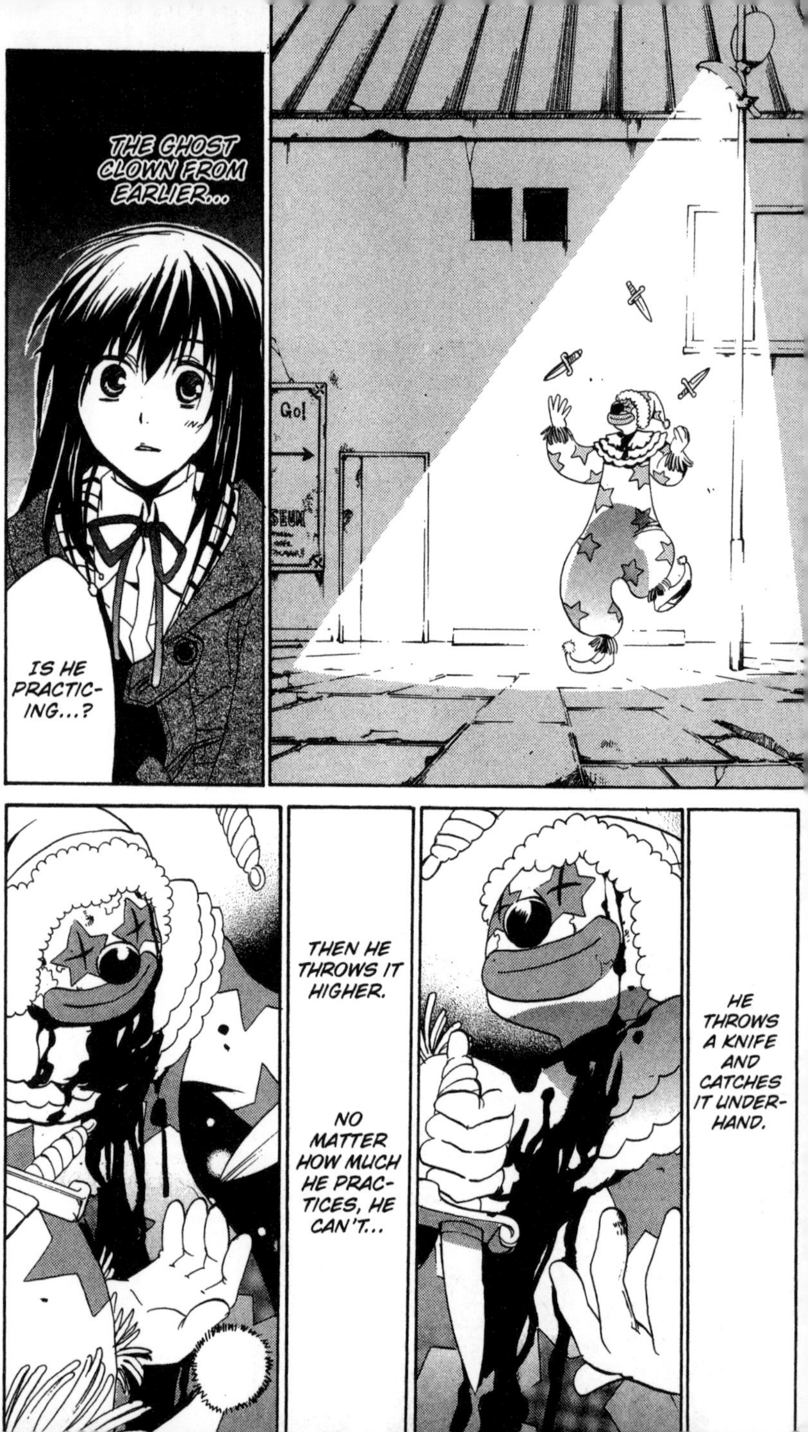
Go!
THE GHOST CLOWN FROM EARLIER...
IS HE PRACTIC-ING...?
HE THROWS A KNIFE AND CATCHES IT UNDER-HAND.
THEN HE THROWS IT HIGHER.
NO MATTER HOW MUCH HE PRAC-TICES, HE CAN'T...

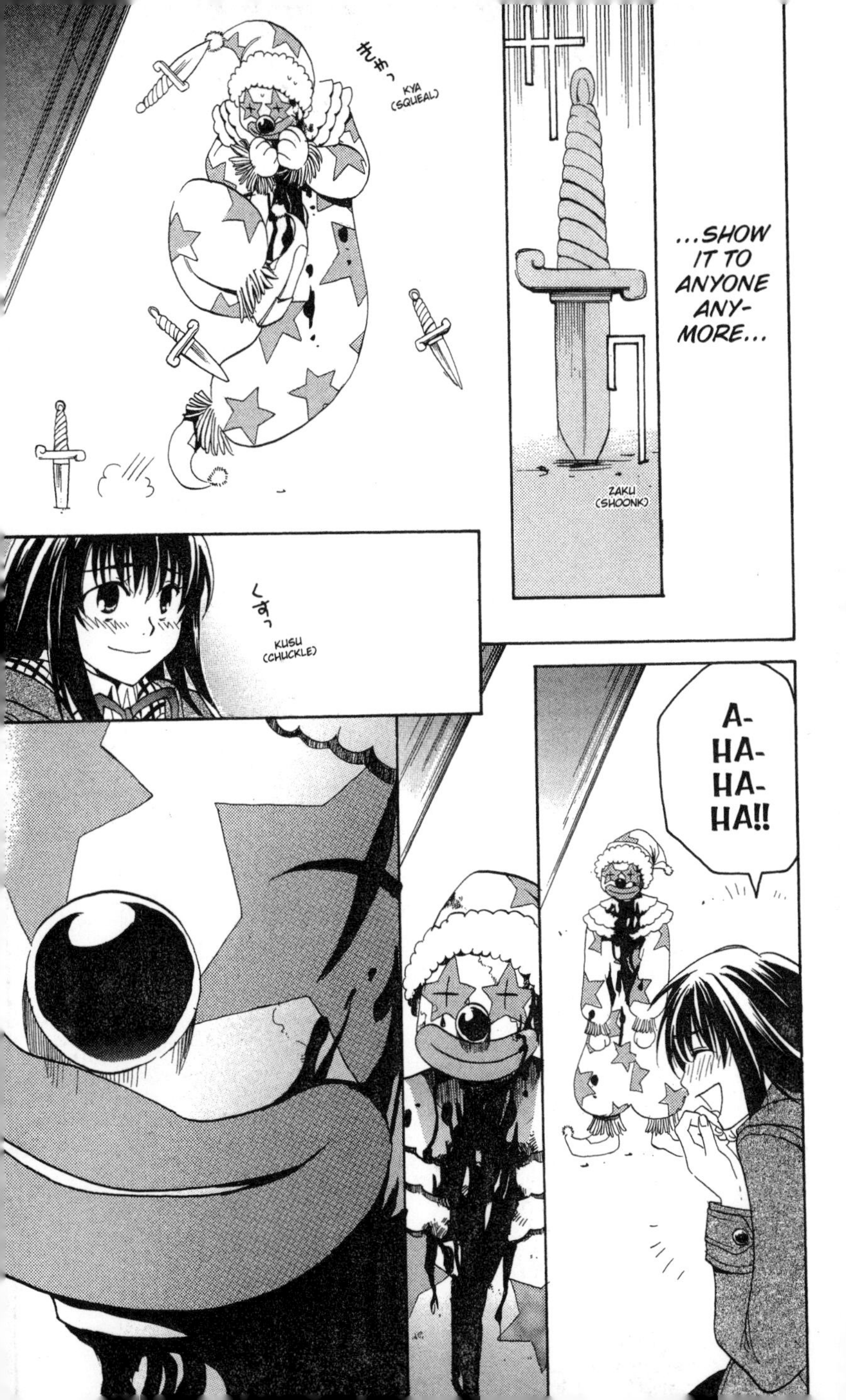
...SHOW IT TO ANYONE ANYMORE...
ZAKU (SHOONK)
きゃっ
KYA (SQUEAL)
くすっ
KUSU (CHUCKLE)
A-HA-HA-HA!!

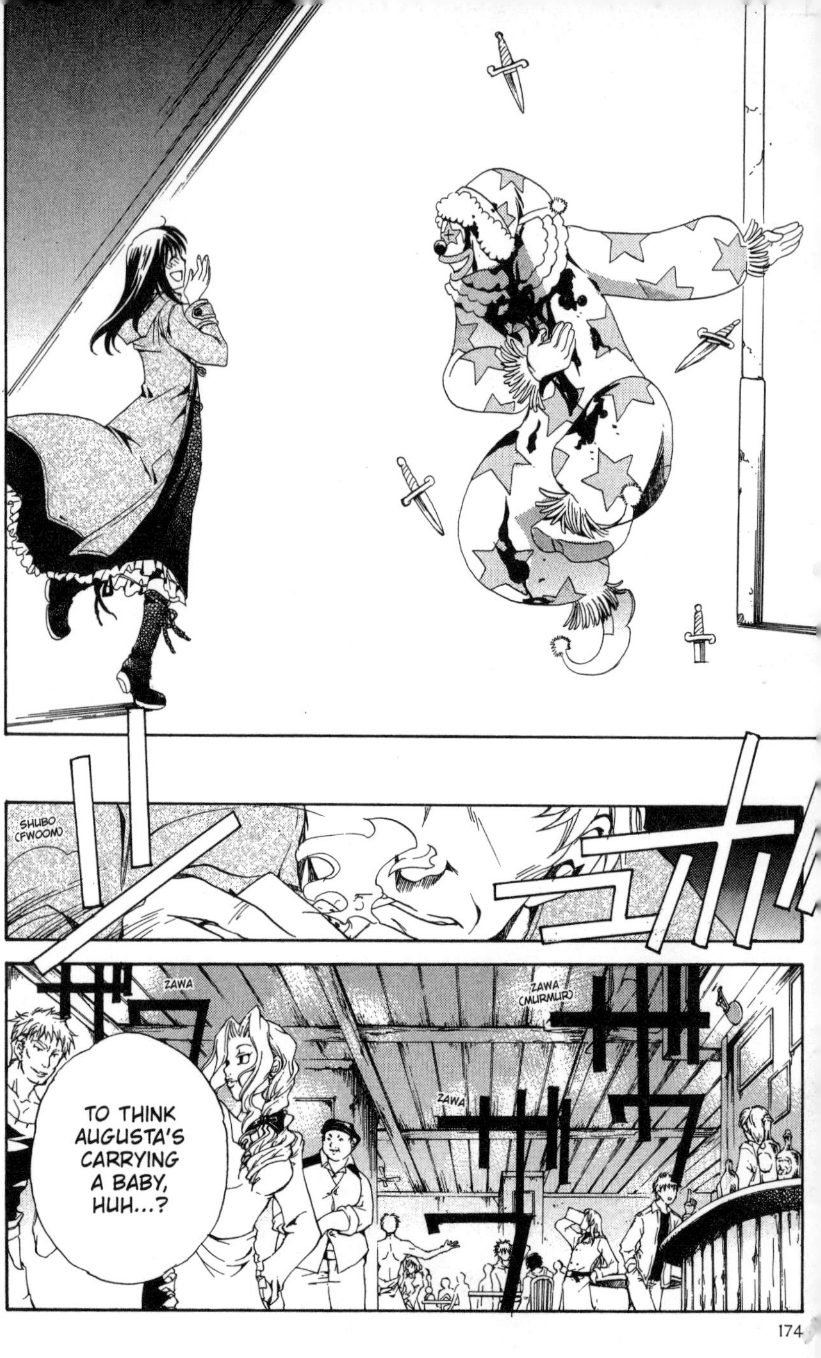
SHUBO (FWOOM)
ZAWA (MURMUR)
ZAWA
ZAWA
TO THINK AUGUSTA'S CARRYING A BABY, HUH...?

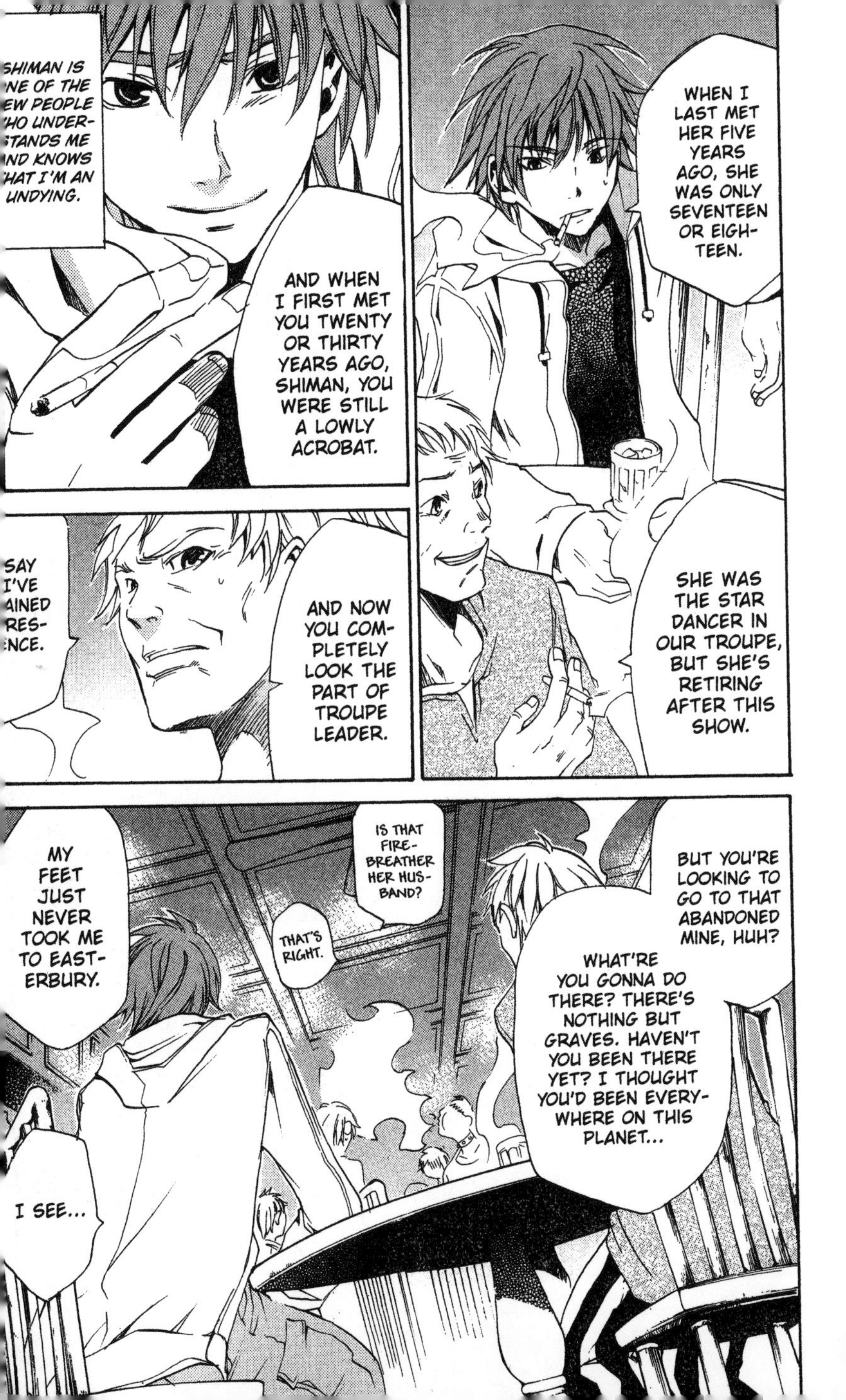
WHEN I LAST MET HER FIVE YEARS AGO, SHE WAS ONLY SEVENTEEN OR EIGHTEEN.
SHE WAS THE STAR DANCER IN OUR TROUPE, BUT SHE'S RETIRING AFTER THIS SHOW.
AND WHEN I FIRST MET YOU TWENTY OR THIRTY YEARS AGO, SHIMAN, YOU WERE STILL A LOWLY ACROBAT.
SHIMAN IS NE OF THE EW PEOPLE HO UNDER-STANDS ME ND KNOWS HAT I'M AN UNDYING.
AND NOW YOU COMPLETELY LOOK THE PART OF TROUPE LEADER.
SAY I'VE AINED RES-ENCE.
BUT YOU'RE LOOKING TO GO TO THAT ABANDONED MINE, HUH?
WHAT'RE YOU GONNA DO THERE? THERE'S NOTHING BUT GRAVES. HAVEN'T YOU BEEN THERE YET? I THOUGHT YOU'D BEEN EVERYWHERE ON THIS PLANET...
IS THAT FIRE-BREATHER HER HUSBAND?
THAT'S RIGHT.
MY FEET JUST NEVER TOOK ME TO EASTERBURY.
I SEE...

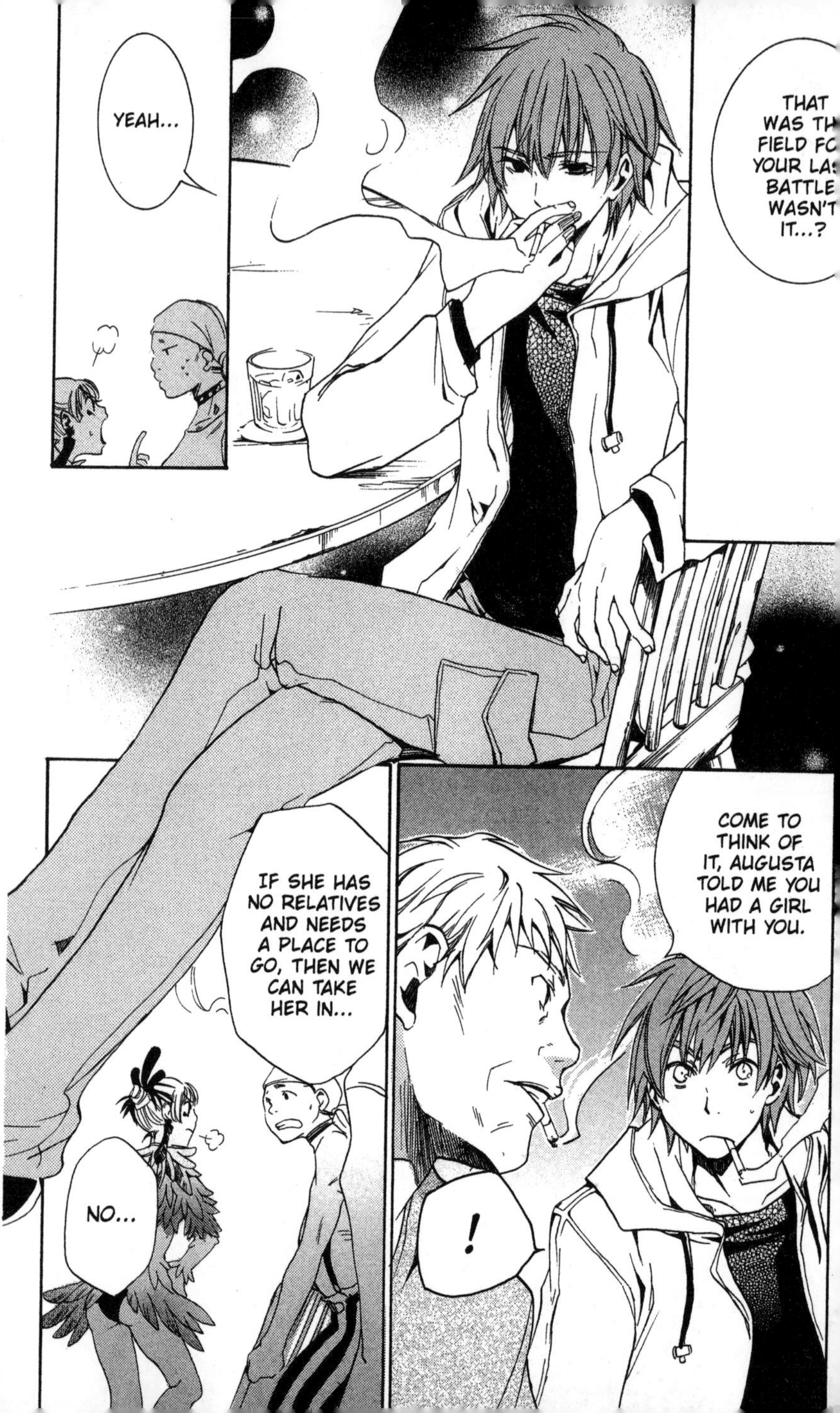
THAT WAS TH FIELD FO YOUR LAS BATTLE WASN'T IT...?
YEAH...
COME TO THINK OF IT, AUGUSTA TOLD ME YOU HAD A GIRL WITH YOU.
!
IF SHE HAS NO RELATIVES AND NEEDS A PLACE TO GO, THEN WE CAN TAKE HER IN...
NO...

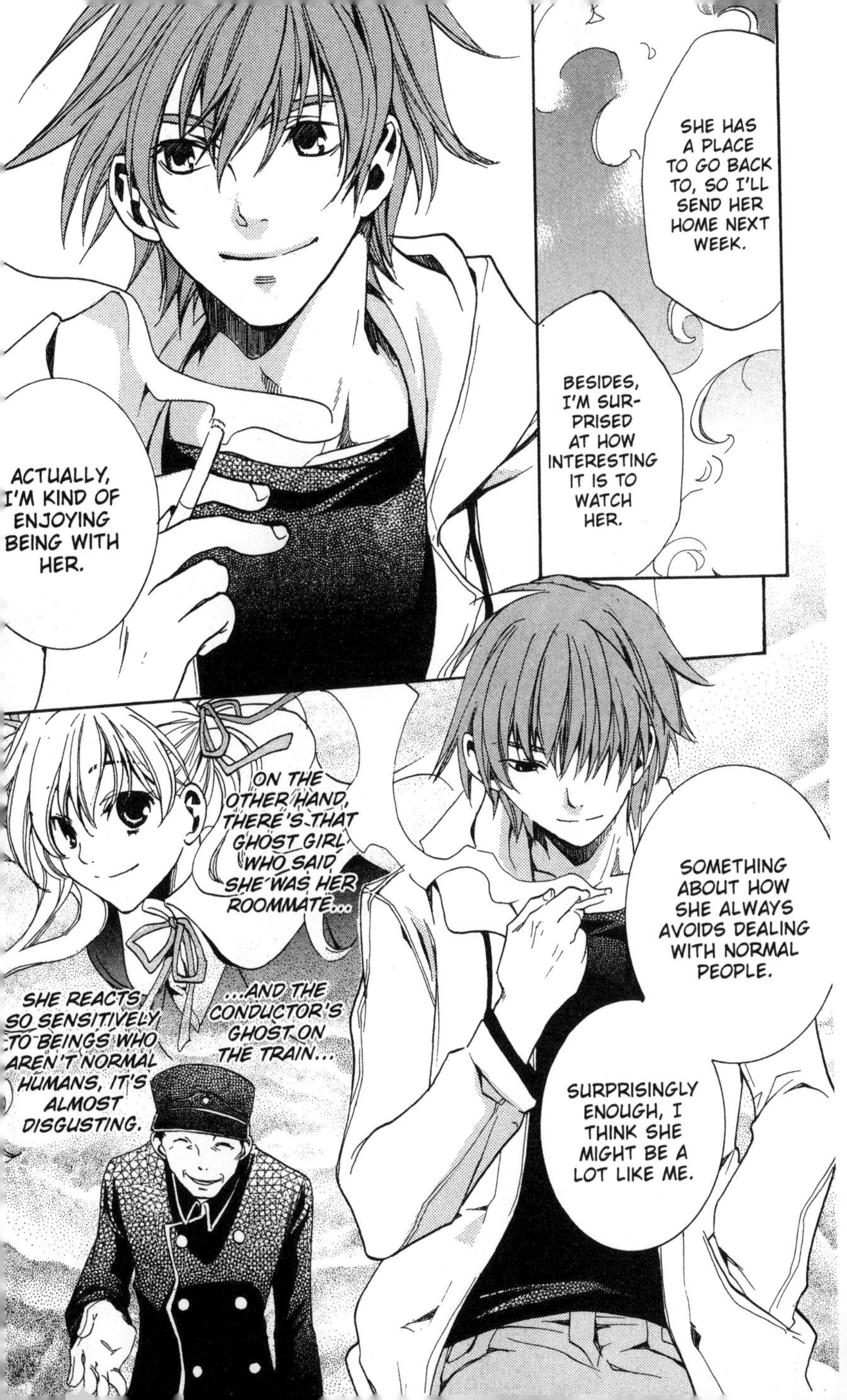
SHE HAS A PLACE TO GO BACK TO, SO I'LL SEND HER HOME NEXT WEEK.
BESIDES, I'M SUR-PRISED AT HOW INTERESTING IT IS TO WATCH HER.
ACTUALLY, I'M KIND OF ENJOYING BEING WITH HER.
SOMETHING ABOUT HOW SHE ALWAYS AVOIDS DEALING WITH NORMAL PEOPLE.
ON THE OTHER HAND, THERE'S THAT GHOST GIRL WHO SAID SHE WAS HER ROOMMATE...
...AND THE CONDUCTOR'S GHOST ON THE TRAIN...
SHE REACTS SO SENSITIVELY TO BEINGS WHO AREN'T NORMAL HUMANS, IT'S ALMOST DISGUSTING.
SURPRISINGLY ENOUGH, I THINK SHE MIGHT BE A LOT LIKE ME.

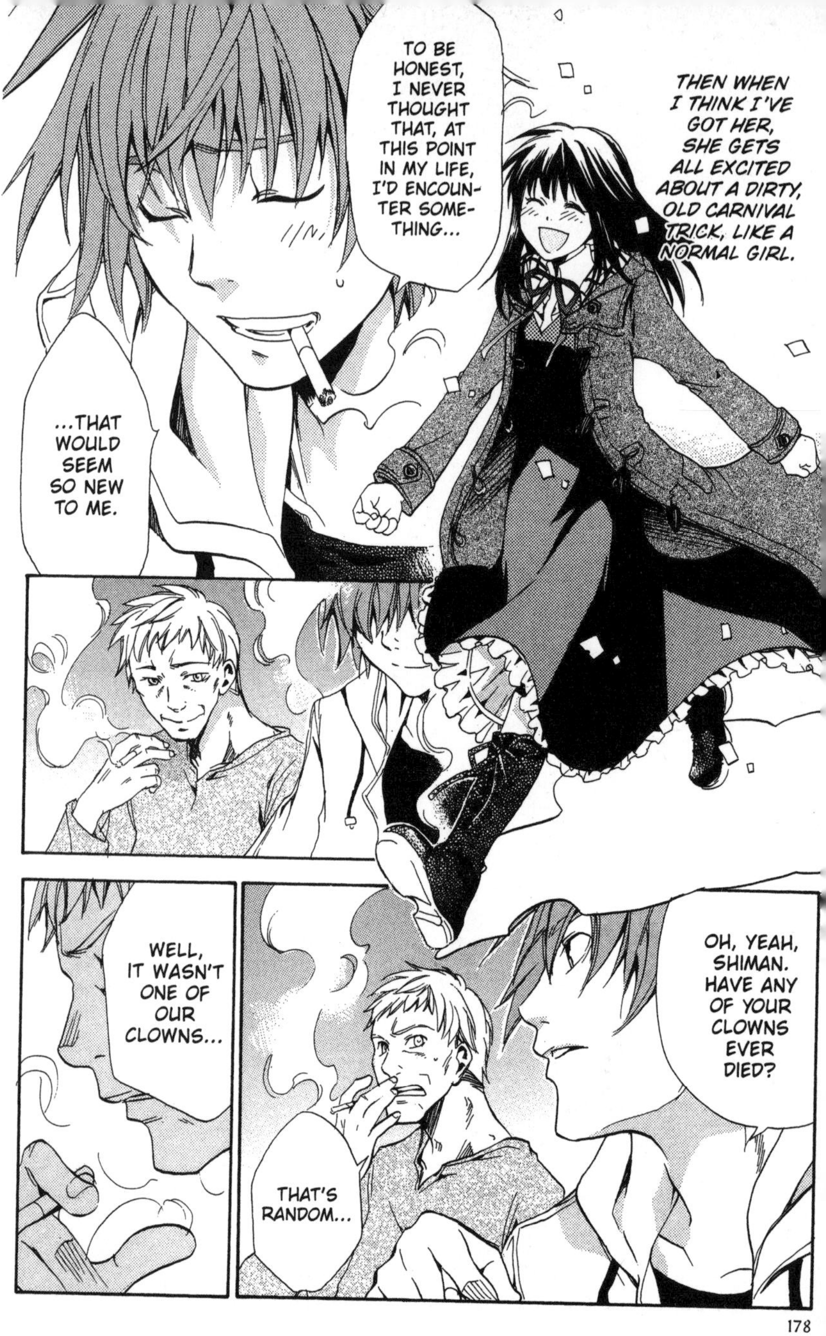
THEN WHEN I THINK I'VE GOT HER, SHE GETS ALL EXCITED ABOUT A DIRTY, OLD CARNIVAL TRICK, LIKE A NORMAL GIRL.
TO BE HONEST, I NEVER THOUGHT THAT, AT THIS POINT IN MY LIFE, I'D ENCOUNTER SOMETHING...
...THAT WOULD SEEM SO NEW TO ME.
OH, YEAH, SHIMAN. HAVE ANY OF YOUR CLOWNS EVER DIED?
THAT'S RANDOM...
WELL, IT WASN'T ONE OF OUR CLOWNS...

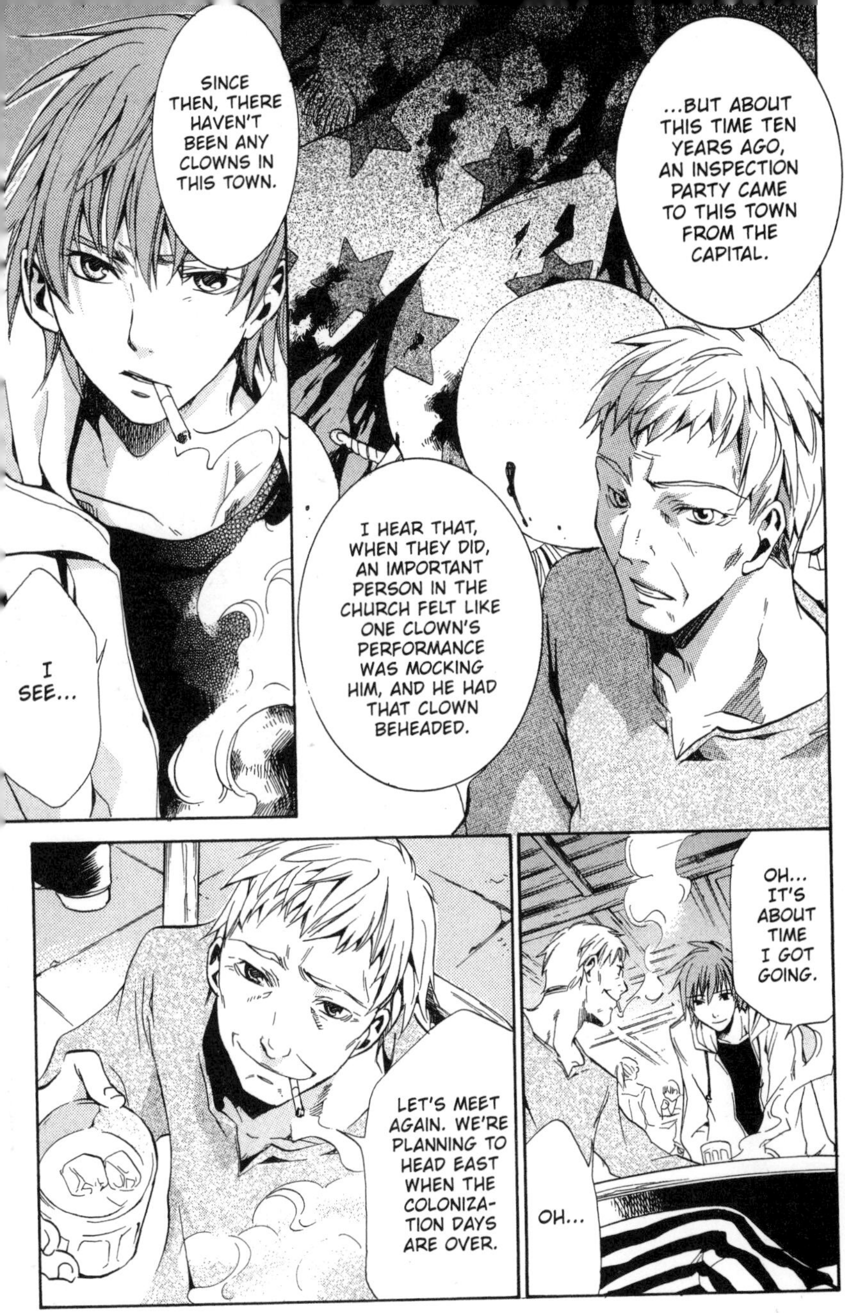
...BUT ABOUT THIS TIME TEN YEARS AGO, AN INSPECTION PARTY CAME TO THIS TOWN FROM THE CAPITAL.
I HEAR THAT, WHEN THEY DID, AN IMPORTANT PERSON IN THE CHURCH FELT LIKE ONE CLOWN'S PERFORMANCE WAS MOCKING HIM, AND HE HAD THAT CLOWN BEHEADED.
SINCE THEN, THERE HAVEN'T BEEN ANY CLOWNS IN THIS TOWN.
I SEE...
OH... IT'S ABOUT TIME I GOT GOING.
OH...
LET'S MEET AGAIN. WE'RE PLANNING TO HEAD EAST WHEN THE COLONIZA-TION DAYS ARE OVER.

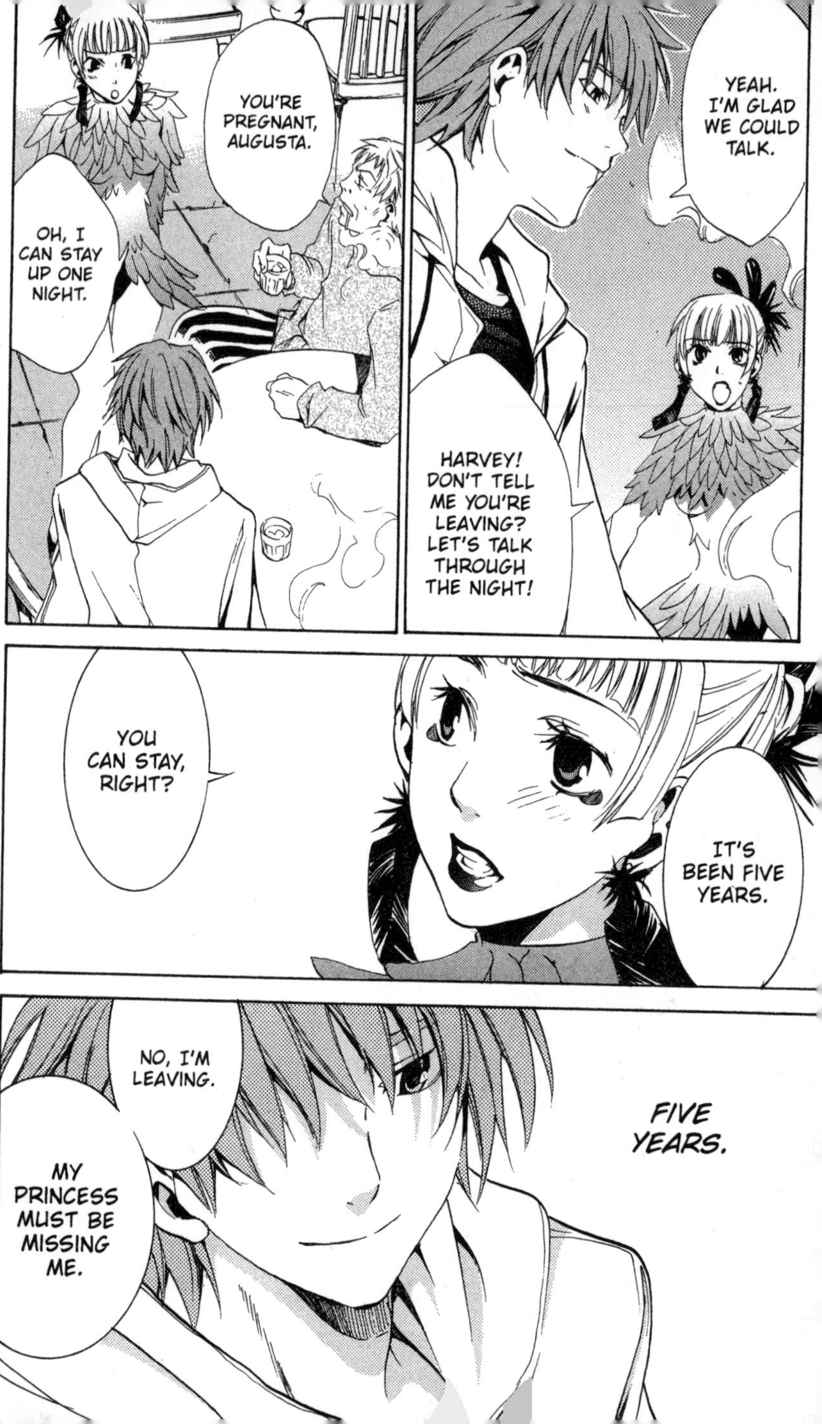
YEAH. I'M GLAD WE COULD TALK.
HARVEY! DON'T TELL ME YOU'RE LEAVING? LET'S TALK THROUGH THE NIGHT!
YOU'RE PREGNANT, AUGUSTA.
OH, I CAN STAY UP ONE NIGHT.
IT'S BEEN FIVE YEARS.
YOU CAN STAY, RIGHT?
FIVE YEARS.
NO, I'M LEAVING.
MY PRINCESS MUST BE MISSING ME.

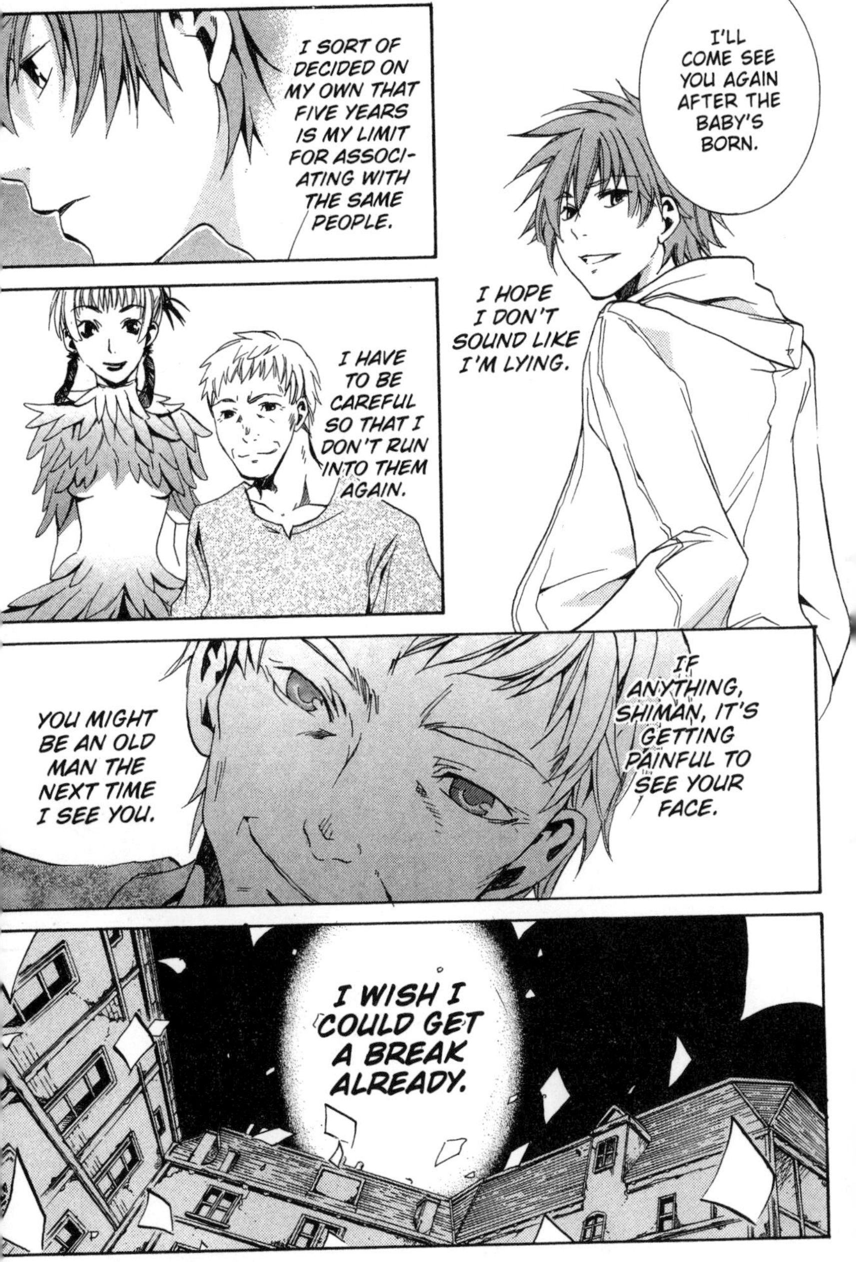
I'LL COME SEE YOU AGAIN AFTER THE BABY'S BORN.
I HOPE I DON'T SOUND LIKE I'M LYING.
I SORT OF DECIDED ON MY OWN THAT FIVE YEARS IS MY LIMIT FOR ASSOCI-ATING WITH THE SAME PEOPLE.
I HAVE TO BE CAREFUL SO THAT I DON'T RUN INTO THEM AGAIN.
IF ANYTHING, SHIMAN, IT'S GETTING PAINFUL TO SEE YOUR FACE.
YOU MIGHT BE AN OLD MAN THE NEXT TIME I SEE YOU.
I WISH I COULD GET A BREAK ALREADY.

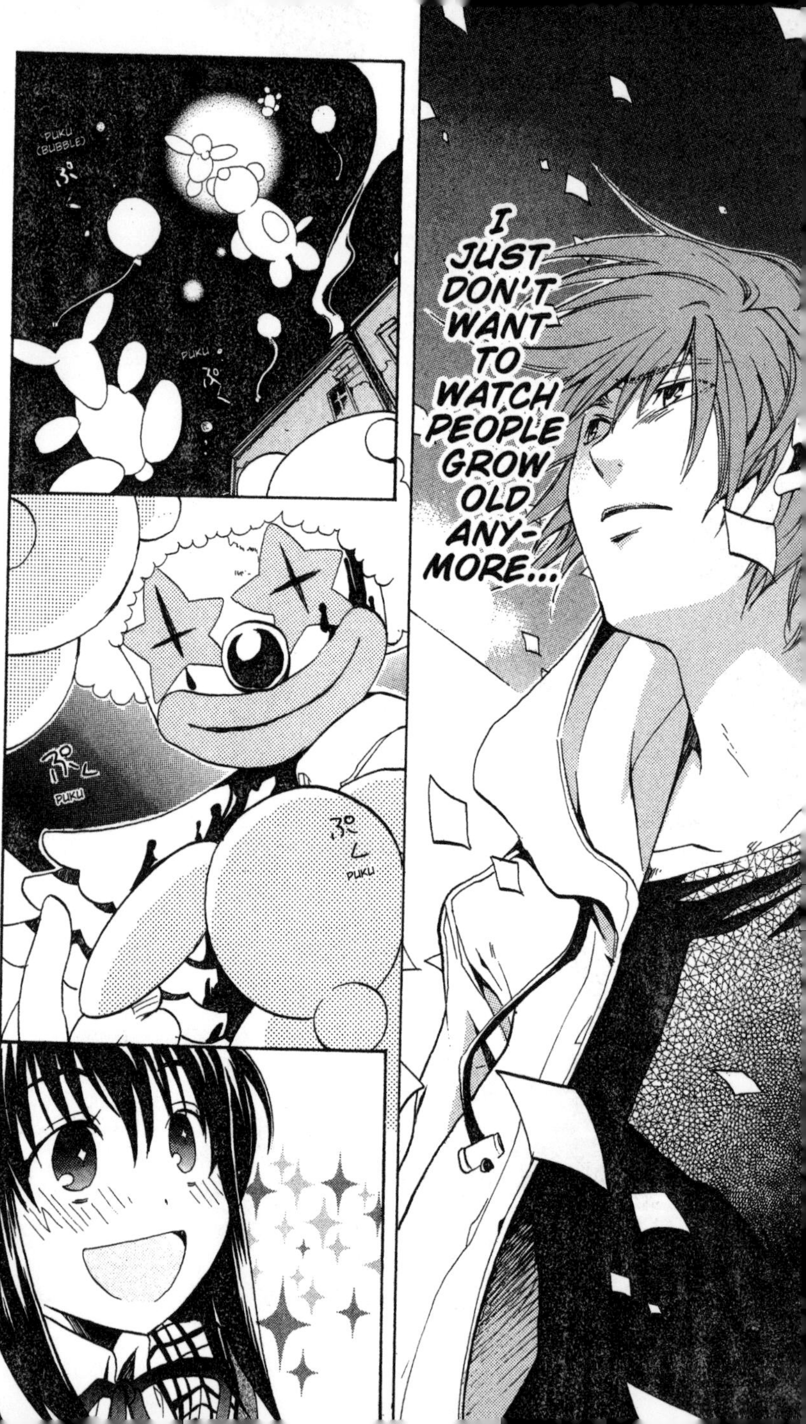
I JUST DON'T WANT TO WATCH PEOPLE GROW OLD ANY-MORE...
PUKU (BUBBLE)
ぷく
PUKU
ぷく
ぷく
PUKU
ぷく
PUKU

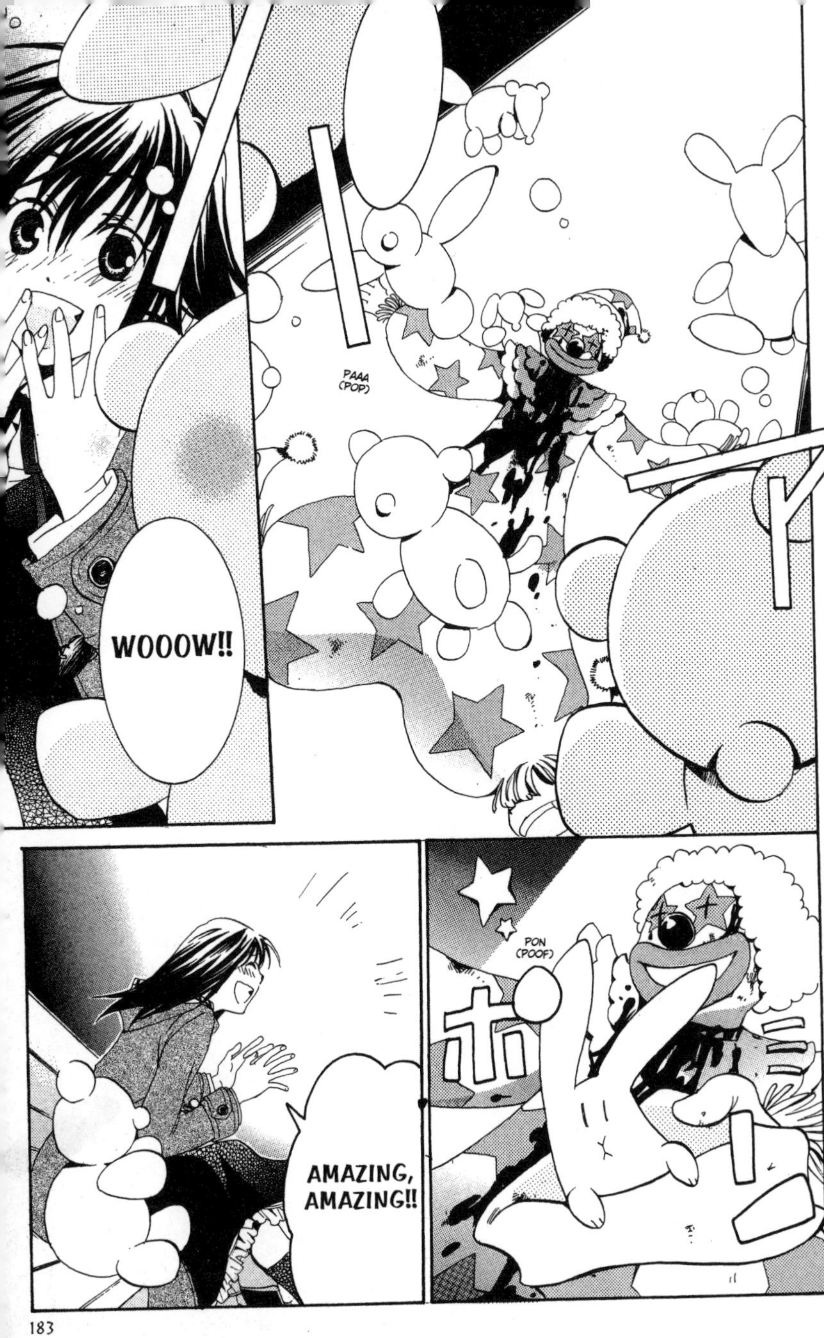
PAAA (POP)
WOOOW!!
PON (POOF)
AMAZING, AMAZING!!

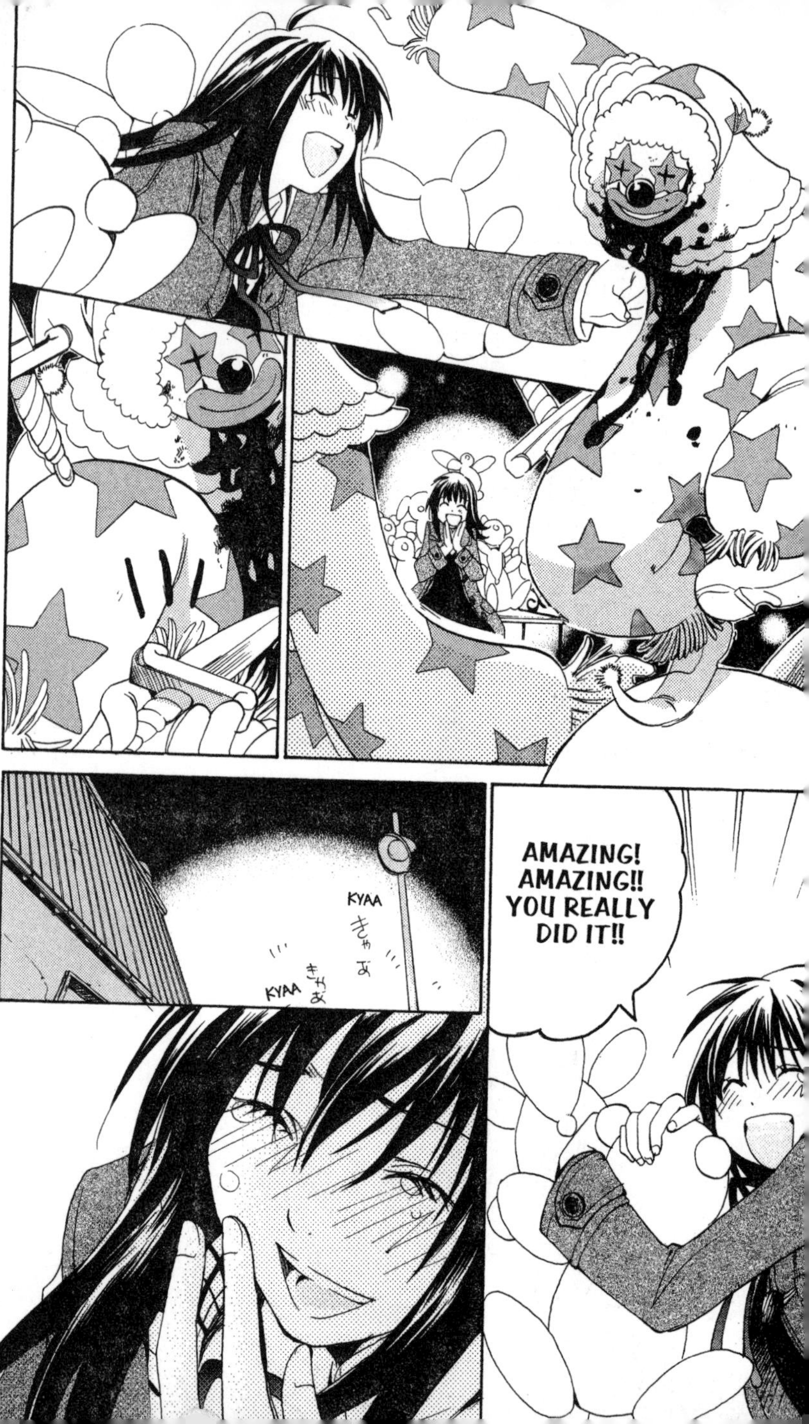
AMAZING! AMAZING!! YOU REALLY DID IT!!
KYAA
KYAA

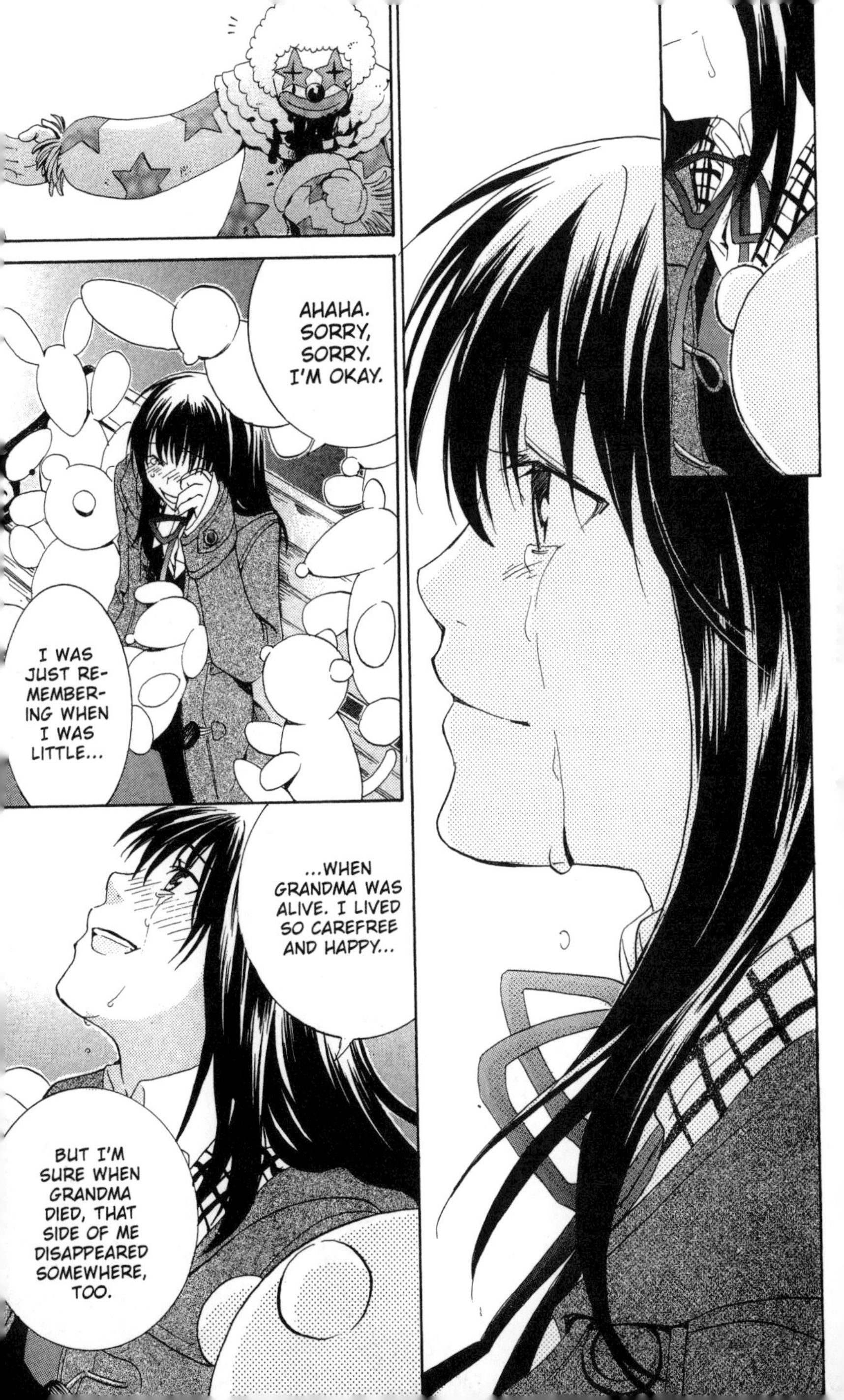
AHAHA. SORRY, SORRY. I'M OKAY.
I WAS JUST RE-MEMBER-ING WHEN I WAS LITTLE...
...WHEN GRANDMA WAS ALIVE. I LIVED SO CAREFREE AND HAPPY...
BUT I'M SURE WHEN GRANDMA DIED, THAT SIDE OF ME DISAPPEARED SOMEWHERE, TOO.

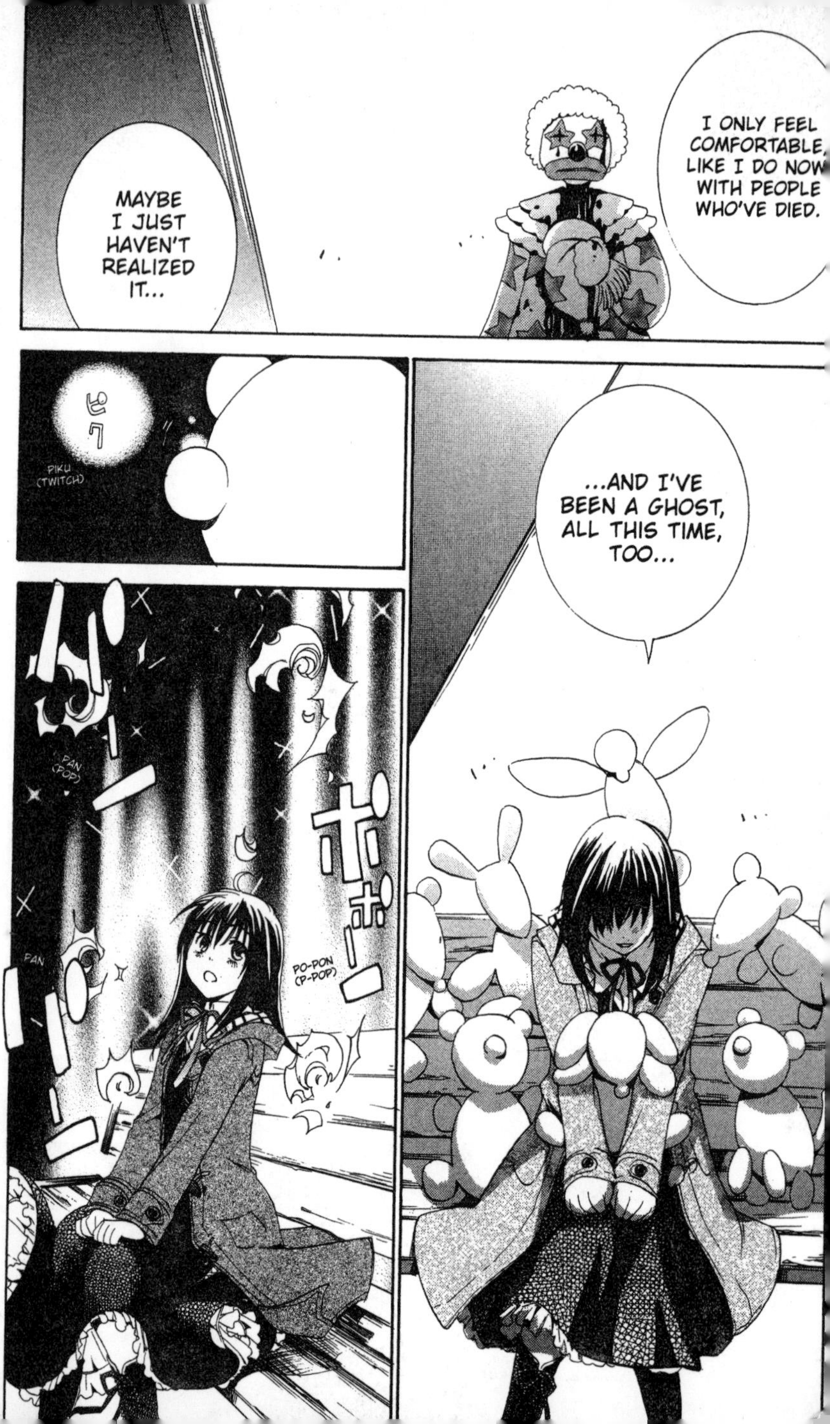

I ONLY FEEL COMFORTABLE, LIKE I DO NOW WITH PEOPLE WHO'VE DIED.
MAYBE I JUST HAVEN'T REALIZED IT...
...AND I'VE BEEN A GHOST, ALL THIS TIME, TOO...
ピク
PIKU (TWITCH)
PAN (POP)
ポポーン
PO-PON (P-POP)
PAN

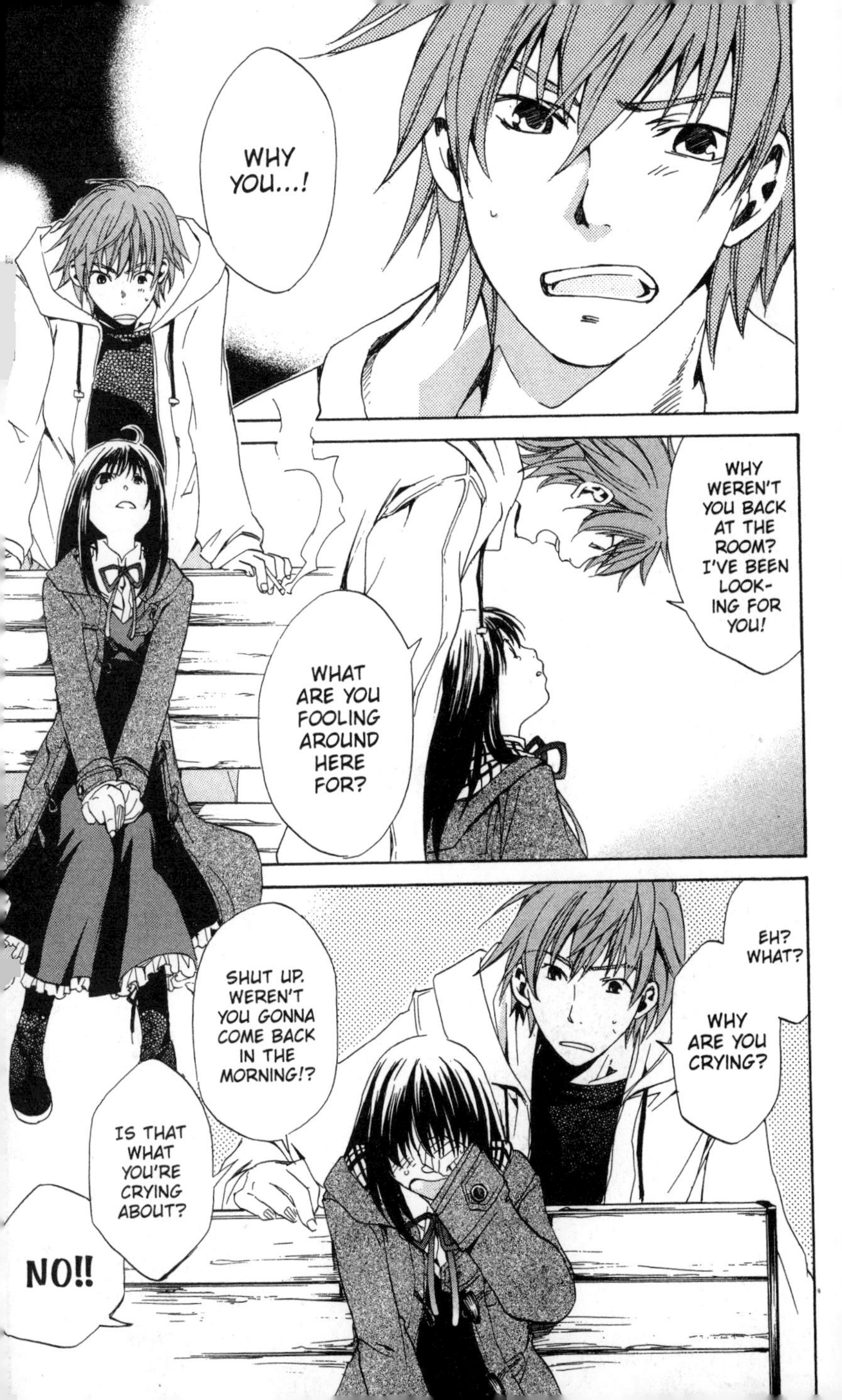
WHY YOU...!
WHY WEREN'T YOU BACK AT THE ROOM? I'VE BEEN LOOKING FOR YOU!
WHAT ARE YOU FOOLING AROUND HERE FOR?
EH? WHAT?
WHY ARE YOU CRYING?
SHUT UP. WEREN'T YOU GONNA COME BACK IN THE MORNING!?
IS THAT WHAT YOU'RE CRYING ABOUT?
NO!!

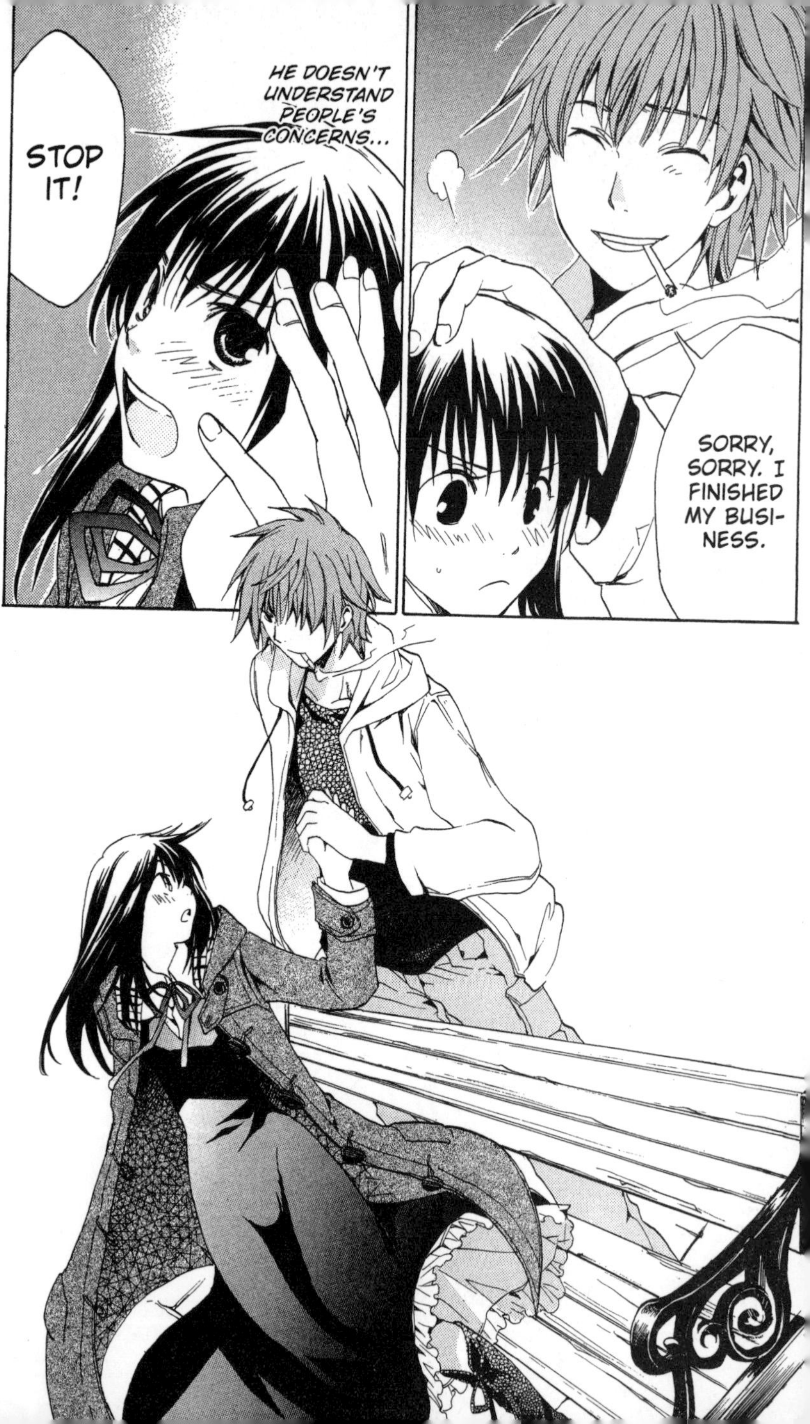
SORRY, SORRY. I FINISHED MY BUSI-NESS.
HE DOESN'T UNDERSTAND PEOPLE'S CONCERNS...
STOP IT!

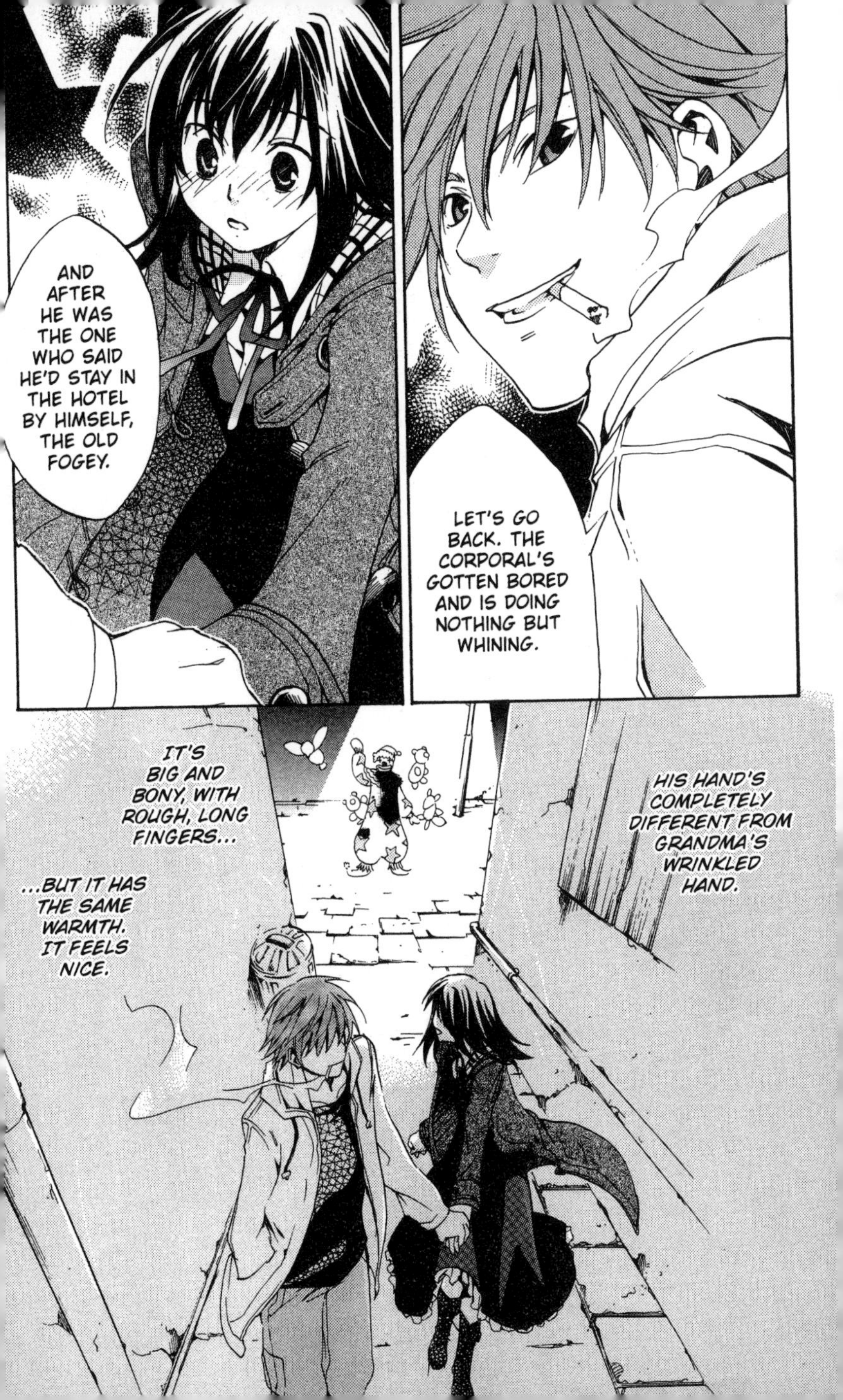
LET'S GO BACK. THE CORPORAL'S GOTTEN BORED AND IS DOING NOTHING BUT WHINING.
AND AFTER HE WAS THE ONE WHO SAID HE'D STAY IN THE HOTEL BY HIMSELF, THE OLD FOGEY.
HIS HAND'S COMPLETELY DIFFERENT FROM GRANDMA'S WRINKLED HAND.
IT'S BIG AND BONY, WITH ROUGH, LONG FINGERS...
...BUT IT HAS THE SAME WARMTH. IT FEELS NICE.

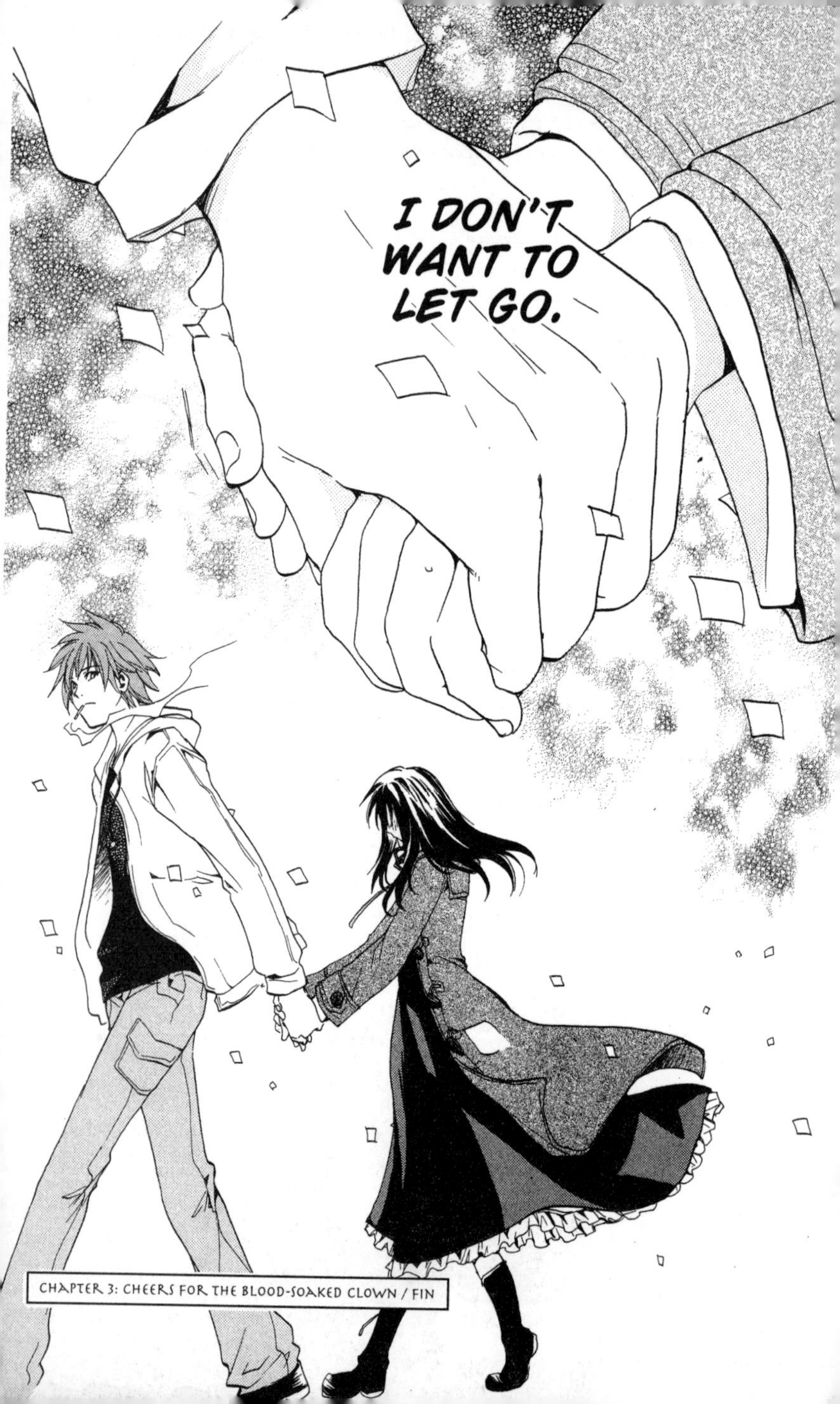
I DON'T WANT TO LET GO.
CHAPTER 3: CHEERS FOR THE BLOOD-SOAKED CLOWN / FIN

Hello, nice to meet you. I wrote the original *Kieli: The Dead Sleep in the Wilderness* novels. My name is Yukako Kabei. This time, I was given a precious extra page. I don't often get this chance, so I'm writing this by hand. These days, everyone relies on computers to write novels, and clean handwritten copies of things are nearly nonexistent, so in the last few years, I've completely forgotten how to write in neat handwriting. Please forgive my scribbles.

Now, the original novels of *Kieli* were published by Dengeki Bunko, and have been wrapped up in nine volumes. *The Dead Sleep in the Wilderness* is the story from the first novel. I never dreamed I'd be fortunate enough to have the editors at Akita Shoten come to me with this idea, but now the series is being made into a manga with beautiful drawings by Shiori Teshirogi-san. When each new chapter came out in Bonita, Teshirogi-san and I would get really excited over strange things, e-mailing each other with, "The blood! The blood!" "You can see his teeth through his cheek!" "His muscle tissue!" and the like. Even the scenes that I made gory in the original without thinking too much about the visuals are re-created beautifully, and I am nothing but impressed by Teshirogi-san's artistic ability. Of course I'm impressed with her adorable Kieli and her good-looking Harvey, too!

Also, I would like to use this space to thank Shunsuke Tagami-san, who was in charge of the illustrations for the novels and gave birth to the visuals of the characters that became the prototypes for Teshirogi-san's characters. And so, I humbly borrowed one of Tagami-san's illustrations below.

The novels continue through nine volumes, so if you liked the characters and the world presented in this work, then please, if you are so inclined, pick up the novels as well.

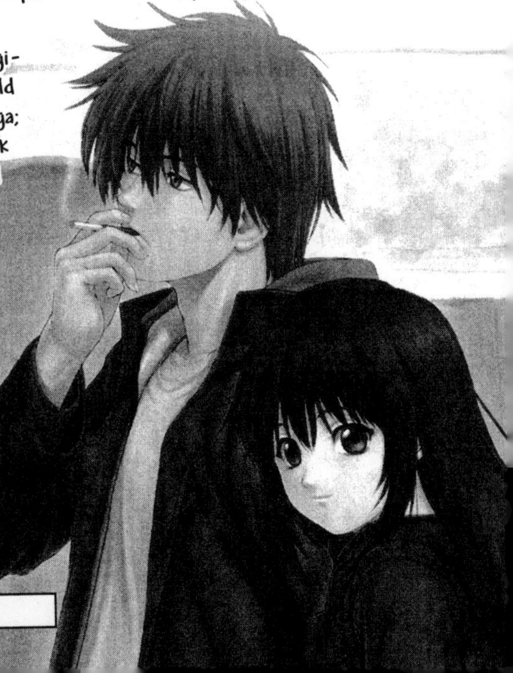

I would like to thank Shiori Teshirogi-sama, who vividly expressed the world of this series in her wonderful manga; the editors at Akita Shoten, who took notice of the original novels; and all the people who took care of me at Dengeki Bunko.

And to you, who were kind enough to pick up this book, I give you my highest level of thanks.

Yukako Kabei
Summer 2006

KIELI VOLUME 1 / FIN

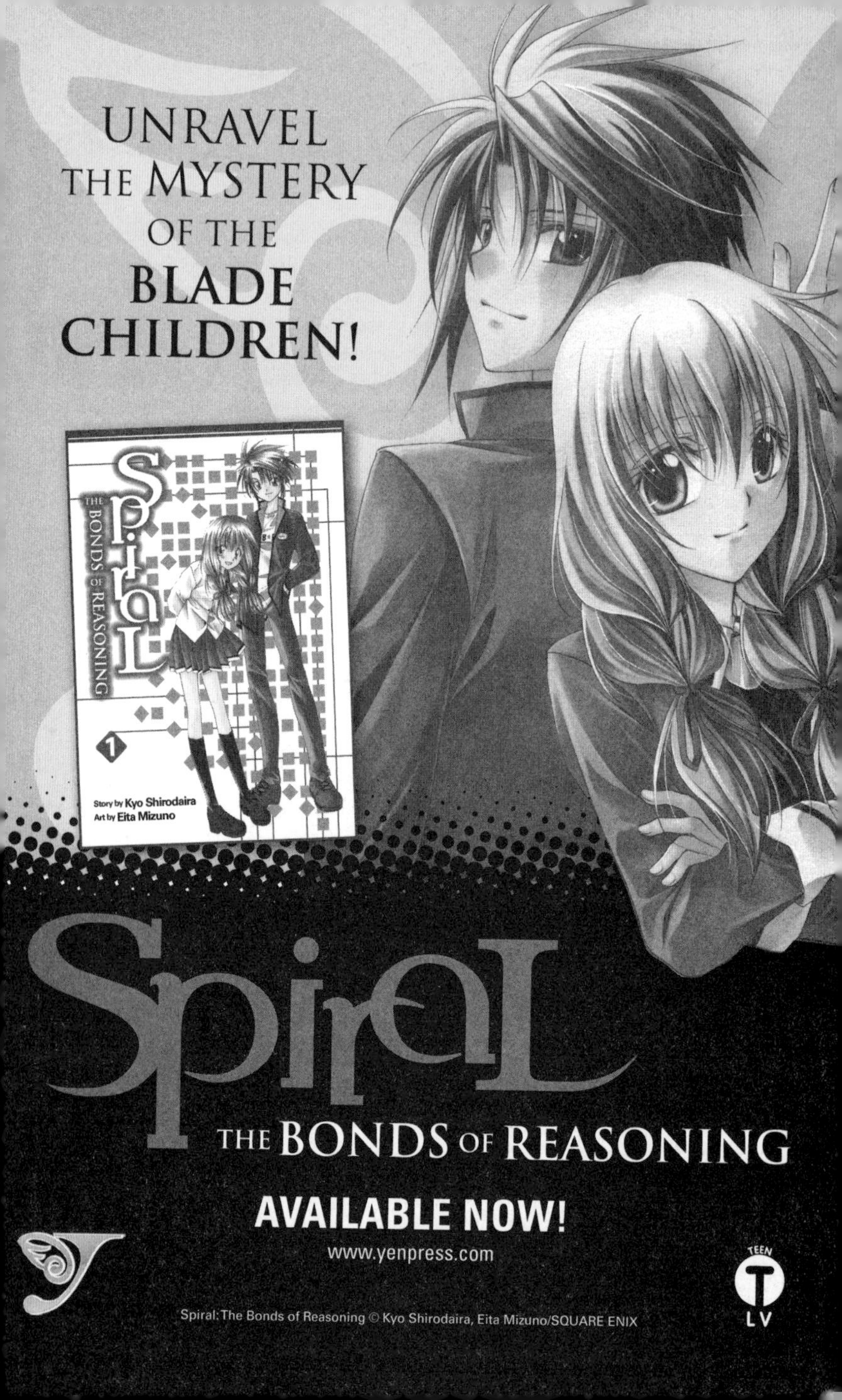

UNRAVEL THE MYSTERY OF THE BLADE CHILDREN!
Spiral THE BONDS OF REASONING
1
Story by Kyo Shirodaira
Art by Eita Mizuno
Spiral THE BONDS OF REASONING
AVAILABLE NOW!
www.yenpress.com
TEEN T LV
Spiral: The Bonds of Reasoning © Kyo Shirodaira, Eita Mizuno/SQUARE ENIX

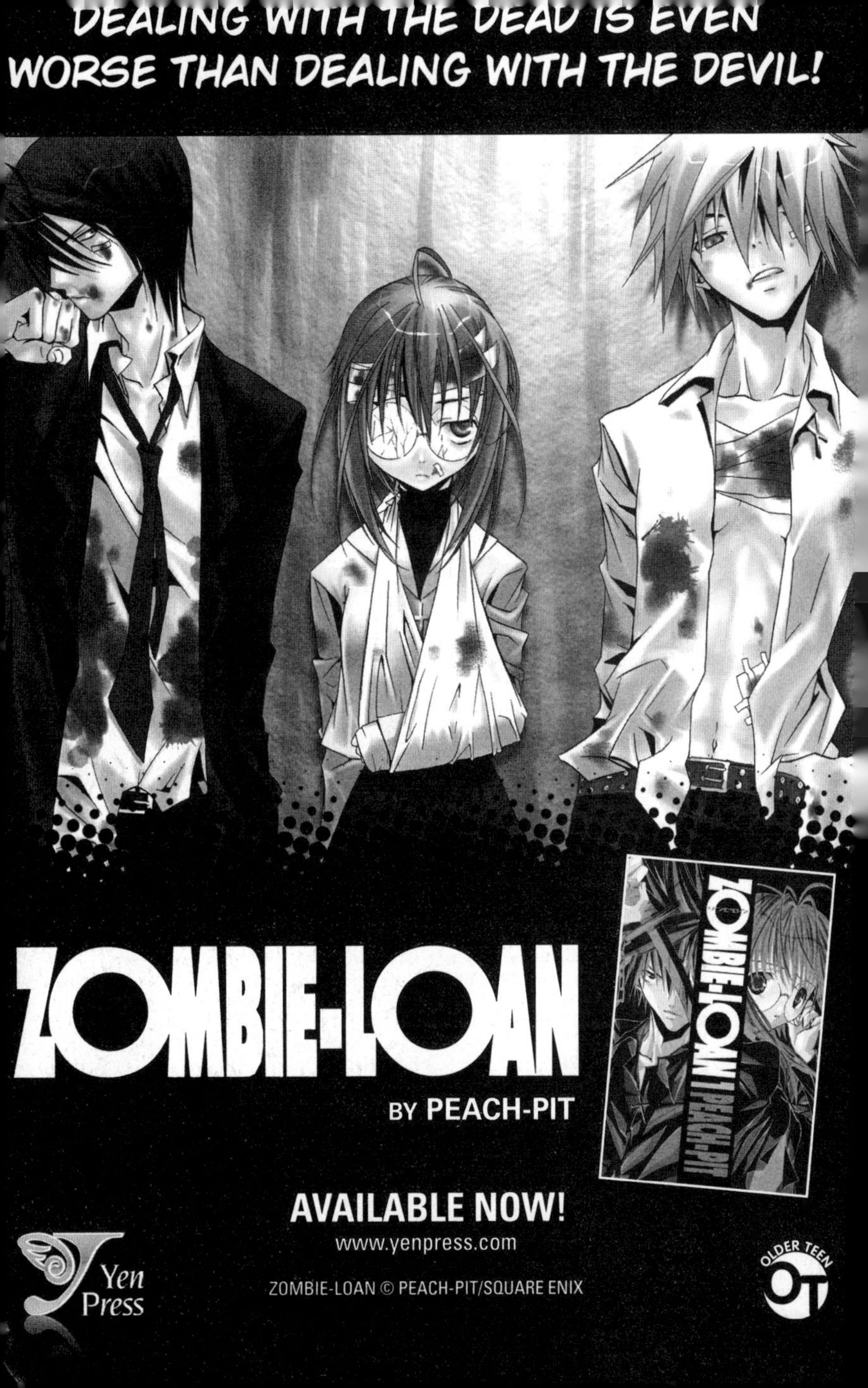
DEALING WITH THE DEAD IS EVEN WORSE THAN DEALING WITH THE DEVIL!
ZOMBIE-LOAN
BY PEACH-PIT
ZOMBIE-LOAN 1 PEACH-PIT
AVAILABLE NOW!
www.yenpress.com
Yen Press
ZOMBIE-LOAN © PEACH-PIT/SQUARE ENIX
OLDER TEEN
OT

KIELI ①

YUKAKO KABEI
SHIORI TESHIROGI

Translation: Alethea Nibley and Athena Nibley

Lettering: Alexis Eckerman

KIELI: SHISHATACHI WA KOYA NI NEMURU, Vol. 1 © 2006 YUKAKO KABEI/MEDIAWORKS, SHIORI TESHIROGI. All rights reserved. First published in Japan in 2006 by Akita Publishing Co., Ltd., Tokyo. English translation rights arranged with Akita Publishing Co., Ltd. through Tuttle-Mori Agency, Inc., Tokyo.

Translation © 2008 by Hachette Book Group USA, Inc.

Yen Press
Hachette Book Group USA
237 Park Avenue, New York, NY 10017

Visit our Web sites at www.HachetteBookGroupUSA.com and www.YenPress.com.

Yen Press is an imprint of Hachette Book Group USA, Inc. The Yen Press name and logo are trademarks of Hachette Book Group USA, Inc.

First Yen Press Edition: April 2008

ISBN-10: 0-7595-2851-9
ISBN-13: 978-0-7595-2851-2

10 9 8 7 6 5 4 3 2 1

BVG

Printed in the United States of America